The
HAWAIIAN
Island Murders

The **HAWAIIAN** Island Murders

A Morgan Crew Murder Mystery

ARTHUR A. LEE

LEEWARD PUBLISHERS, LLC

Orlando, Florida

The Hawaiian Island Murders

By

Arthur A. Lee

ISBN: 978-0692308295

www.leewardpublishers.com

Silver Cat Press
An imprint of Leeward Publishers, LLC

This book is dedicated to The Islands of Hawai'i,
my favorite place on Earth,
and to the Hawaiian People,
who have maintained a culture of beauty
and serenity like no other, a haven for those
who need to slow down
and appreciate life.

Other Books
By The Author

The Morgan Crew Murder Mystery Series

A Storm In From The Sea
The Las Vegas Murders
A Deadly London Fog
The Four Seasons Murders
The Hawaiian Sunset Murders
The Spy Who Would Not Speak
The West Texas Murders

The Mystery and Adventure Series

Three Families

Hawaiian Translation

akua: (ah-ku-ah) the gods or an ali'i who was considered a god

ali'i: (ah-Lee-ee) king or queen, royalty, upper class of Hawaiian Society

hale: (Hah-lay) house

hapa haole: (haa-paa How-lee) half Caucasian

haole: (How-lee) tourist, mainlander, white man

hoaloha ko'u: (ho-a-lo-ha ko-oo) my friend

hoaloha: (ho-a-lo-ha) friend

ho'ohe: (ho-oh-hee) coward

kahuna: (kah-Who-nah) priest

kane: (Con-ay) man

kane nui: (Con-ay New-ee) big man

Kanye: (Con-yea) free

kapu: (ka-poo) forbidden

kihei: (key-hay- ee) a rectangular shawl worn over the shoulder

Leilani: (lay-Lah-nee) heavenly blossoms

moana: (moo-Ah-nah) ocean

mahalo nui loa: (ma-Ha-low New-ee Low-ah) thank you very much

makuakane: (ma-ku-ah-con-ay) father

okolehao: (oh-Ko-lay-Hah-oh) Hawaiian alcoholic spirit distilled from Ti roots

pakalolo: (pak-ah-low-low) marijuana

Palani: (pah-lan-nee) a free man

pupuli: (Poo-poo-lee) crazy

wahine iki nani: (wah-Heen-ee eekee Nah-nee) pretty little woman

THE HAWAIIAN ISLAND MURDERS

By

Arthur A. Lee

Contents

THE HAWAIIAN ISLAND MURDERS

By

ARTHUR A. LEE

CHAPTER ONE

On The Big Island

Cool Island breezes drifted down from Mauna Loa and through the open windows of the little hale that morning. It was hidden away in a forest of tall trees, palms, and clusters of bamboo up in the thick green hills high above Kailua-Kona. Red hibiscus, yellow and pink plumeria, and sweet jasmine added color and a sweet perfume to the deep jungle of green surrounding the house. Fruit hung heavy from the papaya and mango trees. Banana palms held heavy bunches of the fruit. The green leafed trees swayed gently in the breeze. They were filled with birds of bright colors - reds and blues and greens and yellows and white - proudly singing their morning songs, praising the sun and another good day on the Big Island of Hawai'i.

Not too nearby were the nearest neighbors of the little hale, small plantations of Kona coffee trees and a few secretive people who were growing the Hawaiian pakalolo known as Kona Gold on small patches of mountainside dirt, hidden away from prying eyes. A thin dirt track, sometimes patched with the years old remnants of asphalt, but mainly just

1

potholed dirt, twisted and bounced from the hale past the neighbors, finally finding its way down to Ali'i Drive, its touristy beaches, and the blue Pacific.

The small shack's roof was thatched by palm fronds, drying brown but thick enough to keep most of the rain at bay. A heavy storm would blow most of the roof away but the fronds are quickly replaced using the palms that can be found all around the hale and cut from the trees.

The walls were woven of stripped bamboo and whatever scraps of wood could be found in the hills and on the beaches below. The weaving had been done loosely in order to let the cool air migrate through the hale. The walls were sheltered by the wide sloping overhang of the roof on all sides. Dried gourds hung from the roof's eves at the front of the shack over a wood plank porch. Each gourd held flowers that hung long over the edge of the gourd and brought a rainbow of tropical colors to the little hale. Small birds of bright yellow and some of red danced around in the pools of water left from the rain the night before. A few red feathered chickens pecked through the mud for whatever insects they could find for breakfast.

Inside the little hale, Lewis Manaluo slept past the time that the alarm on the old, rusted, wind-up clock had been set to ring. His woman, Leilani, had set the alarm for him the night before. The old wind-up alarm stopped keeping the correct time years before, but neither really cared. When it worked properly, which wasn't often, Lewis would get up, splash some cold water on his face and the back of his neck, and dress in shorts and any T-shirt that was lying around. Leilani would cook whatever they had for Lewis' breakfast, and if he could get his seven year old, faded red Vespa scooter started, he would ride it down the hillside on the dirt road to the construction site where he would work as a laborer, for day-wages, whenever he felt like working. When the urge or the need for a day's work was not there, Lewis would work on some project at home, using the wood that he gathered nearby.

Leilani slept curled against Lewis, her arm across his broad chest. She breathed slowly and deeply, dreaming of the night before, dreaming of holding Lewis tightly against her as they made love over and over again. She had lived with Lewis for almost three years. Those were wonderful years for Leilani; years she could never have imagined before meeting and falling in love with Lewis.

They had a son, Kanye, who in six months would be three years old. Kanye was a bright and rambunctious child, always seeking out things to take apart. He seemed to never be anything but happy. He would chase birds and laugh. He would play in the dirt with toys made by his father, always laughing, always ready to be hugged and loved.

That morning Kanye crawled secretly and quietly on hands and knees into his parents' bedroom at the rear of the hale and tugged at the hand woven sheet covering Lewis and Leilani. The sheet had beautiful images of Hawaiian birds, coconut palms, and fish, all created by Leilani herself on the loom at the back of the house. The loom had been handed down to Leilani from her grandmother, who Leilani told anyone who would listen, was of royal Hawaiian blood.

Leilani woke, rolled away from Lewis and pulled Kanye up onto the bed. Kanye pushed himself onto his father's chest and giggled at waking him. Lewis jumped and laughed as he took the boy and held him up over him. "Oh you kane nui! You wake your daddy up!" He tickled the boy as the boy liked. Kanye laughed and twisted himself free. He crawled off the bed and ran away, laughing.

"What time is it?" Lewis asked, sleep filling his voice. He stretched and yawned, kicking the sheet off. Leilani looked at Lewis. He was young, muscled, and tanned from days in the Hawaiian sun. His shoulders were broad, his arms heavy with muscle. He wore his thick, brown hair long. It hung covering his shoulders until he tied it back behind his head to fall across his wide back.

Lewis' father was a haole, a career Navy enlisted man who met and married Lewis' mother, a pretty teenage Hawaiian dancer who worked the Luaus at the resorts on Oahu. His father died less than a year after marrying Lewis' mother when, in 1987 the frigate USS Stark, was attacked by an Iraqi Air to Sea missile. That day, 37 US Sailors were killed, Lewis' father among them.

Leilani was spellbound with Lewis' body. The look of him stirred the young woman. She pushed herself up from under the sheet, naked as she slept every night, and leaned on one elbow as she put her hand on his back and stroked it slowly, softly, longingly. She didn't answer him when he asked the time. He turned to her and smiled. "Hey, you no hear me, wahine iki nani?" he said. "What time is it?"

Leilani let her hand slip from Lewis' muscled back. She turned and looked at the clock on the small bamboo table next to their bed. The hands on the old clock were stopped at eighteen minutes past three. She said, "The clock it stopped again. But there is light outside and Kanye's awake. Must be time to get up. You want eggs?"

"Sure," he said as he rolled out of bed and stood on the bare wooden floor of their little bedroom. He was naked as he stretched the night's sleep from his body, stretching and flexing the muscles across his back. Leilani wanted him again. She wanted the weight of him on her and the feel of him inside her again. But she also knew that Lewis had to work that day. He had been home for three days and they needed money to buy food. So she stepped out of their bed and took one of Lewis' long T-shirts from the pile of clothes on the wicker chair that Lewis had built last year. She pulled it over her head and let it hang below her hips, pulling her hair out of it to let it hang. She walked to their kitchen.

Leilani was small next to Lewis. She was barely 20 years old and slim, having kept her figure after the birth of little Kanye. Her hair was black as coal, thick, and long, and flowed to the small of her back. Her eyes were dark and had a sparkle to them, like diamonds in the sunlight.

Leilani was of pure Hawaiian ancestry, as proven by her dark skin and eyes. Lewis was hapa haole, the son of the American sailor and the fifteen year old Hawaiian girl.

Lewis walked into the kitchen. Leilani was pleased to see he was dressed in his old, tattered work shorts and heavy, scuffed brogan boots. He would go to work that day, and they would have food for the next couple of days.

He sat at the table Lewis had fashioned from some driftwood planks he had found on the beach one day. He was good working with wood, a real craftsman. The table was handsome and had an artistic flair Lewis found easy to add to whatever he built. He had cut the wood by hand to fit together, and sanded it smooth. He managed to sneak a small can of varnish from the construction site where he worked and finished the table to a high gloss.

He had built their home in the hills himself. It was a mixture of tall bamboo he cut from the forest, wood he gathered from the same forest and drift wood he found on the beaches of Kailua-Kona. He had woven stripped palm frond into mats that he added to the walls and laid on the wooden floor. Although simple, it could have been the model for Gauguin to paint a classic Polynesian lifestyle with the exotic beauty of Leilani in the foreground.

Leilani placed a koa wood dish in front of Lewis. He had carved a set of three of the bowls and would carve a fourth when the new child arrived. The bowl held the last three eggs in the kitchen cooler. Leilani would search through the low bushes for fresh eggs laid by the chickens that morning after Lewis left for work. She had scrambled the eggs as Lewis liked them, alongside of which were two thick slices of Spam and a slice of toast. She had baked the loaf from the last of the flour and toasted it near a small fire she cooked over at the rear of the home. A big, cracked mug was filled with steaming Kona coffee.

He ate the plate clean and drained the coffee. He sat back and lit a cigarette. Leilani disapproved of his smoking but as usual said nothing. Love as deep as hers overcomes disapproval. No one had to tell her this truth; the love she held for him made it natural for her to accept Lewis as he was. The love she had for him would not allow her to ask him to change. She loved him from the first day they met, and she wanted him as he was on that day. He crushed the cigarette out in the triton's trumpet shell that his own Grandma blew to call in the workers from the taro paddies. It was now just an ashtray.

"I guess I try t'get the motor goin'," Lewis said as he pushed himself out of the chair and stood. "I be back late maybe. Gonna' stop for a beer or two, maybe."

Leilani walked to him and, standing on her toes, threw her arms around his neck. Her dark eyes gleamed up at him as she smiled. "You gonna' talk that Mr. Vasco t'day?" she asked.

"Maybe," he answered. "He gets mad an' I ain't got no job. He pupuli, he crazy like."

"But . . ."

"Maybe," Lewis repeated. He bent down and kissed her on the lips. The taste of her lips was sweet and desire rose in him. But he knew they needed money and food so he gently and reluctantly pushed her away.

Leilani touched his arm. He turned to look at her and smiled down at her. She said, "It not really good what that Mr. Vasco, he is doin'. Somebody gonna' get hurt."

"Nobody hurt yet," he said. He was unsure what to do. He wanted to do what Leilani said to do. He wanted to make her happy. "Maybe I talk t'him, anyway."

He lifted her off her feet, holding her up above him. She giggled and he kissed her again as he gently put her back on her feet.

"I gonna' go pick some fruit today," she said.

"Yeah, an' you gonna' get flowers too, if I know you," he laughed. Leilani kept their hale beautiful and colorful by keeping fresh flowers inside and out. The scents of the flowers kept their home smelling sweet.

She laughed as he walked out to the rickety porch of their hale. Kanye was sitting on the top step of the porch playing with his new toy, a set of koa wood toys. There were six fish and three birds that Lewis had carved for him. He patted Kanye on his head; the boy was focused on his toys. Lewis walked down to his tarp covered Vespa.

After several tries, the little motor was grinding but it would not start. Lewis shrugged his shoulders and straddled the Vespa. He pushed it off its kickstand and towards the dirt path leading away from the hale. The Vespa started to roll downhill before it finally caught. It spewed out a cloud of acrid smoke just before rumbling to life. Lewis gave it another big push to get the Vespa going. He waved to little Kanye still sitting with his new toys, and to Leilani, and rode away to work at Mr. Vasco's construction site along Ali'i Drive.

Leilani picked up her son and carried him into their little home to give him a breakfast of the last of the oatmeal, and then spend the rest of the day weaving cloth and collecting fruits and flowers from around her house.

****

The sun had set, burning into the vast Pacific, painting the sky with reds and oranges and yellows Leilani wished she could copy into what she was weaving. She had pulled her Grandmother's loom out onto the front porch of the hale to work as she watched the sun set.

Little Kanye was in his cot, asleep and content after a day of play and laughing. Leilani stopped her weaving, worried because Lewis was not home yet. She was wearing a kihei she had woven herself, bright yellow with red hibiscus and belted with a leather belt Lewis had given her. She pulled it tightly around her against the cool evening air. She lowered herself and sat crossed legged on her porch up in the hills as she watched the sun set, but thinking of Lewis. It was peaceful and quiet; a few birds were signaling their resting places. Thick clouds drifted over Mauna Loa's snowcapped peak from the east, a promise of a little rain that night.

Leilani drifted into her house and crawled into her bed, alone because Lewis had decided to have more than a couple of beers with his friends. He would do that now and then, not often, but she knew a man needed to do that sort of thing occasionally and she never complained. She would worry, but she would never complain. Sleep came quickly to her.

In the morning Lewis was not in the bed next to Leilani, he had not come home. Leilani was worried. Lewis had never stayed out all night before. Yes, he had come home late before, very drunk, but never before had he not been there when she woke.

She had washed some fruit and crushed it into a fine mush for Kanye. Better food would have to wait for Lewis to come home with money from a day's work in the sun.

But a police car found its way to Leilani's little hale instead of Lewis. Leilani walked outside and sat on the steps of her porch. She knew before the uniformed policeman, a thin and pale haole, could walk to her, hat in hand, that Lewis wouldn't be coming home.

She spoke before the young officer could say anything. "He in jail or he dead?" she asked blankly, easily, almost unemotionally.

"I'm very sorry, Mrs. Manaluo . . ."

"We not married," she said.

"I'm very sorry . . . Mr. Manaluo was in an accident."

"Lewis, he dead then?" she asked.

"I'm afraid so, Mrs. . . . I'm sorry, what's your name?"

"Leilani," she said simply, slowly, and softly. She sat unmoved, almost frozen in her all too real nightmare. Kanye was playing on the porch nearby. She stood and went to him, picked him up and held him tightly against her breast. She turned back to the officer and asked, "What you need me t'do? I don't know."

"You should go to the Community Hospital today," he said, both discomfort and compassion in his voice. "Mr. Manaluo is there. If you need a ride, I can arrange that."

CHAPTER TWO

San Marcos, California

"Damn, it's cold out there," Bob Sommers said as he stepped into our home and shook the snow off his brown wool overcoat. He wore an old plaid fedora that he had worn for more years then I could remember. He had bought it one day when he was so drunk I had to go to the tavern to get him and drive him home. He insisted that we go into a second hand clothing store next door to the tavern where he bought the fedora. I suppose I could have knocked him out with one punch; he was so drunk it wouldn't have taken more than that, but he is my friend, and I let him go into the store and buy the old hat.

As with his heavy coat, the fedora was brown wool and limp with age. It too was covered with thick, wet snow. He removed it from his balding head and shook the snow off of it onto the tile floor. He stamped his wet, scuffed leather, wing tip shoes on the bare tile of our entry, leaving a puddle that would need to be wiped up later.

Bob Sommers is my oldest friend. He and I played sports and chased girls through college together. After college we thought it would be a good idea to join the Marines, which we did. Three years later we were out and celebrated hard and fast. Bob signed onto the LAPD and quickly rose to the Detective ranks. He married shortly afterwards and that marriage didn't last long. His wife complained about the hours a detective had to work, often all day and all night. I tried talking to her, explaining that she knew the work he did before they married, but that made no difference to her. She wanted him to work regular hours and be home with her as the other men in the neighborhood were.

He started drinking hard, lost his job as an L.A. cop, lost his wife, and wound up on my doorstep in San Marcos. It took nearly three months to get him straightened out and it was hard work, too. But he finally sobered up and I talked him into staying in San Marcos and not returning to L.A. I got him a job with the San Marcos Police and kept him sober, recently with the help of my wife, Sandy.

He is now San Marcos, California's Police Chief and sole police Detective. He runs the small Police Department in my sleepy little home town. San Marcos is a small town on the Pacific Coast, north of San Francisco that has no use for more than one Police Detective.

Bob is overweight, and he used to drink too much, as I said, but he has given that up in favor of an occasional beer. He smokes too much according to my wife, Sandy. And he likes us to take him to the Country Club for dinner, as often as we will relent and take him there. He stuffs himself with the fine food served there by Chef Paolo, even if he doesn't know what he is eating.

That evening Sandy stood at the open door and took Bob's overcoat and hat from him, looking down at the puddle of wet snow Bob left there. She wasn't happy that he had shaken off all the wet snow on the tiles of our home, but she said nothing. He is our friend, and the snow wouldn't hurt the tiles anyway.

He stepped inside and she shut the door behind him. I came out from the kitchen where I was halfway through putting a lasagna together, something I am long famous for. I had a tomato sauce stained grey apron on and I was wiping my hands on a cotton dish towel. "Hey Bob," I said. "What brings you here on a night like this? Someone told you about my lasagna?"

"Hey, Morgan. I ate already . . . But I'll stay for dinner anyway."   Bob is overweight as I said, and he has been overweight since his troubled couple of years down in L.A. There's no kind way to say that he is fat. He eats everything he sees, and exercise is something he likes to watch other people do as he finishes off a bag of greasy potato chips. Sandy has long worked to get him to lose a few pounds, to no effect yet, but she keeps trying. She frowned when I invited him to stay for dinner.

I had a bottle of agreeable if not expensive Chianti open in the kitchen that had become half empty as dinner was worked on. It was one of those bottles that is wrapped in straw and looks nice on the dinner table.

Sandy followed Bob and me to our kitchen.   Betsy Concanon, who has become part of our family and who is our daughter Caroline's nanny, was there, stirring the red sauce. The smells of the spicy sausage, beef, and pork, the garlic, the onion, the oregano, and the leaves of basil Betsy had cut the way I had shown her – "Chiffonade" I had told her just so I could sound smart and Frenchified – permeated the kitchen and drifted into the rest of our house.

Sandy and Bob stood aside drinking several glasses of Chianti while Betsy and I finished cooking the meal . . . and we too drank Chianti while doing it. By the time the lasagna and salad were on the table I had opened a third bottle of wine, this one a burgundy I had been keeping in my wine cooler for several months. Sandy had set the table with a red checkered table cloth and a set of rustic dishes she had bought the last time we were in Rome. White candles set the mood and soft jazz in the background made for a great atmosphere in which to enjoy a really good dinner.

Dinner conversation was light and we laughed a lot.

Bob can be very funny when he wants to, but that night I sensed there was something serious behind his jokes. Maybe it was just because Sandy cut him off after three glasses of wine; maybe it was something more serious.

Dessert was Bosch pears poached in red wine with cloves and cinnamon that I had cooked earlier, giving them time to cool. They sat in a pool of crème anglaise so that I could brag about my cooking skills. After the meal the four of us sat around the big table, drank gallons of hot, strong coffee and talked. Bob started to take a pack of Marlboros out of his shirt pocket, but a scowl from Sandy stopped him in his tracks. He would have to wait until his drive home for a cigarette.

The bitterly cold early February weather we were all suffering through started the conversation. We all complained about the snow, more than twelve inches on the ground so far and we all wished we could be somewhere warm. We talked about Caroline and our plans for her education. I wanted some snooty private school in Switzerland, but Sandy knew our daughter would go to a local Public School so she could grow into a 'normal' young lady. There would be time, she argued, for Caroline to hang out at the San Marcos Country Club with other very rich young ladies and the boys I worried about.

We talked sports and news events. And when the conversation began to drift away, Bob said what he had come to see us about, confirming my suspicions that there was something other than a friendly visit and another good meal on his mind.

"Morgan . . . Sandy . . . There's a girl who's disappeared. I'm getting a lot of heat on this one."

So there it was again. 'The Unfortunate and Dangerous Life of Morgan Crew' is the name of the biography I will write sometime in the future. My life is to do for others what they cannot or will not do for themselves. My family, the

Crew Family, has wealth beyond dreams and power to be frightened of.   My family wields that power like a sword slashing through whatever is in its path in order to acquire more money and power. I take no part in that acquisition but friends and family come to me for help. My life and the life of my wife, Sandy . . . the love of my life . . . are put in danger with every task we undertake.

And here was Bob Sommers, after eating my food and drinking my wine, asking me to help once again. One day I will learn how to say 'NO'. But Bob is my lifelong friend, as close as a brother to me. How can I say 'no' to whatever he asks of me?

"OK, Bob," I said. "Cut to the chase. What do you want me to do?" I leaned back in my chair anticipating what was coming. The coffee pot had been drained and my wine glass was empty, and the last few drops in the bottle of burgundy had been emptied into Sandy's glass before Bob could reach for it. So I made do with a drink of water from the glass that I had ignored during dinner.

"Like I said," Bob began. He paused long enough to drink some water after seeing me do the same. Even with Sandy limiting what he had to drink, he'd had a little too much wine that night. Over the last year he had limited himself to beer and not more than one of those at a time. When we take him to the Country Club for dinner he has a beer, maybe two, while everyone else is imbibing in hard liquor. He hadn't touched my bourbon in all that time. So he was feeling the effects of the good quality wine Sandy had rationed to him. "Like I said, there's this girl who's gone missing. I'm getting flak from your buddies at your Country Club."

"Who is she?" Sandy asked.

"Sissy McMillan," Bob said. "You know her. Her father is Brian McMillan, the guy who owns all them used car lots all over the State. His face is all over the TV."

"Yes," I said. "I know Brian. He's actually a pretty good guy. He's different in person than what he looks like on TV, and he plays a great game of golf. He's a three handicap. He doesn't wear that big ridiculous cowboy hat when he's not doing a commercial."

Betsy sat forward and leaned her elbows on the table. She said, "I know Sissy. She goes to college at Wrightwood State. I'm in a biology class with her. She's missing?"

"You know her?" Bob asked. I wondered if that was why he showed up. Was he working his missing person's case, knowing Betsy was a student at the same college Sissy was? Was he there to do a police investigation interview? Or was he just visiting friends and stuffing his face with my good food?

"Well, I guess you could say I know her," Betsy said. "I only see her in that one class."

"Tell me about her."

"What's to tell? I mean, she seems like a nice girl. She's sort of pretty; not bad looking anyway. The guys all seem to like her but none of them ever get really close, you know? I'm not sure she's dating anyone at school because I never see her with just one guy. She dresses really well, expensive things, you know? I never put her and the TV guy together as father and daughter. I guess that's how she can afford all those clothes and stuff. I hardly ever speak with her except to say 'hello.'"

Bob's eyes looked down and he fiddled with his empty coffee cup. When he looked up he asked, "Have you ever heard anyone speaking badly of her?"

"No," Betsy said. "She's kind of a loner, you know? Like I said, I've never seen her with just one boy. She's always nice to everyone . . . Smiles all the time, you know? But I don't think she has any really close friends. She's always walking alone when I see her and not talking with anyone. She's smart, probably the smartest one in my biology class."

I spoke up and said, "Bob, if she's in college, she's got to be over eighteen. If she wants to leave home she can, can't she? Why all the fuss?"

"You're right, Morgan. But McMillan makes a lot of political contributions. He's talking about running for Mayor. I'm getting heat to find her." He turned back to Betsy and asked, "How about boyfriends? I know you said she's never with anyone steady but is she dating anyone?"

"I really don't know, Bob . . . Or should I call you Detective Sommers until you're done asking pertinent questions?"

"Just tell me, Betsy," he said, just a little bit of 'cop' in his voice.

"I don't know if Ms. McMillan is dating anyone. I've told you a couple of times. I only see her in that one class and a few times walking the halls, and we don't share a lot of showers. I never hear anybody talk about her, and I've never heard any of the guys talk about dating her."

"That's enough, Bob," Sandy said and stood, signaling that the dinner and conversation were over. "Morgan will talk with Brian McMillan. He will do what he can to make things a little easier for you . . . One friend to another. Betsy has told you she doesn't know Sissy McMillan. Now . . . Thank you for joining us for a nice dinner, but it's getting very late, so we'll say good night."

I stayed seated as Betsy and Sandy followed Bob to the front door. Betsy handed his coat and hat to him, and Sandy opened the door and stood aside. Bob walked into the falling snow. There were no 'Good Nights' spoken.

Back at the red checkered table cloth covered dining table, Sandy made a fresh pot of coffee, filled our coffee cups, and sat. We drank the hot, strong brew silently, all wondering why a pretty girl from a good family with lots of money would just up and disappear.

****

The next morning it was still snowing. February had turned out to be a cold, miserable month. The temperature had not risen out of the twenties for over two weeks. Walking outside to get the newspaper that morning was . . . well, painful. I made the mistake of wearing my slippers and a terry bathrobe over my pajamas. I ran to get back into the house. I slipped a couple of times on the ice frozen under the snow.

It was half past nine, and it was dark as night outside. The wind was blowing the newly fallen snow around along with the snow that covered the ground for the past weeks. It had been a tough winter, and the long range forecast was for more of it.

Up in the hills of San Marcos, above Harborside and its commercial fishing fleet, where our home is, the snow, after the night's fresh snow, was more than fifteen inches deep already, and the weather guy on TV was predicting more over the next three days. Hadn't the snow gods heard of global warming?

I was on my third mug of hot coffee, leafing through the sports pages. Sandy was helping our daughter Caroline with her oatmeal and hot cocoa. Betsy had finished her breakfast and was busy buttoning up a heavy coat, wrapping a wool scarf around her neck, and pulling a knitted ski hat down over her ears. She was going to go to school despite Sandy saying it wasn't safe driving during the snow storm.

"I gotta go, Sandy," she said, smiling gratefully that there was finally someone in her life who cared enough to worry about her. Her parents, whom she hadn't seen nor talked to in more than three years, couldn't care less what she did. "If school was closed we would have heard on the TV. I'll be careful. I'm leaving early enough that I can drive slow and take it easy," she said and started for the front door.

Sandy joined me at the table, filling her mug with hot coffee again. "I worry about her," she said.

"She's a big girl," I said. "She can handle it. Trust her."

We drank coffee without speaking. Caroline was in her highchair scribbling with crayons on the comic page of the newspaper. Sandy was staring out the window at the dark day and falling snow. The wind was blowing plants and tree tops around. The sky was black. We had the heater turned up inside the house, and I kept a roaring fire going in the big stone fireplace, yet it still wasn't really warm inside.

Sandy sipped at her coffee, laid the mug down, and looked at me. "Put the paper down for a minute, Morgan," she said. And of course, I did put the newspaper down. I always do what she tells me to do. I sat back and waited for it because I knew one of her bright ideas was about to be made public. "Let's get out of town," she said. "Let's go someplace warm."

Well, that surprised me. I hadn't seen that one coming. I had anticipated her urging me to go out and find Sissy McMillan. But leaving town was a good idea, a better idea in fact. I'm the first one to want to run away from anything close to trouble.

I had guessed days before that Sandy was fed up with the cold and snow. I was sick and tired of that winter, too. We had the world at our doorstep, anyplace we wanted to be, we could be there. Nothing was out of reach or beyond our means. Why sit inside our house, in front of a fire, bundled in sweaters, watching it snow outside, when we could be playing on some beach somewhere, enjoying a warm sun?

"What about what Bob wants?" I asked. "What about Sissy McMillan?"

"You can phone Brian. Talk to him. Tell Bob you did what he asked, and then let's get the hell outta' here," she said and grinned mischievously, like a child conspiring to steal from the cookie jar.

I smiled, reached out and took her hand in mine, and said, "OK, I'll phone right away. You figure out where we should go."

I got Brian's home phone number from the Country Club. The operator there was clearly uncomfortable giving out a member's phone number, but she knew me and who I am. My name gets me what I want.

"Hello, Brian," I said when he answered the phone, trying to sound affable, hoping I was coming across like that. "This is Morgan. How are you?"

"Oh, hi Morgan. Yeah, I'm just great," he said, sarcasm surrounding the words.

"And how's Brenda?" Brenda is Brian's wife. She is a really nice lady who spends her days working on one charity or another. When she isn't doing that, she is one hell of a tennis player, and she plans a couple of really nice parties every year, too.

"She's fine. Look Morgan," Brian said. "I know you know that our Sissy is missing. How the hell do you think we are? We're very concerned."

"I know you are, Brian. I just wanted to offer our support. Is there anything Sandy and I can do?"

"Yeah, go find her," he said sarcastically. I didn't say anything. After a moment or two Brian said a little apologetically, "I'm sorry, Morgan. I'm just worried sick. Sissy's still just a kid. She has no idea what the world is like away from San Marcos. We've tried to give her everything and protect her . . . probably too much of both. She wanted to go to school down in L.A. but we insisted she stay home and go to Wrightwood instead. We tried to explain how dangerous L.A. is. I don't know. Maybe we were wrong."

"I know, Brian. I can understand how you feel. But she's a good girl . . . I mean young lady," I said correcting myself. "I'm sure she's OK. What do the police say?"

"I should ask you what Bob Sommers told you," Brian said, surprising me that he knew Bob had spoken with me about Sissy. "I think he may confide in you more than he confides in our daughter's parents."

"Bob didn't tell me anything. He asked Betsy some questions. She and Sissy go to the same college . . . You know that. But Betsy hardly knows her. Bob didn't tell us anything."

There was silence on the phone that I broke into by asking, "Is there anything I can do? I know some good Private Detectives."

"I've got an agency down in San Francisco on it already."

"Have they come up with anything?" I asked, trying to sound hopeful.

"Nothing yet. We're still waiting to hear the latest from them."

I didn't know what else to say. I didn't want to get too personal, like asking about the girl's sex life and drinking habits. Sissy McMillan was over eighteen and free to do what she wanted to do. I felt sure she was shacked up somewhere with some college guy . . . at least I hoped she was. But I wasn't about to say that to her father. If she had been in some auto accident or hurt herself, he would have been notified. Barring that, I felt she was probably OK. If Bob had been concerned about a kidnapping situation, or worse, a murder, he would have said so.

It's been my experience that people disappear all the time. Some just disappear, for a variety of reasons that sound good to them but might be crazy to others. A few others are murdered. Only a very few can permanently disappear and not be found. People are all too often hard pressed to give up every detail of their lives. Hobbies and habits stay with a person. I was able to find a person who stole money from one of the family's businesses by getting ahold of the mailing list for Pistol and Rifle magazine. The thief wasn't able to give up that subscription when he disappeared and changed everything else about himself.

Short term sexual flings are common. Young adults, particularly young girls who have been sheltered their whole lives, discover sex and once discovered they can't get enough of it. I was sure that was what Sissy was enjoying. But I wasn't about to tell Brian that, either. So I offered, "Look, Brian. I'm sure Sissy is going to show up soon. I'm sure she's OK. But please let me know if I can do anything. Just don't worry too much."

"Yeah, Morgan. That's easy enough for you to say. Wait 'til that little daughter of yours is eighteen. Then tell me the same thing."

Brian hung up before I could say anything else. Sandy was sitting nearby, listening.

She grinned like the proverbial cat that had caught the canary. I saw it, and I knew what was coming. Sandy had something up her sleeve, something that she had been plotting for some time. She sipped at her coffee, carefully laid the mug on the table and said, "So you did what Bob wanted you to do. Now, is that too expensive resort of yours in Hawai'i open for business?"

A few years ago, before Caroline was born, my family's accountants and attorneys sent me to The Big Island of Hawai'i to save several hundred million dollars of family money. It was a true nightmare that I can't to this day explain. Did ancient Hawaiian gods and evil spirits really protect a pagan religious site? I found it and was trapped in a terrifying storm of spirits and devils determined to protect an ancient altar that had existed in a world centuries old.

No one, except Sandy of course, believes me when I tell the story. People tend to laugh and assume I'd been drinking too much at the time. A couple people have actually laughed and asked if I saw pink elephants, too. The ghosts of the dead of that trip to the Islands still haunt me. Hound, the seventies' hippy throwback who died saving my life, will live in my memories forever. I am sending money to his widow, Nancy Wong and their two children and will continue to do that forever. I owe her that much anyway.

"Yes, dear," I answered Sandy's question, knowing what she had in mind. "The Maika'i Resort is open and doing well. That's where you want to go?"

"It's the good weather I'm after. And I've read that Hawai'i has good weather all year round. I think we could all use a heavy dose of sunshine and sea air."

"Even after what happened the last time back there?" I asked.

"I wasn't with you," Sandy said. The smile left her face and she leaned toward me, touching my arm lightly, almost apologetically. "I'll be there this time . . . to keep you out of trouble."

I thought about it as I walked to the coffee maker and refilled my mug. Turning, I leaned against the counter, drank some coffee, and finally relented. "OK, we'll go. I guess lounging around the resort won't be so bad. When do we go?"

****

Later that day, as we watched Caroline play with a few stuffed animals on the floor in front of the fire, we talked with Betsy about taking a trip to the warmth of Hawai'i. Betsy was looking very serious and not very happy. She was frowning and warming her hands on a mug of hot tea as she twisted it in her hands. Sandy asked her if something was wrong.

"I can't go," she said simply. "I can't take off in the middle of the semester."

"Well then none of us will go," I said.

"That's right," Sandy said. "Your school is too important."

"No . . . No," Betsy said looking up and forcing a smile. "You guys go. C is gonna love the beach and all those surfer dudes. I'll bet she hooks up with two or three of them."

"I don't want to leave you home all alone," Sandy argued.

"Hey, I'm a big girl. I can take care of myself. I just can't miss a couple weeks of classes and hope to pass the end of term exams. I gotta' keep my grades up if I'm ever gonna' get into med school. You guys go. It'll give me time to spend some extra hours studying."

"You're sure?" I asked.

"Yeah, absolutely," she smiled. "I'm gonna' miss C of

course. But she'll have a good time. Just watch her around all the muscly beach type guys," she joked. "I can go next time."

Sandy and I looked at each other and smiled in agreement that we were headed out of town and away from the snow and everything else winter in San Marcos had to offer. But Betsy had lost the smile and was obviously worried about something.

"OK," I said and asked her, "What's wrong?"

"Sissy," she said. "She wasn't in class again today. And thinking about it, I haven't seen her for a long time. I guess I'm a little worried. Did you get a chance to talk to her father?"

"I did," I answered. "But look, Sissy has the right to do what she wants. More than likely she's found a boyfriend. You said she's smart. Does she take school seriously . . . Like you do?"

"I really don't know," Betsy answered. "But I think I'm going to find out."

"Wait a minute," Sandy spoke up. "Don't get involved in something that you have no business being involved in."

Betsy smiled broadly and said, "I've been with the two of you long enough to know how to ask questions. I may not have any business getting involved but like you, it's something I need to do."

CHAPTER THREE

On The Big Island

It was mid-day as the jet raced down the runway but it was black as night outside. Plows on big trucks kept the runways clear of snow long enough for the takeoff.

We quickly climbed above the dark clouds and felt the sun for the first time in a couple of weeks. The flight across the Pacific was a little over five hours long and very smooth after we had climbed out of the turbulence of the storm. I learned during the flight from a very accommodating flight attendant (I am always careful not to call them stewardesses anymore) that the winter storm that had us practically snowed in up in San Marcos had delayed the flights out and the flights in to SFX but hadn't closed the airport yet.

It was a miserable day that Tuesday when we took off. Sandy wasn't as pleased with the pretty young flight attendant who kept checking to make sure I had everything I wanted as I was. But she wasn't too nasty to her; she just didn't smile a lot as the attendant served our drinks and food.

Many years ago, when I was just a very young man and I started taking flights all over for family business, I got used to sitting up front, in First Class. The service back in those days was great and the food was fantastic. I can easily remember meals of beef the 'stewardess' cut from a big roast. I remember great champagne and even hot fudge sundaes.

Today the seats are still wide and comfortable and the booze is still free, but the First Class food and service has gone downhill. What used to be served in the back-of-the-plane common people's seats is now served up front. Oh well. Times change I guess.

I managed to down a couple Bloody Marys and after what they laughingly referred to as 'lunch' I washed the taste away with some barely acceptable bourbon. Caroline amused the other passengers – well all but a few of them who didn't think children should be allowed on airplanes at all – and delighted the flight attendants. Sandy, who had stayed up late packing more clothes than she would ever need for a two week vacation, slept away most of the flight.

As the jet approached the Big Island, I looked out the window at the cloudless blue sky and the snow atop Mauna Kea. I have never gotten tired of looking at snow on the tropical paradise of Hawai'i. Mauna Kea is snow covered all year round, and I promised myself that one day I would take a helicopter to the top and ski down.

We landed at Kailua-Kona Airport and found a freshly waxed stretch limo from the Maika'i Resort. The driver was a smiling and gracious Asian man, in his fifties, grey haired, short and thin, and seemingly unable to stop talking. He was dressed in a very formal grey chauffer's uniform, right down to the peeked cap that he held in his hands as he bowed over and over again, greeting us. He retrieved all our eight pieces of luggage, including Sandy's six suitcases, and led us to the limo.

In what seemed like one long sentence, he expounded on the weather, the ocean tides, the volcano, and where the boats to fish from were docked. And of course, the best of everything could be found at the Maika'i Resort. He was quite conspiratorial in a funny way as he related all the current gossip floating around the west side of the Big Island. The people's names and the places were all unknown to us, but that didn't make any difference.

The best beach, the best swimming pools, the best shopping, the best restaurants, the best entertainment all could be found, he told us, at the resort. And while driving slowly along Ali'i Drive he repeated eight times what a pretty child Caroline was.

The drive to the resort seemed longer than it should have been because the driver kept up the sightseeing litany, driving a little too slow and stopping too often, while turning to look back at us and smile, as he kept doing what he must have thought was a job requirement, being a tour guide. He pointed out every gift shop, restaurant, and beach, every well-known beach bum, muscled surfer, and various other things as he drove. Caroline must have thought him to be very funny because she kept laughing and pointing at him. Oh well.

We arrived at the resort and watched as a platoon of Hawaiians wearing identical red hibiscus flowered Aloha shirts and tan shorts unloaded my two small suitcases and Sandy's six big suitcases. Caroline was loving it all; she was running around the open lobby, exploring all the new things she saw, touching exotic plants and statues, jumping and pointing at the brightly colored parrots on the tall perches, and running her fingers through the water spilling over the edge of a tall brass water fountain.

The resort staff knew we were coming and had prepared well for us. A dozen managers and executives, male and female, surrounded us, all speaking at once and all trying to be the center of our attention. They led us down a white flowered, vine roofed walkway and through flower laden gardens of every imaginable color and scent, over a small bridge spanning a slowly flowing stream stocked with rare, colorful, and expensive Koi. I had to stop Caroline before she jumped into the little stream, attracted by the colorful and very big Koi.

We were followed by four resort porters carrying our luggage. Caroline seemed to enjoy every minute of it, stopping us in our travels every now and then to look and touch things she had never seen before. Our entourage went out of their way to exaggerate their admiration of our daughter, telling us over and over again how pretty and smart she was. But that's OK with me. Personally, I think Caroline is an especially terrific child, brighter and smarter than would be average for her few years.

We arrived at our suite – The Ali'i Suite – a grand and strikingly stunning set of four bedrooms and four baths, a big sitting room with a fully stocked bar, a big lanai with a stone path from it lined with flowering plants and tall palm trees that led to a wide white sand beach. Along the path were tiki torches that would be lit when the sun set and several brightly colored parrots on bamboo perches.

Everything in the suite had been overly decorated in elaborate Polynesian style such as was never seen in Polynesia or Hawai'i before the invasions of explorers and whalers from the East. But Sandy loved it, and Caroline ran around exploring and touching everything. I followed her to make sure she didn't break anything while Sandy stood on the lanai almost overwhelmed at the beauty of everything she saw.

After over tipping the porters and shaking the hands of all the managers and executives, we were left alone finally. I found the biggest of the beds in the biggest of the bedrooms and threw myself on it. I was exhausted and needed a few hours' sleep. Sandy started to unpack but recognized I needed some down time. "I think Caroline and I will go down to the beach . . . or maybe a pool or something," she said. I smiled and closed my eyes.

I was asleep almost immediately, and when Sandy gently shook me awake it was dark outside. She switched on a nightstand light and sat on the edge of the bed next to me.

"Caroline's had dinner and a bath. She's playing in the living room and wants you to tuck her in."

I pushed myself up and sat next to her, rubbing the sleep from my eyes. "How long have I been asleep?"

****

Caroline finally fell asleep in a big bed in a bedroom she chose herself after running from one bedroom to another. She insisted on a nightlight because of the strange bedroom but she seemed happy to have the room.

Sandy had ordered dinner for us to be sent to the suite. Now understand this, I am a red meat kind of guy. A thick steak, a fat burger, a big rack of ribs, and I'm in gourmet-heaven. But I have to admit that Hawaiian fish of all kinds, fresh out of the Pacific, is a treat. I had Ono and Sandy had Mahi Mahi. We finished a bottle of 2003 Dom Perignon as a celebration; I silently wished I could have had a second bottle sent to the room. Sandy must have read my mind because she insisted one was enough. She said nothing as I poured a small brandy from the well-stocked bar the resort provided us, while we sat on the Lanai and enjoyed the cool night air.

It was close to midnight when we shared a shower and eventually wound up in the biggest and softest bed I have ever felt.

The next morning was bright and clear before the sun rose over the mountains of Mauna Kea. At half past seven I was up without waking Sandy, enjoying some good Kona coffee I had made in the little kitchen of the suite, and watching Caroline play with a few toys – a truck and three little cars, ignoring the doll – provided by the resort.

Resort management had no idea why the Crew family

was there. They knew, of course, that the family owned a very big chunk of the place, but was I there for more than a vacation? They were taking no chances; they were providing everything we could want and everything they imagined we might want.

The phone rang and woke Sandy before I could get to it. It was the front desk, the accented voice of a young woman who spoke softly, almost apologetically. "Mr. Crew, I'm so sorry to bother you so early in the morning. There is a Nancy Wong here to see you."

The name Nancy Wong immediately brought images of Hound to my mind. Hound, the 70's hippy throwback who gave his life protecting me the last time I was in Hawai'i, will always remain in my memory. I had arranged an income flow to Nancy and scholarships for their children to see them through college. But I had never thought that I would see Nancy again. Before I could say anything over the phone, that damn little voice in the back of my head started screaming once more, "Get Out! Run Away!" That meant, as usual, I was about to step into trouble.

Sandy was awake and standing at my side. She was wrapped in one of the oversized thick white bathrobes that had been carefully folded and placed in the bathroom. Her hand was on my shoulder. I think she could sense something was wrong. I said into the phone, "OK . . . Have someone show her here."

To Sandy I said, "It's Nancy Wong."

"Maybe she just wants to say hello," Sandy said, trying to ease my obvious worry.

"She came all the way out here at this time of the morning without phoning first? I don't think so. I think she wants something."

"OK, so give her what she wants. I mean, she

deserves it. She did lose Hound after all."

A knock on the door made the decision for me. I would give Nancy what she wanted even if it meant getting into trouble once again. I owed that much to the memory of Hound.

Sandy opened the door and Nancy stood there, smiling but obviously ill at ease. "Aloha," she said. "You must be Sandy. Morgan told me about you. You're as lovely as he said you are." She held out her hand and Sandy took it. Nancy Wong is a stately woman of mainly Hawaiian decent but with enough Asian in her background for her face to be majestically Chinese. She is tall, but not as tall as Sandy. Her hair is black and silky and long. But I noticed a few minor strands of grey beginning to show themselves. The years were catching up with Nancy Wong.

Nancy looked past Sandy to me, smiled again, and said, "Aloha, Morgan. You look better than the last time we talked. I hope you have fully recovered."

I stepped to her and held out my hand but she reached out and took me by my shoulders. She pulled me down, close to her, and lightly kissed me on both cheeks. She said, "Aloha, ko`u maika`i hoaloha . . . Hello my good friend."

Nancy smiled still holding my shoulders, but said nothing more. I asked, "How did you know I was here?"

"I phoned Peter Jascro," she said. "He told me."

Peter Jascro is the managing partner of Harper, Harper, Jascro and Nettles, my family's long time attorneys. He was a close friend of my father and has . . . 'taken care of me' . . . since my father's untimely death.

Nancy looked down to Caroline, still playing on the floor with her new toys. "What a beautiful child," she said. "You must bring her to play with my children someday."

We retreated to our lanai and sat in bamboo chairs with comfortable, overstuffed cushions that surrounded a large, glass top table. The sun had crept over the mountain to the East and was warm on us that morning. Sandy went to the phone and ordered coffee for her and me and a pot of hot herbal tea for Nancy. It took just short of an hour to talk our way through all the niceties; family, kids, weather, catching up on the three years that had passed since my last trip to Hawai'i, etc.

When silence fell and there was nothing left to talk about, it was finally time to get to the point of Nancy Wong's visit, so I asked, "It's good to see you again, Nancy, and I'm glad the children are doing well. Now tell me what you want me to do."

"You do come right to the point, Morgan," she said, smiling uncomfortably, shifting nervously in her chair, and lowering her head. She sipped at the hot tea in the delicate china cup she held. She sipped once again, her eyes lowered to the floor as she tried to think of the right words to use, and then she said in a weak voice, "I have a friend. Her man is dead. They say it was just an accident. They say that he ran off the road on his scooter. I think there's more to it than that. But I can't get the police to do anything. It's been three months now, and they've just written it off as a simple traffic accident."

Sandy put her cup of coffee down on the glass top table we sat around and asked, "Your friend . . . Does she think it was an accident?"

"She doesn't, but for her to do anything more than mourn for her man is not within her. She is a young girl who has been raised in the old Hawaiian way. It may be a good way to live, please understand, but she is naïve from her sheltered life. Look, Lewis . . . that's who died . . . had an old Vespa scooter. That old scooter wouldn't even start up every morning. Lewis hitch-hiked to work half the time. It hadn't gone over 20 miles an hour in years. The best thing it did was spew smoke and fumes whenever Lewis got the engine to start up. And yet the police say he took a turn too fast on some little, barely paved road high up where he had no reason to be, and slid off the road. He would not have taken that road to go home. It was miles out of the way."

"Lewis," I asked. "He's your friend's man? Are they married?"

"Leilani . . . She's my friend. She and Lewis were not married . . . According to what haoles believe anyway. They were joined by a local kahuna; a Hawaiian priest of the old ways," she explained to Sandy. "They've been together for a couple of years. They were very happy and lived a very simple life, hidden away up in the hills. They have a son . . . And Leilani is pregnant with another child."

Anticipating what Nancy wanted I asked, "And when do I get to meet Leilani?"

"Thank you, Morgan," Nancy said. She sat back and relaxed for the first time since arriving. She finally felt comfortable enough to smile at Sandy and me. I imagined it was very difficult for her to come to me and ask for help. People like Nancy Wong, and probably like this Leilani, are very independent of the world you and I are used to. She said, her voice reflecting her relief, "I can take you to her anytime you want. She lives in a very remote area, back in the hills."

CHAPTER FOUR

In San Marcos

It had been a late night for Betsy. She had driven us to the airport in San Francisco and then studied until past midnight after the long drive home in the snow.

The house was dark and quiet when she arrived home and opened the front door. She wished she had left a light on that morning when we left for San Francisco. But the lights came on quickly and the house inside was warm and welcoming. It was home; she had never felt like that anywhere before.

Shedding her heavy wool coat at the door, Betsy went to the kitchen and made a peanut butter and jelly sandwich, the first food she had eaten since a meager and rushed breakfast of toast and two cups of hot tea.

Her pre-med classes were tough even if she wouldn't admit that to anyone. Her High School experience, that ended when she dropped out at sixteen in her second year, was more wild times and cutting classes than studying so she was not as prepared for tough college classes as some of her classmates. But when she came to live with us, she was excited about getting those last two years of High School credits at the local City College. And now she is intent on college at the very private and very expensive Wrightwood College where good grades are tough to earn.

She crawled into bed at half past two in the morning and fell asleep almost immediately. She decided to sleep an extra hour the morning after Sandy, Caroline and I left for Hawai'i. Her first class at Wrightwood College wasn't until twenty minutes past ten that morning. She missed Caroline, she missed helping Sandy with our daughter's bath and breakfast, but she welcomed the extra sleep. Her alarm went off at nine and she rolled out of bed, stretching and wiping the sleep from her eyes. She was excited about the biology class that morning, not only because she liked biology, but because Stanley Douglas, Jr. was in her class. Stanley was her current crush at that time.

Stanley Douglas, Jr. is the son of Marie Douglas, widow of Stanley, Sr. who worked himself to death at the age of 59 while accumulating a fortune that will keep Marie at the San Marcos Country Club for the rest of her life, and will keep Stanley, Jr. a professional college student for many years to come. He was in his fifth year of college and enjoying his sixth major at that time. But he was tall, muscular, handsome, athletic – a tennis star at the Country Club – and popular. And in the summer months he would go down to Monterrey to play polo.

Betsy was in love . . . At an unspoken distance, of course. She wanted to talk to him, to smile and have him immediately fall in love with her. But no one would have ever guessed how shy Betsy is when it comes to men she likes. Her early life and background would have everyone believe she is aggressive sexually. She isn't.

In the biology lab that morning she sat at the lab table, alongside her lab partner, Evan Portman, wishing she could be sitting next to Stanley who was across the room. Evan was a slob of a college student. He wore the same clothes for several days in a row. His face was pimply and his breath was foul. Betsy tried to stay as far away from him as possible, but she had to work with him that semester.

She watched Stanly rather than paying attention to the class. He was smiling and joking and laughing with Lupe Garcia. Lupe, Betsy was certain, was a cheap whore. She wore wild, loud clothing; lots of cheap discount store stuff and lots of heavy makeup. And she had big breasts, and she dressed to show them off. The boys all seemed to like her. Of course Betsy had never met Lupe, never spoken with her, and everyone else thought Lupe was nice and a very smart young lady. But if she was taking all of Stanley's time, at every Wednesday morning biology class, then she had to be a whore, Betsy was certain.

Class started and ended and the eighteen students filtered out, all talking about how difficult the class was. Betsy was silent, staring at Stanley as he walked out ahead of her. Melanie Tufts touched her arm and said, "Still wishing, I see."

Melanie is Betsy's closest friend, another pre-med student. Betsy turned, tried to smile and said, "Yes. What can I do?"

"Why not just walk up to him, tackle him, throw him to the ground, kiss him all over, rip off his clothes . . . And then introduce yourself?"

"Very funny," Betsy said forcing a chuckle.

They walked side by side down the hall towards the door to the parking lot. They each had a Sociology class at a quarter to two that afternoon and nothing to do until then. "Too bad Sissy wasn't in class again," Melanie said. "She's going to get dropped pretty soon."

"I wonder where she is?" Betsy asked. She pulled open the heavy glass door and let her friend walk out ahead of her. They both pulled their thick winter coats up around them to fight off the blast of cold air that met them outside.

They walked quickly, forcing breaths against the icy wind. Melanie said, "She's desperate for a boyfriend. I don't know why she's not popular. She's not bad looking and she's rich. What more do the guys want? Knowing Sissy, she's desperate enough to be shacked up somewhere. Probably with some drug-head up in North Harbor."

North Harbor was once a nice little neighborhood where fishermen and blue collar workers had bought nice little homes and raised nice little families. But that was years ago. Since the 1970s it had gradually, block by block, turned derelict and run-down. North Harbor today is abandoned homes, topless bars, drunks, prostitutes, and drug dealers.

"Could be," Betsy said. She had lived with Sandy and me long enough to know she shouldn't discuss trouble with anyone. Bob Sommers had told her that Sissy McMillan was missing and that meant trouble. "I don't know her very well," Betsy said. "I've only seen her at the Country Club. Do you know her?"

"The Country Club," Melanie said with a bit of derisive humor in her voice. "All you special rich folks get together there? Kind'a nice that you don't have to associate with us average folks."

"OK, cut it out. Do you know Sissy very well?"

"I suppose so. I mean we have an English Lit class together and we talk there."

"So what's she like?" Betsy asked.

"Well, she likes to live fast . . . too fast if you know what I mean. Half the time she comes to class high on something. She did mention someone named . . . I think it was Tommy . . . could have been Fairy Hairy for all I know. She offered to introduce me if I wanted marijuana or anything else. I turned her down, of course. It's a real shame, you know? She's not bad looking and rich and all, like I said."

Betsy stopped as they reached the parking lot. She

said, "You wanna' come over for some lunch? There's some leftover pizza in the fridge."

"Thanks," Melanie said. "But I've gotta' go home and do a load of laundry or I'm gonna' wear dirty underwear tomorrow. I'll see you this afternoon."

Betsy got in my precious MGB that she had driven to class. At first I objected to anyone but me driving the classic, but as usual, Betsy ignored me and drove it anyway. Now it has become her primary means of transport. She does drive carefully, and she takes good care of it, keeping it clean and changing the oil, so I guess I really don't mind.

She started for our home in the hills above the harbor, then suddenly slammed on the brakes and spun the MGB around. She sped off for North harbor. When Betsy was living the 'wild child' life, before she came to live with us, she had spent a lot of time in North Harbor while cutting High School classes. She smoked a little pot and drank a lot of beer. She stayed up late, often for days at a time, and found parties where she fell into heavy metal and punk rock music. Tattoos and wildly colored hair followed. It had been years since she had seen North Harbor, but she remembered the people who she wanted to talk to that afternoon.

She drove the little MGB slowly along Harbor Drive, turning now and then onto a few side streets whose posted names had disappeared a lifetime ago. She stopped once on a street corner outside a dark and dirty beer bar. Two women, prostitutes dressed in tight skirts that barely covered their hips, fish net stockings, torn at the knee of the taller of the two, and tank tops under cheap waist length jackets, were standing on the corner, waiting patiently to earn a few dollars. They were shivering in the winter cold, waiting for a man, any man, who would give them a few dollars for meaningless sex. Betsy recognized one of the two, a woman her own age who once was a North Harbor party girl and who had progressed into a two hundred dollar a day heroin addict.

"Marci," Betsy said, rolling down the passenger side window and leaning to see the woman. "That you, Marci?"

Marci leaned down and looked into the little car. "Betsy? Betsy? That you, babe?" Betsy recognized the dull eyes and slurred voice of someone who had shot up in the very recent past.

"Hey Marci. Have you seen Old Billy lately?" she asked.

"Old Billy? Old Billy?" Marci repeated trying to focus but finding it difficult.

"You know," Betsy said. "Old Billy . . . The guy with tattoos all over."

"Oh, Old Billy! Yeah, I know Old Billy . . . I remember . . . I remember," she said, nodding her head proudly at being able to remember.

"Have you seen him around lately? I need to talk to him."

"Old Billy? That slime bag? You don't wanna' go 'round with him, Betsy. You wan' some shit . . . I can get it. You got money?"

Old Billy was what would commonly be referred to as a dirty old man. He was skinny as a rail, in his sixties and generally filthy. His grey hair was always matted and he scratched at it constantly because of the lice he carried. His beard was grey, thick and filled with bits of old food. His clothes were filthy, old, frayed, and smelled almost as bad as he did, and when he took them off he revealed tattoos over almost all of his body.

Old Billy made a living selling marijuana and cocaine. He would buy beer for underage kids and supply them with marijuana. In return, he would 'feel up' the girls and grope the boys. He liked little children but he also made it his business to know everybody and everything in North Harbor. He listened to gossip and to drunks who talked too much. He made his rounds every day, buying drugs to resell and talking and listening.

"Have you seen him, Marci?" Betsy asked again.

Marci wiped her nose with the back of her hand. She was much thinner than the last time Betsy had seen her. A thought ran through Betsy's mind that this might be the last time she would ever see Marci . . . Alive that is. "Yeah, he's been drinkin' a lot. You got twenty bucks you can lend me, Betsy? I'll pay you back next week. Huh, you got twenty bucks?"

Betsy reached for her purse and dug inside. She knew better than to show Marci all the money she had. She pulled out two twenty dollar bills, one being what Marci had asked for and the other because Betsy felt really sorry for the young girl. She handed both to Marci who grabbed the bills quickly. Betsy said, "Get something to eat, Marci. Now, where do I find Old Billy?"

Marci wiped her running nose again and lusted at the thought of what the forty dollars would buy. "He been drinkin' down at Al's Bar. I saw him there yesterday." With that she turned and ran down the street as best she could in the scuffed high heel shoes that were too big for her, away from Betsy.

CHAPTER FIVE

On The Big Island

Sandy held Caroline in her arms and they both waved good bye as Nancy Wong and I drove away in Nancy's dark brown Jeep with a tan canvass top. The car was not new, its age reflected in the dents and dings on the sides and fenders. But it was clean and the engine was well maintained. The tires were oversized and the treads thick for the back roads Nancy lived on. And as it turned out, they served us well on the mountainous dirt roads that took us to Leilani.

I held on to whatever I could hold onto in the Jeep as Nancy took the twists and turns up the hillside, along the furrowed dirt path that cut through the green forest. The road was paved in spots but was mainly potholed dirt, the asphalt having been poured years earlier and not maintained. She took the turns a little faster than I would have, but I assumed she knew where she was going and was used to the road.

The road took us up the side of the foothills of Mauna Loa, through thick forests and jungle-like undergrowth. As we climbed higher, the air became filled with the sweet smell of Hawai'i's flowers. Every now and then I could see the blue Pacific below us through openings in the trees.

We took a sharp turn to the left and Nancy pulled the Jeep to a quick stop in front of Leilani's home. The Jeep's tires skidded on the soft red dirt. To me, it was something out of a Paul Gauguin painting, filled with exotic colors and thick greenery. The little house was patched together from bamboo and an odd assortment of scraps of wooden planks along with what must have been driftwood. The roof was thatched of old, dried out palm fronds and the small covered porch that leaned to the right was lined with dried gourd flower pots hanging from rough hemp cords, holding flowers of every imaginable color.

Birds were everywhere in the trees surrounding the little hale, all singing their joyous songs in a riotous cacophony. A bright green lizard ran from under the hale's porch and across the dirt to disappear in the forest.

A young woman, a beautiful Hawaiian woman holding a young boy in her arms, stepped from inside the hale. She stood on the porch in the shade of the thatch roof, and smiled down at her friend. She stepped down the stairs and took a few steps toward us.

As we climbed out of the Jeep, I stood back as Nancy and her friend hugged and whispered a few words of greeting, words in Hawaiian that I didn't understand. Nancy stepped aside and introduced me. "This is Morgan," she said. "Morgan, this is my friend Leilani. Lewis was her man."

The little boy, dressed only in faded brown shorts, slid from his mother's arms and scampered around the Jeep and the front of the house. He was barefoot and laughing as he ran around in circles, happily singing some child's song in Hawaiian. His brown hair, bleached from the sun, hung long and uncombed. It was brown rather than the black common to Hawaiians. I learned later that it had been inherited from his father. And his chubby little body was tanned from a life outdoors.

He stopped in his tracks as he ended the song and then ran to Nancy, who scooped him up in her arms, swung him around once and hugged him tightly. She spoke in Hawaiian and he smiled broadly. "This big man is Kanye,"

Nancy said, introducing the boy to me. Slipping from her arms the boy ran back to his mother. He hid behind her, hugging her legs, and looked at me, smiling shyly.

Leilani was obviously pregnant, perhaps four months when I met her. She was a pretty, very young woman, dark and slim, and her black and thick hair flowed over her shoulders and down her back, down to her waist. A white plumeria flower graced her left ear. Her dark eyes were the kind that could swallow a man into their promise of exotic pleasures.

She put a hand on her son's shoulder and with a regal wave of her hand invited us to join her on the porch, under the thatched, sagging roof. There were two chairs, bent wicker, with threadbare cushions. Nancy sat in one; I offered the other to Leilani but she lowered herself cross-legged onto a woven mat on the floor of the porch.

After we were all settled, little Kanye snuggled onto his mother's lap. Nancy spoke softly to Leilani, "Morgan said he could help."

I sat forward quickly and said in my defense, "*Maybe* I can help. I mean, I'm a stranger here. I can only do so much. If you need money . . ."

Leilani interrupted, "No. I got enough . . . And Nancy helps."

"Then what would you like me to do?"

She looked at Nancy who nodded, giving her some support. Leilani said without any emotion, "Lewis, he was working for Mr. Vasco. He the haole owns Vasco Construction down near moana." Nancy interrupted explaining to me that moana is the ocean. Leilani smiled and continued, "That the place supposed to be building big buildings in Kailua. Somthin' funny goin' on down there. Lewis, he seen it. Lewis, he knew." Her face didn't betray the grief she was feeling for the death of her Lewis. Her dark eyes didn't blink; the words were spoken in a soft, gentle monotone.

I turned to Nancy who said, "Lewis said the company was stealing from the people who hired Vasco. He said they were using inferior materials and lying on their books and invoices."

Leilani said, still in a flat voice devoid of feeling, "Lewis, he dead today because he knew. They kill him."

"How did Lewis die?" I asked.

Leilani lowered her head and hugged Kanye; her long hair covered the boy like a silken blanket. I saw a silvery tear in the corner of her eye, the first sign of emotion and grief.

Nancy saw that her friend would have a difficult time talking about her man's death so she spoke up.

"As I mentioned before, Lewis rode an old Vespa motor scooter. Half the time he couldn't even get it started. It produced more smoke than speed when it did decide to turn on. I've been on that old piece of crap. It could only go over twenty if you pushed it downhill. But Lewis was killed when the police said he ran off a road high up in the hills."

"And you think it wasn't an accident?" I asked.

"Two things," she answered. "The road he was on wouldn't be the road he would have taken home. It would have taken him away from home. He would have had to go down from that road almost to Ali'i Drive, and then back up into the hills the way we came. He should not have been going up that road as the police say he was. There wasn't a road or even a path from that road for him to get home. He should have come the way you and I did from Vasco Construction to get home. The second thing is, as I said, his scooter couldn't have gone fast enough for him to lose control and run off the road. Particularly going uphill. He could have walked faster than that old scooter would go uphill."

"But the police disagree?" I asked.

"Yes, of course. I was at the place where he was killed. There are skid marks, but they look funny, not like the scooter made them . . . I don't know. And Lewis' scooter is still lying in the weeds off the road, on the side of the hill, down about twenty or thirty yards. We can go there."

"So you've spoken to the police," I said. "Are they still looking into it?"

Nancy said. "Sure, I've spoken with the police. They're no help at all, and they've closed their file. Maybe you can talk to them?"

"Nancy, after my last visit here I don't think I want to walk into their police station again. I think I'd just like to leave them alone."

"I understand," Nancy said and lowered her head. I had probably brought up memories of Hound and her lost love. I was sorry, but I had said it and there was no taking It back.

We were silent as I thought about all that was said. There I was, in it again, up to my neck. I had been dragged in to help people who obviously couldn't help themselves. But did I want to be dragged into it? I mean, I was supposed to be on vacation with my family, getting away from winter snow back home. How do I say 'no'? I couldn't, of course. I owed Nancy Wong that much. I owed Hound much more.

So I said, "OK, I'll try to talk to the police. They'll probably remember me. And I'll have an attorney come over from Oahu. My attorneys have an office there. We'll see where it goes."

Leilani looked up, and she and Nancy exchanged glances, silently sharing a thought. Nancy turned to me and asked, "What about Vincent Vasco? Leilani and I believe he is hiding something illegal. We believe Lewis knew about this, and Mr. Vasco had him killed."

"Lewis was working for this Mr. Vasco?"

Leilani nodded silently. She hugged little Kanye to her again. But he wanted to run and play, not understanding what was being said. He wiggled free and ran off. Leilani smiled slightly in apology.

"I have a daughter," I said smiling proudly and understanding. "She's about the same age. She can't sit still for more than a few minutes at a time."

Nancy answered my question since it seemed Leilani wasn't going to. "Lewis was a construction laborer . . . When he felt like working that is. I guess you'd say he was a day laborer."

"I don't get it," I said. "Lewis was a day laborer and yet he knew what Vasco was doing? He'd almost have to have access to the company books to know that."

"That's what I thought, too," Nancy said. She stood and walked slowly across the little covered porch. She was clasping her hands together in front of her, almost in prayer. I watched her and waited. Leilani was watching Kanye as he ran and played in the dirt. Nancy paced back and forth four times then stopped and turned to look at me once again. "I have to tell you something."

Leilani looked up at her suddenly. "No! Nancy, no!"

"He has to know," Nancy said softly. "If he finds out from someone else, he won't trust us." Leilani lowered her head; a sad and defeated look clouded her face. Nancy continued what she had to say.

"Lewis Manaluo, that's not his real name. Manaluo is his grandmother's maiden name. His name is Lewis George. His father was a haole, a guy in the Navy. His mother was Hawaiian. In 1987 the ship Lewis' father was on was attacked over in the Gulf and a bunch of sailors were killed, Lewis' father among them. His mother died when Lewis was fifteen. When Lewis was 18 he went into the Army. He wanted to learn some kind of trade. He was always interested in engine mechanics. But he was sent to Afghanistan and they made him a truck driver. On his first leave, he flew into San Francisco, bought some civilian clothes, burned his Army clothes, flew to Hawai'i and took on a new name. He was careful and never did anything that would cause a record of him to be made, not even a driver's license. He and Leilani lived up here . . . hidden away and off the grid as they say."

"But why?" I asked. "He just didn't like the army?"

"He was driving a truck, in a convoy. One of those roadside bombs went off. Three of his friends were killed in a truck near the front of the convoy. Lewis and several others left their trucks and a gun fight started. Lewis killed two men, and two more of his friends were killed before the fight ended. Lewis said that was not why he joined the army. I know that's foolish, but that's what Lewis thought. He'd never killed anyone before, and he believed he couldn't do it again. So he left."

I guess I couldn't argue his reasons for deserting. After all, I have killed people and their ghosts still haunt my nightmares. But desertion from the military was a scary thing and a serious thing. In the end he was dead, and all that didn't make any difference now.

"He was working construction," I asked. "How did he get away with that? I mean taxes and all that."

Leilani answered in her softly flowing voice, "Many people work day labor, what Lewis did. He get paid fifty dollars in cash every day he wanna' work. He don't wanna' work all the time." Leilani laughed a sad little laugh and a diamond-like drop of tear crept from the corner of her eye once again.

I felt that I needed to get more details of Lewis' life, and I felt I needed to speak with Nancy to do that. Leilani was holding in her emotions, perhaps not wanting to break down in front of a haole stranger. I could understand that, and I didn't want to break into her private grief. So I stood and Nancy stood next to me, maybe understanding. Leilani remained seated on the porch. She looked up at us, sadness and heartache overflowing from her.

I wanted to sound sympathetic, but as usual, I never know what to say when someone is grieving. So I said simply, "Thank you, Leilani. I'm very sorry for your loss. I'll do what I can to help you." The young girl forced a smile again and lowered her eyes. Kanye had stopped playing in the dirt and was looking at his mother. He ran to her and she scooped him up in her arms. They hugged each other tightly and cried together.

In Nancy's Jeep, as we bounced along the rutted dirt path, down the hillside I asked, "Tell me about Lewis."

"I thought I did that already," she answered and looked across at me, with a confused frown on her forehead.

"Tell me *about* Lewis. Who was he? What did he like? What did he dislike? Who were his friends? What were his hobbies? Did he practice any religion? I mean, was he Hawaiian in his beliefs? Tell me every detail about Lewis."

Nancy tightened her grip on the steering wheel and seemed to tense up. "Why do you want to know?"

"Lewis was a deserter from the Army. He was on the run . . . even if he was hiding out with Leilani. What else did he do that might have gotten him in trouble? Who were his enemies? I'd like to know everything there is to know about him."

"Lewis and Leilani are . . . were . . . very private. Leilani and I have always been friends, since we were little. Lewis didn't like Jerry. Jerry was a pacifist and . . . I guess Lewis saw him as a coward. So when I visited Leilani and Lewis, Jerry stayed home."

Jerry, known to me as Hound, was a 70's throwback, an aging hippy who lived for surfing, marijuana, and Nancy and their children. On my last trip to Hawai'i, Jerry . . . Hound . . . stepped in front of a bullet meant for me. He sacrificed himself to save me, belying his reputation as a man who was afraid of everything.

Nancy went on telling me more about Lewis. "Lewis didn't have any friends. He was very private. He stopped for a few beers now and then, on the way home from work. But he knew that if he got too close to anyone, his true life might have been found. He devoted his life to Leilani and Kanye. He built their house from what the forest and Island provided. His religion? I think he didn't have any real religious belief. Oh, I think he may have respected all the akua . . . the gods . . . of old Hawai'i. Leilani is a deep believer and keeps many of the old kapu. But not Lewis. I guess that's all I can tell you. Lewis was a good man and now he's dead."

Yes, Nancy Wong's friend was dead. I felt deeply sorry for the very young Leilani and the child Kanye. But I also knew, without putting it into words, that Leilani would find another man. Time would ease, if never heal, the hurt deep in her heart. And little Kanye's memory of his father would fade as do all memories of childhood. I could walk away from Leilani and Kanye, feeling sorrow for their loss, but how do I walk away from Nancy Wong? If not for me, her man, Hound, would be alive today.

And so the hook was set, and I would do what I had to

do.

As we approached Ali'i Drive, Nancy slowed the Jeep, looking for the road that would take us up to where Lewis died. We left the rutted dirt road that had taken us to Leilani and turned onto a paved but not well maintained two lane highway that would take us high up in the hills. We started up the hill and I saw that it was a steep climb.

The road saw little traffic, and much needed repairs went years without being done. The Jeep struggled up the hill in second gear, and if Nancy was not exaggerating, Lewis' old Vespa could never have taken the steep grade of the hill.

Several miles up the hill, Nancy pulled the Jeep to a slow stop along the high mountain road to the spot where Lewis had died. Over the tree tops I could see the blue Pacific stretching out to the horizon.

She jumped from the Jeep and I pulled myself out. There was a metal barrier along the side of the road, rusted, bent, and twisted where Nancy said Lewis' Vespa had hit it. I saw, and Nancy didn't have to point it out to me, that the guard rail was severely damaged. I doubted a small Vespa could have caused that much damage to the steal rail.

"Look behind you," Nancy said. "The road is uphill at this point, and it curves to the right."

I looked and said, "OK, tell me what you see."

"Lewis' little scooter would only go more than twenty miles an hour going downhill. Uphill, it would sputter and spit and barely make it up any hill, no matter the slope. As I said, Lewis could have walked faster than that damn little scooter could move uphill. The police report says that Lewis took the curve too fast and slid off the road. I told you, I've been on that piece of crap scooter. It wasn't going over five miles an hour up the hill. And the curve is to the right, not left. If he did skid it would be to the left, away from the railing, not right towards it. And where are the skid marks? There aren't any from the scooter, only bigger tire marks."

I had to admit that everything Nancy said was right. Nancy is not a stupid or slow woman. She makes a good living using a computer. She helped me easily enough with a locked computer on my last trip to Hawai'i. She is an educated person, and she was seeing things that the police should have seen. I wondered if they had seen what she saw and ignored it.

"So what did happen?" I asked her.

She stepped close to the bent railing and pointed to it. I got close enough to see what she was pointing to. She said, "There are flakes of green paint on the railing that the weather has not washed away yet. Lewis' Vespa was mainly rusted but it had some red paint left on it."

I asked, "And what do you make of that?"

"The trucks owned by Vasco Construction are all green."

I nodded, understanding what Nancy was implying.

She pointed down into the brush along the hillside off the road. There, tangled in the weeds, lay Lewis' old Vespa. I made a mental note to have a towing company retrieve it and to ask the police why they left it there.

We walked back to her Jeep and started down the hillside road. It was a long, slow drive without words being spoken. As we approached Ali'i Drive and the coast, I said as a final thought, while staring out the open window of the Jeep at the clear blue ocean and the soft white waves washing up against the seawall, "I'll talk to Mr. Vasco."

CHAPTER SIX

North Harbor, San Marcos

Marci had told Betsy that Old Billy was drinking at Al's Bar lately. Al's Bar was on Fremont Street, a side street . . . Really just a wide and dirty alley . . . Off of Front Street. When Betsy was a street child, cutting High School and hiding from her parents, it had been a hangout for derelict drunks who had beat the odds and lived long enough to see their fiftieth year. As she turned the corner onto Fremont she saw the same plastic sign, aged with dirt and mildew, hanging over the peeling brown paint on the cracked wooden door of Al's Bar. It hadn't changed much over the years, maybe just a little worse than Betsy remembered.

Many years ago Betsy would find Old Billy somewhere and buy marijuana from him. She had never let Old Billy touch her as so many other girls . . . and boys . . . did. It was always a cash deal, even if Old Billy tried to get too close to her. Once, when he cornered her in the doorway of a vacant shop front, Betsy kneed him in the balls. He backed off quickly and never got that close again.

She pulled the MGB to a slow stop at the curb in front of Al's Bar. There was a stripped down shell of a car sitting on the pavement across the street from Al's. It was covered with graffiti. Its tires and wheels had long since been removed. All its windows had been broken. The dashboard had been emptied and the front and rear seats were gone. No other cars where on the street.

It was a little past two in the afternoon. Betsy looked at her watch and shrugged, knowing she was missing her afternoon Sociology class. It was a bright, sunny day in spite of the cold winter air blowing off the nearby harbor as she stepped out of the MGB.

Dirty snow was piled up along the street and in drifts along the buildings. Empty beer cans and broken wine bottles littered the dirty snow. She stepped carefully over the crusted snow and opened the door to Al's. Heat from inside spilled out onto her along with the fetid smell of stale beer and urine that was mixed with age and dirt. Inside was dark; she took a minute standing in the open doorway for her eyes to adjust. Someone from deep inside slurred loudly, "Hey! Close the damn door! You fuckin' born in a barn or sump'tin?"

Betsy closed the door behind her and looked around the repulsive innards of Al's. The room was not more than fifteen feet wide but it was long, stretching into the dimly lit shadows at the rear. There was a bar to her right, once well carved wood but now broken, chipped, covered with too many coats of cheap paint, and knocked around by too many years in North Harbor.

Six mismatched tables, some round, a few square, lined the wall opposite the bar. Three people sat at three of the tables. One woman had fallen asleep; her gray haired head lay on the table while her arms hung down towards the floor. One man was at the table behind the sleeping woman. He was a thin black man who was singing gospel songs in a drunken mutter. The third, a man in a tattered and torn seaman's pea jacket, was at the last table in the bar. A cigarette hung loosely from his lips. He sat at the table at the back of Al's in what appeared to be a trance. He held a bottle of whiskey in one hand and a glass in the other but he wasn't moving. His eyes were open, but it appeared he was staring off at something only he could see. Betsy recognized the bartender from her street days, but she couldn't remember his name . . . or perhaps she didn't want to.

"Hey!" the bartender said to Betsy as he wiped down the bar with a dirty rag. "You got the right place, lady?"

"I'm looking for Old Billy," Betsy said, standing with her back to the door in case she had to turn and run quickly.

"He'll be here soon," the bartender said, still wiping the bar with the dirty rag, pretending to keep it clean but really only pushing the dirt and spilt beer around. "Come on over here, honey," he said, leering salaciously. "I'll buy you a beer until he gets here."

The drunk in the pea coat at the back of Al's suddenly moved and laughed loudly, spitting onto the table and down his chin. The black man turned and barked, "Quiet! I'm singing t' the Lord!" The grey haired lady who was asleep pushed herself up and slurred, "Shut d'fuck up." Her head fell hard back onto the table top with a loud bang. She started snoring noisily almost immediately. Betsy opened the door and walked out without a word.

She climbed into the MGB and drove a block away. She slammed on the brakes and spun the car around, parking it at the curb where she could see anyone going into Al's Bar. She left the engine running and turned the heater up against the winter cold outside. The canvas top of the little MGB didn't do much to keep the inside comfortably warm.

Betsy was dozing when she saw Old Billy walking toward Al's Bar. She quickly threw the car into first and spun the tires on the slush filling the gutter, getting to Old Billy before he could go inside. She pulled to the curb, startling the old man. He had pulled his wool topcoat around him, holding it closed against the cold with his hands because all the buttons had fallen off some time ago. It was the same dirty coat Betsy remembered him wearing the last time she had seen him, years before. He wore a torn, knitted ski cap, brown and white, pulled down over his ears. On his feet were rubber galoshes, the metal clips left open.

Betsy jumped from the car and stood against it, keeping it between her and the old man, not wanting to get too close to him. Greasy grey hair hung long from under the knit cap. His face had not been shaved in more than a week. Even from five feet away, Betsy could smell the man.

"Betsy? Betsy? That you, Betsy?" Old Billy asked. He squinted behind wire rimmed glasses that he wore low on the tip of his red, bulbous nose. He smiled when he realized it really was Betsy. "My God, Betsy! It really is you!"

He started towards her but stopped when Betsy put her arm up to stop him. "Stay back there," she said. "I don't want you near me."

"Oh, Betsy. That saddens me," he said and faked a pout. "Come give Old Billy a big hug." He opened his arms and his overcoat fell open. His pants were belted with a frayed length of hemp cord. The zipper of his stained pants was broken and open. He wore a sweatshirt, grey from both color and age that held the spilt food that had missed his puffy lips over the last couple of weeks. He was the same disgusting individual Betsy remembered from years ago.

"Not likely," Betsy said. "Do you know Sissy McMillan?"

"Darling little Sissy?" Old Billy said with a disgustingly leery grin on his dirty face. A few drops of spittle dripped from the corner of his lips. "Of course I know Sissy. Her beautiful breasts are soft and white. Let's see if they're like yours, little darling Betsy."

"Not likely," Betsy repeated. "She's hanging around with someone named Tommy. Do you know him?"

"Oh, darling little Betsy. You're asking so many questions of me and not offering me anything in return. Now, I think I deserve a little something, don't you? Why don't we step into an alley where we can be alone?"

"Not likely," she said again. She opened her purse and looked inside her wallet. She had two twenty dollar bills and four singles. She pulled a twenty from the wallet without letting Old Billy see the rest of her meager supply of cash. "Twenty bucks," she said, holding the bill out in front of her. "Now tell me, do you know this Tommy?"

"For twenty dollars . . . yes, I know Tommy. He's a nasty little boy. Likes his drugs but he isn't very friendly . . . won't share himself with me."

"How do I find him?" she asked. "What's his last name? Where does he live?"

"Now that's yet more questions, my darling little Betsy. I think I deserve something more, don't you?" He was drooling through his lascivious leer. Spittle hung on the stubble covering his chin. His nose was running and dripping onto his coat without Old Billy knowing or caring if he did know.

Betsy reached into her wallet and pulled out the four one dollar bills. "This is all I have," she lied, holding them up with the twenty. "Take it or leave it."

"Oh, alright," Old Billy said. "If that's all I get, that will have to be enough." He took a step forward and started to reach for the bills. Betsy pulled them back and said, "Tell me first. You're a lying son of a bitch and we both know that."

"Oh, alright my darling little Betsy. But I am very disappointed. Tommy DeVito is his name. He lives down by the harbor. He has a little place above the Mancini Warehouse."

"That place has been abandoned for years," Betsy said.

"Yes," Old Billy said. "Tommy has made a place for himself on the top floor. There used to be an office there. Ragged little place, but he's a real stoned out drugger. I was there once. I heard about a party with all kinds of pretty little boys and girls. Damn Tommy and his friends beat me up and stole some marijuana I had wanted to sell them. Nasty little boys, those were."

Betsy balled up the five bills and tossed them at Old Billy. They fell to the sidewalk at his feet. He bent and picked them up too quickly, coming close to losing his balance. He fumbled with them and let them fall to the sidewalk again. He quickly snatched them up, struggling to bend through his layers of clothes enough to reach them. He held them tightly in his dirty fists while Betsy opened the door to the MGB but before getting in she turned back to Old Billy and said, "If you're lying to me I'll come back and do more than knee you in the balls. Understand?"

CHAPTER SEVEN

On The Big Island

Nancy pulled her Jeep to the curb in front of the Kailua-Kona Police Station. She left the engine running and looked across the seat at me. I really didn't want to get out of the Jeep and walk up the stairs and into what I knew would be waiting for me inside. But I finally got up the courage and walked into the Police Station. It hadn't changed much in the years since I had last been there. It was still a cold and unwelcoming place, but maybe the paint on the walls had been changed, I couldn't really remember. It was a pale green that day.

I stopped at a glass walled reception desk and waited for the woman on the other side of the wall to look up at me. I thought maybe I should tap on the glass but I didn't. Finally, she slowly looked up and asked, "Yes, what can I do for you?"

"I'd like to speak with someone about the Lewis Manaluo death, please."

"And who is Lewis Manaluo?" she asked.

"He was in a reported auto accident some time ago. He died. I would like to speak to someone about that."

"And who are you?" she asked. So far her welcome wasn't too welcoming. She hadn't smiled at all nor had she said even a simple 'good morning'. But I was used to that kind of reception and brushed it aside.

"I'm Morgan Crew," I answered and smiled a lot.

She reached for a phone and turned in her chair, her back to me. I tried but I couldn't hear what she was saying. When she turned back to me she hung up the phone and said, "Have a seat over there," pointing to the wall behind me. I turned and saw a wooden bench that I went to and waited.

I looked at my watch every fifteen seconds or so; a nervous reaction to waiting for something to happen. Twelve minutes went by; I was hoping Nancy was still waiting for me outside so someone could testify that I had in fact entered the Police Station if I never came out again. Then a side door opened and Police Chief Daniels stood in the doorway, looking at me.

"I thought I'd gotten rid of you," he said.

"Yeah, sorry," I answered as I stood up. "I just need a couple of minutes. I need to speak to someone about the Lewis Manaluo death."

"Why?" he asked.

"Is there someplace we can talk?" I asked. "I mean, maybe we could go to your office?"

"Why?" he asked again.

"I just need to clarify a few things about Lewis' death, that's all."

"Why?"

I took a few steps toward Chief Daniels, but I stopped when his hand went to the very big pistol hanging at his side. He rested his hand on the butt of the gun, and I got the message. That old feeling of challenging authority once again overwhelmed me. So I smiled broadly and said, "OK, have it your way. You know my attorneys. I'll just have them file whatever papers they think appropriate to get you into court bright and early tomorrow morning. Then you can explain to the judge why you won't talk to me about a closed police accident investigation."

"You'd do that, wouldn't you?" Daniels said snidely.

"You should know me by know, Chief Daniels," I said and took another step towards him just to test his resolve. "I get what I want, when I want it."

"In my office," Daniels spit out; he turned and let the door start to close behind him. I ran to it, grabbed it before it could close and followed him. The inside of the police station hadn't changed at all, except for all the new faces. Daniels had added several new officers to his station.

He sat behind his desk, and without him asking me to sit, I took a chair and sat, keeping the desk between us. I tried as best as I could to look in charge and not worried, but I was. Daniels asked, "So what the hell do you want?"

"Lewis Manaluo died in what has been classified as a motor vehicle accident. I was up where he died. There are things I'd like to make sure made it into the file before it was closed."

"And how the hell do you know the file is closed?" he asked angrily.

"My friend, Nancy Wong, has been following the case. She told me."

"Is that the Nancy Wong that was married to the drug head you dragged around with you the last time you were here?"

I had no intention of arguing with the man, I wouldn't have won. So I said simply, "Yes."

"And if I tell you to go t'hell, you'll run off to your attorneys, right?"

"As fast as I can," I answered.

Daniels picked up his phone and pushed two numbered buttons. He said into the phone, "Bring me the accident file on a Lewis Manaluo."

He hung up the phone and leaned back in his chair, his hands folded in his lap, and stared at me with what I can only describe as pure hate. I said nothing as we waited, but I kept forcing a smile onto my face.

It seemed like hours passed very slowly but in fact a woman in civilian clothes brought the thin file to Chief Daniels within minutes. He laid it on his desk without opening it and said, "So, what the hell do you want to know?"

"Can I see the file?" I asked.

"No, you can't."

"OK, then tell me if the accident scene was diagramed and photographed."

Daniels stared hard at me and then said, "Say please."

I laughed trying to hide just how scared I was. I leaned forward and whispered, "Please, sir."

Daniels opened the file and held it up so I couldn't see what was inside of it. He leafed through the few pages inside one by one, closed the file and laid it back on his desk. He said, "No photos . . . The scene was described verbally."

"Is that usual?" I asked, surprised that no photos were taken nor diagrams made.

"In certain cases . . . such as this one," he answered.

"Why?" I asked, pleased that I got to ask 'why' as Daniels had done.

"Because that's the way we do it."

"What about insurance claims?" I asked.

"Bums like Manaluo don't have insurance. He didn't even have a driver's license."

"Is there a record in the file of the green paint on the railing where the scooter went off the road?" I asked.

Again Daniels picked up the file and leafed through it slowly. He closed it and said, "No . . . Why?"

"Because it's there," I answered.

Daniels glared at me, his face starting to turn red. He asked, "And how long has that damn green paint been there? Could have been months."

"Wouldn't it be nice to know that for sure? And why is the scooter still down the side of the cliff? Why hasn't it been pulled up and examined?"

"For what?" he asked.

"I have a witness who has been on the scooter. It could just barely run and couldn't have made it up that hill fast enough to skid off the road."

"Who?" Daniels asked as he sat forward and leaned his elbows on his desk.

I didn't tell him my witness was Nancy Wong. I asked, "Does the file mention there are no skid marks made by the scooter at the scene, only large tire marks, and that the road turns to the right?"

"Why?" Daniels asked without opening the file.

"Because Lewis went off the road to the right. If he had been going fast enough to take the turn too fast, he would have skidded to the left, not to the right. And the scooter would have left skid marks."

Chief Daniels leaned back in his chair and glowered at me. Then he picked up the phone and punched in two numbers. When someone answered he growled, "Get the hell in here!"

A uniformed officer almost ran into Daniels' office and stood, apparently frightened more than I was. Daniels tossed the thin file to the officer and said, "You fucked that up! Get out there right now and complete the scene! And get somebody to pull that damn Vespa up the hill. Get it to our motor pool and have them tear it apart! I want that done today, got it!"

The officer fumbled with the file and just stood looking at his boss. Daniels slammed his fist down on his desk and yelled, "Well, get the hell going!"

The officer, a very young haole who was probably a very new recruit, turned and ran from the office. Daniels opened his top desk drawer and took a pack of Winston cigarettes out. He took one and held the pack out. "You want one?" he asked.

"I'd love one," I said. "But my wife would kill me."

"Yeah," he laughed. "And I wouldn't even charge her. Might give her a medal though."

He lit the cigarette, coughed as he inhaled the smoke, and then asked, "Why the green paint? Is that important?"

His voice had finally taken on a reasonable tone. I relaxed a little and decided to open up to him. I explained, "Lewis lived up in the hills with a young girl. They were married by a Kahuna. They have a child and one on the way.

He worked as a day laborer at Vasco Construction. His woman said he thought something fishy was going on at the construction site, but she doesn't know what. All of Vasco's trucks are green like the green on the railing."

"Vasco Construction," Daniels said. "There's a lot of money there. The Island Government encourages development. I need more than that to go out and bother them."

"Vincent Vasco runs the place," I said. "I just think you need to talk to him. Find out if he had anything to do with Lewis' death. That's all."

"Yeah, that's as good as everything else you've brought to me. I need more than speculation to go after a multi-million dollar developer. But look, I'm going to see to it that the accident is investigated properly and if anything turns up . . . I'll follow up on it."

"Will you let me know what you find out?"

"Where are you staying?" he asked.

"At the Maika'i."

"Of course," he said derisively. "Your resort is OK but Vasco's isn't. Yeah, I'll let you know," Chief Daniels said. "Now, how about you get the hell out of here and go back to your too expensive playground."

It wasn't a question so I got up and left.

Nancy was waiting for me at the curb. I got in and she asked what I had found out.

"Nothing really," I said. "They're going to go to the accident scene again and do a more thorough accident report. They're going to pull Lewis' Vespa into their motor pool and have their mechanics look it over. Chief Daniels said he'd let me know what they find out. Don't be too surprised if he doesn't tell me, though."

****

It was late into the afternoon when I pulled myself from Nancy's Jeep at the grand marble and polished brass of the Maika'i Resort. I stood on the marble floor under the polished wood roof and watched her drive away. In our suite, Caroline was just waking up from a nap. She stumbled and crawled around the main room, rubbing sleep from her eyes. When she looked up and saw Sandy with her arms around my neck, kissing me, she squealed and ran to us. Sandy stepped back, and I reached down to pick up our little girl and spun her around.

The three of us sat on the floor and played with Caroline and her toys. She giggled and laughed and crashed one toy truck into another, again ignoring the dolls supplied by the resort. Suddenly she stood, smiled broadly and said, "Let's go swimming!" So on with our swim trunks and bathing suits, and we ran out to the pool. I jumped in and held my arms up for Caroline who without hesitation jumped into my arms and the water. We splashed and laughed until the cool evening air set in.

Retreating to the lanai, Sandy ordered drinks for us and dinner for Caroline, who insisted on chicken nuggets, French fries, and chocolate milk. All my objections that I wasn't allowed such a gourmet treat went unheard or maybe ignored. But the bourbon eased things for me.

We watched the sun begin to set into the wide Pacific as Caroline, after her dinner, played with one of the toy trucks on the lanai. She again ignored the doll and the Teddy Bear.

We hadn't talked of my visit with Nancy's friend in the hours since I returned. I really didn't want to bring up the subject because that damn little voice that lives in the back of my head was screaming once again, "RUN AWAY! RUN AWAY!" Whatever the source of that voice, it seems to know every time I start to step into that swamp full of gators and snakes. All I wanted to do was pack our bags and get on the first jet out of there. But as usual, I knew that wasn't going to happen.

I think Sandy sensed what I was feeling. When the sun had set and little Caroline was beginning to slow down, Sandy poured another bourbon for me, to keep me busy as she put Caroline to bed for the night. She picked her up and said, "I think its bedtime." Caroline yawned and hugged her mother tightly. "When I get back we'll talk," she said to me.

I sat in the cool of the evening, listening to the faint melodies of the Hawaiian music coming from the beach bar. A slack string guitar and soft vocals floated on the hibiscus scented air. I wished I had a cigarette and another bourbon. Sandy had quietly returned and sat next to me without me noticing.

"Your daughter would like you to tuck her in," she said. "And leave the light on until she's asleep, OK? I'll order some dinner while you do that. How about some shrimp?"

I went to Caroline's bedroom and found her fast asleep. I kissed her lightly and left the room, leaving the light on even though she was asleep already.

I returned to the lanai and found Sandy had relented and poured a third bourbon for me. As I sipped at it, the suite's doorbell rang and dinner was delivered; grilled shrimp with an Asian sauce, steamed rice, and bok choy. Sandy pulled a split of a good Riesling from the suite's wine cooler. By the time I was done I was feeling the effects of the three bourbons and wine.

I moved from the table to a chase lounge on the lanai,

leaned back and closed my eyes. My thoughts were deep into the beautiful mysteries of the Islands and the death I had to find answers to. "A penny for your thoughts, Morgan," Sandy said surprising me.

"Yeah," I answered. "For a penny I'd give them to you forever."

"It's that bad?"

"Yeah . . . It's that bad."

"Tell me," she said and reached a hand out to touch my arm.

"Nancy believes her friend was murdered. Leilani . . . that's Nancy's friend and the dead guy's . . . girlfriend . . . wife I guess. They lived together anyway. Nancy says they were married Hawaiian style. Anyway, she thinks he was murdered. The police don't. Nancy and Leilani want me to prove he was murdered."

"And you want to go home," she said. It wasn't a question. We have been together long enough for her to know me perfectly, to know what I was thinking without words being spoken. I think that evening she also knew I wasn't going to go home.

"I want to . . . But as usual I can't. Damn it! God damn it!" I slammed my fist down on the little bamboo table next to my chaise lounge.   "I'm sick of people coming to me all the time!"

It was only a few months before that I had been captured and tortured in that warehouse in that ugly West Texas compound. All those people, Mary Lou Perkins and her whole operation, they were all dead. But the memories of the beatings I took; the cracked ribs and broken teeth out on that remote desert road; the rubber hose Colonel Max used on me in the warehouse; the days without food or water; and the death of all those good people who gave their lives for me, stay with me still. The memory of the feeling that I was going to die back there, without ever seeing Sandy and Caroline again, still haunts my nightmares today. I was sure I was going to die back in that damn compound, and no one would ever know.

And then there were the frightening memories of my last visit to Hawai'i. Was it all just a bad dream? Or did it actually happen? I believe, an unspoken belief, that the ghosts and demons, and all the ancient legends are real. No one else believes what I saw and what happened to me. I had been close to death once again, that time to just save my family from losing some money they really didn't need.

"Why me? Why not someone else?" I asked, more to myself than to Sandy.

"Because, Morgan, you are who you are. It's your life. It's your purpose in life. You're here to help people. You're here to do what others can't do for themselves. And that's why I love you so much."

I smiled at her and said, "It's not the money, huh?"

"Well . . . Yes, of course," she laughed. "Of course the thought of all that money just makes your expertise between the sheets all that much better. I often dream of making love on piles and piles of hundred dollar bills!" Then the mischievous grin left her face and she said very seriously, "Morgan, I'd love you if you were the poorest man on earth. You know that. Go ahead and give away everything and let's move into a shack here on Hawai'i. I'll still be there with you. Now what do we do about helping Nancy Wong?"

"I went to the police," I said. "I spoke with Chief Daniels . . . Remember? I told you about him. Anyway, I convinced him to reopen the accident investigation. There are too many things that were passed over. He said he would let me know the results, but I doubt he really will."

Sandy said nothing, she knew how torn up inside I was at having to go through yet another task that I really didn't want to take on. She squeezed my hand and we watched the stars in the cloudless sky until it was very late.

****

The next morning, after a light breakfast of fresh pineapple, yogurt, and great coffee, I rented a car from the Avis desk at the resort lobby and without too much trouble I found Vasco Construction's building site, where Lewis Manaluo worked. It was a thirty-five mile drive south of the Maika'i Resort and twenty three miles south of Kailua-Kona in an area that once was undeveloped trees and jungle-like foliage. There was an occasional small hale, sometimes fenced and with maybe a goat or two grazing here and there on the thick, green grass, but little else. I took a slow curve in the road and then in front of me was a big gash that had been cut into the thickets. A sign along the road read: *VASCO CONSTRUCTION*.

I pulled from the paved road onto the cleared, rutted, red dirt road that was the entrance to the building site. About twenty five yards off the paved road I stopped at a tall chain link fence with a wide double gate crossing the entrance. It was closed and locked with a heavy chain and padlock. To one side was a small wooden gatehouse. A uniformed man stepped from it.

His long tan pants were fresh and crisp. His pressed and wrinkle free shirt was light blue, with long sleeves rolled down and buttoned at the cuff despite the heat. There was a silver badge pinned to the shirt over his heart. He wore a wide brimmed grey hat with a similar silver badge pinned to the front of it. And he had a sidearm, a big semi-auto pistol, carried in a polished black leather holster at his hip. He was almost military in appearance.

He carried a clipboard as he walked slowly towards the center of the gate, eyeing me suspiciously. He stood inside the locked gate and stared out at me. I rolled down the window of the car and leaned my arm, as casually as possible, out the window. If he was waiting for me to get out, he had a long wait.

Finally the guard reached down to a ring of keys that were clipped to his black leather belt and unlocked the gate. He pushed one side of the double gates open just enough for him to squeeze through and closed the gate behind him without locking it.   He approached me very slowly and suspiciously. But instead of walking to the driver's side of the car, he walked very deliberately to his left, his hand on his holstered pistol. He circled the car officiously, looking inside each window as he walked. When he was on my side of the car, he stopped just behind the door, as cops do when preparing to ask for a driver's license.

"May I help you, sir?" he asked as he leaned down and peered into the car.

"I don't need help," I answered, trying as hard as I could to be a wise-ass. I have always enjoyed challenging authority, especially when people think they have authority when they really don't.

"This is private property, sir," he said.

"No it isn't," I said. "Inside your fence may be private property but out here it just ain't."

"I assure you, sir . . ."

"Let's cut the crap," I said. "I want to see Mr. Vinnie Vasco."

"Your name, please sir?" he asked.

"Morgan Crew."

The guard looked at his clipboard, flipped through a few pages, then said, "I'm sorry sir. But I don't see your name on my list. Is Mr. Vasco expecting you?"

"Go inside," I said. "Pick up your phone and tell Mr. Vasco that Mr. Morgan Crew is here. Tell him I own steel companies, concrete companies, shipping companies, construction companies, electronic companies, and a few banks . . . Tell him I own a lot of shit like that and he's probably doing business with a couple of my companies. Tell him I want to speak with him right now."

The guard stood up straight, hesitated, at first looking down at me wondering if I was crazy, joking, or serious. Then he walked quickly back inside the gate. He closed the gate but didn't lock it once again. I watched the guard through the window of his little guard shack as he picked up a telephone and spoke into it. He nodded, hung up the phone, turning his back to me. If I wasn't going to get in, he would have locked the gate and walked away. So I waited, rolling up the window to let the air conditioner do its job. It was hard to believe that back home, in San Marcos, it was probably snowing and cold and miserable.

I waited in the car, wishing I had a cigarette, for not more than a few minutes before I saw the guard quickly pick up phone again. He listened but said nothing. Hanging up the phone, he left his little guard shack and came back to me. This time he came directly to me and bent down before asking, without officious fake authority, "May I see your driver's license, please, sir? Mr. Vasco wants to make sure you are who you say you are."

That seemed reasonable enough, something I would do if the situation were reversed. So I let him look at my driver's license, but pulled it back when he tried to take it from me. "Look," I said, "but don't touch." He smiled a knowing smile and looked carefully at my California Driver's License. He looked at the photo and then at me and back at the photo. He wasn't going to take any chances.

The guard stepped back and glared down at me, the knowing smile having disappeared from his face. For a minute I thought he might draw his gun and shoot me. Instead he walked as slowly and deliberately as he could manage to the double gates, pulled the right gate open and waived me on. My small Japanese rental car just barely made it through the one open gate without scraping paint off of it. Just as I made it through, a brand new Dodge pickup truck, green in color as Nancy Wong had mentioned, drove directly at me and stopped a few inches away from the front bumper of my car. Two men, in the same kind of uniform the gate guard wore, climbed out of the truck and approached me.

"Good morning, Mr. Crew," one of them said in greeting, bending down to look at me while the other circled my car, looking inside through the windows. "You'll need to leave your car here and come with us. Mr. Vasco is waiting for you in the construction office." He tried to open the door for me but I had locked all the doors. I smirked, feeling satisfied. I waited a long few seconds, and then unlocked the door. It was opened for me and I followed the two to their pickup truck.

The Dodge was what is called a "six pack", a front and rear seat in front of a long open bed. I sat in the rear seat, making sure they didn't lock the door that I planned to jump out of if necessary.

We bounced along slowly for a few hundred yards. It certainly was a construction site; there was no doubt about that. There were big and small trucks, back hoes, excavators, bulldozers, and a dozen or so men standing around holding shovels and smoking. Piles of dirt were everywhere, and two bulldozers were pushing two piles of dirt into two new piles. There were holes in the ground, a couple big holes and a lot of small holes.   Stacks of steel beams and piles of wood, plywood, concrete blocks, and heavy lumber lined the road. A couple dozen big roles of cable, some red, some blue and many black in color lay unused at one side of the road, while cardboard boxes that obviously had been sitting out in the weather for a long time were stacked up on the other side. But I didn't see any real building in progress.

We came to a stop outside a long double-wide trailer, painted green like the pickup truck. A set of unfinished rough wooden stairs led up to an even rougher wooden walkway that stretched around one side of the trailer and across the front. There was a small metal table and two metal chairs on the walkway at the front of the trailer, painted the same green as the trucks and trailer.

I couldn't help but notice that the wood of the stairs and the walkway, although unfinished, was nearly new and not worn as I would expect to see at a construction site. It was weather beaten but appeared little used. Standing at the top of the stairs could only be Vincent Vasco.

He was middle aged, perhaps forty-five years old, and in great physical condition. He stood a little taller than me, perhaps 6' 3", slim and muscular. His grey suit was cut to show off his slim waist and broad shoulders. His hair was black, thick and curly, combed back off his forehead and shiny from whatever grease he used to hold his hair in place. His eyes were deep set and very blue, yet he was dark, Mediterranean dark rather than tanned by the Hawaiian sun.

He wore a black silk shirt open at the collar, two buttons down to make sure everyone could see the black hair on his chest. And to finish off the outfit he wore highly polished dark green shoes of some sort of lizard skin. I had been around professional crooks enough to take quick notice of the slight bulge under his left arm. Mr. Vasco may be a lot of things, but a man who worked in construction . . . he was not. He *was* the type to carry a gun, however.

And I had seen his type before. Mr. Vasco was connected. Mr. Vasco was East Coast connected. Mr. Vasco was a man who demanded respect. Mr. Vasco was part of an organized crime family.

I had seen them before. I had seen them years before in San Marcos when they tried to turn my quiet little town into a major drug import point. I had seen them in Las Vegas when one of their kind almost murdered Sandy. Mr. Vasco might as well have had a sign pinned to his coat saying 'MAFIA'.

I stepped out of the truck and started towards the stairs up to Mr. Vasco. A guard, uniformed like the others, standing at the bottom of the stairs raised his hand like a traffic cop stopping cars. As I said, I like to challenge authority, particularly feigned authority, so I did stop, but not until his raised hand touched my chest. He didn't move, but Mr. Vasco laughed and said, "It's OK. Let him come on up here."

His voice was a painful whisper, gravelly, deep, almost like an injured bear in the forest. As I started up the stairs, he took two steps closer to the top of the stairs. My eyes were drawn to a nasty scar, red and jagged, across the left side of his throat, from under his ear down and more than halfway to his right ear. That would explain his voice. I wondered if the person who gave him that was still walking around.

I was one step below the wooden deck. Mr. Vasco stood at the top blocking my way up. He smiled down at me. His right hand slowly reached into his jacket. At first I thought he was going for his gun. He pulled a cigar from a black leather case that he took from his inside jacket pocket, slowly bit the tip off, spit it to his left, and lit it with a gold gas lighter that shot a two inch triple flame out. I waited, one hand on the railing, and said nothing, exchanging smiles with him. Finally he said, "So what the hell you waiting for? Come on up."

"I would if you weren't in my way. And I have no intention of playing King of the Hill with you."

He laughed broadly, sounding more like an injured bear trying to laugh, and stepped aside. There was a glass sliding door on the trailer at his right hand which he opened, and he stepped back for me to walk past him, into the trailer. Inside, I remember thinking that I hoped I was eventually going to walk out again.

Rather than an ordinary looking construction trailer, with big work tables and papers and blue prints and tools, the interior was another world. We were in a reception room, paneled in dark stained oak, carpeted with a lush pale green carpet, free of mud stains from the outside. It was furnished with expensive tan leather chairs and a long red leather couch outlined in big shiny-brass tacks. A Las Vegas type beauty, with mounds of blond hair piled high on top of her head, was sitting behind a desk, smiling brightly through exceedingly large and very red lips, as Mr. Vasco led me through a door into his office, which took up two thirds of the long trailer.

It was decorated – how do you say it? – overly masculine in style. Everything was big and bold, failing in an attempt to look rich and sophisticated. In one corner there was a big table on which rolls of construction plans were piled neatly. The rest of the place was dark cherry wood, red velvet, over stuffed leather, and a really big desk that looked elaborately hand carved and polished to a mirror finish. The walls held framed photos of Sinatra and his Rat Pack, Edward G. Robinson, James Cagney, and other movie and stage stars, both male and female, most of them autographed. And there was a marble top bar with a brass rail at the foot; behind it on glass shelves were a dozen crystal decanters filled with a dozen different liquors.

Vinnie stepped behind his desk and sat, leaning back in

the tall red leather chair, and drew deeply on his cigar. He continued to smile; I think it was his way of intimidating people, and he did it very well. I stood for the moment or two it took him to say, "Hey! How come you're standing there? Sit down. You wanna' a drink or somethin'?"

I pulled a chair away from the desk and sat, trying as best as I could to not look frightened. The game was on and I was willing to play, so I sat back quietly and smiled back at Mr. Vasco. I would bet my money and family power against his money and family power, and we'd see who would win. I crossed my legs and sighed, feigning boredom, waiting for him to say something. When he did speak I grinned, knowing I was a point ahead in our little game.

"So, Mr. Morgan Crew," he asked. "How come you wanna' see me? You wanna' invest some of your millions in my comp'ny?" His injured, raspy voice had a definite East Coast accent to it. Maybe New York, but with the damage done to it, it was hard to determine for sure.

"No, Mr. Vasco. I've got enough investments. I want to talk with you about a friend of mine. Lewis Manaluo. He works for you . . . Here on your construction site."

Vasco frowned theatrically and sat forward, holding his cigar out and leaning his elbows on his desk. There must have been an A/C vent or fan hidden somewhere because the smoke from the cigar was being blown directly at me. Another little means of intimidation. He, of course, had no idea that I enjoyed it and wished I could join him with a cigar of my own. But Sandy would surely know.

"Lewis who?" he asked. "I never heard the name before. What kind'a work did he do here?"

I caught the mistake and ran with it. I sat forward, made it a point to take a deep, enjoyable breath of the cigar smoke, and said, "You asked what kind of work '*did*' he do here. You mean he doesn't work here anymore?"

"I don't know. I got no idea."

"Actually, he's dead, Mr. Vasco," I said as I leaned back, very satisfied with having scored another point in our little game. His expression and the smile on his face didn't change.

"That's too bad. He worked here, huh? When's the funeral . . . I'll send some flowers."

"What was he working on?" I asked, ignoring his obviously sarcastic remark.

"I got no idea. I told you, I don't know the guy. I got a lotta' guys work here . . . Day labor most of 'em. Too damn lazy, most of 'em, t'work full time, ya' know? Sure, they get paid cash . . . Off the books. I gotta' do somethin' to make this damn place pay off. This damn Island is expensive, ya' know? I got investors wouldn't be happy if it didn't. So, you wanna' go report that off the books crap, go ahead. But unn'erstand that if you do, my investors wouldn't be happy about that neither."

"Your investors," I asked. "Is that supposed to be threatening to me?"

"Threatening?" he said and forced a rough laugh. "I ain't said nothin' threatenin' to nobody, Mr. Crew." He took in a deep mouthful of cigar smoke and blew it directly at me. It smelled like a really good cigar, maybe a little stronger than I like. I prefer them on the mild side and with Dominican Republic grown tobacco with a light Connecticut shade wrapper. But I get so few chances to enjoy a fine cigar that I took advantage of the cloud blown at me and inhaled deeply. I made such a big show of enjoying it that Vasco didn't bother repeating the attempted intimidation.

I sat back again and crossed my hands in my lap. I

looked Vasco right in his eyes and said, "Mr. Vasco, I've dealt with guys from big families before. You don't frighten me. I've got a big family, too." I'm certain he took my meaning. "Now let's cut out all the bull crap and just let me know what Lewis Manaluo was working on here. I'm just trying to help his family, nothing else."

Vasco leaned back in his tall chair, the back of it hitting the wall behind him and causing a big framed photo of Marilyn Monroe to shake. He chewed on the end of his cigar, stared at me and grinned as he was thinking. The room was filling with smoke at the ceiling. I looked at my wrist watch twice before he spoke. "OK, go on out and find my foreman. Name's Mario. Ask him. If this guy was working here, he'd know."

"I'll do that," I said. "But one thing before I go. You've got a big construction site here. You've been at it for . . . How long? More than six months, right? Yet all I see are holes in the ground and guys standing around doing nothing."

"Yeah, so what? You some kind of fuckin' engineer or somethin'? What the hell you know about my business?" His injured whisper of a voice took on a meanness to match the scowl on his face.

I smiled. I had an idea what was going on. Proving it would be difficult. And did I really have to prove whatever criminal activities Vinnie Vasco was involved in? All I needed to do was to find out why Lewis died. If the two things were somehow connected, so be it. But for the time being, I convinced myself that I didn't need to know what Vinnie Vasco was doing. So I just got up and left to find Mario.

CHAPTER EIGHT

San Marcos

Betsy pulled the MGB to a stop at the curb across the street from the Mancini Warehouse where Old Billy had told her Tommy DeVito lived. Snow plows had recently been there and had pushed the street's snow to the curb, piling it high where cars were supposed to park. Betsy had to park almost in the middle of the street. But there wasn't much traffic at Harborside that day. In fact, the snow of the last few weeks had kept almost everyone away. The gift shops and restaurants were closed, to re-open when the weather cleared and people returned to the harbor and wharfs.

She left the engine running on the MGB as she sat inside trying to stay warm against the icy weather outside. She was wondering if she should go in to the warehouse . . . hoping to find Sissy McMillan there . . . or to just say 'The hell with it' and go home for an afternoon and evening of homework. "What would Morgan do?" she said out loud. Knowing the answer, she turned the key, quieting the engine, and opened the door. A blast of cold winter wind hit her as she ran across the street. She clambered over the snow pile left by the plows. Snow found its way into her boots as she climbed the banked snow. She skidded and slipped across the icy sidewalk, managing to keep to her feet.

The dilapidated building used to be, once years ago, a warehouse where fish were cleaned and packed in ice, awaiting trucks to take them to wherever the fish could be sold. Today it is a rotted wooden hulk with only a faint hint of the paint from years past that it used to be clothed in dotted here and there. The tin roof was rusted and bent and failed many years past to hold back the rain.

The walls were covered with spray painted graffiti and remnants of posters and homemade signs for lost dogs and cats. There were four windows along the street-side wall but the glass had long since been broken out of all of them. And on the sidewalk in front of the building was a tarp covered motorcycle. Betsy thought that might belong to Tommy DeVito, and if it did, then he was inside. But why leave it outside when inside it could at least be out of the weather? Crazy, she thought. Maybe Tommy was crazy?

At the side of the building, there was a single door with four small windows that were boarded up next to two large sliding doors that once allowed trucks inside the warehouse. Betsy knocked on the door, softly at first, then a little harder. After trying a third time, she put her hand on the door knob and hesitated. But she did turn the cold knob and the door swung open on noisy hinges.

Inside was grey and as cold as it was outside. The old walls could not stop the winter wind from blowing with an eerie whistle though the warehouse.   Betsy took three steps inside and stopped. She called out, "Hello! Anybody here? Hello!"

She had a small pocket flashlight on her keychain, meant for little more than finding a keyhole at night. But she switched it on. For as little good as it did, it did keep her from tripping over rubbish that covered the concrete floor.

A big rat ran across the floor a dozen feet in front of her and made her flinch. "Oh great!" she said, again out loud. "That's all I need." She walked carefully and slowly, further into the building. Twice more she called out, "Hello! Hello! Anybody here!"

She walked the perimeter of the warehouse and found a staircase at the rear of the building. She fought back the feeling that to run was the best thing she could do and took the stairs one at a time.

Each tread squeaked loudly, and one bent as she stepped on it, making her think it would break under her, but it didn't. There was trash on every tread; empty potato chip bags, candy wrappers, old take-out food containers. It all reassured Betsy that someone was in fact living there.

At the top was what used to be an office; a room with a big glass wall in front. Half of the glass wall was broken, and plywood had been nailed to the frame to cover the opening. The other half was cracked and filthy but not broken. She wiped some of the grime away with the sleeve of her coat and tried to light the inside with her tiny flashlight, but all she could see were dark shadows and the movement of little things scurrying across the dirty floor.

There was a door to her left, hanging open a few inches. She went to it and stepped cautiously inside the office. Piles of rags and garbage were everywhere. A torn and beaten up old couch sat against the wall at the back of the room; dirty, torn blankets lay on it.

Betsy gasped, "Oh my God!" Tommy DeVito lay sprawled, half on the couch and half off the edge, his head on the floor. His eyes were open; his mouth was frozen in a silent scream. His chest was covered in blood from the three bullets that had killed him.

CHAPTER NINE

On The Big Island
Vinnie Vasco's Construction Site

I brushed past the security guard who was standing at the top of the stairs at Vinnie's construction trailer-office. The guard, bigger than me and nasty looking in spite of his clean and crisp uniform, didn't move aside for me. The better part of valor told me not to challenge him. I squeezed past him and walked down the steps onto the red dirt below. I had quickly gotten the impression that I wasn't welcome at the Vasco Construction site. The best thing I could do right then was find Mario and then get the hell out of there.

The guard who had driven me to Vinnie was waiting at the green pickup. I walked up to him and asked where I could find the construction foreman, Mario.

"Don't know," he said simply. "You gonna' leave now or what?"

I thanked the man and walked past him and the truck's open door that he was holding for me. The sky was beginning to turn dark; clouds were rolling in over Mauna Kea which meant rain that afternoon. Near one of the piles of red dirt, a group of men were standing around, several leaning on shovels stuck in the ground. A few others were sitting on the dirt; several more were smoking and walking back and forth aimlessly, talking amongst themselves. I went to them. I must have looked pretty strange to them, being dressed in tan slacks and a bright red and yellow Hawaiian shirt, because they all stopped what they were doing and looked at me.

When I reached them I was tempted to bum a cigarette, but I knew Sandy would smell it on me. The few breaths of smoke from Vinnie's really good cigar had to be enough. I smiled, trying to look friendly and asked, "Is Mario around?"

A young man, showing off his muscles under a tight fitting dark blue T-shirt and equally tight fitting shorts, stepped from the group of men. A cigarette was hanging loosely from his lips. He had a wise-guy sort of grin on his tanned face. He looked around at the men, smiled like he was about to be really funny, and then turned to me and said, "Mario who? And who says he's round?"

The men behind him all laughed, some of them obviously forcing the chuckles, maybe because they didn't understand the joke or maybe because they were scared not to laugh. I answered, "Gosh, you must be the resident comedian. You been on T.V.? You been on the show they call World's Best Dumb Ass Jokes?"

The grin vanished quickly and the laughing stopped as quickly. He snatched the cigarette from his lips, threw it to the ground, and took a threatening step towards me. I held my ground, but inside I was ready to take a punch from this guy.

The uniformed guard who had tried to block my way at the top of the stairs a minute earlier had come up behind me, without me noticing. When he spoke it startled me, caused me to flinch a little, but I tried to hide it. He said, "Mr. Vasco says it's OK for this guy to talk with Mario."

One of the men standing in the group stepped forward. "I'm Mario," he said. He was the shortest of the workers he was with, but he was built like a bull. In fact he reminded me of pictures I had seen in newspapers of Sammy 'the Bull'

Gravano of New York Mafia fame and Tony Spilotro, the 1970's Mafia enforcer in Las Vegas. He put his hand on the shoulder of the man who had moved towards me, quieting the man instantly. He pushed his way past the man and stood in front of me, looking up at me with what I was sure was contempt.

"I need to talk with you about a former employee," I said. "Let's walk." I turned and walked with Mario back towards the construction trailer. Mario, shorter than me, walked quickly; I had to quicken my step to keep up with him. Vinnie was outside, on the wooden porch, smoking his cigar and smiling, looking at us. He seemed to be enjoying the show.

When we were out of earshot of the men behind us, I grabbed Mario by the shoulder to stop him. He turned, gave me a nasty look and brushed my hand away. I asked, "I need to know about Lewis Manaluo."

"Why?" Mario asked.

Mario was a good foot shorter than me, but I had no doubt that he could rip me apart if he wanted to. His shoulders were broad and his arms were thick. His left bicep bore a tattoo of a dagger dripping blood. His hair was cropped short, almost leaving his scalp bald. He had this message of danger in his dark eyes. I wasn't about to piss this guy off. So I said simply, and smiled as I said it, "He's dead. His wife wants to know why."

"He ran off the road I heard," Mario answered. "Been drinkin' with the guys. Simple as that."

"What guys?" I asked.

"The guys," he said. "You know. Guys that work here. Other guys that are his friends, like. I don't know what guys. That all you wanna' know?"

"Work here? It doesn't look like much work is being done," I laughed.

"You find that funny? This your place or somthin'?"

"No, I'm just asking. I want to be able to tell Lewis' wife what happened to him, that's all. What kind of work did Lewis do?"

"He swung a damn shovel," Mario spit out. He was getting angry. It has been my experience that when people get emotional . . . angry in Mario's case . . . they often say things they wouldn't ordinarily say. But I had to be careful with Mario. If he got too angry, I'd wind up on a hospital bed.

"Who did he swing that shovel at?" I asked and tried to laugh again.

Mario grinned but his dark eyes burnt into mine with an unmistakable message of danger behind them. "You got yourself a good God damn sense of humor, don't you?" he sneered.

"Please," I said, trying as best as I could to feign pleading, dropping the comedy. "Just tell me what you know about Lewis and I'll be on my way. That's all . . . Please."

He looked up at me, still grinning but with a vicious tint to the grin. I wondered if he was thinking if a left to my jaw was better than a right to my gut. He turned his head and looked up at the porch of the construction trailer and Vinnie Vasco. I looked up at Vinnie also and saw him, with a dangerous grin on his face, nod slightly.

Mario turned back to me and said, "Lewis was only a fair worker. He didn't show up for work every day like he was supposed to. But when he was here he did good work. He would never be more than a dirt mover laborer. He went out with the guys every now and then and had a few too many beers. He didn't talk much . . . Kind of a guy that maybe had something to hide, ya' know? That's all I know."

"Where did the guys go to drink?"

"Some little place out by Keelakula Beach.   Papa Keoni's it's called. Been there once or twice myself. Cold beer and big cockroaches. Tourists don't go there."

"Do the guys get paid every week?" I asked.

"Why? What's that matter to you?"

"I want to know if he was hiding anything from his wife," I lied. "He stayed out late too often considering he had a really good looking woman waiting at home for him."

Mario thought about that, his eyes tearing into mine, and then answered, "Laborers work by the day. When there's work for them, they get paid in cash at the end of the day. Other guys . . . The more reliable ones, you know? . . . They get paid weekly by check. Lewis, he was one of the guys who got paid in cash at the end of the day. Mostly 'cause he couldn't be counted on to show up every day. His kind are like that. Lazy most of 'em. When they got a couple dollars in their pocket, they go to the beach or lay under a tree with a six pack of beer."

I didn't know where Keelakula Beach was and I wanted to go there, but I figured I had asked enough questions of Mario. Pushing it might not be too smart. I thanked him and held out my hand. He looked at my hand and the grin left his face long enough for him to turn his head to the right and spit. I assumed that was a signal for me to go, which I did as quickly as I could while restraining myself from running.

I had to walk back to the construction gate; the truck that had brought me to Vinnie Vasco had long ago disappeared. The ground was wet; I struggled to walk across it, hoping not to lose one of my shoes in the mud. And to top everything off, to make it an all-around really good visit to

Vinnie Vasco, it started to rain.

I was muddied half way to my knees by the time I reached the gate. My car had been moved outside the fence and the gate was closed and padlocked. The guard was inside his little shack. He stood there looking at me, not making any movement toward coming outside to open the gate for me.

I went to the door of his guard shack and pushed it open. "Do I climb over the fence . . . or do you open it?" I asked him. He said nothing. The phone inside his little guard shack rang. He let it ring three times while staring at me before answering it. I could see him through the open door of the shack. He said nothing but was nodding his head over and over again.

When he stepped outside, he walked quickly to the locked gate, unlocked it and pulled one side open. He held it while I walked past him. As soon as I was outside he quickly closed the gate and wrapped the chain through, locking the padlock. He turned and walked back inside his little shack. My guess was that Vinnie had told him to get me out as quickly as possible and not let me back in.

I sat in the car, wondering what to do next. I was wet and muddy. I weighed going back to the Maika'i Resort against trying to find the place where Lewis went for his beers. I chose looking for Papa Keoni's.

****

I had one of those tourist maps you can pick up at the front desk of every hotel and in every gift shop. It wasn't much of a help, but it did have Keelakula Beach listed, and it wasn't too far away. I backed out of the entrance to the construction site and drove away.

After getting lost twice, making a couple of U-turns, and taking a few wrong turns, I found Keelakula Beach. It was at the end of a tight little dirt road that cut through several small farms that supported a few cows and gardens. Mainland folks wouldn't take a second look at the road. I bounced along slowly. The rain had stopped but the potholes were full of water. A mile along the road, I turned a corner and found myself looking at the Pacific Ocean.

The road ended at a rocky black sand beach. I parked the car at the end of the road, in the shade of a tall tree, not wanting to get stuck in the sand. It was a nice little beach, not more than a hundred yards wide. It was sort of horseshoe shaped, making it a cove where waves found their way in and crashed on some big rocks and the black sand. A half dozen young Hawaiians were surfing the waves that day, and a few others sat on the beach under tall palms that swayed in the light breeze, watching the surfers. The sky had cleared, and the Hawaiian winter warmth was returning as I walked across the beach.

Papa Keoni's sat on eight wooden poles sunk into a little rise of grass covered sand at the back of the beach. There were a couple trees around the small building, providing a semblance of shade. It was a very small thatched roof shack, walled in a collection of whatever scrap wood and metal Papa Keoni had come up with years before. I walked along the back edge of the beach to Papa Keoni's. The people lying back on the black sand turned to look at me, a stranger, a haole with mud stained pants, who would not normally be there.

There were four steps from the beach to the front door. The front door hung open, skewed awkwardly on one hinge, the top hinge having been ripped from the frame and unrepaired. An old, rusted metal sign that once advertised some kind of drink I couldn't recognize had been nailed to the wall next to the door. A painted portrait of a pretty Hawaiian woman was the sign's main attraction.

Inside I could hear the recorded soft sound of a slack string guitar and the alto voice of a pretty good Hawaiian singer being played on cheap speakers that did not do the recording justice. I stepped inside and stood in the doorway, looking around. The music stopped suddenly as the five young men inside turned and looked at me. I imagine I looked pretty strange, dressed in my light cotton slacks that were muddied almost to my knees and a loud Hawaiian tourist shirt open at the collar. I was a tourist, dressed like a tourist, pale like a tourist. Maybe the first they had seen at Papa Keoni's.

I took the few steps necessary to reach the bamboo bar and pulled a rusted metal stool away to sit on. An old woman, enormously fat with thick dark grey hair that hung down below her hips, was standing behind the little bar of bamboo, her hand on the CD player she had just turned off. She was wearing what could have been someone's tattered blue table cloth wrapped around her, under her fat arms, and almost covering her huge breasts. She leaned on her elbows against the bar and asked, "You lost, honey?"

"No," I answered smiling as sweetly as I could manage. "Just thirsty. How about a bottle of beer?"

She laughed uproariously, her whole body shaking, as she reached under the bar and pulled up a frosted bottle of Budweiser. She twisted the top off and slid the bottle across the bar. I went to it and lifted it to my lips. It was cold, and it was really good. I drank it quickly.

"Now, honey," she said. "Why you not tell me why you come here?"

"I heard you had good beer," I said.

The smile disappeared from her round brown face. The five men who had been sitting listening to the recorded music all stood in unison and turned to me. The old woman said, "These here boys, they good boys. They plenty strong, too.

You tell me why you here or these boys they gonna' hurt you bad. You some kinda' cop?"

I took another mouthful of the cold beer, emptying the bottle and put it down carefully on the bar. I said, "Lewis Manaluo. I want to know why he died."

One of the five men who had stood looked at me and asked, "You that man been talkin' with Leilani?"

I turned to him. "Yes," I said simply.

He asked, "You that friend of Nancy Wong and her man, Hound?"

"I am."

He looked around him, to the others standing with him. They all nodded and sat, leaving the man standing alone. He said, "You come sit with us. Mama Keoni gonna' bring us more beer, right Mama? I think maybe you gonna' pay for the beers, eh haole?"

The old woman laughed again and managed to walk from behind the small bar with a distinct waddle that shook layers of fat. She was holding six bottles of beer, three in the fingers of each of her fat hands. She laid them in the center of the table.

I pulled a metal chair with a torn plastic seat from the next table to the round table the men were sitting at. A bottle of beer was pushed towards me. I grabbed at it and drank thankfully, quenching my thirst. The first bottle of beer was good, the second one was better.

It was amazingly cool inside the little bar, considering there was little to keep the heat out. Above me the roof was browned palm fronds. I could see blue sky through holes in the thatch. But there must have been enough shade from the few trees, combined with a breeze coming in off the Pacific, to cool the shack.

The five men, three pale enough to be haoles who wore beards on their dark, tanned faces, sat in silence, watching me drink the beer down to an empty bottle. I put it down on the table top with a sharp crack in the quiet little barroom. "So what?" I asked them. "Do I ask the questions or answer them?"

"What you wanna' know?" the same man who invited me to the table asked.

"How about your name? You know mine, I'll bet."

"Sure. You that Morgan Crew fella'. Everybody 'round here know that. I'm Palani. I knew Lewis. He was a good friend . . . A good man."

"He knew something about the Vasco Construction site, didn't he?"

"He said he did. He that type a'guy. Me . . . I take my pay and buy a beer . . . Maybe do some surf, ya'know?"

"So you work at Vasco's with Lewis?" I asked.

"Sometimes," Palani answered. "I got other sometimes work, but when I got a day here an' there I sometimes work there . . . Like Lewis do."

"Do you have the same suspicions Lewis had?"

"Lewis . . . he that kind'a fella' thinks other people's business maybe his business. He a right kane. But he thinks maybe he's supposed to make wrong stuff right. Not me."

"And what wrong was he trying to make right?" I asked. The second bottle of cold beer lay empty in front of me. I waived to Mama Keoni, the fat lady behind the bar, to bring six more beers to the table.

"Hey, I don't know," Palani said. "I keep my nose where it belong. He say he know somethin'. Lewis, he a right kinda' guy . . . But he would'a been better off just goin' home."

"So what *did* he tell you? You said he told you he thought something was wrong about Vasco. What?"

Palani pulled the new bottle of beer towards him. He looked around at the four others at the table. Three of them were concentrating on their beer. Number four, a big, dark skinned man with Asian features on his face, grasped his bottle of beer tightly in both of his bear-like hands, looked at Palani and shrugged his shoulders.

Palani drank down half the bottle of cold beer, put the bottle down and looked at me. He began, "Lewis, he told me he got into Mr. Vasco's office one night. Lewis, he was curious why everybody workin' there all gettin' paid for doin' nothin'. Vasco payin' everybody and all them security guys big money. He drivin' 'round in this big car. Lewis say lots of men come visiting couple of times each month and walk away with these suitcases they not come with. Lewis, he think somethin' crooked goin' on. You know, criminal stuff. So Lewis, he sneak into Vasco's office and looked through some drawers and things. He told me lots of paper but he don't know what it all means."

Palani paused and drank some more of his beer. He put the bottle down on the table and looked at me, saying nothing more.

I asked, "Is that it? Did he tell you anything else?"

"That's it. Lewis says he thinks maybe these guys are crooks stealin' money from people who send Vasco money . . . You know?"

"And you think that's why Lewis died?" I asked. "You think he was killed because he knew something?"

"Maybe he was killed 'cause he talk about it too much, like," Palani said. "Everybody all know somethin' not right out there. But everybody they all keep their mouths shut and get their money for doing nothin'. Lewis, he talk too much."

"Where else do you work?" I asked Palani.

"I got this right good job at a warehouse . . . Drivin' d'fork lift truck." He laughed at that.

The man at the table, number four with the Asian features, spoke up. "I work down there, too, at Vasco's place," he said. His accent was Hawaiian telling me his ancestors had come to the Islands many years ago. "I drive d'heavy stuff . . . You know . . . Dozers and things."

"What's your name?" I asked.

"Mikey Chung," he said.

"And you know what Lewis knew?"

"No, man. Lewis, he maybe thinks he knew but he has other problems."

"Like what?"

"That for you to find out. Lewis make like he a good guy but he got secrets."

"What secrets?" I asked. I knew Lewis was a deserter but how many other people knew that?

"Like I say, I know but you gotta' find out. I know stuff . . . But you gotta' find out."

I thought about what Palani had said and the hints that Mikey Chung had given me. If Lewis knew something about Vinnie Vasco, that could explain his death. But if there was something else, some other secret he carried, maybe his desertion, then there might be another explanation.

I held onto the empty beer bottle but two were enough for me. I wasn't about to indulge in a third even if the five Hawaiians did. I said out loud, more to myself than anyone else, "The question now is what the hell do I do?"

Mama Keoni was standing at my side. I hadn't noticed the big woman until she spoke, "Maybe you don't do nothin'. Maybe that Vasco fella', maybe he be takin' care of for what he does."

"What does that mean?" I asked.

Mama Keoni just laughed, her whole body shaking like Jell-O, and walked away. Palani was smiling, maybe a little embarrassed. He said softly, "Mama Keoni, she still believe in the old kapu."

Now some people might laugh at anyone still believing in ancient gods and devils, and the ancient laws. But I'm not a total disbeliever. My last visit to Hawai'i brought me in direct conflict with . . . something. If it was just my mind playing hallucinatory tricks on me, or if it was really the ancient gods and demons protecting what is theirs, I still don't know. I am just thankful to be alive, to have survived . . . Whatever it was. So if Mama Keoni believes in the ancient kapu, more power to her I say.

****

I got up and walked outside into the sunshine and heat of the day. It was a slow walk across the soft black sand to my car. My feet sank into the sand, and I felt like I should just sit down in it and enjoy . . . Enjoy what the Hawaiians were enjoying. Then someone called to me and I turned. Mikey Chung was walking to me.

"Hey! Mister!" he called out. When he was near me he

said, "I think I wanna' talk to you."

"So talk," I said.

"Not 'round here. Maybe I come to you tonight. What place you stayin' at?"

I told him I was at the Maika'i Resort. He said he would come there that evening. He turned and walked back to Papa Keoni's.

I walked across the black sand to where I had left the car, parked behind some bushes. It was past noon; the sun was overhead and hot in a clear blue sky. Thankfully, there was a cooling breeze blowing off the Pacific. I wished I was back with Sandy and Caroline, playing in the cool ocean and building sand castles on the beach.

As I turned past a big flame orange bougainvillea a big bright red and blue bird flew out of it. I flinched and ducked away, laughing finally. The colors of the Islands are always surprising and amazing to me.

The car sat where I had left it, but a piece of paper had been added to the windshield, under the wiper blade. It surely wasn't a parking ticket; I was off the road and in the trees just off the beach. It just couldn't have been a 'no parking' area. I pulled the paper off the windshield and held it for a minute without unfolding it.

It was a scrap of white paper, torn roughly from a larger sheet. I had the feeling it had to be some kind of a threat, a warning, and that little voice in the back of my head started screaming again, "Get out! Run away! Get out!" One of these days I'm going to start listening to that warning.

I opened the paper and found in a handwritten scrawl, roughly printed letters in pencil, "HANAMAIA DRIVE. RIGHT NOW. I WON'T WAIT LONG."

I pulled the Island map from the glove box of the car and found Hanamaia Drive. It wasn't too far away, not too far into the hills. As it turned out, I drove past the little road and had to turn around. Finding it, I turned onto one of the many almost paved roads that twisted and turned its way into a forest.

About a mile along the road a man stood leaning against a fence post that barely held his weight. He was a big man, not more than 5'8" but fat to say the least. He had to be pushing 300 pounds or more, and he was sweating in the afternoon heat. He wasn't Hawaiian; he was olive skinned with thick, jet black curly hair combed straight back off his forehead. When he saw me coming, he stood from the fence post and waived me down.

I stopped and opened my window down half way, leaving the car in gear and ready to slam my foot down on the accelerator if I had to get out of there fast. The man waddled to the side of the car, breathing hard at such small exertion, and leaned down. He was wearing black slacks and a white long sleeve shirt that was open at the collar. Both his pants and shirt were soaked with sweat. I guessed he wasn't used to the Hawaiian heat of winter.

"He's waitin' f'you inside," he said, his breath full of garlic that mixed unpleasantly with strong body odor.

"Who's waiting for me?" I asked, trying to lean away from the stench.

"You wanna' know about Vasco Construction?" he asked. He spoke slowly; his voice had a distinct Brooklyn twang to it.

"I guess . . . Yes, I do."

"He's waitin' f'you inside," the fat man repeated. Leaning down to look into the car must have been too much for him. He stood and took a deep breath.

I sat looking up at him, trying to decide if I should 'see the man' or get the hell out of there. The decision was made for me when he pulled a big .45 Colt semi-auto from under his shirt and used it to break the half open window of the car. Before I could brush the broken glass off of me, he reached in and unlocked the door. He pulled it open and grabbed me by my hair. He dragged me out of the car and onto the dirt and broken pavement.

I lay there with my face in the dirt as he held onto my hair. I felt the business end of the gun being pressed against my temple. Then he said, "I tol' you . . . He's waitin' f'you inside."

"OK, OK, I get the message," I said. "Let me up and show me where inside is."

He let go of my hair; I hoped I hadn't left a handful of hair with him. I pushed myself up and got to my feet. I checked the top of my head to see if I had any hair left or if I was bald. He held the gun pointed at my stomach and motioned with his left hand up a narrow path through some bushes that had started growing over the thin path. I started up the path, pushing bushes aside, and he followed a few feet behind me. I could hear him breathing hard. If he suddenly collapsed, I told myself, I would run as fast as I could, get Sandy and Caroline and get on the first jet out of town.

But he didn't collapse, despite his struggle to walk under his weight in the heat of the early afternoon. Then in front of me, I found an old barn, obviously unused for many years. Vines were crawling up the sides, and a few of the decaying boards on the side of the building had rotted away.

"Inside," the fat man wheezed trying to speak while breathing hard. "He's waitin' f'you inside."

I went to a door that was partly open. I pulled hard at it with both hands. It opened on its squeaking hinges. There was enough space for me to walk into the dim light of the barn. Before my eyes could adjust to the light, the fat man hit me from behind. I felt the barrel of his gun on the back of my head as I collapsed into blackness.

I don't know how long I was unconscious, but I woke up with a throbbing headache. I rubbed the back of my head and felt some warm blood. The room was spinning around me as I pushed myself to my knees. Standing would be impossible, I decided, so I pulled myself around and sat on the dirty floor, pulling my knees up to my chin.

I heard a voice, different from the voice of the fat man. He was saying something, but with the pounding inside my head I couldn't make out what he was saying.

I rubbed my eyes and coughed, and little by little sight was returned to me. Then I started to understand what the voice was saying.

"Are you alright, Mr. Crew?" the voice asked. His voice wasn't rough and guttural as was the fat man's. It carried an accent I had heard before, well-educated Western European.

As the fog left my eyes, I looked around the room. In some shadows across the barn from me was a man sitting in a metal folding chair. He was dressed in a grey suit, a good quality suit, and highly polished shoes. He sat cross legged, his leather gloved hands folded on his knees as he sat forward, looking down at me.

"Mr. Crew," he asked. "Can you hear me?"

I nodded, my hand on the swelling at the back of my head.

"I am very sorry Bruno hit you," he said. His voice seemed refined, soft, the words well spoken. He seemed almost to care that my head was throbbing and bleeding.

"Yeah, well I'm sorry, too." I said.

"I was hoping to make my point in a gentler manner."

"And what point would that be?" I asked.

"The point being that you need to leave Mr. Vincent Vasco alone. You should not bother him anymore."

"I get the point," I said looking at the blood from my skull on my fingers. "Say, who the hell are you anyway?"

"I am the man, Mr. Crew, who will climb your tree and rip all its branches off."

"What the hell does that mean?"

"It means that if you bother Mr. Vasco again . . . I will kill your wife and your child. I will kill your friends and all your relatives . . . Anyone you care about will die. I will go so far as to kill your daughter's pet dog in front of her as she watches. If she doesn't have a dog, I will buy her a dog and then kill it." He laughed at his little joke. "And when I have done all that, after you have seen everyone you love and care about killed . . . I will kill you. On the other hand, if you leave Mr. Vasco alone you will never see me again. Do I make myself clear, Mr. Crew?"

"Answer one question for me and then I promise to never bother him again," I said.

"And what is that question?" he said, leaning back in his chair. In the dim light I could make out a vicious grin on his face.

"Did Vinnie have anything to do with Lewis Manaluo's death?"

He turned his head to look behind me, and the fat man kicked me hard in my back. I screamed and rolled over as he kicked me again and again. I quickly rolled into a fetal ball to try to protect what parts of me were important. He kept kicking my arms and back, and when I rolled onto my side, he kicked me at the side of my head. He pulled me to my feet and started hitting me with his fists. I tried to protect my face with my arms but he was good at what he does. I fell to the floor, and the kicking started again.

The pain didn't stop until I was unconscious. When I woke up I was alone, lying on the dirty floor of the old barn and in pain. I hurt everywhere and I was bleeding from my mouth and nose. But I had gotten the message.

CHAPTER TEN

San Marcos

Betsy huddled inside the old MGB in the street outside the warehouse. She had found Tommy DeVito's body inside the old building. When she shined the tiny flashlight on the body, her stomach revolted and she ran away to vomit at the top of the stairs in a dark corner.

It took her time to settle herself and to stop crying. It wasn't the first time she had seen a dead body; she had been framed for murder in Texas when she woke up in a room with a young man lying dead on the floor. But in finding Tommy DeVito, all the memories of that terrible experience, the time she spent in jail, the beatings she had been subjected to, all came back in a flood of emotion.

She managed to take the stairs down, stumbling once or twice. She made it outside, into the fresh, cold air. She breathed in deeply and retched once again on the snowy sidewalk. When she was able, she phoned Bob Sommers. She told him of the death through tears she couldn't stop.

She waited inside the little MGB for Bob to arrive, letting the engine run, hoping the heater would keep the cold away. It was snowing hard outside, and she was shivering, but she wasn't about to go back inside where the body of Tommy DeVito lay. As she waited, the tears finally stopped flowing. She wiped her eyes and cheeks with a tissue.

When the two police cars arrived, Betsy spoke to Bob through the open window of the car. She felt weak and her whole body was throbbing. She was worried that if she were to get out of the car, she might faint and fall to the street. She told Bob that she had found Tommy DeVito inside. He shook his head and told her to wait where she was, but he didn't say anything to her for doing what she had done.

Betsy waited inside the car while Lt. Bob Sommers was inside with three of his officers and someone from the County Morgue. Time dragged by for Betsy; she wanted nothing more than to throw the car into first gear and speed away. But Bob had told her to wait, and she did.

Finding Sissy once had been something Betsy felt she needed to do for a classmate. Now that quest had grown into a dangerous and fearsome murder case. In her mind she was tossed between saying, "T'hell with Sissy," and wanting to go on and find her. Betsy's years with Morgan and Sandy had instilled in her the overwhelming desire to do for others what they cannot do for themselves. She had learned the lesson well. So she stayed and waited to hear what Bob Sommers would tell her.

She turned on the radio and ran through all the stations but found nothing that could take her mind off of the dead Tommy DeVito. A knock on the passenger side window made her jump. It was Bob Sommers.

He opened the door and squeezed his bulk into the small car to sit next to Betsy. Bob is a big man, over 200 pounds, and the MGB is small inside and out. But he managed to get in and sat for a moment, the door hanging open, his right leg hanging outside the little car. He looked sideways at Betsy. She wiped a few remaining tears from her eyes and said, without looking at Bob, "Well, what do you know?"

"It's not what I know, Betsy," Bob said. "It's what you

know. Tell me again why you came here?"

"Sissy McMillan," she said simply. "Like I told you."

"You came here because of Sissy McMillan?"

"Yes," she answered and wiped away another tear. "Sissy is missing, and I want to find her . . . To find out if she's in trouble or something."

"First of all, you're not supposed to be looking for Sissy. That's my job," Bob said. "Second, what the hell brought you here? And I want the truth, Betsy. Don't play Morgan Crew with me. You don't have the influence he does. Tell me everything."

Betsy took a deep breath and started, staring out the snow covered windshield, without looking at Bob, "I heard that she might be involved with drugs and some drug-heads up in North Harbor. I found a guy who deals drugs to kids . . . Old Billy. Do you know him? Anyway, he told me Sissy was shacked up here with Tommy DeVito. He said Tommy was a drug head and was feeding drugs to Sissy. So I came here hoping to find her. If she was here, I was going to try to talk her into leaving Tommy and coming home with me. I know, that's probably stupid, but I had to try. But all I found was . . . was what was inside. He was murdered, wasn't he?"

"It looks that way," Bob said. "I doubt anyone would commit suicide by shooting themselves four times in the chest and stomach. So Sissy was living here? That makes her someone I want to talk to. Tell me what else you know."

"That's it, Bob. I swear; that's it. All I was trying to do was find Sissy because in a lot of ways she reminds me of what I used to be. That's all."

"I understand," he said. He was quiet for a moment or two and then said, "I suppose it's stupid of me to tell you to go home and stay out of this. Morgan's rubbed off on you, I'll bet.

You're going to go on looking for Sissy, aren't you? And there's nothing short of locking you up in one of my cells that will stop you, is there?"

Betsy smiled and for the first time looked at Bob.

"OK," Bob said. "As long as you know that Sissy is now involved in a murder, and that could be dangerous for you. I want to know whatever you find out . . . Immediately, understand? And for God's sake be careful. Morgan will kill me if anything happens to you."

Bob leaned into the open car door and had a hard time getting out. An icy and wet wind blew inside the car as he struggled. When he was finally on his feet, on the sidewalk, he closed the door and watched as Betsy threw the car into gear and sped away.

CHAPTER ELEVEN

Honolulu

I had gotten back to the resort and our suite in the late afternoon. I must have looked like a well-dressed Island bum as I walked through the lobby in dirty clothes with dried blood clotting my wrinkled hair, with a black eye that was swollen shut, and a swollen lip and cheek that curled my mouth unnaturally.

Sandy almost screamed as I walked into the suite. "Oh my God! Not again!" she cried out. A doctor was called by the resort management. While waiting for him, Sandy cleaned up my face and wiped the blood from my hair. The Doctor put a couple of stiches on the back of my head and assured me I had no broken bones. He prescribed ice to reduce the swelling and left after Sandy wanted him to take me to the hospital. I refused and for once I won an argument with Sandy.

Little Caroline was standing aside watching this whole thing, not sure what to make of it all. I think she knew I had been hurt but in the end, as any two and a half year old would do, all she did was stand there and cry. Sandy comforted her and I held her on my lap to stop the tears.

After the Doctor left, Sandy poured a very strong and large bourbon for me. I told her to hold the club soda which she did. I took it thankfully and drank half of it down quickly. A knock on the door stopped me from finishing the tall drink.

I started to get up from the chair I was in, but Sandy stopped me. "I'll get it," she said.

"I forgot," I told her. "There's a guy coming to talk to me. Mikey Chung. That's probably him."

Sandy shook her head but she knew there was nothing that was going to stop me at that point. She opened the door and Police Chief Daniels was standing there. He took off his hat and told Sandy who he was.

"I assume you want to see Morgan," Sandy said. She was standing in the doorway to keep him out. Beside him was one of his officers, a woman who was built like a football player. I remember thinking when I saw her, 'I wouldn't want to tangle with her.'

I stood little Caroline on the floor and was able to get out of the chair, painfully, and stand looking towards Chief Daniels. I hoped he wasn't there to arrest me. Maybe he had heard somehow of the trouble I had after leaving Papa Keoni's.

"It's OK," I said to Sandy. "Let them come in."

She stepped aside to let the two cops in but left the door open. Daniels asked her, "You must be Mrs. Crew?"

"Yes. And why are you here?" she answered.

Daniels turned to me and said, "You been hit by a truck?"

"Sort of," I answered. "What can I do for you?"

"Do you want to file a complaint against someone?" he asked.

"No. Just tell me why you're here."

"Do you know someone named Mikey Chung?"

There was no sense lying to a cop . . . At least not right then. There might come a time when I had to lie, but at that time I figured the truth would be best.

"Sure," I said. "I met him earlier today. He's coming to see me tonight."

"Why?" Daniels asked. He walked into the suite, holding his hat in his hands and looked around. He had this look of disdain on his face. I guess he didn't appreciate all the luxury he saw. His officer stood at the open door, I guess to keep me from running out, which I'm sure she could have done.

"I'm not really sure," I answered. "He said he wanted to speak with me and he would come here tonight. You can wait for him if you want."

"Yeah, well, he won't be coming," Daniels said as he picked up a piece of Asian statuary and examined it.

"Why not? Did you arrest him for something?"

"No," Daniels said. "We found Mikey Chung's body in a trash dumpster about an hour ago. He was stabbed. We haven't finished counting the number of times he was stabbed."

I didn't know what to say. First Lewis and now Mikey Chung. But were the two related or was Mikey's death something else? Mikey said he worked full time for Vinnie Vasco. He also spent time at Papa Keoni's. Those two things connected him to Lewis. And he said he knew something about Lewis' death.

Chief Daniels walked around the room, looking at the expensive furnishings, touching a few things and picking up some others. He stopped when he got to Caroline. He looked down at her and smiled. She didn't move; she looked up at him, I think perhaps knowing he wasn't her daddy's friend.

Daniels walked around her and without stopping he asked, "I want to know why he wanted to talk with you. Don't pull any of your shit with me. I know all about you from the last time you graced my Island."

"Honestly," I said. "I don't know. He stopped me as I was leaving a bar and said he would come here this evening. That's all I know."

Caroline had come to me and was hugging my leg tightly. Maybe she didn't understand all the words, but she knew what was going on and she was frightened.

"Where did he stop you and say he would come here?" Daniels asked.

"At a little place called Papa Keoni's."

"Yeah, I know the place. Unlicensed, but I don't really care so long as there's no trouble there. Why the hell were you there?"

I started to feel that this wasn't going where I wanted it to go. I needed some freedom if I was ever going to find out why Lewis died. Chief Daniels, not liking me anyway, might take that freedom of movement away.

I sat back down and took Caroline onto my lap. "They have really cold beer," I said. "I was thirsty."

Daniels had picked up a small crystal decanter that was filled with a very good cognac. He lifted the top and smelled the liquor. He nodded his approval and put it down. He turned to me, the first he had looked directly at me since walking into the suite.

"OK, yeah, I get it," he said. "You may be able to get away with that shit back home, but here . . . this is my Island, and you won't get away with it here. One more time, why were you at Papa Keoni's?"

"For the beer," I said and smiled, knowing I could win that one. "Go ask them."

"Go ask who?"

"Mama Keoni and all her customers. They're all there almost every afternoon after work. And probably late into the evening too. If you hurry you might still find them there."

Daniels wanted to spit to show his contempt, but he didn't. He started for the door but stopped, his back turned to me.

"Where were you after you left Papa Keoni's?" he asked without turning around.

"Nowhere important."

"Who kicked the crap out of you?"

"Nobody," I lied. "I just walked into a door, that's all."

"I think maybe you killed Mikey Chung," Daniels said.

"Yeah, sure I did," I said. "I was really angry that he wanted to talk to me so I killed him."

"Mikey Chung was a black belt in Karate. He could have beat the crap out of you and left you like you are."

"And after he beat the crap out of me, I was able to stab him . . . How many times did I stab him?"

"Did you kill him?" Daniels asked.

I waited for a silent ten count and then said, "Are you going to arrest me?"

"No, not yet," he said. He turned slowly and looked at me with a really frightening stare. "I want you at my station in the morning. I want to compare your blood and prints to what we found on Mikey Chung."

"Do you have a warrant?"

"I can get one if that's necessary," he said.

"Good, get one and I'll have my attorneys get in touch with you as soon as you do."

I stopped Chief Daniels as he was at the door. I asked, "What about the accident investigation? What have you found out?"

Daniels turned and said, "Forget it. You don't get anything from me."

"Suppose I trade blood samples for the accident report?" I asked.

"Forget it," he said maliciously.

Daniels left with his officer following behind him. She slammed the door closed loudly.

"What was that all about?" Sandy asked.

"Later," I said. I let Caroline slip from my lap. She ran to Sandy who picked her up. I quickly drained my glass and held it out towards Sandy. She held onto Caroline as she refilled the glass with good bourbon and brought it to me. Caroline was looking worried. She couldn't understand, but she knew something bad was happening. Sandy hugged her and told her there was nothing to worry about. "It's just Daddy's job. You'll get used to it."

****

Later that night, after Caroline had dinner and a bath and was safely tucked into bed, I told Sandy all that had happened.

"So this Mario guy told you about Papa Keoni's," she said. "That's how the two men who beat you up knew you would be there. This Vinnie Vasco must have sent them. There's no other way they could know you'd be there."

"And that means we're going home in the morning," I said.

"Oh no we're not," she said. "Look, you were told to stay away from Vinnie Vasco. So stay away from him. You can do what you need to do without ever seeing him again. After all, he's not going to tell you anything anyway."

Our dinner had sat on the table out on the lanai, uneaten, cold, and a gathering place for flies. Without words being spoken we knew we needed clear heads, so booze was out of the question. Two large pots of coffee kept us going while we talked into the night.

"These people are Mafia," I insisted. "They will kill you and Caroline, for God's sake."

I was trying to convince both Sandy . . . and myself . . . that we needed to go home. I was scared, I admit that. Alright, not scared so much for myself because I know what my life is all about. It is my station in life to put my own life at risk to save others. I don't like doing that but I have resigned myself to accepting that fact. I would much rather sail off into the Pacific on some stinking old fishing scow and never see any of the money or responsibilities again.

I had faced up to criminals of all kinds, even Mafia killers. I was scared for Sandy and Caroline. I knew what people like Vincent Vasco would do. They would kill anyone without thought if it meant money in their pocket. I looked at my watch. It was past three in the morning.

"And let's not forget that there has been a second murder. Mikey Chung. He must have known something to get himself killed," I said.

"All the more reason," Sandy said, "to find out what Vinnie Vasco is doing."

I sipped on the cup of the last of the cold coffee, thinking about all that had happened. The night air was cool; an ocean breeze was blowing the tall palm fronds around and carrying the smell of the Pacific with it. The moon was full and the dark sky was bursting with diamond-like stars. A few clouds drifted by, like shadowy ghosts seeking refuge from the world. I watched the white foam of the ocean.

"Remember what they did to you back in Las Vegas?" I asked. "They almost killed you."

"*Almost*," Sandy said touching my knee softly and smiling gently in an attempt to ease my worry. "I'm not scared. You can't spend the rest of your life worrying about me. Who saved your bacon in Texas? We beat that awful criminal in London. We are who we are."

"What about our daughter?"

"If we play this smart, nothing will happen to anyone. Don't bother Vinnie Vasco again, stay away from him, and do whatever else needs to be done. If Vinnie isn't bothered he will leave us alone. We need to help Nancy and Leilani. That's not debatable. Now, how do we do that?"

"If Lewis was murdered because of what he knew about Vasco Construction then I need to find out what is going on out there," I argued.

Sandy was silent and for the first time since I've known her she was not able to tell me how to solve the problem we were facing.

"I don't have any idea what the hell's going on out there," I said. "They have a construction site that's apparently months old, yet nothing is being done. Dirt's being moved around. There are piles of rusted steel and rotting wood.

There are holes in the ground and a bunch of guys are standing around smokin' and jokin' . . . But no work is being done. And Lewis' friends told me Lewis had stuck his nose in where it didn't belong. He said Lewis thought they were stealing money from investors. But all that may just be guesses. If Lewis had really gotten into Vinnie's construction office . . . which I doubt . . . how do I do the same thing? Something illegal is going on or I wouldn't have been beat up and threatened. But is that any way connected to Lewis' death? And now a second Vasco employee is dead. What the hell do I do if I don't go near Vinnie again?"

"So we have to find out what they're doing out there," Sandy answered. "If Lewis was really murdered, it has to have something to do with what's going on out there. And if this Mikey guy was murdered because he knew what Lewis knew, then Vinnie is hiding something illegal. What other reason could there be? Maybe Lewis really did know something . . . Maybe he saw something? Maybe he told Mikey? Maybe his friends are right?"

I finished the bourbon and the cup of the last of the cold coffee, thinking about all that had happened. Off in the distance, at the end of the sandy beach, the white foam of the ocean rode on top of waves that crashed onto the beach, the only sound that filled the night.

"I'm lost here," I said finally. "I don't know anyone here. I don't know where to go. If I can't go back to Vinnie, then what do I do? I don't know anyone who can help or anyone who can even give us some cheap advice." I was trying to come up with an excuse to get on the next jet and just go home. But Sandy wasn't buying any of it. "And let's not forget that Mikey Chung was killed, too. He must have known something to get himself killed. If I find out what Vinnie is doing . . . Who is he going to kill next?"

"All the more reason," Sandy said. "If we don't do something and Vinnie is really killing people to cover up what he's doing, who will stop him?   The police certainly aren't going to run out there and question him."

Again I could say nothing.

Sandy leaned back and stretched out her legs. She was smiling one of those sly-fox smiles of hers. She had an idea. She said, "Doesn't that pack of wolves you call your attorneys have an office on the Islands?"

"Yes, on Oahu."

"Then go there and get some advice. Stay away from Vasco and anything that belongs to him. Find another way to find out what's going on."

We talked for another hour. It took that long for me to be convinced that I was going to do what I had to do. We went to bed a little after four in the morning. Sleep was difficult, but after a lot of tossing and turning, I managed to fall into a deep sleep without the nightmares of the devils and ghosts of my last visit to the Islands.

I slept until past nine AM. Sandy was awake and up before me, keeping Caroline busy and quiet so I could sleep. I woke up once and found Sandy at the bedroom's vanity, brushing her thick, dark hair. Caroline scampered into our room. Sandy scooped her up quickly and carried her from the room so I could sleep some more.

By the time I was awake and out of bed, Sandy had packed an overnight bag for me, phoned the inter-island airline to reserve a seat, booked a suite at the Hyatt on Oahu, phoned the local office of Harper, Harper, Jascro, and Nettles, the Crew family lawyers, and told them to expect me that afternoon. I was on the lanai, drinking the strong, dark Kona coffee I love and rubbing the sleep from my eyes when Sandy told me I was leaving for Oahu in three hours. That should have surprised me, but it didn't. That's what Sandy does.

Caroline was on my lap squeezing a stuffed elephant, bouncing around and pushing the toy in my face. Her fingers were sticky with the remnants of her breakfast of oatmeal, toast and jam.

Later that morning we took a taxi to the airport north of Kona. Caroline was in Sandy's arms as I checked in at the Island Air counter.

****

I got off the inter-island jet and managed to get lost in the airport for a while. I wandered around through the crowds of tourists heading home, wearing their loud Hawaiian shirts and sun dresses with flower leis hanging around their necks, and straw hats they had bought at the Island's open air markets.

You can tell the people who are heading home because of the way they are dressed and the tans and sun burns they are bringing with them. The people from States where winter is raging usually are burnt red, ignoring the fact that their pale skin would fry in the Hawaiian sun. The new arrivals wear blue jeans, heavy shirts and sweaters, and slacks and carry heavy coats that they needed when they left the snow back home. They look happy but very out of place. I finally found a taxi and headed for the Hyatt.

Checking in at the Hyatt a little after 1 PM, I decided to forgo lunch and head directly to Harper, Harper, Jascro, and Nettles' offices, which were on the twentieth, twenty-first, twenty-second, twenty-third, and twenty-fourth floors of a thirty floor office building in the center of the city. Walking into the lobby of the building was a pleasure as I felt the cool air inside waft over me after the tropical heat outside. I walked to the reception desk which was at the other side of the big, marble floored lobby.

At the desk a young woman sat in front of three large computer screens. She was wearing a light blue Hawaiian patterned dress that went well with her very dark black hair. She looked up at me and smiled a toothy smile. She asked, "Yes, sir. Can I help you?"

I told her my name and that I was there to see someone at Harper, Harper, Jascro and Nettles. She told me I was expected and directed me to an elevator to my left which would take me to the twenty-third floor. As I walked to the elevator, she picked up a phone to tell the attorneys I was on my way.

When I stepped off the elevator, a young woman was waiting for me, smiling businesslike and welcoming. She was tall and slim with long brown hair that flowed softly to her shoulders. She wore a very businesslike white blouse and a black skirt, short healed black shoes, and a simple white pearl necklace. She was the oh-so typical young attorney that I have seen in every office of Harper, Harper, Jascro, and Nettles' all over the world, wearing the uniform of the young ladies who hoped one day to move up the company food chain. She was either a new graduate from some prominent Law School or a Paralegal with extraordinary talent who would one day be a lawyer.

"Mr. Crew," she said and held out her hand. I shook hands with her and waited for her to say or do something. She took her hand back and just stood there and smiled, her hands folded. Finally I had to say something. "I expect you're supposed to lead me to someone's office."

"Certainly," she said, still smiling. I was beginning to think Harper, Harper, Jascro, and Nettles had hired a robot.

"So, shall we get going?" I suggested.

"Certainly," she said . . . smiling still. "Who would you like to see? Where would you like to go?"

I was getting frustrated, and considering the fact that I really didn't want to be there, I was beginning to feel that maybe I had an excuse to turn around and leave. But before I could, a man walked around the corner to the elevators where we stood. He was dressed in not too expensive grey slacks that were wrinkled and well worn; pants you might find at some discount mall or big box warehouse store. He wore a very faded and old, blue flowered Hawaiian shirt that was also wrinkled and hanging loose outside his pants. The shirt and pants were sporting the remnant stains of his lunch. I wondered, today's lunch or yesterday's?

I saw a slight irregularity in the way the tail of his shirt hung, a slight and almost imperceptible bulge that I had seen before. The man was carrying a pistol under his shirt, and by the size of the bulge, it was a big gun. He wore brown leather sandals, scuffed and dirty, without socks. Hardly the uniform for a prestigious law office.

His hair was dark blond and combed straight back, shiny, and slightly long and curly around his ears and at the back of his neck. He needed to see a barber. The stubble on his face was speckled with grey; he had not shaved that morning and possibly the morning before. He was tanned, and his muscled arms pushed at the short sleeves of the shirt. He stopped and held his hand out to me. I took it quickly and then pulled away. "And who might you be?" I asked.

He turned to the still smiling young lady and said, "Thank you, Diane. That will be all." She turned mechanically and marched away, all without a word and without losing the pasted-on smile on her attractive face.

"I'm Harris Esposito," he said to me. "Most people call me Harry. I don't like Harris but my mom did. It was her father's name. Let's go to my office." He turned and walked down a hallway to our right. He walked slowly, casually, maybe a little unsteady on his feet. He kept glancing to his right and left as he passed offices. I followed.

We walked down the long hallway decorated expensively in cool colors of beige and pale greens and blues, with splashes of bright paintings of Hawaiian landscapes, seascapes, birds, and fish hanging here and there. Potted bamboo and other greenery were placed in just the right places. We walked on soft, thick, plush carpet woven in a red and gold Asian pattern of mountains and rivers and birds and fish. The whole place was professionally designed and decorated to let a visitor know there was money there.

There were offices, glass walled, spaced appropriately along both sides of the hallway allowing occasional solid walls for the decorations. In each were young lawyers dressed in dark business suits, white shirts, and ties, studiously working over papers and computers.

Harry stopped and opened a wooden door that at first I thought might be a storage room or broom closet. There were no glass walls on either side of the door. He stepped aside for me to enter. Inside was a small room, with only one small window that looked out over the roofs of other smaller buildings. It was crowded with old, dusty, metal file cabinets, cardboard boxes stacked high along three of the walls, and an overflowing trash can. An open pizza carton with a two-thirds eaten pizza shared space on a beat up leather couch with piles of paper and two old shirts. On the old wooden desk, partially hidden by a pile of well-worn manila folders, was a glass ashtray filled to overflowing with cigarette butts and ash. The room smelled of cigarettes, stale food and burnt coffee.

Harry picked up a pile of manila folders from a wooden chair, looked around for a place to put them, and when he couldn't find one, simply dropped them on the floor. He said, "Please sit down, Mr. Crew."

I stood in the open doorway and asked, "I gather you're not an attorney."

"How the hell did you guess that?" he said laughing.

He sat in a tall black cracked imitation leather chair behind his desk; the chair squeaked loudly as he leaned back. "Please, sit down."

I took the vacated chair and said nothing, waiting for an explanation. Harry lit a half-smoked Marlboro that he retrieved from the overflowing ashtray and said, "Look, the guys in charge had a meeting . . . after your wife phoned. They got Peter Jascro on the phone."

Harry paused, maybe waiting for a reaction from me. He didn't get one. Peter Jascro is the managing partner of Harper, Harper, Jascro, and Nettles, and a personal friend of my late father. Since my father's death, when I was a young man still in college, he has taken care of me and advised me as my father would have.

So Harry continued, "Mr. Jascro told them to help you. The problem is they don't know what to do, so as they normally do when they're confused, they told me to talk to you. So, what can I do for you?"

"Just who the hell are you, Harry?" I asked. I sat forward, elbows on my knees, and I tried to look interested when what I was really feeling was that I should get up and walk out.

Harry stubbed out his cigarette and opened a drawer in his desk. He pulled out a pint bottle of what I imagine was supposed to be some kind of whiskey because it was dark brown in color. But I'd never heard of the brand before – 'Red Hat Irish Whiskey'. "You thirsty?" he asked.

"No . . . No . . ." I stammered not really understanding what was going on. "Who are you?" I asked again.

"I told you," he said as he poured a good amount of the whiskey into a coffee cup. "They call me Harry."

"But *who are* you? I mean . . . Do you work here? Are

you an attorney?"

"Oh my God, no! I do work here, I mean. I'm sort of the go-to guy around here. Officially, I'm a licensed P.I. They pay me to handle the stuff they don't want to get close to. You know, the tough stuff. Anything that might get their two thousand dollar suits dirty."

"OK," I said. "I can understand that." And I did because in the Crew family, I did the same kind of work. Harry and I both handled the dirty work that others didn't want to get near.

Harry paused long enough to drink half the whiskey in his cup and light another cigarette stub he pulled from the ashtray. "I used to be a cop in Detroit . . . A detective actually . . . Homicide . . . You know. I got in some trouble back there. I quit and moved out here four years ago."

I asked, "But is there enough work here in Hawai'i to keep you busy?"

"Unfortunately not," Harry said, smoking the cigarette down in quick, deep breaths. "They send me all over . . . But I always like coming back here. It's peaceful, you know? They want me to move back to the mainland, work out of the New York office, but I'm not going to do that. I've got two ex-wives back on the mainland and a bunch of cops who don't like me. I like being this far away from them."

"So why did you leave Detroit . . . Other than trouble with ex-wives?"

Harry laughed and coughed on a lungful of smoke. He crushed out the cigarette and said, "Gotta' quit these damn things." He pulled a very used handkerchief from his back pocket and blew his nose into it, very loudly. "Anyway, I was working a double murder. Drug connection; which isn't unusual back in Big D. It turns out a couple of uniformed cops were being paid to transport heroin and cocaine around town while on duty. A couple of dealers decided they didn't have to pay the cops. They thought they could blackmail them. The dealers wound up dead instead. I arrested the cops and put them in jail. They were stupid enough to use their own issued guns to kill the dealers. Dumb, huh? Anyway, turns out they weren't alone in the transport business, and a contract was put out on me by the cops involved. So I quit and moved out here. I love it here. Lots of single women from the mainland come here on vacation, if you know what I mean. They're looking for sun, sports, and sex they don't get at home."

"How come I've never heard of you?" I asked. "Peter Jascro is a lifelong family friend. We've had this firm on retainer since before I was born. I should have heard of you."

Harry laughed and sat forward, leaning on his cluttered desk. He said, "I've heard of you. The stuff you get involved in is amazing. I'm really surprised you're still alive. Well, the firm thinks you don't need me to help you. The whole damn bunch of lawyers knows that. Why pay me when you do it for free?"

That was news and something I'm going to remember the next time someone from Harper, Harper, Jascro and Nettles wants me to go off and risk my life. But the matter at hand – Lewis' death – remained and I had to do something. So I told Harry the whole story, up to my visit with Palani and Mama Keoni. I wanted Harry, or someone other than me, to find out what was going on at Vasco Construction and if Vinnie had Lewis murdered. So I wouldn't make waves. The warning I had received was a very good warning and one I would heed.

Harry dug through his ashtray three times while I told him everything. Halfway through I paused and asked, "Do you want to take a minute and go out for a pack of cigarettes?"

"Nah," he said as he came close to burning his nose lighting a short stub. So I finished my story and waited for

Harry to say something. He didn't. He leaned back and
rocked in his squeaking chair. He poured another double shot
of his whiskey into the cup without offering any to me, which I
would have refused anyway.

So, I spoke up. "What do you think?" I asked. "What
can be done?"

"Hell, I don't know," he said, shrugging his shoulders
and crushing out the remnants of the butt he had smoked
down to the filter.

"What do you mean, you don't know? Why the hell am
I here? Why am I wasting my time with you?"

I started to get to my feet to walk out of his office.
Harry sat forward and stopped me, saying, "Wait a minute. Sit
down. Cool off, will you. Don't get your shorts in a knot."

When I sat down again Harry asked, "So do you want
to prove this Lewis guy was murdered? Or do you want to
prove this Vasco guy is a crook?"

"I think the two are connected," I answered. "I believe
Lewis knew something and Vasco had him killed because he
knew something."

I waited again while Harry dug through his ashtray, this
time not finding anything that could be re-lit. He opened the
top drawer of his desk . . . It squeaked loudly as he pulled it
out. He reached in and grabbed a pack of Winston's. He tore
off the cellophane and ripped at the foil, finally shaking a
cigarette from the pack. He lit it and drew deeply. He blew
the smoke towards the ceiling and then looked at me. He
said, "Proving Lewis was murdered is probably impossible
since the police already said it was an accident and whatever
on-site evidence there may have been is long gone."

I hadn't told Harry about my troubles with Police Chief
Daniels or of Mikey Chung's murder. That was my problem

and I would handle that.

Harry took two more long drags on the cigarette and said, "Proving Vasco is a crook may be easier. I have an idea."

I waited while he smoked and stared at me, but he said nothing. I asked, "OK, how about you let me in on your idea?"

"Can't do that right now," he said. "I gotta' talk to this guy I know. See if he wants to help. I'll get back to you."

Harry stubbed out the half smoked cigarette and stood. He walked around his desk to the door, opened it and said, "Go on home. I'll phone you soon."

I left Harry's dump of an office noticing that my jacket smelled like cigarettes. I would have to have it dry cleaned before going back to The Big Island or Sandy would get all over me for smoking. While I was on the elevator going down to the street and the warm Hawaiian sun, Harry was on the phone.

He held the black phone to his ear, hugging it with his shoulder, listening to it ring seven times on the other end as he struggled to get another cigarette out of the pack he had just opened.

When the call was answered he said, "Hey Rog. Got a job for you guys."

CHAPTER TWELVE

San Marcos

It was late in the evening on Friday, schools were closed for the weekend and kids would be filtering into North Harbor looking for pot to smoke, beer to drink, and maybe something harder. It was snowing outside again. There was no wind that night. The snow was falling in thick, slow, dreamlike drifts. Betsy was at Morgan's home in the hills, trying to decide if she was hungry enough to eat something or go back to North Harbor and try to find something new on Sissy.

She was scared but there was another lesson she had learned from Sandy and Morgan:

"Everyone is scared of something; some people are scared of everything. Fear is a terribly controlling emotion and is a very hard thing to overcome. But to do what must be done you must push past the fear, stand in front of it, and then do what must be done."

And so she stood, and as she was putting on her coat, the phone rang.

"Hello," she said brightly, expecting it to be Sandy or maybe me, checking up on her.

"You the one tryin' to find Sissy?" the man's voice asked. He was speaking in a whisper but his voice was not deep or harsh. It was a young man, Betsy thought.

"Who are you?" she asked.

"You the one tryin' to find Sissy McMillan?" he asked again.

Betsy didn't answer. She waited for the man to say something else. She knew she should be getting information, not giving it.

Finally he said, "You wanna' find her, meet me at Longview Park . . . Northeast corner . . . Stay away from the street lights." The line went dead.

"OK," she said out loud as she hung up the phone. "So do I go or phone the cops?" she said aloud once again. When she realized she was talking to herself she knew she had to go. If she didn't, she would carry the fact that fear took control of her with her forever. It would be a terrible weight to carry, that she let fear stop her from finding Sissy.

She walked to Morgan and Sandy's bedroom. In Morgan's nightstand was his .38 revolver. She opened the drawer and looked down at it, lying black and cold. The memory of the time she had shot a man who was going to kill Morgan flooded into her head. The red blood pouring from the man clouded her eyes as she thought about it. If she took the gun with her, could she use it again? If she pulled it from her purse would she freeze? Would whoever she was to meet take it from her and shoot her? She slammed the drawer shut, leaving the pistol where it rested, and left the house.

****

Longview Park was, in the summer months, a pleasant, green pasture where children played, dogs chased sticks thrown by their people, flowers bragged loudly in many colors, and birds brought music to the warm air. In winter months it was covered in snow and ice in a silent black and white. The birds, the flowers and the dogs were all gone. When the storms subsided, children might be seen playing in the snow or sledding down hills.

It lay along the border of the San Marcos Country Club, and in the summer it could be seen by golfers as they tried to make it down the long 16th fairway. The park was sunken below the street level, and several broad concrete steps led from the sidewalk down into the gardens.

Rose bushes lined the terraced banks on either side of stairs. In the spring and summer, they gave the park a look of elegance, like a palace garden. But now, the many rose bushes lay dormant in their winter's sleep. The leafless trees stood against the snow like black skeletons in the night. The park's several fountains were still; the several ponds were frozen over.

Betsy slowly pulled the MGB to the curb. It was ten past ten that night; it was snowing again, and the wind had begun blowing the snow around in thick clouds. She left the motor running and the wipers on, trying in vain to keep the snow off the windshield. She was shivering from both the cold and from the fear she was trying to ignore.

Along the curb, streetlights cast eerie pale yellow light along the snow blanketed sidewalk. She had been told to stay out of the streetlights. She looked ahead and behind her. The light at the rear of the car was working but the next was dark. There was a shroud of blackness there until the third light, which was working. She took a deep breath and pulled herself from the car. She left the MGB in the light, to be seen readily by anyone passing, hopefully a patrolling police car.

She took the first step towards the darkness, and then another. She forced herself to keep walking, her feet sinking into the new fallen snow, until she reached the streetlight that was not working.

She stood in the frigid darkness under the dead light pole, shivering, pulling her wool coat tight around her. Icy flakes of snow were hitting her face. Stamping her feet against the cold, she waited. She jumped when someone came up behind her and asked, "You Betsy?"

She turned quickly and looked at a boy, perhaps it was a man. He was not more than five foot five inches tall. He was skinny, and his hair was long and greasy and hung under a dirty wool knitted cap. He wore a dark blue Seaman's Pea Coat that was covered with snow. His hands were shoved deeply into the coat's pockets. He was maybe young, maybe just an older guy who looked young. Betsy was unsure, but she was sure the guy was cold. He was shivering and his nose was red and running. He quickly wiped the back of his bare hand across his nose and shoved his hand back into his coat pocket.

"Who are you?" she asked.

"Never mind that," he answered. It was the same voice that Betsy had heard on the phone, almost high pitched as a young boy's would be. He was small enough and skinny enough that a lot of the fear Betsy had felt was gone from her. She felt confident she could take the man in a fight. When she was young and wild she had been in fights and had learned quickly. Hit first, hit hard, and hit again and again. Don't stop and don't feel sorry for the person being hit.

"You wanna' know where Sissy is . . . It'll cost ya'," he said grinning.

"OK, how much?"

"I want a thousand bucks," he said with greed in the words.

"That's ridiculous," Betsy said. "I'm a student. I don't

have a thousand dollars."

"That Morgan guy does. Get it from him."

"He's away . . . On vacation," Betsy said. "Make me an offer that's not stupid."

The man said nothing. He was obviously thinking, and it was clear to Betsy that thinking wasn't what this guy did very often.

"I can give you about forty bucks right now," she said. "I can get maybe another two hundred at the bank in the morning."

The little man frowned in thought, obviously having a hard time weighing his options. Then he said, "Give me the forty . . . Be here tomorrow night with the two hunnert'."

"You're kidding, right?" Betsy said and laughed a little. "If I give you forty dollars I'll probably never see you again. No, you tell me what I want to know . . . Then I'll give you forty dollars . . . And you'll get another two hundred tomorrow."

He wiped his wet nose again and shivered against a sudden gust of icy wind that blew from the harbor. "OK, give me the money," he said.

"Tell me first," Betsy said.

"Shit! . . . OK . . . She's OK . . . She's not in trouble . . . She's with her boyfriend and she's OK."

"Where is she?"

He stared at Betsy, his mouth hanging open, his cloudy eyes wide. Finally he said, "I don't know . . . ya' know . . . They keep moving 'round . . . She's ok . . . She loves the guy, ya' know." He held out his hand expecting Betsy to give him money.

"That's not good enough," she said. "I want to talk to her. Where is she?"

"I tol' ya' I don't know . . . They move around . . . You promised me forty bucks."

"Can you talk to them?" Betsy asked.

He hesitated, and then answered, "Yeah, I guess so . . . Why?"

"Go tell her I want to talk to her," Betsy said. "Come back tomorrow about ten in the morning and I'll give you one hundred dollars."

"You said two hunnert," he demanded.

"One hundred," she said. "Take it or leave it."

"Give me the forty," he said, holding his hand out.

Betsy took two twenty dollar bills from her purse and held them out, inches from the man's hand. "What's your name?" she asked.

The little man smiled and said proudly, "They call me M."

"M what?" she asked.

"That's what they call me . . . That's my name."

He quickly snatched the bills from Betsy's hand, turned and ran down the concrete stairs into the snowy darkness of the park.

CHAPTER THIRTEEN

On The Big Island

Sandy wasn't very happy when I told her what I had accomplished on Oahu. "Accomplished?" she said. "You call that 'accomplished'? I was hoping those damn attorneys would do something so we can get back to our vacation."

"And just what the hell do you want me to do?" I said trying to be defensive without being too nasty. "I went there and they knew I was coming. Peter Jascro said they were to help me. I talked to this Harry guy and he said he would handle it. What else could I have done?"

"I don't know," Sandy said, understanding but dejected anyway. I think she wanted the problem solved quickly. She obviously was worried about Vinnie and what he could do. And I think she wanted some fun time with me and Caroline. I hadn't spent a lot of time with her and Caroline, and I hadn't had much time to lay back and relax either. "I guess I just thought a dozen attorneys would fall on this Vasco guy. Sue him, you know? Do something."

"We'll just have to wait and see what Harry does. He said he'd take care of it. I guess I feel like if Vasco is crooked, Harry will find out. In the meantime, I need to go see Lewis' woman, Leilani, again."

"You think she can tell you something else about Lewis?"

"That's the idea. I think Lewis did more than sleep, eat, surf and go to work when he feels like it. I need to know more about him. Something inside of me tells me there's more to this guy than that. I'm going to try to find my way back there in the morning. You wanna' come with me?"

"No," Sandy answered. "I think I'll take the baby to the beach."

****

At the front desk of the resort I rented a new Toyota 4 wheel drive SUV. As it turned out, managing the narrow and rocky back roads into the hills that would take me to Leilani were almost too much for the car. Nancy's Jeep had a hard time, but she was familiar with the ruts and pot holes, I wasn't and managed to drive into and out of most of them, missing only a few.

I bounced along slowly, trying to avoid as many rocks and low hanging tree branches as I could. I got lost twice and had to squeeze the big SUV through a couple of U-turns to retrace where I had come from, but finally I turned a corner and there was Leilani's little thatch roofed piece of heaven in front of me.

I stopped the car in front and rolled down the window, expecting to see little Kanye scampering around, but I saw no one. The green all around was thick, like a jungle, but somehow welcoming and not dangerous. There were dozens of birds flying everywhere, jumping from tree limb to tree limb. The red chickens were pecking and scratching in the dirt. The smell of the flowers and fruit trees that were everywhere was like nothing I had ever experienced before. I breathed in the perfume deeply and smiled. I remember thinking, "I could live like this."

I got out of the car and walked up the steps to the door. It was partially open; I called out, "Hello . . . Leilani . . . It's me . . . Morgan Crew."

There was no answer but out of the corner of my eye I caught movement. I turned and found Leilani and Kanye walking around the corner of the house. Both were naked and Leilani was drying her long hair with a towel. Her belly was swollen with her unborn child and I found that to add to the sexiness of the woman. Her body was young and lush with promise. Lewis had been a lucky man.

"I am sorry, Morgan," she said, walking slowly towards me and smiling, seemingly not caring about being naked. "Me and Kanye, we were bathing back at the creek. Come inside, I will fix some tea."

I stepped aside and followed her into the little hale. She pointed to a small couch that had a woven cloth of Hawaiian design with birds and flowers decorating it, slung casually across it. I sat as she and the little boy walked into what obviously was the only other room of the house.

While I waited, I looked around the room. Besides the sagging couch I sat on there were only a few other pieces of furniture. A bamboo and wicker chair with beat up cushions that had seen better days sat on the other side of the room. Two small tables fashioned from bamboo sat nearby, one with a gourd bowl that held fresh bright yellow flowers. Both held fat candles that had been burned half down. There was a fishing net hanging from a wall and a surf board propped up next to it. Another larger gourd had been fashioned into a vase, hung from the wall, and brilliantly red and pink plumeria rose from it.

There was a small gas stove at the back of the house and a small sink next to it. The floor was covered with woven thatched rugs, not laid in any pattern, just placed where they needed to be. On the floor, next to the couch I sat on, were two Coleman camping lanterns. There was little else there, but I thought that maybe these people didn't need much else. The 'things' that filled my life probably didn't bring as much happiness to me as these few things had brought to Leilani and Lewis.

She returned from what must have been her bedroom, dressed in a white and blue cloth wrapped around her, tied at the left shoulder, and belted with an old leather belt. Her hair was still wet and shown like silk infused with sparkling diamonds as it hung down her back.

"You like tea, Morgan?" she asked and smiled as she walked to her little kitchen.

"Yes, of course," I answered, wishing the tea could be a bourbon.

As if she read my mind she said, "Lewis, he keep some okolehao here. You want some of that?"

"What is it?"

"Lewis, he make it himself. I show him how. Maybe you wanna' try some?"

I had tried several different kinds of moonshine booze over the years. Most of it would probably burn out the lining of a person's stomach if too much of it were taken in. But what the heck, maybe Lewis' okolehao was good. So I said I would try a glass of it.

Leilani pulled a small glass from the sink and rinsed it in a small ceramic bowl of water. From under the sink, behind a red and white cloth hung from the cabinet, she pulled a glass jug that was full of a clear liquid. She filled the glass half full of Lewis' okolehao from the jug.

She walked to me, holding the glass, smiling and looking like something out of a beautiful dream. I took a small sip of the homemade booze. At first it tasted good, almost sweet, but then the burning began.

I smiled gratefully, not wanting to insult Leilani, but I decided one sip of the strong liquor was enough. Placing the glass on one of the bamboo tables nearby, I smiled my thanks and asked, "Leilani, I need to know more about Lewis. Tell me about him . . . What he liked and disliked . . . His friends . . . And his enemies if he had any . . . If he wasn't at work or here at home with you, where did he go . . . Anything might be a help to me."

Leilani curled herself like a delicate vine, lowering herself to the floor and sitting cross legged on one of the woven mats facing me. Her forehead frowned and she gazed into her memories. When she spoke, her voice was almost a whisper, like a soft murmur carried by a light breeze.

"Lewis, he a good man . . . He don't hate nobody . . . He liked being here with Kanye and playing with him. He like to make things with his hands. He make this hale and things." She paused and thought more, then said, "Lewis, he kind and he like simple things. Nobody ever heard him say nothin' bad 'bout nobody."

"Was his job at the construction site his only problem?" I asked. "Did he ever mention anything else that was bothering him?"

Leilani thought some more, her forehead wrinkling again. "Last month . . . 'bout a month ago I guess . . . he come home and Lewis, he was . . . not happy, I guess. I ask him but he wouldn't say nothin'. Late at night, before we go to sleep, I ask him again. He says he talk with somebody that day . . . somebody that I guess scared him. I never saw Lewis scared of nothin' before. He a strong man. He never scared before. He a good man, and nobody I know hate him."

"Who was this person he spoke with? Was it someone

from Vasco Construction? Where did he talk to this man?"

"Man?" Leilani asked. "You think this was a man . . . not a woman?"

"If you think Lewis was cheating on you . . . I'd bet against it. I can't imagine anyone taking the chance of losing you and everything you have here. To anyone, to me, this is paradise and nothing could be better. No, if someone frightened Lewis, it had to be a man who knew something about Lewis. Maybe he knew that Lewis had found out what was going on at Vasco Construction?"

She smiled and a few tears filled her dark eyes. She wiped them away with her small hand and tried to smile. She said, "I don't know if this man he was from Vasco. I think Lewis, he had a few beers before coming home that day. Maybe he talk with this man there? I don't know."

"Where?" I asked. I wondered if it was Papa Keoni's.

"I don't know. I don't know," she said as she wiped some more tears away. "Soon after that . . . Lewis he killed soon after that."

I tried to drink some more of the okolehao but left the glass with little of it gone when I left Leilani's little hale. She was crying openly. Little Kanye ran to her and hugged her wanting to stop her tears. All I could do was stand, touch her shoulder, thank her, and walk away.

CHAPTER FOURTEEN

San Marcos

Bob Sommers came to Morgan's house in the hills after Betsy had phoned him. It took her some time to decide to phone Bob. She sat at the kitchen table drinking hot tea, forgetting or perhaps not realizing just how many cups she was drinking as she thought about what she should do. In spite of her trepidation, every hour that passed increased the driving force inside her to find Sissy McMillan. She still wasn't sure why she felt she had to find the girl. Sissy wasn't close and not even a friend. But Betsy couldn't lose the feeling that she had to go on.

Telling the police what she was doing was another thing. She had to decide if she was going to go on, on her own. Or should she tell Bob everything she was doing? He had told her to be careful and to let him know what she found out. To be safe, to be sure she was free to find Sissy, she felt she had to keep Bob happy. So she phoned him and he came to her.

They sat around the table in the kitchen, Bob drinking hot coffee, Betsy drinking more of her tea. They finished a whole package of Oreos between the two of them. Betsy finally told him about the phone call and meeting M in Longview Park.

"Betsy," he said when she had finished. "That wasn't very smart. You should have called me. Suppose he had hurt you?"

"Bob, I can take care of myself. M is just a little twerp. I could have kicked the shit out of him easily."

Bob sat back in the chair, staring hard at Betsy. He knew, of course, of her years on the street. It was Bob Sommers who convinced Morgan and Sandy to take her in. He could see, even back then, that there was something good left inside of her, something that could be saved if she could be brought to the right environment.

"I have to ask. Did you carry a gun?" he asked after a couple of uncomfortable moments.

"No, of course not."

"But you thought about it, didn't you?" he asked. He knew that Morgan kept a .38 revolver in the house. He also remembered that strange night when Betsy shot a killer who was about to kill Morgan and Sandy. He could never prove that it was Betsy of course. Morgan stepped in to protect Betsy. He said he had done it and then Sandy did the same, saying she had done it. In the end every spy agency in the U.S. had stepped in and taken all the evidence of everything that had happened, refusing any of it to Bob. So Bob couldn't charge anyone. But he knew what had happened. He knew that Betsy had killed the man. The thought spun around in his head, 'Could she do it again?'

Betsy avoided the question. Of course she had thought about it. She had gone to Morgan's bedroom nightstand and stared down at the pistol. She had come very close to taking it with her and that might have meant real trouble. Did M frighten her enough that she would have threatened him with the gun? What would M have done? If she had the pistol, could she have shot him? All those thoughts had been spinning around inside her head for hours before phoning Bob.

"Who is this M guy? Do you know him?" she asked rather than answer his question.

"Yes," he answered. "He's got a rap sheet here and just about every other place he's ever been. He tries to sell drugs. He talks too much about it and gets busted. He does botched burglaries and leaves all kinds of evidence behind and gets busted. He's tried his hand at auto theft but he's a lousy driver and smashes up most of the cars he steals . . . and gets busted. He's stupid, and he wants to be a criminal, which makes him easy to catch."

"I kind of got the idea he wasn't the brightest light in the chandelier," Betsy said and laughed a little.

"His name is Emmanuel Bottoms," Bob wet on. "Apparently he hates his name and insists on people calling him M. It's probably his own short version of Emmanuel. I don't know. He's a troubled kid. His mother raised him. I guess he never knew his father. Whoever that was. His mother is some kind of religious fanatic . . . I don't know if she goes to a church or not. She stands on corners and reads from her bible and preaches doom and destruction, asking people for money. I guess the State supports her. I'm told a lot of welfare money goes her way. Emmanuel went through High School here in San Marcos. At least when he wasn't in jail for something."

"You called him a 'kid'?" Betsy asked.

"Yeah, he's nineteen, maybe twenty years old. But to look at him you'd think he was maybe fourteen or fifteen," Bob said. "He was real skinny the last time I busted him. And short, too. He talks like a kid of maybe thirteen or fourteen. I think he may have some mental limitations, if you know what I mean."

"You mean retarded?"

"Hey, be careful talking like that. That's a bad word

anymore. The wrong people hear you saying that and you could get sued royally."

Betsy sipped at the cup of tea, by that time only barely warm, but said nothing.

"So he said Sissy is shacking up with some boyfriend?" Bob asked. "Isn't that what Old Billy told you about her and Tommy DeVito?"

"Yes. I guess Sissy gets around, doesn't she? I mean, if M knows she's with someone other than Tommy. Do you think he was talking about Tommy, not knowing he's dead?"

"I don't know," Bob said. "If the kid meant someone other than Tommy, I don't suppose it has occurred to you that her current squeeze might have killed the DeVito kid out of jealousy?" he asked.

"The thought crossed my mind," Betsy said. "What should I do to find her now?"

"You don't do anything. You should stay out of it. Go back to school. Forget about all this and leave it to me. I know what you want to do but this is too dangerous now. There's been a murder and now this idiot M is involved. There's no telling what that idiot might do. It's too dangerous for you."

"Will you talk to this Emmanuel Bottoms?" she asked.

"As soon as I leave here I'll have him picked up."

"Will you let me know what he tells you?"

"I can do that . . . If you promise to stay out of this," Bob said very seriously.

Betsy looked down at her cup of tea and answered, "If I can help you in any way, I will."

"That sounds like something Morgan would say," Bob said, exasperated. "I don't want to have to lock you up in one of my cells 'till this is all over. Just be careful, OK? There's been a murder, remember. Morgan would hold me personally responsible if anything happened to you."

After Bob had left the house, Betsy sat in her room, trying to read through her biology assignment. But her mind was filled with thoughts of Sissy McMillan and the dead Tommy DeVito. She closed the book and went to bed, but sleep eluded her just as the attempt at study had.

****

The next morning she stood in the winter's morning cold waiting for the bank to open at nine AM. She was first in line and withdrew $200 from her account, leaving $82.43 left in her life's savings.

Fresh snow had fallen overnight, and the little MGB spun and slid across the nearly deserted roads as she headed for Longview Park. She doubted M . . . or Emmanuel . . . would be there. Bob would have picked him up the night before and probably was still holding him. But she had to try.

Black clouds darkened the morning enough that the street lights remained on at ten in the morning. She found the one that was out the night before and parked under it. She again left the engine running, trying to stay warm from the tiny amount of heat thrown off by the car. She made a mental note that when she could afford a car of her own, it would be bigger and better than the MGB, and it would have a hard top and a good heater. And it would be an automatic. She hated having to shift gears in the MGB all the time.

An hour passed. She was shivering with the cold, and the gas gage told her the car was running low on fuel. Bob had M; she was becoming sure of that. But if she phoned Bob, he would know she was not doing what he told her to do.

A tap on the passenger side window made her jump. It was not M, it was Bob Sommers. Betsy rolled down the window and could not keep the guilt from flooding across her face.

"How long have you been here?" she asked as he crouched down to see into the small car.

"As long as you have. I've been with you since you left home. I kind of thought you wouldn't listen to me."

"Well . . . Thanks for caring anyway," she said trying to smile but it was just too cold to feel happy. "You have M, of course. You picked him up last night like you said, right? I was just sitting here shivering for nothing right?"

"No," Bob said. "I put the call out, but we couldn't find him. A guy like that, he's got dozens of rat holes to hide in."

That surprised Betsy. Then she realized that if the police didn't have M, he just wasn't going to show up. "I guess I just lost forty dollars," she said. "I kind of knew he wasn't going to show up."

"Me too," Bob said. "You going home now?"

"No," she answered. "I have a class I have to get to."

"Do I need to follow you to make sure you go to school?"

"No, I've waited long enough," Betsy said as she shifted into first. "And I'm freezing cold."

Bob stepped away and walked back to his car, which was parked at the corner behind a row of tall, snow covered bushes. He waited to watch Betsy drive away and turn left, the direction she needed to go to get to school. But after Bob had driven away, Betsy returned and parked once again under the dark street light.

Within a few minutes a shadow approached the MGB. Betsy opened the car door and stepped out. "Hello, Emmanuel Bottoms," she said and smiled.

"Don't call me that!" he said harshly. "I tol' you I'm M. That's what you call me! An' you think I'm stupid or somethin'? I seen the cop back there. You think I'm stupid?"

"No," Betsy said, trying to stay calm. "I don't think you're stupid. I didn't know the police were here, either. I didn't plan that. They're not here now, so tell me where I can find Sissy. I've got one hundred dollars for you, and I want to know where Sissy McMillan is." She had decided not to tell M that she had withdrawn $200. She would hold that other hundred in reserve for emergencies.

"Gimme' the money," he said, holding out his dirty and boney hand.

"Not until you tell me where I can find Sissy."

"An' suppose I tell ya' and you don't give me the money?" he sneered.

"Are you telling me you'd hurt me?" Betsy asked and took a threatening step closer to M. She was taller than M, and she outweighed him. If necessary, she told herself, she would do what she had to do to get some truth from him.

He pulled a six inch knife from his pea coat's pocket, but his step back as he drew it told Betsy he was more scared of her than she might be of him.

"Look," she said forcing a smile and trying to sound nice. "Let's just make this a business deal. You tell me where Sissy is, and I'll give you the money. No tricks on either side, OK?"

She took one of the hundred dollar bills she had withdrawn from the bank out of her pocket and held it up, showing M she was sincere. He reached for it but she was quicker and pulled it away.

"OK," he said. "She's in this here motel outside of town . . . On Highway 1 . . . Trav'ler's Rest or somethin' like that. You'll find it. Just drive and you can't miss it. Guy's name is Bobby or Bob or somethin' or other. Don't know his last name. Now give me that money."

She held the bill out and wanted to ask him how he knew this, but instead she said, "If you're lying to me I'm going to find you and take my hundred dollars back in your teeth and blood. Understand?"

M grabbed the bill and ran into the park as he had done the night before.

****

Betsy went to her three classes that day, but her mind wasn't on them. She drifted up and down the hallways between classes, skipped lunch, had a too strong and bitter coffee at the school's espresso stand, and walked out of her last class before it was over.

It had stopped snowing finally, and the sky cleared for the first time in days. Not knowing what to do, she drove around town aimlessly for hours until the MGB ran out of gas. She left it on the side of the road while she walked to a gas station.

Back at home she put together a ham and cheese sandwich for dinner but was only able to eat half of it. For two hours she paced around the house, drinking cup after cup of hot tea, wondering if she should do anything or just phone Bob

Sommers.

She was about to crawl into bed, having slipped into soft woolen pajamas. She had not slept much the night before and exhaustion was setting in. The next day she had no classes. A free day left her in limbo, whether she would catch up on her studying or go find Sissy. All she wanted right then was a few hours' sleep, and then she would either go back to concentrating on school or go on searching for Sissy.

She stood at the side of her bed, one hand on the spread ready to pull it down. But the thought of Sissy missing for almost two weeks filled her thoughts. Quickly, she dropped the spread and pulled on jeans and a heavy, wool, plaid shirt over her pajamas. She slipped her bare feet into her Nike running shoes. She grabbed her wet wool coat and started to slip into it. She tossed it on the floor and pulled her ski jacket from the closet. Rubber boots were at the front door but she ran out without looking at them.

The snow had begun to fall once again, harder and faster than the day before as she drove the little MGB down the icy roads from the hillside where Morgan and Sandy had their home. The car slid into a curb once as she tried to turn a corner, and from that point on she drove very slowly out to Highway 1. She thought, 'If I kill myself what good will that do Sissy?'

She stopped at the junction where she could turn onto Highway 1 and for the first time realized she didn't know if she should go north or south. She slapped herself on the forehead and realized she should have looked up the motel in the yellow pages before leaving the house. Rather than head back home she turned left and headed north.

The highway was thick with fresh snow and a layer of ice under it. There wasn't much traffic on the road at that time of night. She crept along as slow as the little car would go, riding the clutch, which Morgan wouldn't appreciate if he ever found out. Twenty miles out and several hours later, she had not seen a motel as M had described, so she turned around and went south.

It took hours, but the snow was slowing, and a black sky was beginning to grey as morning approached. A few stars could be seen between the layers of clouds. Twenty five miles south of San Marcos she pulled to the side of the road. M had lied to her, she realized. She had lost $140.00 for nothing.

She was mad, but she was also holding back tears for being such a fool as to trust someone like M. Bob Sommers had told her that M's mother preached the bible and took handouts on the streets of San Marcos. She slammed her fist against the steering wheel and slammed it again, swearing the most foul words she knew. She would go home, make some strong coffee to keep her awake and have something to eat. Then, when it was daylight, she would go out and find M's mother. But sleep and school would have to wait.

CHAPTER FIFTEEN

On The Big Island

Vinnie Vasco liked his comforts. He had been born poor in Brooklyn, New York. His father was a not very smart, low level, wanna-be gangster who hung out with hoods on the neighborhood street corners. He liked to act tough and look like what he thought a gangster looked like. But he was always just someone who wanted to be a gangster; he never made it into those ranks.

When Vinnie was very young, and his father had a few dollars in his pocket, he had bought a used black leather jacket rather than pay some of the back rent on their apartment. The bill collectors were frequently at their door. Vinnie's father would act tough and threaten them, but they all knew he was nothing, just a lot of talk. Vinnie's mother worked as a waitress now and then when the bills piled up too high or when food was short. His father never gave up the hope of becoming a made Mafia soldier.

The real gangsters Vinnie's father liked to be around gave him a few dollars to run errands, bring them sandwiches for lunch, and occasionally take part in small thefts. But that connection gave Vinnie the opportunity to meet people, Mafia connected people, as he grew into his teens. These connected men liked Vinnie and Vinnie liked them. As a young boy he was smarter than his father and the street corner mob saw that. Vinnie used his intelligence to work his way up to meeting the people who gave the orders. He rose from taking part in hijackings to planning them. Soon he had his own money 'out on the street', loaning it out at high interest rates and doing his own collections. Slowly, over a few years, the young man was brought into the world of organized crime, the world of Mafia leadership.

Vinnie gained a reputation as a fearless enforcer who liked to use a knife for the bosses. At sixteen he acquired a 'street name', Vinnie Cuts. He worked his way up to a trusted position of the Brooklyn mob and soon was working 'angles' to bring money to his Mafia bosses.

Things were going well for Vinnie. At nineteen he was wearing expensive suits and driving a new Lincoln. He had his own apartment and his own women. Life was good for Vinnie for many years. He had his own 'crew' and gave his own orders.

Until one hot summer night, Vinnie was out to collect an overdue debt. He had sent two of his crew out to collect the debt, but they came back bloodied by the man. The debt was owed by a big man, bigger then Vinnie anyway, who took Vinnie's knife away and cut his throat. It was bad enough for Vinnie to be out of action for months but not bad enough for him to die. When he had recovered, his voice was the harsh rough voice that people soon got used to.

But Vinnie never got used to it. He hated what the big man had done to him and would never lose that hatred. Three days after he was back on the streets, the big man Vinnie had tried to collect a debt from was found hacked to pieces behind a triple X rated movie theater. He had been beaten to death. His skull was fractured in two places. Three ribs were broken. Both arms were broken. His balls had been cut off and were stuffed in his mouth. All his fingers had been cut off and were never found. His eyes had been cut out; his tongue had been cut out. What was left of the big man was hard to identify, but dental records let the police know who he was.

Money began to flow into Vinnie's pockets again, after months of recuperation. The murder of that big man, that no one ever talked about openly but everyone knew about, sealed Vinnie's reputation. He began doing hits for the mob and strong arm extortion. He was on call by every Godfather in New York when a murder needed to be done.

Vinnie discovered as a teenager that he liked expensive clothes, expensive cars and expensive women. On warm, dry days he would walk the sidewalks of Brooklyn where he had grown up just to feel the sensation of people, everyone, stepping aside to let him pass. People would smile and say hello as they stepped into the street or into a doorway. He never looked at them or spoke to them. He just smiled and walked past them.

One day as he walked down Mulberry Street, a black Cadillac pulled to the curb next to him. Tony Armono leaned out the open window.

"Hey, Vinnie," he called out, stopping Vinnie in his tracks. Vinnie knew that Tony Armono was a mid-level member of the Calabresse Family. One never walks away from Tony Armono.

Tony said without smiling, "You gotta' meet wit' some people, over at il Diavolo Rosso, ya' know? You gotta' go there now, OK?"

He had been called into a meeting in the backroom of il Diavolo Rosso – The Red Devil. It was a neighborhood Italian restaurant that had been in business since the mid-1920's and since then was a place for local mobsters to meet and discuss business. People of the neighborhood went there for good Italian food, the food many remembered from their years living in Italy before coming to America. They were safe there, even into the late night hours. No street thug would dare assault anyone near il Diavolo Rosso.

Adamo Fizulli had started working at the restaurant when he was ten years old and spent long days washing dishes in the hot kitchen. He was an old man the day Vinnie had been called to the meeting. When Vinnie walked into the restaurant, the old man who stood every night at the cash register at the front door looked at the door at the back of the small room and said, "They waitin' for you back there."

Vinnie hesitated. He was either going to be given a job to do . . . or he was going to be executed. He tried to think about what he could have done or said to cause his death. Either way, live or die, he had to walk into the back room. No one could run from the Calabresse.

He opened the door slowly and looked inside the dimly lit room. There was one round table and three chairs filling the room. One chair was occupied by Roberto Zappone, a high level Capo of the Calabrasse Family. The other was occupied by someone Vinnie didn't know and had never seen before. He was dressed well in a business suit, shirt and tie. He wore thick, black-rimmed glasses and stared across the room at Vinnie.

Zappone was smoking a thick, black cigar. The smell was strong and harsh, and filled the room. He put the cigar down in a metal ashtray and said, "Vinnie, thank you for coming."

Vinnie almost laughed because no thanks were necessary. There was no way he could have said 'no.' "You're welcome," he said anyway.

"Please sit," Zappone said pointing to the third chair at the table.

Vinnie sat, leaned back, and crossed his legs casually, trying to not appear frightened. He smiled and looked back and forth, from man to man, waiting to hear what his fate would be.

The man with the glasses then spoke, "We have a business planned, Vinnie. We think it's time to move you up. We'd like you to manage this operation for us."

Vinnie's smile rose from a grin to a broad smile, more in relief knowing he would walk out of the back room. "Thank you," he said to the man in the glasses. "But can I ask . . . who are you?"

Zappone said, "This is Thomas Wright. He's our accountant and business manager. He handles the books and the money. You gonna' get to know him real well."

"I'm glad to meet you, Mr. Wright," Vinnie said. His raspy voice was rougher than normal. His throat was dry. He wanted a drink of water, but should he ask for one?

Thomas asked, "I'm sorry to ask, but . . . your voice . . ."

Vinnie said, "Don't worry about it. People get used to it."

"Anyway," the accountant said, "We're starting an operation in Hawai'i. The job will last a year, maybe a little longer. You will run the operation and you will be cut in for fifteen percent of the profit."

Between Wright and Zappone they explained the operation to Vinnie. Similar scams had been run before, they said. Vinnie would sell stock in the proposed resort on The Big Island. He would sell to investors as much of the resort as people would buy, hopefully two or three hundred percent, or more, of the resort. And when these investors found out they had been scammed, the Family's soldiers would enforce the thefts. They would threaten, they would assault, and if necessary they would kill the people who lost money.

At first his assignment to run the construction scam in Hawai'i wasn't what Vinnie wanted to do. It would take him away from his Brooklyn neighborhood and streets. He enjoyed the collections and enforcement, he enjoyed the occasional thefts and hijackings, and he enjoyed the respect he was shown on the streets, brought on by fear. But in his business you never say 'no' to a boss.

Then Thomas Wright told Vinnie that the goal was fifty million in the year it was planned to run. Vinnie did the calculation in his head as he listened. His fifteen percent of fifty million would be $7,500,000. That changed his opinion of the job he was handed.

When Vinnie first arrived on The Big Island, a taxi took him to the construction site of the never to exist resort. It had been fenced, and a few big earth moving machines were there, but nothing was happening. No workers of any kind were there. His office trailer was there, and a smaller trailer was next to it, intended to be his home while on the Island. 'Yeah, well that ain't gonna' happen,' he thought.

He told the taxi driver to take him to the best and most expensive resort on that side of the Island. He liked his comforts. An hour later the taxi dropped him off at The Hawaiian Palms resort, and he started the process of throwing out fishing lines to reel in suckers who would give him their money. The small trailer was soon sold and dragged away from the construction site.

In Hawai'i it didn't take Vinnie long to like the luxury provided for vacationing visitors to the Islands. He took up residence in the two bedroom suite at the resort along the Kohala coast. He drove a cream colored Jaguar F-Type convertible back and forth between the resort and his construction site every day, loving the sun and the blue sea, and the sounds of the waves crashing onto the beaches and rocks. His expensive clothes, expensive car, and thick roll of hundred dollar bills attracted a lot of the vacationing women at the resort to him. He liked that; he liked everything he found on Hawai'i.

And he enjoyed 'selling' the never-to-be-completed resort to the suckers that flooded to him to give him money for a percent of the resort's ownership. Mario DeSante had joined Vinnie and worked as 'foreman' at the construction site. Mario was Vinnie's enforcer when an enforcer was needed. He was a good man in Vinnie's opinion, although Vinnie had always enjoyed being his own enforcer. It felt good to have someone to do whatever Vinnie commanded. It was yet another step up in the organization.

By the time a week had passed since Vinnie had spoken with Morgan at his trailer, he had forgotten completely that someone named Morgan Crew had come asking questions. The man the Family had imported from France would scare that Morgan Crew person away. No one was a danger to him; he honestly felt that. Any danger, even a hint of danger, could be taken care of with his knife or with the gun of one of the Family's soldiers, or with Mario's fists.

That Friday he left his construction site at four in the afternoon and drove north to The Hawaiian Palms resort. He was feeling very good. An 'investor' from somewhere – Vinnie didn't care where the money came from – had written a check for $350,000 to become an investor and shareholder in the resort that Vinnie assured him would triple his money within a year. He looked forward to a weekend by the pool or maybe on the beach, drinking very silly looking tall drinks with flowers stuck in the glass, and watching all the young female tourists parade by in their skimpy bikinis.

He had dinner sent to his suite because he hated eating alone in the restaurant. He really didn't care what stupid names they called the fish there; he liked what he got and ate some kind of fish almost every night. The steaks were good, but he liked the fresh fish better. And the service at the resort was terrific as far as Vinnie was concerned. He didn't realize that people were standing in line to do something for him for the big tips he gave them from the thick roll of hundreds, fifties and twenties he carried. When he went to one of the bars for a drink, he never asked for change from a twenty. Everyone there loved him.

For dinner that night he ordered a bottle of rough Italian red wine, even though the wine did not do justice to the excellent fish. He sat on the lanai and finished the wine, watching the sun blaze to a fiery red as it sank into the Pacific. He heard some music coming from one of the lounges at the resort. It sounded good, soft and flowing on the cool night air. It was too early for bed, so he slipped on sandals and went to the Marlin Lounge for a drink or two, hoping the music was coming from there.

The Marlin Lounge is a rustic cocktail bar overlooking the beach. It is walled three feet tall in lava rock and roofed in palm held up by tall koa wood beams allowing customers to look out onto the white sand beach and the waves riding up from the Pacific. Fans line the ceiling of the lounge, spinning slowly more for decoration than comfort. They allow the cool ocean breezes to comfort the guests enjoying their overpriced fruity drinks.

Vinnie stood in the wide doorway looking around for a table or a place at the bar to sit. The lounge was crowded that night. Winter is high season on Hawai'i. The snow and cold weather on the mainland draw thousands of people to the warmth Hawai'i offers.

Everyone was dressed in their new gaudy Hawaiian garb: loud shirts and flowery dresses that Hawaiians laugh at and wouldn't wear. Everyone that is, except an exceptionally beautiful and elegant woman who was sitting by herself in a small booth on the other side of the room. She was dressed in a cool and simple beige linen dress, sleeveless and not too low-cut. A single strand of pure white pearls graced her pale white neck.

She was tall and slim and very European in the way she looked and held herself as she sat. Her hair was aristocratically blond and fashioned the way visitors to the islands would never think of.   It was thick and pulled up dramatically high against the warm air into a French twist.

Vinnie had been to Italy once on business.   He remembered seeing rich young beauties from all over Europe parade themselves on warm summer evenings with hair done as this woman's hair was.   This woman, he thought, wasn't from the mainland.

He stared at her as she slowly brought a tall flute of champagne to her rose colored lips.   Her eyes were on the flute and on the small plate of strawberries on the booth's table in front of her.   Then she slowly looked up, and her eyes locked on Vinnie's.   He had never been affected by a woman's eyes the way this woman's blue eyes locked on his.   There was something hypnotic to her deep blue eyes, something that called to him, something he knew immediately he had to have. At first he wanted to flinch, to turn away, but he couldn't.   The stare entangled him in a net of wonder and wouldn't let him go.

She smiled a little and then looked away.   Ripping her gaze away was almost painful to him.   Vinnie hesitated and then weaved his way across the crowded lounge to her.   He bumped into people without seeing them.   He didn't hear the people complaining, and he didn't notice the waiter who spilled a tray of drinks when Vinnie shoved him out of his way.   At the booth, he stood, looking down at her, not knowing what to say.

The woman raised her head slowly, dramatically, and a small, elegant smile crossed her perfect lips again.   "Are you here to fill my glass?"

"I ain't . . . I mean, I'm not a waiter," he stammered in his gravelly voice.   She looked at the scar across his throat and understood his voice.   Her eyes returned to his.

"Then why are you here?"

"You're beautiful," he said, not realizing he had said it. "I ain't . . . I mean, I've never seen anyone as beautiful as you."

"Thank you," the woman said without smiling again. She carefully placed the flute on the table and looked back at Vinnie. She said in a silky voice, "Now, if that is all you want, please go away."

Her voice was plainly not that of an American. It was accented, European, educated and formal, perhaps even royal. This was not an ordinary woman. This woman was sophisticated, of a higher European class, not at all what Vinnie was used to.

He shifted back and forth on his feet nervously and then managed to say, "No . . . I mean . . . Who are you? What's your name?"

"I am not used to introducing myself to strangers in a bar."

"I'm sorry," he said. "My name is Vinnie . . . Vincent Vasco. I run a construction company here on the Island. I don't mean to be rude, but you are amazing."

"Thank you, Mr. Vasco. But if we are to talk further, I will need a formal introduction."

Vinnie stood still for a moment and then quickly turned and walked away. A few short minutes later he was back with the resort manager in tow. They stood next to each other as the woman gazed down at her empty champagne flute, seemingly ignoring them.

Vinnie looked at her, poked the manager on his arm and said, "Introduce us."

The manager swallowed hard and then said, "M'Lady, this is Mr. Vincent Vasco. Mr. Vasco, this is Lady Catherine

Hamilton."

"Lady?" Vinnie asked. "Lady Hamilton. I'm very glad to meet you. I've never met a lady before . . . I mean someone with a title . . . Lady, you know."

The manager quickly and silently backed away without either of them noticing.

Lady Catherine looked up at Vinnie and then at her empty glass. Vinnie quickly filled it from the bottle of Crystal in the silver ice bucket. She sipped at her champagne, placed it carefully on the table and looked up at Vinnie. After a moment's gaze she said. "My glass is empty again, Mr. Vasco."

Vinnie quickly filled her glass, pouring too much until she held a hand out and told him that was enough. The wine foamed over the top of the flute.

"I'm sorry," he said, his face blushing. "I ain't . . . I mean, I've never met anyone like you. I guess I'm just a little rattled."

Catherine smiled again but said nothing.

"You're alone, right?" Vinnie asked.

"Quite alone . . . at the moment," she answered.

"But you're so beautiful. You shouldn't be alone."

"Mr. Vasco," Catherine said, her voice a patronizing octave higher. "I am seldom alone. I have come to Hawai'i, in fact, to be alone. Now, what else may I do for you?"

"You can let me sit down with you. I'll get us another bottle of champagne."

"I am perfectly capable of buying my own champagne, sir," she said sounding a bit insulted.

"Please," Vinnie pleaded. "Just let me sit with you for a while. I just want to talk with you."

Catherine held her now full flute of champagne delicately in her sculptured finger tips. She was silent for a moment and then said, "Alright, Mr. Vasco. You may sit, but only for a few minutes. I dislike rudeness as much as I dislike being rude."

Vinnie quickly slid onto the red leather bench but not too close to Catherine. He waived to a passing waiter and ordered another bottle of Crystal champagne. They sat in silence as they waited. Vinnie could not take his eyes from her even as the waiter opened the champagne and filled two fresh, tall flutes for them.

Vinnie could not come up with words to speak to her. He had never seen anyone as beautiful as Catherine. And he had never been at a loss for words with women. She had to be, he thought, real royalty, descended from kings and queens of old Europe. She could be nothing else.

"Tell me about yourself," Vinnie said finally, his rough voice quaking as he tried to think of something to say to her.

"What!" she said, a front of astounded disbelief in her voice. "I am not accustomed to telling my life's story to strangers."

"I'm sorry," Vinnie said. "I just want to get to know you. You have a title, I know that. But who are you? Where are you from?"

She sipped at the champagne and regally placed her glass on the table. "Well, sir, if I must. I am Lady Catherine Hamilton. I am from Hungary. My husband is English. I reside on the continent and this is my first voyage to Hawai'i."

"Your husband?" Vinnie asked. "You're married?"

"Of course," she said. "And you? I know you are some sort of common laborer or some such thing. Are you married?"

"I'm not a laborer. I own the company. And I'm not married. Is your husband here with you?"

Catherine sipped again at the champagne and then said, her eyes down, "No, he isn't."

"Why not?"

"Mr. Vasco, if you must know, I enjoy time alone . . . away from my husband."

Vinnie felt joy rising in him. She might be available after all. He smiled and asked, "Where is he?"

"We have an estate in the South of England," she answered, not looking at him.

"Is that yours or his?" Vinnie asked. He was uncomfortable and unsure of what to say. But he needed to keep speaking with her; he needed to have more time with her. He couldn't just let her go out of his life so soon.

"My family estates in Hungary were lost during the war. My Grandfather fled the Country when the Nazis invaded, and when he returned, the Communists had taken over. All was lost forever. He stayed, but my father and mother went to England."

"So your title," Vinnie asked, hesitating for fear of asking too much.

"It is my husband's. My Grandfather was a Count. His title went back to the Hapsburgs. But that is all gone now," she said with great sadness in her voice.

"I'm very sorry," Vinnie said sincerely. "What can I call you?" he asked.

"You *can* address me any way you please . . . You *may* address me as . . . I was going to say M'Lady, but I think I would prefer Catherine. It has been a long time since anyone called me that."

"Alright Catherine. Then let me show you around the Island. There are some fascinating things to see here."

CHAPTER SIXTEEN

San Marcos

The morning was crisp and clear, the sky was blue, and there was no sign of new snow promising to fall that morning. The air was cold, but it actually felt good after days of dark storms and blowing wind and snow. For the first time in more than a week the temperature rose above freezing. The roads were still covered with last night's snow, but under it the ice had begun to soften. Betsy took no chances, and as she drove the little MGB down the hillside roads from Morgan's home to North Harbor she kept the car in low gear and took the turns slowly.

At first Betsy drove around the North Harbor area, slowly navigating the main streets, looking for M's mother. Then she drove the same streets again but found only homeless derelicts sleeping off the night in doorways and alleyways, trying to stay warm any way they could. 'How many of them would never make it through the night?' she thought. And she knew that without Morgan and Sandy Crew, she might well have ended her days where these sad people lay.

She was about to give up, telling herself she was just wasting time and gas, but she figured a few minutes more couldn't do any more harm. So she drove out of North harbor and to the San Marcos Harbor, Harborside as it is known. It was Saturday and a clear day. Tourists would take advantage of the break in the weather and begin arriving at the waterfront to shop for souvenirs and to have lunch at one of the seafood restaurants.

And as soon as she turned the corner at the Harbor Master's office onto Harbor Drive, she saw her. The woman was old, her tangled grey hair hanging long and uncombed. She wore a threadbare coat as grey as her hair, the collar turned up against the still chilly air. The coat hung limp almost to her ankles; her feet were hidden inside ragged and wet bedroom slippers, a hole in the left slipper exposing her unwashed toes.

She held a tattered book, her Bible, open in her hands as she read from it. There was a cracked and mended ceramic soup bowl at her feet. Some coins and a lone dollar bill were in the bowl. Her voice was high pitched and hoarse from her daily preaching. It cracked as she spoke as loud as she could manage. She read a passage from her Bible and then explained to the world that what she had read portended the end of the world, when judgment would befall all of Earth's sinners. She called on all the sinners to repent and be saved.

Betsy pulled the car to the curb across the street and watched the woman for a few minutes. She was waving her right arm above her head while she held her Bible in her left hand, reading from it, and shivering at the same time. Her face was gaunt and colorless. She was terribly skinny and looked like she needed a good meal as much as a new coat.

Betsy pulled herself from the MGB and crossed the street, stepping carefully through the wet slush that covered the road. A car drove by, not caring that she was in the street and splashed her with wet snow. The preaching woman saw her, so Betsy decided not to yell a string of profanities at the car. 'Best not to piss her off,' she thought.

She made it across the street and stood a few feet in front of the woman who smiled gratefully that someone was taking an interest in what she had to say. Her shrill soprano voice rose an octave in her joy.   Betsy took a dollar bill from her purse and dropped it into the soup bowl. "God bless you, my child," the woman said.

"I hope so," Betsy answered and smiled. "I'm going to need all the blessing I can get."

"God forgives all who repent."

"I hope so," Betsy repeated. "Are you Mrs. Bottoms?"

"Why, yes, I am. Do you know me? I don't think I know you."

"I know your son, Emmanuel. I'm trying to find him."

"Emmanuel?   My   son?"   Mrs.   Bottoms   asked suspiciously. "Why? What sin has he committed now?"

"None that I'm aware of. I owe him some money, and my conscience has been bothering me. He did me a favor, and I need to repay him."

"My son did you a favor?" she asked suspiciously. "Emmanuel has never done anything for anyone but himself. God's judgment will fall hard on those who live in falsehoods. If you think Emmanuel has done something for you . . . then rest assured he has done nothing. His soul is lost to sin. He is damned to God's judgment."

"I'm sorry to hear that," Betsy said. "But do you know where he is? I really need to give him the money I owe him."

"Give it to me and I'll give it to him," the woman said, a little smile of lust cracking across her wrinkled face.

Betsy smiled and then said, "Does God forgive liars who steal other people's money? Look, I'm sorry. I've got a twenty dollar bill for your collection bowl if you tell me where I can find your son."

"Are you the cops?" the woman asked, her forehead wrinkling suspiciously again.

"Do I look like a cop? I'm a college student. I've given M more than a hundred dollars already and I want to talk to him. Do you know where he is or not?"

"A hundred dollars! He must be in trouble again."

"Please," Betsy said as she pulled a twenty from her purse. "Tell me where I can find him."

Mrs. Bottoms took the twenty dollars, moved close to Betsy and whispered, "You didn't hear it from me . . . but he sleeps during the day on an abandoned boat . . . The Mary D . . . on pier 3 . . . Where he is in the moonlight is anybody's guess. He roams around in the dark mostly. That's when the devil's work is best done, you know. Be careful of him. He is the devil's hand-picked worker."

Betsy thanked her and turned away to walk to pier 3. Mrs. Bottoms called after her, yelling loudly, "Tell him to repent! Tell him to give up the ways of the devil!"

****

Betsy found pier three easily enough. Small boats, old sailboats for the most part, and a few small motor boats were tied up there. Piers 1 and 2 were where the bigger and better boats, the commercial fishing fleet, moored. Halfway down pier 3 and on the left was the Mary D.

The Mary D was a 25 foot wooden hulled sail boat that was perhaps one or two winters away from sinking to the bottom of the harbor. It appeared to have been abandoned to the weather. The mast had broken some time before and lay across the open deck. The hull held very little paint; the exposed wood was warped, dark with mold, and covered with black barnacles.

A mass of seagulls jumped into the air from the pier as Betsy approached. They screamed and threatened, but Betsy was used to them and ignored their loud cries. She stood on the dock next to the Mary D and called out, "M! . . . M! . . . Are you there?"

There was no answer. She called out again but no one answered. She stepped from the pier over the rail onto the deck, and the boat rocked under her on the calm harbor water. She was ready to jump back onto the pier should the rotted old scow suddenly capsize and sink.

A dirty blanket hung across a doorway that led down into the cabin. She pulled it aside a little too hard, pulling it off of the two nails that had been holding it in place. She stepped cautiously down into the cabin. Inside, the small cabin was dark and clammy and cold. A lingering odor of tobacco smoke, marijuana, and stale urine hung in the musty air. But M was not there.

The walls were covered in wrinkled and well used Playboy centerfolds. The single bunk was filthy; the once white sheets and bare pillow were almost black. Betsy decided to search through the cabin, opening drawers and forcing herself to search under the few dirty clothes lying in piles everywhere. She quickly pulled the filthy sheets away from the bunk and tossed them aside onto the floor. The thin, torn mattress followed the sheets onto the cabin's floor. She knelt and peered under the bunk. Piles of pornographic magazines and pictures had been jammed under the bunk, along with untold amounts of dust and dirt.

And there was a manila envelope there, too. She pulled it out and opened it. Eight handwritten letters, written in pencil with childishly misspelled words, were inside. They were not addressed to anyone, but they said the writer loved someone and described in vivid detail all the unnatural sex acts the writer wanted to perform on his lover.

The words made Betsy feel sick to her stomach. She felt sick at the thought that M might have written these sick letters to or about Sissy. But that, she told herself, had to be silly. How could M even know Sissy?

She took the envelope with her as she left the boat. It would have to go to Bob Sommers, she knew that. Bob would have to know about M, and maybe he could protect whoever M had written the filth to.

CHAPTER SEVENTEEN

On The Big Island

Sandy and Caroline and I had spent a fun couple of days together. We splashed in the pool and the warm ocean. We rented a car and drove into Kailua-Kona to tour the shops there and eat a great lunch at The Kona Inn. Caroline insisted on some plastic toy fish, and Sandy just had to have three Hawaiian dresses and a bright pink broad brimmed straw hat. I settled for a new pair of sandals that were more comfortable to wear in the afternoon heat than shoes.

The last day of that week, I played on the beach with Sandy and Caroline throughout the morning. The air was cooler in the morning than it would be in the afternoon. The ocean was lapping casually up onto the white sand. I was showing Caroline how to build a sand castle, but every now and then she would get up and run to the water, with me after her. Sandy was watching our fun and laughing wildly as she lay back on a chaise under the shade of a broad palm tree with a tall icy glass of some fruity rum drink with one of those ridiculous little umbrellas stuck in it.

We had lunch together, delicious fish sandwiches for Sandy and me, and a bowl of mac and cheese for Caroline. I was tempted to steal some from her, but I didn't. And then while Caroline was taking a well-deserved nap, Sandy and I sat on the lanai enjoying some iced green tea. Without speaking the words, I had been hoping for one of those tall fruity rum drinks with flowers and a little umbrella stuck in it like Sandy had enjoyed earlier. But Sandy is intent on keeping me healthy so I suffered in silence.

We were quiet for a long time, staring out onto the white beach and the clear blue ocean. I was feeling a little sleepy and I was about to take a short nap when Sandy asked quietly, almost in a whisper, "So you're going back to that beach bar again?"

"I guess I have to," I said in a sleepy voice. "Leilani said Lewis had some kind of run-in with someone while having a beer after work. He wouldn't talk to her about it, and the only bar I know of that he went to is that Papa Keoni's place. They talked to me last time, so maybe they'll talk to me some more. I mean, I have no place else to go."

"Do you want me to come with you?" she asked.

"No, not really. It's not the kind of place a lady would like."

"So, you think I'm a lady now?" she asked, teasing.

"You're always a lady, always have been . . . even when you're kicking the shit out of somebody."

She laughed at that, and we finished the pitcher of tea, enjoying the warm weather and the sounds of the ocean. I guess because I was going off into danger once again, Sandy relented and let me have a bourbon over ice from the bar inside the suite. It was good and gave me a bit of false courage to do what I had to do.

I rented the same Toyota 4-wheel drive I had last time and found Papa Keoni's without too much trouble. It was mid-afternoon when I pulled to a stop under the same palms at the edge of the black sand beach as I had the last time I was there. The shade was as near to the little thatched roof hut that passed for a bar as I could get without driving onto the black sand.

I walked slowly across the sandy beach, the afternoon sun just starting to approach the Pacific. I didn't mind the Hawaiian sun, in fact I love it. The warmth of Hawai'i and the beauty it grows on the Islands is what I dream of when I think of a place I really want to be.

It was a quarter past four; I wanted to be at Papa Keoni's before the locals got off work. I wanted to speak with Mama Keoni alone. I needed answers without being threatened by a bunch of her 'good boys'. I reasoned that Mama Keoni would have been at the bar every day, even when the regulars were not. She may have seen something the others didn't. She may have seen who Lewis was arguing with. And I didn't want to have the others influencing what she would tell me.

I walked, avoiding the high tide that splashed up on the beach. I was wearing my new sandals and a pair of tan shorts as well as a brand new Hawaiian shirt Sandy had insisted I get for myself. As I got close to the bar, Mama Keoni stepped outside, a long handled broom in hand. She started sweeping off the little porch and wooden steps before seeing me approach her.

"You back again," she said without smiling. In fact she looked angry.

"Yeah. I just had to have another one of those ice cold beers."

"You like other haoles. You don't know how to speak true," she said.

"OK," I said as I walked to the bottom of the three worn wooden planks that served as steps up to her bar. "I can be truthful."

Mama Keoni made no effort to move from the doorway; her bulk filling the door completely. She was wearing a dark blue muumuu with a white lace collar. Her feet were bare, and her dark face held an angry expression.

"I want to speak with you about Lewis again," I said standing on the first step, looking up at her. "His woman wants to know why he died. Can I talk to you?"

She stood in the doorway, staring down at me, her face wrinkled in thought. Then she stepped backwards into the barroom, and I took the stairs to follow her inside. As soon as I walked into the little tavern I felt shaded, cool air, and I smelled the fragrance of hibiscus and plumeria. It may be a hangout for locals but I liked it anyway. I imagined myself retreating to the Island, living on the beach in a small grass hale, catching fish for dinner; or in the hills like Lewis had, and enjoying beer after beer at Papa Keoni's. There would be no more pleas from lawyers, family and friends. I simply wouldn't tell them where I was.

Mama Keoni walked behind the bar, still holding onto her broom, and waived at a rickety stool, one of four mismatched benches along the bamboo bar. I pulled it away from the bar and sat.

"So, what you wanna' know, haole?" she said.

"How about one of those cold beers?" I asked and smiled as best and as broadly as I could.

She reached under the bar and pulled out a bottle of Budweiser, pulled the top off barehanded and put it in front of me. I drank half of it down quickly, feeling the coldness of it refresh me.

I smiled again and asked, "Is Papa Keoni around? I mean, the name of the place, you know? Is he here?"

"Papa Keoni, he my man. He dead now. He out fishing on his boat. He never come back. I think maybe mano get him."

"Mano?" I asked. "That's a shark, isn't it?"

"Yes, mano is the shark. Too bad but Papa he liked bein' out on moana. Maybe he now where he happy. I hope so, anyway. He stay in my heart forever."

Mama Keoni's grief was real. I felt bad for her, but as usual I didn't know the right words to express my regret. I find it impossible to say the right thing to people who are suffering. When friends are in the hospital, I try everything I can to not visit them because I always say the wrong thing.

So, not knowing what to say I got right to the point. There was no sense trying to grease her with flattery or lies. This woman, like so many other Hawaiians I have met, was not dumb. She could see the truth when truth was being hidden from her. I believe native Hawaiians have some special ability to do that.

I asked, "Lewis stopped in here to have a couple of beers after work every now and then. Leilani told me that one night he came back upset about something. She said he had talked with someone that night while having a beer. I need to know who he was speaking with and what they talked about."

"So you think Lewis in some kind'a trouble?"

"I think he was in some kind of trouble with someone. I think his death wasn't an accident. I think someone killed him. Maybe it was someone from Vasco Construction, maybe not. But I need to know."

"The boys here, they good boys. They not gonna' hurt a good hoaloha, a good friend. Lewis, he a good friend these boys."

"OK," I said. "So did Lewis ever talk here with anyone who was new to you? Someone who isn't one of your good boys?"

Mama Keoni leaned back against the wall of the little hale, her dark forehead wrinkled as she stared deeply at me; her black eyes peered into my eyes trying to learn the truth. Then she said, "Yes, I remember once Lewis, he was here and this man he walk in. He not looking happy, you know? He waived at Lewis, and Lewis, he walk outside with this man. The boys here, they say they go with Lewis, but he say no to them. He go outside with this man. They talk loud like, angry. Lewis, he come back inside and he walkin' in circles, really mad maybe. The man, then he leave an' I don't see him again."

"Who was this man?"

"I don't know. I not seen him before."

"Can you describe him?" I asked.

She stood away from the wall and said, "This place I got . . . This place, I got no license for. Trouble here not good for nobody. I don't want no police here asking questions."

"I'm not the police," I said. "All I want to do is help Leilani and Nancy Wong. They are my friends, my hoaloha. Now, what did this guy look like?"

"OK, this guy he dark, but he not no Hawaiian. I seen haoles like him before. He maybe Mexican. And he some kind'a soldier."

"How do you know that?" I asked, sitting up straight because it was the first solid lead I had in this morass of swamp.

"His hair cut like soldiers cut hair. He got lots'a muscles and a big tattoo on his arm."

"What kind of tattoo?" I asked. I needed something, anything, to use as a lead to find this man. If he was in the military, maybe the tattoo would tell me which branch of the military.

"I don't know . . . Some kind," she said. "Maybe you wait 'till Palani come here. That boy he was in the army or somethin'. Maybe he know."

"Did Palani see this guy?" I asked.

"Yes," she said. "Some of the boys they here when he showed up. I know the boys they don't like this guy. They Lewis' friends. That haole, he make Lewis mad, worry like, you know? The boys they don't like that. Maybe they help you. You wait. Have another beer, maybe," she said as she pulled another bottle of beer from under the bar. I pulled a twenty dollar bill from my money clip and laid it on the bar. Mama Keoni snatched it up. There was no change coming to me, but I really didn't care if it would bring some truth to me.

And so I waited until Mama Keoni's 'boys' left their jobs and came for their usual few beers. The afternoon sun was heading west, and it started to get warm inside Papa Keoni's. Mama Keoni walked to a big fan hanging on the back wall and switched it on. It made more noise than anything else and did little to cool the room. I watched as the sun peered in through the thatched roof and drift wood sides of the little bar. The sky began to turn red and then burst into flames as the sun sank into the ocean. As night fell, the air began to cool with the breeze from the Pacific.

Mama Keoni brought me a couple more icy cold bottles of Bud, and I retreated to a dark corner table. The afternoon heat and the beer combined to make me sleepy. My eyes became heavy and I struggled to keep them open. My mind wandered to the beauty of the Island, the greenery and the sweet flowers, the smell of the fresh breezes down from Mauna Loa and the sounds of the Pacific crashing onto the beach. I leaned back in the chair and looked up through the thin palm frond roof and saw birds of so many exotic and loud colors flitting around, searching for a place to rest and sleep the night away.

As my eyes began to burn, crying for sleep, I tried to think what I would need to do to move Sandy and Caroline and me to these Islands and hide away in the hills, perhaps near Leilani and Kanye. The peace and simplicity of life would be wonderful. I would fish in the ocean in the morning while Sandy gathered fruit. Caroline would play in the dirt with Kanye. Trouble would become a memory, a thing of the past. Then reality pulled me from the muse.

Alone and in pairs, men started walking into Papa Keoni's. It took three bottles of beer for the first of Mama Keoni's boys to arrive. They arrived in twos and threes, all of them from jobs that had to be tough based on the sweat and dirt they carried with them. Finally, Palani and his three buddies walked to their usual table, all drinking the beer that Mama Keoni had waiting for them.

I stepped from the shadows of the corner and walked to them. The four all looked at me, none too friendly or happy to see me again.

Palani glared at me and said, "Mikey Chung is dead. Why? Is he dead because of you?"

"Mikey said he wanted to talk with me," I said. "I think he knew something about Lewis' death. I think he wanted to tell me what he knew. I think whoever killed Lewis killed Mikey to shut him up."

"That's what you think?" Palani said. "I think maybe all this trouble 'cause of you."

"Does that include Lewis' death? Because that happened before I got to the Island."

"Don't make no difference. You ain't here, maybe Mikey be still alive."

There was no use arguing with Palani. He and his beer drinking group were obviously close friends. Nothing I could say would change Palani's mind, or the minds of anyone else at Papa Keoni's. So I said, "I need to talk with you about the man who talked to Lewis and made him angry. Leilani told me Lewis came home one night from here and he was upset and mad. I need to find that man."

Palani, obviously the spokesman for the bunch, said, "Why you gotta' do that? We Lewis' friends. We gonna' take care of that. You don't need to. Go home haole."

"Is that right?" I said. "You're going to go to work every day then come here and drink a few beers, maybe eat some fish or something, talk about what you'd like to do, go home, sleep and get up the next morning and do the same thing all over again. That's how you 'take care of that' as you say?"

"What the hell business is it of yours?" one of the others said. He wasn't Hawaiian but he was tanned as dark as any Hawaiian. His hair was dirty blond and long and uncombed, and he smelled of fish. He was one of the few who went out early every day to catch fish to sell to the restaurants. Like the commercial fishermen I know back in San Marcos, he would spend the afternoon cutting and cleaning the fish before heading off to Papa Keoni's.

"It's my business because Leilani made it my business. I can find this guy . . . If you'll help me. I don't think you guys can do that. If this guy was mad enough at Lewis he could have killed Lewis. I can see him prosecuted and put in jail. I don't think you can do that. Now, you guys would all have been here that night. You must have seen something. I need to know what you saw when that guy was here. I need to know anything you know about this guy. When I find him, I'll let you know after I call the cops. Is that OK with you?"

The five men looked at each other without speaking. In silent agreement Palani turned back to me and said, "OK. Pull up a chair and buy us a beer. There ain't much, but we gonna' tell you. You do us wrong, and that ain't too smart."

Mama Keoni brought five bottles of cold beer to the table and stood nearby as I listened to each man tell me what he knew. Each of the four spoke, one after the other, each adding something.

They agreed the man I wanted to talk to was military, big, olive skin, hair cut high and tight in military style, as Mama Keoni had said. He wasn't very young, perhaps mid to late thirties, and he wasn't happy to see Lewis. He was Lewis' height but heavier muscled with thick arms and a thin waist.

They told me that this man had walked into the bar and stood in the doorway, silhouetted against the bright light of the setting sun outside. He stood still, staring angrily across the small room at Lewis' back. When Lewis turned to look at the man he froze, the color quickly draining from his face. The man spoke one word very loudly, "Outside." Lewis stood, told the others to stay inside, and followed the man out the door and down the steps into the sun and onto the black sand.

Palani and his friends had walked outside and stood on the porch, in the doorway, watching, waiting to see if Lewis needed help in a fight. Lewis and this man spoke to each other outside of the bar, in raised voices, angrily. But none of the four could tell me what was being said, other than the fact that the stranger was calling Lewis a liar and traitor.

Lewis looked and sounded defensive. The stranger was livid. The man poked a finger at Lewis, and Lewis pushed his hand away. No one there could tell me what was said in any detail, but all were sure they had never seen this man before, and he definitely wasn't a worker at Vasco Construction. He was too clean. His clothes were not the clothes of someone who 'swung a shovel'. He wore pressed and clean blue jeans and a black T-shirt that fit tightly over his muscled arms.

I asked Palani, "Mama Keoni told me you might be able to identify the tattoo on his arm."

"No," he said. "I guess I wasn't looking. I was watching to see if Lewis needed help."

One of the others, the haole who worked on a fishing boat, said, "Yeah, I seen it. It was this eagle wrapped in an American flag . . . You know, stars and stripes."

Then a voice crackled from across the room, behind me, near the open door of Papa Keoni's. The man said, "I seen him, too."

I turned and saw an old man, thin, grey hair and beard, and skin like old, cracked, weathered leather. He wasn't Hawaiian, but he must have been on the Islands for a long time. He sat at a table near the door. I hadn't seen him come in, and apparently no one else had either. He was that kind of man who is almost invisible to people nearby. The kind of person who is not looked at as people pass them on the street.

Mama Keoni looked at the old man and said, "Henry, this bad business. You don't get no free beer trying to lie to this man."

"I'm not lyin', Mama. I was walkin' here that day. I had three dollars that day, 'member? I bought my own beer. You 'member, don't you? I bought my own beer that day."

"I remember," she said and smiled. "It not all the time you buy your own beer."

She turned to me and explained, "Henry an old time bum 'round here. He don't hurt nobody so people sometime buy him a beer or two. Lewis, he buy Henry a beer a lot. I think Lewis maybe feel sorry for the old Henry, you know? I think Lewis don't hate nobody."

I turned around and asked Henry, "So tell me. What do you know about the man who argued with Lewis?"

Henry struggled to stand. He pushed his chair away and used the table to brace himself as he stretched his thin and stiff legs to pull himself to his feet. He wore old, dirty cutoff jean shorts, frayed at the bottom, and a tank top T-shirt that was two sizes too big for him. It was torn across the front. He was little more than wrinkled skin and bones.

He held tightly to a can of Coors with both hands. He weaved his way towards us on unsteady feet. He wore old rubber flip-flop sandals and skidded across the wood floor as he walked. He stopped near us, and I stood to let him sit rather than see him collapse to the floor. He took the chair gratefully and smiled at me.

He started, "I did some sweeping that day. Took out some garbage. I got paid three dollars even though the guy promised me five. Son a'bitch, that guy. Then I came here. I walked like I always do, down the beach and 'cross the rocks. It's tough getting here, but this here place is the only place they let me drink my beer without gettin' the shit kicked outta' me. When I got here, I seen Lewis and this big guy out on the sand. They was arguing and like they was about to get into a fight. The big guy was calling Lewis a son of a bitch and a lot of other stuff. I stood away because I didn't want to get involved, ya' know? But I saw, and I heard some of it.

"The big guy said he was gonna' get Lewis," Henry continued. "I heard him say Lewis was as good as dead. I guess I got there too late 'cause I missed the beginning, ya' know? So I don't know why they was mad at each other, ya know? Then the big guy just turned and walked away to this motorcycle and sped away kicking up a lot of sand and dirt."

"What kind of motorcycle?" I asked hoping for another good lead.

"Hell, I don't know," Henry said. It was big and black . . . You wanna' know what the license plate was?"

"You know the license plate number?" I asked, astonished. "Did you write it down?"

"No," the old man said sounding insulted. "Why should I write it down? It don't mean nothin' to me."

"But you asked me if I wanted the license plate number."

"Sure . . . You wanna know or not?"

"Yes I want to know!" I said, quickly getting exasperated.

"Cost you a beer . . . or two, maybe," Henry said and grinned like the cat that had just caught the canary.

Mama Keoni said, "Henry! You don't try to steal from this man!"

Henry looked up at me, smiling still, and asked, "You wanna' know or not?"

I pulled a twenty dollar bill from my money clip and held it out. Henry reached for it but I pulled it away. "Tell me," I said. "If you're not lying there's another twenty in it for you."

"FOUR-EIGHT-T-R-A-N-S," he said. "That was it. The number 48 and the letters T-R-A-N-S after it."

The haole fisherman spoke up and said, "Hey that means the 48th Transportation Division. My buddy, he was in the National Guard . . . The Army . . . He knows them things and we talk about it. That guy is an army guy."

I handed Henry two twenty dollar bills and gave two more to Mama Keoni. I told her, "Get Henry some food . . . As much as he can eat. But he buys his own beer, OK?"

Mama Keoni smiled knowingly and took the twenty.

I laid a fourth twenty on the table and told Palani and his friends, "The beer's on me."

CHAPTER EIGHTEEN

San Marcos

Lt. Bob Sommers and Betsy sat at the kitchen table in Morgan's house in the hills above the San Marcos harbor. The clear and promising morning had turned dark and cold with black clouds that came in from the Pacific and carried more icy rain and then snow with them.

Betsy had heated water for tea, but Bob preferred a can of beer, which Betsy pulled from the back of the refrigerator. There were three cans of Coors left. Sandy had long ago relented and kept a supply of beer in the fridge, more for the fact that without it, Bob might find his way to the bar and the hard liquor. It was her way of trying to keep him away from it.

Bob was paging through the handwritten letters Betsy had found on the Mary D. There were nine pages of lined yellow paper that had been roughly torn from a pad. "You say you found this stuff in an abandoned boat down at the harbor?" he asked her as she stirred her cup of tea without knowing she was doing it.

"Yes. M's mother told me he sleeps on the boat."

"You talked to this kid's mother?" he asked.

"Yes, I'm sorry . . . I guess," she said, even though she wasn't sorry.

"So even after I asked you to stay out of this, you didn't

. . . or you couldn't," he said, shaking his head in disbelief. "You've been with Morgan and Sandy too long. They're rubbing off on you, and you're going to wind up in trouble like they do. Except you don't have the pull they do to get yourself out of trouble."

"Bob," she said as she touched his arm lightly. "I was in trouble. They saved me, remember? And I think it was your bright idea that they take me in."

"Yeah, but I thought it was just a good idea. To try to get you out of trouble, you know? Had I known you'd become some amateur Sherlock Holmes, I would have thought of something else. Hell, Betsy, you don't know what you're doing out there. Do I have to lock you up to keep you safe?"

"I'm sorry, Bob," she said again although she knew she wasn't really sorry. Inside of her there was a driving urge to find Sissy McMillan because also inside of her was the feeling Sissy was in real trouble. It was more than a young girl running off for some sex and fun, Betsy knew that inside of her. It was bigger than that. It was all about drugs. Everything and everyone she had come across was involved in drugs, and that kind of thing never works out well for anyone involved.

Betsy knew the streets, and she knew what drugs had done to the people she used to know and hang out with. If Sissy McMillan were in trouble with drugs, Betsy had to find her and help her. That could have been her, she knew. Had not Morgan and Sandy taken her in, she could have wound up on the streets, hooked on drugs and doing anything to get the drugs.

"Sorry don't feed the bulldog, Betsy. You've been off talking to prostitutes, drug dealers, and a demented child molester. And now some crazy old religious fanatic who might hear God telling her to kill you. That stuff's dangerous."

"It's not like I haven't been there before," she said in the only defense she had. "Those people used to be my friends and the only family I knew . . . before Morgan and Sandy that is."

"Yeah, I know. But now you're all grown up, going to college. You're not some kid anymore. You've got a future ahead of you. You need to smarten up and get your sights set on what's important."

"Sissy McMillan is important," she answered, trying to sound convincing.

"Yes, she is," Bob said. "And she needs to be found. That's what I get a paycheck for. I've asked you . . . Now I'm *telling* you. Go back to school and stay out of this."

"That's coming from Lt. Bob Sommers of the San Marcos Police Department?" she asked, grinning slyly.

"Yes, it is. I will throw your tattooed little behind in jail for interfering with a police investigation if I have to."

Betsy sipped at the cup of hot tea, grinned, and said sarcastically, "And how do you know I have a tattoo on my ass?"

Bob finished his can of beer. Neither said another word. Bob finally got up and left Betsy sitting at the table as he left the house. There was school the next day; she finished her tea and opened one of her books. She put Sissy McMillan out of her mind, at least temporarily.

****

Betsy had a 10 AM biology class the following morning. She was up early after a restless night that found little sleep. She was early to class, anxious to make up for the days missed while she searched for Sissy. She was first in the classroom, sitting at a lab table, waiting for the rest of the class to arrive. She was flipping through her biology book and reading through the notes she kept on her iPad. How much had she missed, she wondered? But biology seemed to come easy to her, so she wasn't too worried about catching up.

Sissy should have been in that class. Betsy kept looking at the door as students filtered in, hoping Sissy would be one of them. But she wasn't. Mr. Thatcher, the biology professor, started the class, but Betsy had a hard time listening to him. Her mind was filled with Tommy DeVito and M and M's mother. She couldn't shake the feeling that she should be out looking for Sissy and not sitting there listening to some discussion on biology that she already knew.

When the class ended and the students started running for their next class or wherever they would go, Mr. Thatcher stopped Betsy as she started to leave.

"Betsy," he said. "Would you please wait a minute?"

When the classroom was empty save for the two of them, he said, "I've been told you've been looking for Sissy McMillan."

"I guess I'm just worried about her," she said defensively, expecting a lecture on not missing any more classes.

"I am, too. She's missed too many classes. I'm going to have to drop her pretty soon. Do you know where she is?"

"No," Betsy said. "I have a feeling she's in trouble . . . But . . ."

"Trouble? What kind of trouble?"

She hesitated at first then said, "I'm not sure."

Betsy felt she shouldn't be talking to anyone about the questions she had been asking and the answers she had gotten, anyone except Bob Sommers of course. In looking for Sissy she had learned personal things about some people, personal things that she felt she should keep to herself.

She had learned about people from Morgan and Sandy. She had learned that people were always curious about other people's business. Morgan would say 'sticking their fat noses where they don't belong.' Betsy knew things about Sissy that she was reluctant to talk about. She knew personal things about Sissy, things Sissy herself wouldn't talk about. These things should be kept private, Betsy believed. Mr. Thatcher may well be wondering if he should drop Sissy, or maybe he was just 'sticking his nose where it doesn't belong.' So she wouldn't tell him what she knew.

"I'm going to phone her parents," Mr. Thatcher said. "I need to know if she is going to continue with school. If you know something, you should tell her parents. Tell me if you don't want to talk to them directly. I'll tell them if you feel uncomfortable talking to her parents."

"There's nothing to tell," Betsy said. "I mean, all I've been doing is asking questions of people who don't know anything. The police are looking for her. I know that, and I'm sure Sissy's folks know that. I'm sure the police have spoken with Sissy's parents."

"The police?" Thatcher said. "Well, that's good. I guess I'll have to put her on some kind of probation. I'll talk to admin about it. If you hear anything, let me know. I really would like her to continue with school. It would be a shame to see her just drop out."

Betsy turned quickly and walked away, out of the classroom, and started for the parking lot and Morgan's old MGB. It was a bitterly cold morning with a clear blue sky. She was walking as fast as she could towards the car when someone called her name. She stopped and turned to see who it was. A gust of icy wind blew into her face making it hard to breathe.

A tall, handsome, and athletic looking young man walked towards her. He was carrying two text books under his left arm, and he carried a canvass computer case in his right hand. He was wearing the school's athletic jacket, not enough against the bitter weather but school jocks were a proud bunch.

'A student,' Betsy thought. But she didn't recognize him. 'Doesn't mean anything. He's just not in any of my classes. Maybe he just wants to meet me?' she thought and tried to smile. 'He's cute enough,' she thought.

She waited as he approached. "What do you want?" she asked and smiled as best as she could in the cold.

"I want to know why you're out asking questions about Sissy," he said.

Betsy was a little disappointed. "Who are you?" she asked.

"I'm Ron Porter. I know Sissy. We were going out together for a while."

"So then you know where Sissy is?" Betsy asked.

"I was hoping you could tell me. I haven't heard from her for a couple of weeks."

"Look," Betsy said, taking a couple of steps back, away from the young man. "I'm feeling uncomfortable here. I don't know you . . . We're all alone here . . . And I'm cold."

"I'm sorry. I didn't mean to scare you. I'm just curious why you're out looking for Sissy. Is it because she's one of your Country Club friends?"

"I don't get it," Betsy said annoyed at the way Ron put the question. "What the hell are you talking about?"

"Why aren't you asking about the other girls who are missing? Aren't they as important as Sissy McMillan? Is that what you think?"

"Others?" Betsy asked. "You mean Sissy's not the only girl who's missing?"

"You really don't know do you?" he asked, realizing Betsy really didn't know about the other girls.

"You live with that Morgan Crew guy, and you really don't know. Doesn't he know? He's got that big damn habit of using all his damn money to run people's lives. He hangs out at that damn Country Club and runs everybody's lives from there. And neither of you know? That's a bunch of shit. You know something, and you won't tell me because you think I'm not in your damn Country Club class of rich-bitch people."

He was angry. He was obviously envious of what other people had and he didn't, Betsy reasoned. That envy, she knew, was a result of a generation being brought up believing they are 'entitled' to everything without having to go out and earn it. She had heard this before. She lived with Morgan and Sandy Crew who have everything and didn't earn it. But Betsy knew that Morgan and Sandy earn every penny they have by risking their lives doing things for people that they cannot or will not do for themselves. So Ron Porter could be jealous and envious, he could be angry and nasty. It made no difference because Betsy knew the truth.

She could feel that old temper of hers rise up inside of her. It had been a couple of years since she had been living rough on the streets, and she liked to think she had grown up. She was feeling more angry than frightened of this boy now. Rather than step away from Ron, she took a threatening step towards him.

Looking dead square up into his eyes, she said, "Cut the crap, Ron. I don't give a good God damn what you think of Morgan and Sandy, nor what the hell you think of me. Tell me who these other girls are."

He looked shocked at Betsy's words. He took a defensive step backwards without knowing he was doing it. "Mary Ortiz and Diane Kohn," he said quickly.

Having lived with Morgan and Sandy Crew for a couple of years, Betsy had become known around San Marcos. Some of the influence Morgan carried around with him had attached itself to her. Ron realized quickly that he wasn't going to intimidate Betsy. People who knew her and who she lived with treated her with some deference. Ron reacted as anyone else who knew Betsy Concanon would have if she stepped towards them and spoke so strongly. He answered quickly and tried to smile to hide his sudden discomfort.

Betsy locked her stare on Ron and asked, "How long have they been missing, and have the police been notified?"

"I . . . I don't know for sure," he stuttered.

"Then why did you come across so tough with me?" she asked.

"I guess . . . I guess a lot of us . . . well, we think . . . I mean Sissy McMillan is from a rich family, the Country Club and all that. Mary and Diane aren't."

"And you and your friends got the idea I don't care about them? That I'm only interested in Country Club types? Is that what the hell you think?"

Ron didn't answer, he was afraid of telling Betsy the truth, which was in fact that he thought she really didn't care about Mary and Diane. Many students at the college knew Betsy was out looking for Sissy, and because they didn't know the truth, it had become common agreement that she didn't give a damn about the other two.

Ron remained silent. She could see the unease on his face. Betsy shook her head and turned away from the young man. He stood watching her as she walked to the car. Ron wanted to do something, to say something, but he was scared. He turned and walked back to the school as Betsy jumped into the MGB and drove away as fast as the wet roads would allow.

CHAPTER NINETEEN

On The Big Island

I left Henry with his twenty dollars and a fresh bottle of beer that he drank greedily and quickly. Mama Keoni brought beer for her boys and went to her small kitchen where she grilled two pieces of Spam and two eggs, adding them to a plate of steamed rice and some macaroni salad. She carried the plate to Henry and said, "You eat this whole t'ing like the haole said you to do. If you don't, I don't bring you no more beer." Henry looked at the plate, and although he would have preferred another beer or two, he started to eat the food.

I took the winding back roads from Papa Keoni's slowly. It was a thin road, almost paved to be kind to the road. The car bounced along hitting nearly all the pot holes because my mind wasn't on the driving.

I now had two people who could have killed Lewis. Vinnie Vasco, of course, was an obvious choice. I know Mafia types and he fit the mold. That meant he was a killer. His foreman, Mario, had to be his enforcer. And any of Vinnie's security guards could have been told to kill Lewis. I was sure they were the type to carry out that type of order. If Lewis had found something illegal going on at Vinnie's construction site, then Vinnie would have had no second thoughts about killing him to keep the money flowing. He would have set Mario or one of the guards on Lewis.

But now there was a second person, an unnamed

military type who several people saw at Papa Keoni's. This man was angry, and that anger was aimed at Lewis. Lewis, I knew, had been in the Army and had deserted. If this stranger knew that, he could be angry enough to have killed Lewis.

One thing kept creeping its way into my thoughts. There was green paint on the road side barrier. Vinnie's trucks were green. It would have been easy enough for Mario to run Lewis off the road. But why was Lewis on that particular road? Where was he going? It wouldn't have taken him home according to Nancy.

There were too many questions, but at least I had a lead to follow that didn't involve Vinnie Vasco. I had a license plate, and I had a man in the military. I smiled as I turned the wheel to navigate a tight turn, scraping the side of the car on some low hanging branches. The first bullet smashed the windshield. The second smashed the side window just inches from my head as I floored the accelerator.

The car spun into and out of a big pothole and finally caught the road as two more bullets hit the side of the car. I was picking up speed as the fifth hit the front left tire.

The car slid to the right and I lost control of it. It spun 180 degrees into a ditch at the side of the road and hit a tree hard. I had been too busy thinking about who had killed Lewis to fasten my seat belt. Because of that I was flung forward. My head hit the windshield and my chest smashed against the steering wheel.

For a moment I was blacked out, but the realization and the fear that someone was trying to kill me quickly brought me around enough to know I had to get out of the car. The car was leaning to the left, in the ditch. The driver's side door was jammed shut but the engine was still running and the power window still worked. I crawled out, trying as best as I could to ignore the pain. On my feet, I quickly stumbled into the jungle along the side of the road.

I fell to my knees onto the damp earth. I had to get away from the car because whoever was after me would go there first, looking for me. I crawled and clawed my way through the thick undergrowth. My clothes were being ripped apart by the scrub I was pushing my way through. My hands and knees where cut and bleeding, and added to the pain in my chest and on my head; I hurt like hell all over. Blood was dripping from my forehead into my eyes. I wiped it away with my sleeve, and I forced myself to go on.

In my dazed condition, it seemed like I had crawled a dozen miles when in fact I was only a short distance from the road. It had to be far enough; at least I hoped it was far enough because I couldn't go any further. I collapsed to the ground and pulled myself into some bushes. I lay there trying to be still, trying not to breathe too loudly. I had to push past the pain that was everywhere. And the black cloak of unconsciousness was folding over me. I felt it coming and shook my head to keep it away. I couldn't moan or cry out as the spasms of pain whipped across me. All I could hope for was that whoever was out there wouldn't come looking for me.

After a few minutes I tried to move again. Each pull I made at some bushes or tree caused racking pain to shoot across my chest. 'Broken ribs,' I remember thinking. I pulled at something again, paused for the pain to subside, and then pulled myself forward another couple of inches.

One last pull at a thorny bush and I rolled down into a shallow stream. Before the water could do anything for me I blacked out.

I woke up lying on a dirty blanket on the floor of an old Airstream trailer. It took a moment or two for my eyes to finally focus. I looked up and to the left and right. Whatever that place was, I thought, it was a mess. There were dirty dishes and piles of clothes everywhere. Cigarette butts and ash crowded every dish and cup and Styrofoam takeout container. Flies were buzzing, and spiders had spun webs to catch them. I pushed myself up on one elbow and looked around. At the back of the trailer a man was lying on a bench, his back to me, snoring loudly.

I got to my feet and tried to stand against the trailer spinning around me. I rubbed my eyes and shook my head and the spinning stopped. I realized my clothes were torn rags, and I was cut and scratched everywhere. My chest was still sore and my head ached where I touched the open cut from the windshield.

"Hey!" I called out to the sleeping man. He didn't stir. I held onto a wall cabinet with a broken door so as not to fall as I went to him. I touched his shoulder and shook him. "Hey," I said again. He groaned and rolled over.

It was the old man from Papa Keoni's, Henry, Mama Keoni called him.

"Yeah," he mumbled. "You awake finally."

"What the hell . . ." I started.

"Nah," he said as he pushed himself to his feet. "Wait 'till I get me a beer."

Henry went to a small dented and rusted, green refrigerator and pulled a can of Coors from it. He made it back to the bench he had been sleeping on and sat down. "You want one?" he asked.

"What I want to know is what the hell happened," I said. I had to hold onto a crowded counter top so that I wouldn't collapse to the floor.

Henry drank the can half empty and said, "Hell, I don't know. Heard the shots and found you in the damn creek. You was alive so's I dragged you here. You a heavy son a'bitch, you know that?"

"You heard the gun shots?" I asked. "Did you see who

was shooting?"

"Nah. I ain't too fast on the feet no more. I done seen the car, though. Got bullet holes in it."

"You came from Papa Keoni's?"

"Yep. I was eatin' the food and drinkin' the beer. Mama heard the shots, too. Me an' her was all that was there, so's I went to look."

"What about the others?" I asked. "Where were they?"

"They all left after you did. Them guys don't like me. They say I talk too much when I drink. An' they say I smell bad, too. Screw them, ya'know?"

I looked around the small trailer; it couldn't have been more than fifteen feet long, and it was very close to being a garbage dump. Cockroaches were running up and down the walls. Empty beer cans were everywhere. The smell was appalling.

"Do you live here?" I asked, not believing anyone could live like that. "Is this your home?"

"Yeah, great ain't it?" Henry answered. "I done found this whole thing laying out here . . . I don't know, maybe a year ago, maybe more. I think somebody just dumped the damn thing. Don't belong to nobody, so's I took it. I sleep here. Better than sleeping outside, ain't it?"

Although I felt sorry for the old man, I had other things on my mind at the time. I pushed into the back of my memory that after this was all over I might be able to do something for him. On the other hand, I had seen people like Henry before. They are so deep into alcohol, sometimes drugs, that nothing can be done for them, except perhaps give them a meal or two.

"OK, look," I said. "I need to get out of here. How far from the car am I?"

"Not too far," old Henry said. "There's this here path that'll take you to the road you was on."

"A phone," I said. "Do you have a phone?"

"Shit no," he said and laughed.

"Can you take me back to my car? Can you show me the way?"

"Yeah, I can . . . But I'm almost outta' beer. You got money . . . I checked."

I pulled my money clip from what was left of my pants pocket. "You didn't take my money. Why?"

"Hey mister! I ain't no thief! You think I am an' you can get the hell outta' here on your damn own!"

"OK, sorry," I said. I pulled two twenties from the clip and held them out towards Henry.

He looked at them and said, "I said I ain't no thief. I ain't dumb neither. You got more than forty bucks and you need me to show you the damn way back to your damn car. How much is that worth t'ya?"

I had a little over five hundred dollars left in the clip. I handed Henry two hundred dollars, and he took it. It was probably more money than he had seen in one place in many, many years. I knew it wouldn't go for food or anything good. Two hundred dollars' worth of beer might just last him . . . Until what? An untimely death? A predestined death?

He quickly finished his can of Coors and dropped the empty can onto the floor. He pushed himself to his feet once again, kicked some trash out of his way, and started for the door. Opening the door, he stopped, turned to look at me, and said, "I ain't gonna' carry your fat ass. You know that, don't ya'?"

"I can walk," I said.

"Yeah . . . Well, if you fall, you gotta get your own damn ass up again, got it?"

It was early evening as Henry led me through the trees, brush and jungle that he lived in. The path was merely flattened grass that Henry had used for so long it might be called a path. I had to duck under tree branches and push underbrush out of the way. My chest was aching, and the cut on my forehead began bleeding again. I wiped the blood away and tried to ignore it and the other scratches I had gotten trying to crawl away from the car.

The air was cooling as night approached, and I felt drops of rain through the tall trees. We kept walking; I was amazed at how fast Henry could walk. He was little more than sunburnt leathery skin over old bones, yet he was able to keep up a pace I had difficulty matching.

Then Henry stopped; he was looking and listening. He put a finger to his lips to tell me to be quiet. I could not hear what he must have heard.

He turned and took a step closer to me. He whispered, "There's people out there . . . By your car. I ain't goin' no further, understand? You go if you want."

With that, Henry pushed past me and almost ran back towards his little trailer. I tried to listen for what he had heard, but my head was spinning, my ears were ringing, and I hurt on almost every inch of my body. 'What the hell,' I thought. Henry said there were people there, not just one person. Maybe they could help. On the other hand, maybe they were the people trying to kill me.

So I continued along Henry's thin path, and shortly I

could see the road ahead of me. The car wasn't there, but maybe I had run off the road someplace other than at the path.

I could hear faint voices above the din inside my head. They were on the road, to the left and not too far away. So I decided to take the risk and step out of the bushes and onto the road. It was dark and raining lightly but I recognized two uniformed policemen maybe twenty or thirty yards away. I tried to call out. My voice was weak, and my head was spinning. I called out again and fell to my knees. They saw me and ran to me.

They picked me up by my arms and carried me back to their car. They laid me down in the back seat. I was not completely unconscious, perhaps a little delirious from the exertion of getting back to the road.

"Who are you?" one of them asked.

"Morgan . . . Morgan Crew," I managed to whisper.

"Was that your car?"

"Yes . . . Someone was shooting."

"Yeah, we know. The car was towed back to the station. You need a hospital."

"Good," I said. "Good . . ." and then I blacked out.

I woke up in bed at the Kona Community Hospital. Sandy was standing at the bedside. She was holding my hand. She smiled a little as a tear or two crossed her cheeks. "Hi," she said.

"How long?" I asked. My throat was dry, and it was hard to talk.

"Just a couple of hours," she said. "You've been beat up pretty well . . . Again damn it . . . But nothing is broken.

Just a lot of bruises and cuts. Your ribs are badly bruised and they probably feel broken, but they aren't. The doctors want you to stay the night. The police are waiting for you to wake up. Do you feel you can talk to them?"

"Yes," I said. I tried to sit up a little in bed, but my chest hurt. "Can you crank up the bed a little?" I asked Sandy.

She found a button on a wired remote, and the head of the bed rose. I cringed a little as the bed forced me to sit up.

"I think you should rest some more before you talk to the cops," she said as she wiped a tear away.

"Why are you crying?" I asked.

"Why! You stupid jerk! I almost lost you . . . again! What the hell do you expect me to do?"

"I'm OK," I said and squeezed her hand. "Don't worry. You won't get rid of me that easily. Where's Caroline? I don't want her to see me like this."

"She's back at the resort. Managers, maids, and a couple other people were lined up to take care of her. She'll be alright."

"Good. I'll just rest here a little while, and then I'll get outta' here."

"Not until the doctors say it's OK," Sandy insisted.

"Yeah, right. Now tell the police to come in."

She bent down and kissed me quickly on my lips, stood and wiped another tear away. She opened the door and stood aside. Police Chief Daniels walked in. I could see the two officers who had brought me to the hospital waiting in the hallway. Sandy closed the door and went to my bedside. She took my hand, sort of protecting me if I needed protection.

Daniels looked down at me, examining all the bandages and bruises, using his experience to determine just how far he could go in questioning me. I got tired of waiting for him to say something so I asked, "Did you come here just to look at me?"

"So what happened?" he asked finally.

"I was leaving Papa Keoni's. I was going back to the resort. Someone took some shots at me. You have the car, you know that already."

"Yeah, I know that. Now tell me what happened. Why was someone shooting at you?"

"Because I'm asking questions about Lewis Manaluo's murder," I said. My throat was raw and Sandy could hear that. She poured a glass of water from a pink plastic pitcher, put a glass straw in the glass and held it for me to drink. Daniels waited.

I took a sip of water, cleared my throat and said, "I guess I'm asking the right questions, and someone is getting scared."

"Who do you think is getting scared?"

"So far, my only suspect is Vinnie Vasco. I told you that already."

I wasn't about to tell Chief Daniels about the military type stranger who argued with Lewis at Papa Keoni's. It has long been my experience that police, any police including my good friend Bob Sommers, get bent out of shape when I start doing their job. So I am in the habit of telling the police only what I want them to know. Eventually I will tell them everything, after I have figured out everything.

"And that's it?" Daniels asked.

"That's it," I said and smiled, even though a simple

smile hurt.

"My guys found you walking out of the bush," he said.

I figured telling him about Henry wouldn't do any harm. And if Henry was trespassing by living in somebody's abandoned junk trailer on someone else's land, maybe the authorities would place him somewhere he could be taken care of. Of course, I knew that was fantasy. I have never seen any government authority take care of people the way they should be taken care of. Subsistence welfare and government housing are nothing more than a quagmire of quicksand for people to get stuck in. But Daniels might pick up Henry and put him in one of his cells. A few days or a couple of weeks in jail, with good food and some medical attention, might do him some good.

So I told him. "When the car ran off the road I managed to get out and crawl into the forest. I was trying to get away from whoever was shooting at me. I was hurting really badly, and I guess I passed out. I woke up in this old trailer where someone named Henry lives."

"Yeah," Daniels said ominously. "I know Henry."

"Anyway, Henry somehow managed to drag me away from the road before anyone could find me. I woke up in his trailer. I gave him two hundred dollars to show me the way back to the road. I found your two officers, and here I am."

"What were you doing at Papa Keoni's?" Daniels asked.

I knew Papa Keoni's was unlicensed, and I was sure Daniels knew that, too. He hadn't closed it up yet, so I assumed he didn't care if a few locals got together there after work. I said, "I was having a couple of beers." He didn't need to know anything more at that time.

"That's all? Just drinking beer? That's a load of

bullshit," he said.

Sandy, faking being insulted as best as she could, said, "Please! The language! I'm not used to hearing words like that!"

"Yeah, right, I'll bet," Daniels said. "Look, the two of you are in trouble here. You've got that little child to worry about, too. I know your reputation, the both of you. I also know that to stop you, I'd have to lock you in my jail. But I'm not going to do that. I think maybe one of two things will happen. You'll either get killed and be out of my hair, or you'll find what you're looking for and you'll stop doing what you're doing and go on home, in which case you'll be out of my hair."

"Is that it, Chief Daniels?" I asked. "You just want me gone?"

"That may happen sooner than you think. You'll probably go home when you find out what's happening."

"What's happening?" Sandy asked.

"Vasco's lawyers filed an action against you, Mr. Crew. Slander and defamation. Good luck with that one."

"Well, I guess I'd better get my own lawyers working on that. Sandy, see if you can get a telephone in here . . . after Chief Daniels leaves."

As Daniels turned to leave, I stopped him and asked, "What have you found out about Lewis' death?"

"None of your damn business," he spat out.

Daniels left without saying another word. Once again, my experience with the police is that in the back of their minds they would like to see me get myself killed. I think Daniels was hoping for just that.

Sandy started to go for a telephone when I stopped her.

"Forget the phone," I said. "It'll take weeks to get something like that into court, and we'll be done and out of here long before that."

She pulled a chair to the side of the bed and said, "OK, now tell me what really happened."

****

The next morning, as I was checking myself out of the hospital in spite of what all the doctors said, Vinnie Vasco woke up to a bright and warm morning. In his bed, lying next to him was Lady Catherine. Every night with Lady Catherine had been like nothing Vinnie had ever experienced before. There had been a lot of women in Vinnie's life, some hotter than fire in bed, some cold and demanding. But Lady Catherine was different. She knew things Vinnie never imagined could have existed. Sex with Lady Catherine was ecstasy; a wild frenzy of delights Vinnie had never thought was possible.

He lay under the soft, cool sheets wondering if it had all been just a dream, spurred on by too much champagne the night before. Was she really lying next to him? Was she real or just a dream? Was she only human or some kind of mystical, heavenly being?

Turning on his side, slowly so as not to wake her, he leaned on his elbow and looked at her. Her soft blond hair had been let down and lay across her white shoulders like clouds of exotic silk. 'She is beautiful,' he thought. Beyond beautiful, if that was possible. She was like a sculptured masterpiece from some master artist. Her skin was creamy white and unblemished. He ran a finger from her shoulder down her arm. It was as if she had been woven from the finest soft golden cloth of kings.

She moaned softly at his touch, and she turned slowly towards him. Her eyes opened slowly, and she looked up at him. The deep blue of her eyes on him was like an electric shock. Her hand pulled the sheet away exposing her breasts, perfect breasts, Vinnie thought, like none he had ever seen before.

She smiled and reached out for him, slowly pulling him down to her. They kissed deeply and he rolled over onto his back, bringing her on top of him. Her hair covered his face, and he could smell a spring-like rose garden. She whispered in his ear, "I'm hungry. I need coffee."

He held her tightly to him, crushing her breasts against his chest. "I want to spend the day with you."

"Of course," she said softly, as if that were a foregone conclusion. "And the night also."

Vinnie smiled, thanking the God he had been taught about by the Sisters when he went to school. Maybe, he thought, there really is a God. Someone . . . something, perhaps fate, perhaps something more, had to bring this woman to him.

After a breakfast of rolls, papaya, and hot Kona coffee that was brought to Vinnie's suite, they spent the day driving around the Big Island in Vinnie's Jaguar. They laughed and made up imaginary stories about the things they saw. Lady Catherine moved closer to him and rested her hand on his thigh. She slowly, lightly, ran her hand up his leg, stirring him to pull off to the side of the road where they made love on some thick and soft grass, behind an old stone wall that was covered in flame red bougainvillea. Three old boney cows with fat utters that had been grazing there watched them, and they laughed when they realized they had an audience.

They drove south and stopped at Kealakekua Bay where Catherine told Vinnie the history of British sea captain and explorer Captain James Cook and how he had died at that very spot. Some Hawaiian, she explained, had stolen a small boat. An argument arose and the Hawaiians attacked Cook and a few of his men, killing them all.

Then on to the very southern tip of the Island, where they watched the lava from Mauna Loa flow into the Pacific and boil away, filling the air with steam clouds of hot gas. They stopped at Kilauea Crater and ate a light lunch at the Lodge there.

Driving on, they stopped to sample chocolate covered macadamia nuts at the Mauna Loa Macadamia Nut Factory and stroll through the botanic gardens. At Hilo they stopped for cooling rum drenched drinks and returned to the resort in time to linger together in a warm shower before dinner.

Vinnie sat at the table in the dining room near the beach. The cocktail lounge where he had met Lady Catherine was near enough for them to hear the music being played there.

He listened to the waves brake onto the rocks in the dark of the night that was lit by a million stars and a glowing full moon. Cool breezes filtered in from the ocean. He gazed at the woman who sat across from him, realizing at that moment that he was in love. For the first time in his life he was in love. He had lusted after women and spent weeks with one woman or another. Once he married a woman, but that lasted less than three months. Never before had he felt for a woman as he felt for Lady Catherine.

This woman was fascinating, educated, and elegant. She knew things Vinnie would never know without her. Her beauty was beyond beauty; she was soft, her skin was pale as pearls and flawless, her eyes had an exotic darkness to them and drew Vinnie into them like a moth to a flame.

He knew he could never let this woman go from him.

Nothing would stop him from having her. At that moment a man walked up to their table. The man was middle-aged, perhaps early fifties with soft skin, more feminine than masculine. He was pale with a redness on his puffy cheeks that was caused by the Hawaiian sun. He was dressed in a silk shirt of light cream, open at the collar, and dark brown cotton slacks, well pressed. He had white leather slip on shoes on his feet, and he didn't wear socks.

He looked down at Lady Catherine and said, smiling graciously, "My dear! I had no idea you were on the Islands." He spoke with a very upper class British accent. His eyes were pale green and hooded by lashes that hung heavily.

"Oh, Clive," Catherine answered. She smiled but Vinnie felt the smile was somewhat forced. "I have been meaning to phone you, darling."

Clive looked at Vinnie, and Catherine said, "Please excuse me. Clive, darling, this is Mr. Vincent Vasco. Vincent, this is my husband, Sir Clive Hamilton."

"Your husband," Vinnie said, not just a little surprised. His fists clenched without him realizing it. He felt anger mixed with jealousy that this man could possess such a woman. "Glad to meet you . . . I guess," he said.

Clive held out his hand. Vinnie hesitated, then took it, and they shook hands lightly and briefly. Sir Clive's hand was soft and a little damp, like a wet sponge, and his grip was limp, almost feminine. Vinnie felt a little uneasy holding the man's hand.

"Clive, dear," Catherine said. "Would you like to join us? We were about to have coffee."

"Thank you, my dear," he answered. "But I've had my coffee already. Please do join me on the terrace for drinks when you are done."

Clive walked away towards the open cocktail lounge that was lit by tiki torches, where a four piece band was playing soft Hawaiian tunes for the guests. Vinnie watched the man. His steps were slow, almost dancelike. He wondered how such a man . . . if you could call him a man . . . would have a wife like Lady Catherine. At the table, Vinnie asked in his raspy whisper, "Your husband?"

"Yes," Catherine said in a wondering tone. "I did tell you I am married."

"But I didn't know your husband was here. Did you know?"

"Of course," she said in a wondering tone, as if it should have been obvious to Vinnie.

"But . . . But why?" he asked.

"Vincent, my dear," she murmured sweetly, reaching across the table to take his hand in hers. She held his hand gently and patted it to comfort him. "Clive and I have an arrangement. He pursues the men and boys he likes, and he earns the money we both need. I am free to be with whomever I wish. It works out well for us."

"But . . . But . . ." was all Vinnie could manage to stutter.

"You see," Catherine explained. "Clive is a titled heir, a Knight of the Realm. His family goes back generations. There are certain functions, royal functions as well as government and social, he must attend, and he needs a wife at his side to dispense with any of the rumors that fly around about his being homosexual. I am that wife. I am his wife in exchange for a lifestyle I was born into but cannot attain on my own because of the Nazis and then the Communists. Clive supports me and takes care of me . . . in grand fashion. I do love the man for all he does for me, please don't mistake that."

"And what about me?" Vinnie asked.

"Vincent, you are very special to me," she said, squeezing his hand gently.

Vinnie wanted to burst out loudly and tell her he loved her, but he couldn't find the words or the guts to say it. What if she laughed? What if she rejected him? What if she got up and walked away and he would never see her again? No, he had to wait, but if he had to, he would fight for her. Yes, he told himself, he would kill Sir Clive Hamilton if he had to.

They did sit with Sir Clive on the lanai and drank cognac and listened to the music. Few words were spoken. Vinnie was not comfortable. He wanted to get up and take Lady Catherine to bed and make love to her while Sir Clive stood aside and watched. But, he thought, if the guy was gay, would he really care?

CHAPTER TWENTY

San Marcos

Betsy drove home faster than the roads and weather would safely allow when she left the college parking lot and Ron Porter. She was angry, and she felt stupid. She had been out looking for Sissy McMillan not even knowing that there were two other college girls missing. How could she look at the other students again? How could she go back to school carrying such a weight of embarrassment with her?

Why hadn't Bob Sommers told her? He must have known; a lot of other people including Ron Porter knew, and she was angry that he hadn't told her. She slammed on the brakes of the MGB in time to avoid driving into the closed garage door. She slammed the front door closed and threw her purse and books on a chair and ran to the phone before taking her coat off. She dialed Bob Sommers' cell phone number. She was so shaking with rage that she misdialed twice before taking a deep breath and slowing down.

Bob picked up his phone on the third ring. Betsy shouted into the phone, "Why the hell didn't you tell me? What the hell! . . . I mean Bob! . . . What the hell! I thought you were a friend!"

"Hi Betsy," he said. Bob was sitting at his cluttered desk trying to complete some personnel reports. He hated that part of his job, but the San Marcos Police Department was his, all six officers, four cars, and an office staff of three.

"Glad to hear from you, too. You sound like your old self."

"Bob," she said trying to control her temper. She knew it would do no good at all to yell at him and have the cop, Lt. Bob Sommers, mad at her. She knew she needed Bob Sommers the friend on her side if she were ever to find Sissy. At first she had her doubts about Sissy being in any kind of trouble. But with two more girls missing, those doubts were all gone. "I just found out that there are two more girls missing," she said after taking a deep breath.

Bob said nothing; Betsy waited and then said, "Bob, are you still there? I asked you a question."

"No you didn't. You told me you found out that two more people are missing. What do you want me to say?"

"I want you to tell me you know that Mary Ortiz and Diane Kohn are missing and you have an investigation going."

"Investigation of what? All these girls are over eighteen. They have the right to do whatever they want to do."

"So you are aware of the three of them."

Again Bob said nothing.

"OK," Betsy said, taking another deep breath and speaking slowly. "Do you have files open on the three of them?"

Again Bob would not answer.

"You know about Sissy," Betsy said. "I know you are looking into that because you told me not to interfere with the police. Should I assume you have files open on the other two? If I go looking for them, are you going to tell me not to interfere with the police there, too?"

Silence.

"Tell you what Bob," she said, feeling very frustrated and angry. "I'm going to be asking questions and I'm going to be looking. How about I keep whatever I find to myself? How about I don't tell you anything just like you're not telling me anything?"

"You aren't the police around here, Betsy," Bob said. "I am, and I get to tell you what to do. You don't tell me what to do."

"Is telling you to screw off telling you what to do? I'm really pissed off, Bob. I feel like a fool, and you made me feel that way. How do I face the people at school? How do I explain to them that I'm not some rich bitch country club girl?"

"I made you feel like a fool, huh? I did, huh? How's that?" he asked.

"I was confronted in the parking lot at school by a student, Ron Porter. He knew two other girls were missing and I didn't. He accused me of not caring because they aren't Country Club girls. Do you have any idea how I felt?"

"That's too bad, Betsy. But it doesn't change anything. I'm the cop . . . You ain't."

"Too bad, Bob. You can't stop me from looking for Sissy."

"Betsy," Bob said finally. "I hope you remember what the inside of a jail cell looks like." The line went dead.

Betsy didn't have any classes the next day, but she drove to the campus anyway. She was determined that she would find out where the three missing girls were, even if they were only off with their boyfriends somewhere. As she drove, she wondered if the three of them were all shacked up together somewhere. No, she shook her head at the thought. That was unlikely. They were in some kind of trouble, she was sure of that. But could the three be in separate trouble, not connected somehow? 'How could she know?' she thought. All she knew was she had to find Sissy, and if the three were connected somehow, she would find all three.

To her, the most logical place to start was to get some background on the three. There had to be something in common between them if they were all in the same trouble. And the only place she could think of was to start at the college since all three were students there. That fact was the only thing the three had in common, at least as far as she knew.

The administration building is a two story red brick building that had been converted from a warehouse when the college had been built eight years ago. Inside it is bright and finished with light colors of beige and pale yellows. Nice prints of spring flowers and summer pastures were framed inexpensively and placed almost randomly along the ground floor hallways.

On the ground floor, behind a large receptionist's desk, are small cubicles of light grey that are lined up like soldiers on parade and occupied by the people who do all the administrative work at the college.

The second floor holds large glass-walled offices with better quality, well framed pictures and potted plants along the hallways. The offices are furnished with more expensive desks, leather chairs, and file cabinets than can be seen on the ground floor. The walls of the offices are painted in soft colors, and each has a large window overlooking the campus. They are the offices of college executives and Deans.

After some gentle demands made to people on the first floor, demands that included mentioning Morgan Crew's name, Betsy was shown upstairs to the office of Mrs. Elizabeth Gordon, the Dean of Students.

"Why hello, Betsy," Mrs. Gordon said, standing and

shaking hands with Betsy. "And what brings you here today?"

Mrs. Gordon knew, of course, that Betsy had been out looking for Sissy McMillan. A lot of people knew that. The word had spread all over town and all over the campus. And a lot of people knew that Betsy Concanon carried the influence of Morgan and Sandy Crew with her. The Crew family had financed a large part of the building of Wrightwood State College.

Mrs. Gordon anticipated that Betsy would eventually come to her, asking questions. She knew that she had to be very careful of what she told Betsy. There were privacy laws, after all. But it was common knowledge in San Marcos that the law seldom applied to Morgan Crew. Mrs. Gordon, as with so many people in San Marcos who weren't members of the Country Club, was silently jealous and envious of the power wielded by Morgan and Sandy Crew. Oh yes, they did a lot for the community, but they also demanded a lot in return.

Betsy sat in a chair and tried to look comfortable, but Mrs. Gordon recognized that she was not. Betsy was sitting forward on the edge of the chair, and her hands were clinched so tightly in front of her that her knuckles were white.

"I've been looking for Sissy McMillan," Betsy said quickly before realizing that Mrs. Gordon must have known that.

"Yes, I know," she answered calmly, still smiling. "Is Sissy a friend of yours?"

"Not really . . . I just know her from Biology class. I just want to make sure she's OK."

"I'm sure she is," Mrs. Gordon said. "Have you spoken with her parents?"

"That's part of why I'm here. Can you give me her home address, please? And the addresses for Mary Ortiz and

Diane Kohn, too."

Mrs. Gordon, smiling still, hesitated while she thought. 'This girl,' she said to herself, 'has no legal right to school records. But Morgan Crew might come here if I don't do something.'

Rather than face the wrath of the entire Crew family and their lawyers, who, she felt, would surely descend on her if Betsy didn't get what she wanted, she reached down to the lower drawer of her desk and pulled the San Marcos telephone directory from it. Betsy sat back in the chair, embarrassed that she hadn't thought of that.

The San Marcos phone directory is a thin tome, not more than an inch thick. The very rich are not listed; the drug dealers and hookers are not listed. Only the average people can be found there.

Flipping through the pages, Mrs. Gordon stopped and then looked up at Betsy. She smiled and said, "The McMillan's are not listed." Turning more pages, she stopped again and said, "Mary Ortiz's parents live at 1219 Pine Avenue. Shall I write that down for you?"

Betsy was blushing, and she felt like running away, but she knew she couldn't do that. She said in a weak, trembling voice, "Please, Mrs. Gordon. I can do that. You know I want more than that."

Mrs. Gordon closed the phone book with all the drama she could find and put it back in the desk drawer. She asked, "And just what is it you do want, Betsy?"

"I want to know *about* them. What classes were they taking? Who were their friends? What kind of students were they? How did their tuition get paid? I want to know who they were so I know where to go to look for them."

"You're speaking about them in the past tense, Betsy.

You said 'who they *were.*' Does that mean you know some tragedy has happened?"

"I just have this . . . this gut feeling, I guess."

"And Mr. Crew approves of you trying to find them?"

"Morgan and Sandy are away on vacation. I guess I can get them on the phone if you want. I mean, if you need to hear from them that you should help me that is."

Mrs. Gordon sat silently, staring at Betsy. It was a threat, she knew that, but it was a weak threat. Betsy's face was crimson, and she could not look directly at the Dean. Betsy didn't want to really phone Morgan and Sandy, at least Mrs. Gordon hoped that was the case. But she also knew that Betsy could, in fact, phone Morgan Crew if she had to, and Mrs. Gordon would have to do what he said.

She stood and walked around to the side of her desk. She said, "Student records are in that file cabinet," pointing to a grey metal, four drawer file with a vase of fresh flowers on top next to a framed photo of her son and daughter. "I can't just let you see the records. There are privacy laws and rules. I could get in a lot of trouble, maybe lose my job. I'm going to go down the hall and speak with Dean Atkins. If he says it's OK to let you see the records, I will show them to you. I'll be gone about five or six minutes or so. You stay here . . . alone, with the door shut."

When Mrs. Gordon had closed the door behind her, Betsy jumped up and started rifling through the files of student records. She found the files on all three girls and quickly wrote down what she thought was important: addresses and phone numbers. There wasn't enough time to go through the files page by page, but, she thought, it was a place to start.

Replacing the files, she started to run from the office and found Mrs. Gordon sitting in a chair in the second floor lobby, near the stairs. She smiled and nodded as Betsy walked past her and down to the front door.

CHAPTER TWENTY-ONE

On The Big Island

I awoke the next day to find Sandy and Caroline under the shade of the covered lanai, sprawled out on the tiled floor, coloring pictures in several coloring books and laughing at their play. When I walked out to the lanai, little Caroline jumped up and ran to me. She saw the bruises and cuts all over my face and arms. I scooped her up in my arms. I didn't let her see the pain. She touched my face and began to cry.

"It's OK, baby," I said. I hugged her tight to me and whispered, "It's OK. Don't cry."

She touched the bandage on my forehead and said, "You're hurt."

"No, baby. I'm OK. Don't cry."

When she pulled herself away from me, she knelt on the floor and handed me a crayon. She tried to smile past the tears filling her eyes. "You color with Mommy and me," she demanded. "You color, and you feel better," she said smiling as best as she could.

I managed to get down on the floor, lying prone, trying not to let the pain show on my face. I found myself coloring in the black outline of a cartoonish little Hawaiian girl. While I was doing that, I brought Sandy up to date on what I had learned. And I realized that as I spoke, Caroline was listening intently rather than coloring her picture.

"So you have a license plate number, and you know that guy is in the army. That means you know who he is, she said." She got to her feet and walked to a small table where a large coffee pot and two mugs waited. She poured a mug full and brought it to me. I was able to struggle myself into a cross legged sitting position on the tiles, only moaning a little as I moved, and she handed the hot mug to me. It was good and did the job of washing away the last bits of sleep from my eyes.

"Not really," I said. "I have to run the plate, and how do I do that here? The cops hate me from my last little adventure here. And so far, I haven't made friends with them doing what I'm doing now."

"Morgan," Sandy said in her exasperated voice, one I have gotten used to every time she manages to outthink me. "I know if it weren't for your accident you would know what to do. Get on the phone to Peter Jascro."

"Maybe I should get Harry over on Oahu to run the plate? He's closer, and he surely can do that sort of thing," I suggested. My mind wasn't working as clearly as it should. There was a grey blanket of pain covering my brain that slowed down my thought process.

"Sure," Sandy said. "Harry can do it, but do you really trust that guy to do anything? He sounds like a real flake. Maybe you should stay away from him and do what you're sure will work."

Caroline was lying on the floor, on her elbows taking all this in. She said, "I like Uncle Peter."

That was all I needed. If the two of them thought going to Peter Jascro was the best idea then I would phone him. And I did. That was the only sensible thing to do, and I like to think that if I had been fully awake and not in so much pain I would have thought of that, too. But then, Sandy has a habit of out-thinking me all too often.

While I waited for Peter to call me back, I colored some more and Sandy ordered breakfast. Caroline insisted on pancakes. In deference to the work I still had to do, Sandy ordered a three egg omelet with cheese for me – a luxury I seldom get to enjoy.

An hour later, after Peter phoned and as usual warned me to be careful and not get myself killed, I knew the man's name. Julio Aguilar. Leilani had told me that Lewis had been a truck driver in Afghanistan. The license plate on Julio's motorcycle told me he probably was a truck driver also. That connection made sense.

With that connection I felt sure the argument Lewis and Julio had at Papa Keoni's was about Lewis deserting from the Army. So I wondered if Lewis had not died several days later, would the Army have sent someone out to pick him up? Would this Julio Aguilar have reported that he had found a deserter? Or did Julio murder Lewis? Unlikely, simply because of the way Lewis died and of course the green paint on the railing where he died. I would not put Julio aside as a suspect, but my money was still on Vinnie Vasco, his green trucks, and his thugs. Vinnie would kill to protect what was his.

I got a lot of stares and looks when I went to the front desk offices of the resort and asked to use a computer. No one asked what had happened to me, but I guess I looked like the walking dead.

The front desk staff nearly ran to show me to a desk in the office and a computer. Three of them stood over me, turning the damn thing on and all talking at once, telling me how to use it. Their hands were everywhere, pushing buttons and keys and getting in my way. I held my hands up and said as nicely as I could but maybe a little too strident, "Enough. I can take it from here.   Thank you."   All three walked backwards from me, all saying they would be nearby if I needed anything, all hoping they hadn't offended me in any way. Money does wonderful things sometimes.

It took a minute or two, but I managed to learn that there was only one U.S. Army facility on the Big Island. Pōhakuloa Training Area is a large facility hidden away in the high plateau between Mauna Loa and Mauna Kea. Pōhakuloa is where small and large arm training is conducted. There is a small airfield there, and about two thousand troops are stationed there for training at any one time. There is a support staff including elements of the 48th Transport Battalion. Julio Aguilar had to be there, and being on the Big Island, he may have inadvertently run into Lewis or seen him somewhere. However he had found Lewis, he had been able to confront him at Papa Keoni's. I needed to find out how he had come across Lewis and what he did after arguing with him.

Although I wanted to speak with Julio, my money would not be on him to be a murderer. Vinnie Vasco still held that top spot and I hoped Harry Esposito was doing something about that. I would leave Harry alone for a few days, maybe a week, taking Sandy's advice. Then if I hadn't heard from him, I planned to phone him. If he wanted my money, he needed to do the job. In the meantime, I would focus on Julio.

I had found what I needed to find using the resort's computer. I went back to the suite and found both Sandy and Caroline in swim suits. Caroline said, "Let's go swimming, Daddy!" So it was on with the swim suit and a T-shirt to try to hide my bruised and discolored ribs, and off to the beach, where Sandy and I each held one of Caroline's hands as she stood in the small waves as they lapped up onto the beach. Caroline was in heaven.

Lunch was chicken nuggets and fries for Caroline and coconut shrimp with a mango sauce, salad, and a good if not remarkable white wine for Sandy and me. Then Sandy and Caroline waived goodbye again as I went to the front desk of the resort. I once again rented a Toyota 4-Wheel drive. I anticipated the drive into the hills might need a four wheel drive. I was waiting for someone at the rental desk to complain about wrecking one of their cars the day before, but no one did.

I asked at the resort's concierge desk for directions to the **Pōhakuloa Training Area**. To my surprise, no one had ever heard of it. But a good map from the AAA was found, and between the concierge and her secretary, we managed to locate where I needed to go.

I headed off for the mountains and Julio Aguilar. I got lost a couple of times, but finally I found my way to the training base. Except for the mountainous terrain and thin, winding roads that saw few cars, it wasn't too hard a drive. There were lots of twists and turns, and the passing countryside was green and lush most of the way. I crossed a rickety wooden bridge over a small stream and a field with big black cattle who watched me pass with a great deal of curiosity.

I found the main entrance to the base and drove past an unmanned gate, into what looked like an administration area. I found a building with a small sign near the only door in the building. The sign was painted white with black letters that read "Commanding Officer." I stopped in the street in front of the building and looked around, waiting for someone to ask me what the hell I was doing there. There were young men in fatigues walking around and a few in shorts, T-shirts and loud Hawaiian shirts. A couple of young women, both in full camo fatigues, walked by me as if I might be invisible. No one seemed to care I was there, so I parked the car near the door of the building where I hoped to find someone to talk to. I walked up the two wooden steps to the office, first thinking I would knock and then just opening the door and walking inside.

There I found a Sergeant in crisp fatigues with a lot of stripes on his arms and sleeves rolled up showing off good biceps. He sat behind his desk and looked at me, perhaps wondering who I was and how I got there. I took a quick glance around the room. A few metal filing cabinets that had been painted khaki lined the wall behind the Sergeant. Another desk, which was clean on top and seemingly unused, was across the room. Some framed pictures of officers and a few of groups of enlisted men hung on the walls. In the back corner was an American flag on a pole. There was a door across the room, behind the Sergeant, with frosted glass panels and a sign that read Lt. Col. Brighton.

The room smelled of fresh paint, and I saw that the walls of the office were clean and a cool light beige color. It was an old building but newly painted on the inside. The room reminded me of the barracks Bob and I were in during our basic training at Camp Pendleton. Uninsulated wooden boards and exposed 2 X 4's for walls. I wondered just how long that building had been there.

"Hi," I said being as friendly as I could to allay any suspicion that I might be a spy or saboteur. "I guess I need to speak with someone in charge. Maybe Colonel Brighton? Is he here?"

"Who are you?" the Sergeant asked. "And who beat the crap out of you?"

"I was in a little auto accident," I said explaining my bruises and cuts. "Nothing serious. Can I speak with the Colonel, please?"

"Once again, who are you?" he asked.

"I'm Morgan Crew," I answered. "I just need to speak with one of your people. Who do I talk with to do that? Is your Colonel around?"

"Who is it you want to talk to?"

"Julio Aguilar," I said. "I think he's stationed here."

"You a cop?"

"No, I'm not," I tried to say with a slight laugh, and it hurt to laugh, but the Sergeant was being a little too tough for me to be comfortable. Maybe that's why he wore all those stripes on his sleeve.

"You a bill collector?" he asked.

"No," I said. "Look, I just need to speak with Mr. Aguilar. It's a personal matter, that's all."

"Does *Sergeant* Aguilar know you're coming to see him?" he asked, emphasizing Julio's rank.

"No, he doesn't," I said. "Look, do you greet everyone who comes here this way?"

"We don't get many visitors . . . Sir," he said with maybe just a little bit of sarcasm in his voice.

"So anyway, where do I find him?" I asked. "Do I need someone's permission to talk to him or not?"

The Sergeant picked up an old black telephone with one of those twirled cords that had seen better days and punched in a four digit number. I remember thinking I had entered some kind of Twilight Zone episode and gone back in time about fifty years.

"Sergeant Aguilar?" he said into the phone. "This is Sergeant McMichael, there's some guy here to see you." He waited and listened for a few seconds and then said, "Says he's Morgan Crew." Again he listened and then said, "I don't know. He's some kind of civilian. Maybe you should ask him yourself, *Staff Sergeant*," McMichael said with a very military gruffness to his voice, obviously pulling rank on a lower ranking NCO. He hung up the phone quickly.

He looked up at me, flipped his thumb over his shoulder, and said, "Drive straight down this road. Take the second right. Follow the signs to the Motor Pool. Sergeant Aguilar will be looking for you."

I left without thanking the guy. Right out of college, Bob Sommers and I signed onto the Marines. A three year hitch was enough for me. That experience allowed me to know that the standard attitude of professional military people is tough and obnoxious. That may be standard and very necessary to get the job done inside the Military, but it isn't for me.

Outside I heard gun fire from some distance away. I hoped it was just firing range practice and not the last civilian visitor, or perhaps a bunch of soldiers warming up to use me as a target.

The sky was darkening, and a few drops of rain were hitting the car's windshield. I resigned myself to the fact that I would probably get wet. But it was still warm, and as I drove slowly down the road, I thought of all that snow back home and poor Betsy having to deal with it. I hoped she was OK and not having to shovel too much snow to get to school. Actually that thought made me feel a little guilty since I was enjoying the sunny and warm Hawaiian version of mid-winter.

I found the Motor Pool without any trouble and saw a big, muscular man standing in the shelter of a doorway, keeping dry. He was wearing camo fatigue pants tucked into highly polished high top black combat boots, and a khaki T-shirt that fit him like a second skin. He fit the description of the man who had been arguing with Lewis back at Papa Keoni's Bar, big and muscular, and his short sleeves revealed the tattoo Palani's friend had described.

"Hi!" I said as I walked to him. He was standing in the open door and stood there for a moment or two, letting me get wet, before stepping back to let me in out of the rain. 'Nice guy,' I thought, but rather than say anything, I just smiled and said, "I'm Morgan Crew. You're Julio Aguilar?"

"*Sergeant* Aguilar," he said firmly, making sure I heard him say Sergeant. He held out his hand. His grip was strong, almost too strong, but I didn't let him know that. He was smiling; that was a good thing.

"You get hit by a truck or something?" he asked, looking at my cut and bruised face.

"Just a fender bender," I said brushing it aside.

"What can I do for you, Mr. Crew?" he asked quickly.

Although he continued to smile, I got the impression he wasn't too happy to see me and wanted me to get to the point quickly, and then leave. I guessed I was interrupting some work he had to do. I decided that small talk wasn't on the menu. And I figured there wasn't much sense in trying to run a scam on this guy. He seemed too smart to fall for fast lies. So I asked, "You know Lewis Manaluo?"

The friendly smile and attitude dropped away like a ton of proverbial bricks. He crossed his arms across his chest, showing off his really big biceps under his T-shirt sleeves and fully exposing the tattoo Palani's friend told me about.

"Why?" he asked. "You his lawyer or somethin'?"

"I'm not a lawyer . . . Or a cop . . . Or anything else. I'm a friend of Leilani Manaluo. She is Lewis' woman."

"Woman? You mean they ain't married? That figures. That guy don't believe in too many rules. Too many people around that don't believe in rules no more."

"So you know him then?" I asked again.

"Yeah, I know the son of a bitch. I called the CID. That son of a bitch is goin' to Leavenworth for a God damn long time."

He was talking about Lewis in the present tense. If he knew Lewis was dead, he wouldn't do that. I decided to wait to mention the fact that Lewis had been murdered.

"CID?" I asked, not knowing what that is.

"Criminal Investigation Division. That's Army cops. They chase down fucking deserters . . . Like that Lewis son of a bitch."

"You know he deserted? How do you know that?"

Julio turned around and walked towards a long table on the other side of the room. The room was a combination office, work shop, and tool room. What struck me about the room we were in was how neat and clean it was. Up on a hoist was a small pickup truck that had its wheels off. Parts were spread out along a work bench, all lined up in perfect military order. There was no grease on the concrete floor, not even the smallest oil stain. It was like no other auto workshop I had ever seen.

The walls were painted olive drab green. Two walls were lined with wrenches, hammers and tools I could not identify, all lined up and hanging on peg boards in very neat and military fashion. Four desks were along another wall, facing each other back to back, and each was devoid of the usual papers and files one might expect in an office. The only decoration on any of the walls was a calendar hanging next to the first of the desks, each page a nice picture of some picturesque part of the U.S.

Julio saw me looking around and seemed to know what I was thinking. He said, "I'm a professional soldier, Mr. Crew. I like the order and uniformity of the military. This is my work place; I'm in charge here. I keep it neat."

I nodded but said nothing. Julio asked, "I just made a fresh pot of coffee. You want a cup? It's good stuff, not that Mess Hall crap they put out."

He walked to a wooden table where a very clean Mr. Coffee maker sat next to a tray of very clean white ceramic cups, turned upside down. There was a covered bowl of sugar and a carton of dry creamer next to a drinking glass that held some metal spoons. Everything was lined up like soldiers on parade. The table was otherwise clean.

"I've never turned down a cup of good coffee in my life. But you never answered my question. How do you know Lewis deserted?"

"I was in Afghanistan with him. A lot of other guys were with him, too. We was all in transport, like him. We was all under fire and took our chances, like we was supposed to do. Nobody else deserted, only that fucking coward."

"Did you kill Lewis?" I asked bluntly.

I watched Julio's face closely. Surprise of any kind would confirm that he didn't know Lewis was dead. There was the slightest flinch that ran across his face, a slight look of surprise that he managed to hide very well. Other than that quick reaction, all Julio did was smile and lean back against the table. He had poured one cup of coffee and held it tightly. I guessed I wasn't going to get a cup after all. He said nothing.

"I assume you already knew Lewis is dead?" I asked.

"No, I didn't know," he answered, almost too coolly. "But I'm glad the bastard is dead. I hope he's burning in hell."

"Why?" I asked. "Do you hate him that much just because he was scared? You must have been scared a little, too."

Julio stood up straight and took a few steps closer to me, thinking as he walked. He stopped and said, "Look, me and everybody else was scared. But we didn't run. He went on leave. Me and a lot of other guys knew we was shorthanded and postponed our leaves. Lewis didn't. He jumped at the damn chance to get the hell away. The day he was due back from leave, I had assigned the bastard to drive a truck in a convoy I was leading. When he didn't show up, I had to assign a rookie Private who just got in from basic training to drive Lewis' truck. The kid had been in Afghanistan for three fucking days . . . Three fucking days. He was a nice kid, too. Just nineteen years old. He was married. He had a wife and kid on the way back home. He had no experience or training avoiding those IED's . . . Roadside bombs if you didn't know. Lewis had that training. Lewis would have avoided that bomb. The kid hit it, and we couldn't find enough of him to ship all of him back home. That kid died because Lewis deserted."

"If Lewis hadn't seen that bomb, would he have been killed in that truck?"

"I don't know. He had training; the kid didn't, like I said. Me and the guys who were there for a long time had the training. He knew what to look for. He knew what to avoid. That poor kid didn't."

"Lewis is dead now. I think he was murdered. Lewis had a family, too. He had a son and another child on the way. If someone killed Lewis, tell me how that's different," I argued.

"He was married then?" Julio asked snidely, knowing the answer already.

"I think you know he and his woman weren't married," I said. "Not married like you and I know. They were married under old Hawaiian law . . . by a kahuna."

"So he wasn't only a coward . . . He was also living in sin with some whore."

"How can you say that? How can you judge the man? And you've never met his family. How can you call his woman a whore?" His words offended me, but I also knew that Julio had never met Leilani. If he had, maybe he would have a different opinion of her.

"Mr. Crew," Julio began as he started to pace back and forth in front of me, holding his cup of coffee tightly in both of his big fists. "I'm a professional soldier. I'm in for the long haul. I love my Country. I'm also a Christian. I believe in Jesus Christ and the Bible. The Country I love is being ripped apart from the inside with immorality of the most obscene kind. Marriage is the basis of the family, and family is the basis of our society. If Lewis had been a good man, and if the woman he cohabitated with were a good woman . . . they would have married under God's law. No, I have no respect for either Lewis or the woman he was fucking."

"You know Lewis as Lewis Manaluo?" I asked.

"I know he enlisted as Lewis George. Yeah, I know he was calling himself Manaluo since he deserted."

"How do you know that?"

"I was told," he answered.

"Who told you?" I asked. If that were true then someone on the Island had to have told Julio. Lewis lived an almost hidden life, almost totally off the grid. No one off or on the Island could have known. There was no public record of him on the Island.

"None of your business," he said.

"Did you kill him?" I asked again.

Julio smiled again, drank some of his coffee, and then said, "No . . . I wish I had. I wanted to kill him. I wanted to see him suffer. But I believe in the morality of the law. I fought off the urge to break that bastard's neck. I prayed on it, and finally I made a report to the CID on Oahu."

"When did you see him last?"

"Do you think I'm stupid? You know I saw him at that bar . . . What's it called . . . Papa something or other. I confronted Lewis there. I wanted him to come with me and turn himself in, to do the right thing for once in his corrupt damn life. I tried to convince him that it would go easier on him if he just walked in and confessed. But he wouldn't. Too much of a damn coward to do that I guess. Yeah, I got mad, but I didn't kill him. I walked away before I did something I shouldn't have done. I never laid a hand on the bastard."

"So, someone told you that you could find him at Papa Keoni's. What else did this person tell you?"

"Why?" he asked. "Why is that important?"

"I just need to tell Leilani. I promised her I'd find out what happened to Lewis," I explained.

"Ok, so I know where he worked and that he went to that bar once or twice a week."

"Why didn't you go to where he worked? Why wait until he went to Papa Keoni's?" I asked.

"Oh, I tried but I couldn't get past the front gate. That's damn tight security down there. Wish this place had security like that. We don't even control who comes in here," he said, looking at me. I know he was talking about me. "What goes on down there anyway?"

"I don't know," I said, avoiding a change in the subject. "So you waited until Lewis went to Papa Keoni's. Did you wait there every day for him to show up?"

"You're pretty damn smart, aren't you? You know I didn't. No, I got a phone call telling me he'd be there that day."

"You got there soon after he did. It took me almost two

hours to get here today. It would take you about that long or longer to get to Papa Keoni's. That means you got the phone call before Lewis left work that day. Right?"

"Yeah, right."

"Ok, thanks," I said. "I think you've told me who killed Lewis."

"What!" he said. "How the hell did I tell you who killed that son of a bitch?"

CHAPTER TWENTY-TWO

San Marcos

Diane Kohn's address was listed as one of several apartments that were rented to out of town students at the college. They were in a small neighborhood of apartments a couple of blocks square and situated right next to the campus. In the summer months, when school closed and most of the students went home, they were empty and repairs were done. Repairs took most of the summer months because the students were hard on the apartments. Parties and fun and pet dogs necessarily did a lot of damage to them.

There were twenty one apartments and a small laundry room in the two story building where Diane had lived. It was definitely a student apartment building needing paint and repair. A few broken windows had cardboard taped over them. Most of the doors were cracked. There was spilled trash outside lying all over the snow. Dog feces spotted the snow that was covering what should have been a lawn in the spring and summer but would be little more than dirt and weeds when the snow melted. And old bicycles were chained overnight to rotting wood fences and a few metal posts of stop signs in hopes that they would be there the next morning.

Diane's address according to the college's records was apartment number 7. Only a few of the apartments had numbers on them. But Betsy was able to figure out that even numbered apartments were on the ground floor. She walked up ice and snow covered concrete stairs, holding tightly to the handrail, and knocked on the door that had the number 7 painted on it in rough black paint.

"Yeah!" someone inside yelled. "Come on in! It ain't locked!"

Betsy opened the door a few inches and peered inside. Two young men and one young woman were inside; one of the men was stretched out on a beat-up old couch, apparently asleep with a tattered brown blanket pulled up to his chin. The other man was at a small desk, a laptop computer in front of him. He seemed to be engrossed in whatever he was doing. The woman was in a small kitchen stirring a pot of something that was heating on a small and old two burner stove. The smell wasn't very appetizing but was once something Betsy would have looked forward to. She had become used to better food in the two years she had lived with Morgan and Sandy.

The apartment was small, a living room and tiny kitchen was all she saw. Two doors, one closed and the other open, led to two bedrooms, and a third, closed door in the tiny hallway must have been the bathroom. The living room was painted a thick, heavy, cheap yellow, obviously layered on top of multiple layers of more cheap paint. The one indication of human living conditions was a small glass vase on the floor under the lone window in the living room. It held four red roses.

"What'a'ya want?" the man at the desk asked without taking his eyes away from his computer. "I'm busy . . . Got a damn math class this afternoon."

Betsy opened the door all the way and stood without entering the small apartment. She asked, "Does Diane Kohn live here?"

"Yeah, but she ain't around," he said. "Now go away, will ya'? And close the damn door! You born in a barn or sumpt'in!"

Betsy stepped inside and closed the door behind her, but not all the way, leaving it open a crack for a quick getaway if she needed a quick getaway.

"Do you know where she is?"

"No! I tol' ya' that. Now go away so I can study."

The girl in the kitchen smiled in apology and waved at Betsy, calling for her to go to her. She was dressed in an old T-shirt that was a couple of sizes too small for her, being that she was not slim to say the least. She had rolls of fat from neck to waist and her stomach was like a man's beer belly. Her arms were fat and flabby.

Her blue jeans were old, torn at the knees, and needed a trip to the washing machine. Her mousey brown hair hung long and uncombed. As Betsy got closer to whatever was on the stove the smell became stronger. The young student didn't look dangerous, so she walked gingerly to her.

"You're Betsy Concanon, aren't you?" she asked in almost a whisper.

"Yes. I've seen you at school. But I don't know your name," Betsy answered, lowering her voice also.

"I'm Theo . . . short for Theodora. I used to share a room with Diane. I'm a music major, so you and I wouldn't be in any classes together." Theo said it with a bit of snide sarcasm.

"Do you know where I can speak with Diane?" Betsy asked.

"No . . . I guess I figured she just got tired of school and split, you know."

"So she hasn't been here for a while?"

"No . . . A couple two or three weeks now, maybe a little less," Theo said. "Me and her, we don't hang around a lot together. But she might be with the guy she's been seeing."

"Who's that? What's his name?" That was what Betsy had been looking for. If Diane wasn't in serious trouble she would be with a man, somewhere, in bed probably. Knowing who the man was and where they were would end Betsy's search for Diane at least.

"I don't know," Theo answered. She took the pot from the stove and poured some of the hot soup – if that is what it was – from it into a cracked cup, spilling a few drops onto the torn green Formica countertop. The spilt soup went unnoticed by Theo. "You want some?" she asked. "There's enough."

"No, thanks," Betsy said. "Look, I really need to talk with her. Can you tell me anything? Have you ever seen the guy she's dating? Anything?"

"No, she was always very secretive about him. Wouldn't tell me anything. I don't think he's a student though. I never saw her walking in the halls holding hands with anyone, you know? But she smokes a lot of pot. I used to get mad when she smoked in our bedroom. I don't do that stuff, ya' know? She used to get it from some creepy, dirty little guy. He came here a couple of times. Calls himself something stupid . . . N or M or something like that."

Diane Kohn and M? Betsy was surprised about that. That was the first connection between the missing Sissy and the missing Diane. Morgan's voice echoed through her mind. 'There's no such thing as a coincidence.' Betsy now had to consider that Diane's disappearance and Sissy's disappearance were connected.

"Did she take her clothes when she left?" Betsy asked.

"No . . . As a matter of fact I'm getting ready to pack up her stuff and take it to the school's lost and found. I need to get someone in here to help with the rent. It's tough with just the three of us, you know?"

"Can I look at her things?" Betsy asked.

"Sure, go ahead. Take it all with you if you want. In the back bedroom. Door on the right. Her things are in the pink bureau and on the left of the closet. Leave my stuff alone, though. OK?"

In the bedroom, Betsy found two single size beds, one made neatly and the other with a blanket pulled roughly up to a small, thin pillow. A guitar was leaning against the side of the unmade bed telling Betsy that must be Theo's. Three of the walls were white; the third had been painted an out of place dark blue. Posters of rock musicians hung on the blue wall.

There were two small desks next to each other. One was neat, the other a mess of papers and books. Betsy assumed the neat one belonged to Diane. She searched through the desk. Only school papers and a few books were in the desk's drawers. And she opened each of the four drawers of the pink bureau. Stuffed into the drawers, unfolded and wrinkled were the usual clothes that any young woman would have.   That made Betsy wonder. Diane's bed and desk were very neat, yet the clothes were not. Then she realized that Theo must have been 'borrowing' Diane's clothes and stuffing them into the bureau when she was done with them. She pulled a few of the sweaters and blouses out and held them up. They were obviously too small for Theo but she had worn them, stretching out a few and ripping a few others.

In the small closet, on the left side, a few blouses hung on wire hangers alongside a light blue buttoned sweater with sequins across the shoulders and front. Next to them were two pairs of good quality tan cotton slacks. On the floor under the sweater and pants were three pairs of blue jeans tossed in a pile. More of Diane's things that Theo had been squeezing into, Betsy thought. Maybe Theo had found them too small and just tossed them onto the floor.

Betsy pulled the jeans out one at a time, searching through the pockets. In the back pocket of one was a small scrap of paper, wrinkled into a ball and stuffed deep into the pocket. Written on it in printed penciled letters was, *'I want to see you tonight. 9 PM on the Mary D.'*

"The Mary D," Betsy said out loud, not realizing she had said it because of her surprise. The Mary D was where M was sleeping. Could Diane have been with M? She had a hard time visualizing any halfway good looking college girl with someone like M. He was creepy and dirty. But he had a supply of drugs. M might have been a source for the marijuana Diane had been smoking. Betsy wondered if Diane was exchanging sex for drugs. So many of the young boys and girls of San Marcos did that in North Harbor.

Betsy had smoked her share of pot in years past. She had a hard time imagining that any young woman would screw someone like M just for some pot, when pot was so cheap and so readily available. No, there was something else to the note. Someone other than M must have written the note. Diane's boyfriend. It must have been. And that meant her boyfriend was connected to M somehow.

She folded the scrap of paper and put it in her purse. There was nothing else of interest in the bedroom, but as she was about to leave the room, she realized that Theo had a few framed photos of what must have been family and friends, with Theo in each of them. Diane had nothing personal in the room, no photos, nothing. The posters of rock stars, hanging near the unmade bed had to be Theo's.

She went back to the kitchen where Theo was leaning against the counter, drinking the soup . . . or whatever it was. She had spilt drops of the dark brown liquid down the front of her T-shirt, obviously not caring about it. Betsy again whispered, "I found a note in one of Diane's jeans. Did you see it when you wore them?"

"Wore them?" Theo said, embarrassed that Betsy knew she was 'borrowing' Diane's clothes.

"Look, I don't care if you wear her clothes or what you do with them. Burn them if you want to. It's none of my business. But the note might be. Now, did you know about the note?"

Theo's face was blushed and her eyes looked away from Betsy. She took another drink of her soup and said, "Let me see the note."

Betsy took it from her purse and held it out, not letting Theo take it from her. The girl looked down at it and then admitted, "Yeah. I guess I saw it. I just shoved it back in her jeans."

"So the note wasn't written to you?" Betsy asked. She had to be sure it was to Diane and not Theo.

"Me? No, of course not. It was just in her jeans pocket, that's all. I didn't know what it meant so I just put it back."

"Were you anyway curious what it meant?" Betsy asked. "Did you think it might be something about where Diane is?"

"Look, me and Diane . . . I mean Diane and I . . . we were just roommates, not friends. I have all I can do to take care of myself right now."

Betsy put the note back in her purse and left the apartment, without thanking Theo. As Betsy was walking out the door Theo ask her to let her know if she found Diane and if Diane was going to pay the month's rent she owed.

Betsy stopped and turned to look at the girl. "Is that all you care about?" she asked. "Do you care that Diane might be in trouble somewhere?"

"Don't bother letting me know," Theo said sharply as she drank her soup from the cracked mug. "I'm going to clean out her room this afternoon anyway. I'm gonna' throw out her stuff. I'm gonna' try to find a new roommate."

As Betsy walked out, she thought that Theo would probably keep whatever she wanted of Diane's clothes, anything that might fit her, and throw away very little.

****

Mary Ortiz's address in her college record turned out to be her parent's home on the outskirts of North Harbor. For that part of San Marcos it wasn't a badly kept house. It was old but unlike many of its neighbors, it was clean, well maintained, and the lawn was not full of weeds and garbage poking above the snow. There were snow covered bushes lining a flagstone walk from the sidewalk to the front door. The walk had been cleared of snow and ice. A large area to the right that was surrounded by neatly laid out red bricks suggested a flower garden when the weather permitted. And hanging from a pole attached to the wall near the front door was an American flag, fresh and clean which meant it was taken in at night.

Betsy knocked on the door. She stood under a porch roof, pulling the collar of her wool coat up around her neck. The sunny morning had turned grey and cold, and dark clouds rolling in signaled more snow that afternoon and evening. A freezing wind was blowing in off the harbor and the Pacific.

The door opened, leaving a wood framed screen door, painted bright green, closed. A woman, Latino, whose attractive face had not faded with age, said, "Yes, what do you want?" She was dressed in a flowery house dress and pink fuzzy slippers. Her hair, black and streaked with grey, hung limp and uncombed.

"Mrs. Ortiz . . . You are Mrs. Ortiz, aren't you?"

"Si . . . Yes . . . Who are you?"

The woman's eyes were red from recently shed tears. She was twisting a very used tissue in her fingers. She stepped back, a little fear inside of her, perhaps from having lived in that neighborhood for so many years. Her hand went to a small hook door latch on the screen, closing it.

"I'm Betsy Concanon. I go to school with your daughter."

"My daughter? Maria?"

"Maria?" Betsy asked. "I thought her name is Mary."

"Si, she calls herself that. But her name is Maria," Mrs. Ortiz said. Tears welled up in her eyes again. "Do you know where she is? Have you seen her?"

"That's why I'm here, Mrs. Ortiz. I don't know where she is, but I'm trying to find her. May I come in? May I speak with you about Mary?"

The woman hesitated once again. In that neighborhood, it wasn't safe to let strangers into your home. But it was the only home Mrs. Ortiz had known for the past twenty-two years, and she wanted to live as normal a life as she could. The young girl standing on her porch didn't look dangerous; she was well dressed, and she was smiling. So Mrs. Ortiz unlocked the screen door and pushed it open. She stepped aside, holding the screen door open, and Betsy walked into the house. Mrs. Ortiz closed the front door, and Betsy watched as she at first started to lock the door, then changed her mind and left it unlocked.

The house was clean and neat, but nothing inside was

new. The furniture was old but well cared for. There were framed photos on every table and every wall, and more photos filled a mantle above a brick fireplace. And there were small statues of Saints and Jesus. The photos all had to be family, Betsy assumed, and the young girl in the photos had to be Maria. She seemed to grow up in the photos, starting in many of them as a young child and then a pretty young woman in the more recent color photos.

The air inside smelled wonderfully fragrant from whatever was simmering on the stove in the kitchen. It reminded Betsy that she hadn't had anything to eat for . . . In fact she couldn't remember her last meal.

Betsy stood with her back to the closed door as she looked around the house. She smiled at the woman but said nothing. Mrs. Ortiz pointed to a wooden chair with a cushion on the seat and asked Betsy to sit. She sat across the room, on a couch, a wooden coffee table separating them, and asked, "Do you know my Maria?"

"I'm afraid I don't, Mrs. Ortiz. But I want to find her and talk to her."

"Why? What business is it of yours?" the woman asked suspiciously.

"There are two other students at the college who are missing, Mrs. Ortiz. I'm worried about them. I don't want to frighten you, but it seems strange to me that three girls would disappear all at the same time."

"That is what the police said," she told Betsy. She wiped tears from her eyes with the tissue that had seen more tears then it could handle. "I am very worried. Have you told the police what you know?"

"Yes," Betsy answered. "I've told Lt. Bob Sommers."

"So, you are working with the police, then?" Mrs. Ortiz

asked.

"Not really . . . In fact Lt. Sommers told me to go back to school and stay out of this."

"But you won't do that, will you?" she asked.

"No, I won't. Now please, tell me about Mary . . . Maria," Betsy asked, correcting the girl's name for Mrs. Ortiz's sake.

"Alright. I'll tell you what I told the police," the woman said. She wiped tears from her eyes; her Spanish accented voice was quaking and weak.

"Maria, she was always a good girl. She studied hard in High School and did very well. She went to Mass twice a week and went to confession every Friday. She graduated at the top of her class. My husband and I wanted her to go down to Los Angeles and work in my sister's shop. She is a dress maker. That, we thought would be a good profession for our daughter. But Maria, she wanted to go to college. She is so smart that the Wrightwood College gave her a scholarship," Mrs. Ortiz said, smiling proudly. "But in her second year of school she began to change. She didn't go to Mass as often as she should, and for months she didn't make a confession. She began to wear too much makeup, and she was buying clothes, short dresses and things. Where did she get the money? We don't have the money to give her, and the things she buys are so expensive. And she started seeing someone; someone who kept her out late at night. Often she would come home . . . Dios Mio! . . . She would come home drunk."

"Who was this man?" Betsy asked.

"I don't know. My husband and I, we asked but she wouldn't tell us. She got very angry, and she yelled at us. She used foul words, too. Dios Mio! She is gone now . . . with this man I think."

"I'm very sorry, Mrs. Ortiz, but I have to ask. Did Maria ever use any drugs?" Betsy asked nervously. She didn't want to offend this woman but she had to know.

"Oh Dios Mio!" the woman cried. "Once when I was doing laundry I found a plastic bag in her things. My husband, he said it was marijuana. Maria, she became very angry. She took the bag away from her father and cursed terribly. She said it was not what he said it was, and she ran up to her room."

Mrs. Ortiz broke down into tears, sobbing her daughter's name over and over again. Betsy went to her and sat next to her on the couch. She took the woman into her arms and let her cry on her shoulder. She whispered, "I'll try to find her, Mrs. Ortiz. I'll try."

Betsy stayed with the woman until her tears had subsided. When she left the house and got in the MGB, she was certain that there was a connection between the three missing girls. School and marijuana was that connection. And M had to be where the three connections met.

She was sure that Bob Sommers knew all that she knew and that made her a little angry at Bob. She felt certain that he must know of the marijuana connection between the three girls and how M would fit into everything. So, as she sat in the car with the engine running and the heater turned up, she weighed going to Bob Sommers or going to find M. 'What the hell,' she thought. She decided to spend her time looking for the girls and not waste time going to Bob Sommers. All he would tell her, she was certain, would be to stay out of his case and go back to school.

She sat in the cold for a long time, thinking. What should she do next to find the three girls? She finally put the little MGB in gear and drove away.

CHAPTER TWENTY-THREE

On The Big Island

Vinnie Vasco was still a young man, barely forty years old. His history with women had been long and varied, from High School girls who were anxious to give him their virginity, to young, rich college girls looking to tame a 'bad boy', to whores who made money by screwing the neighborhood gangsters, to a married neighborhood woman or two who fell in love with his good looks and muscles. Now and then Vinnie thought he might be in love, but that sensation drifted away as he became bored with the woman he was with.

But Lady Catherine Hamilton was something he had never experienced before. She had a royal manner about her. Her etiquette was always perfect regardless of where they were. Her speech was always as grand as a Princess. And she had the body and mind of a sexual animal who never seemed satisfied and who never tired of wearing Vinnie out.

They lay in bed that morning, eating the biggest, sweetest strawberries Vinnie had ever seen, drinking ice cold papaya juice and filling delicate china cups with never ending hot Kona coffee. Vinnie wanted a steak and half a dozen eggs but he wanted Lady Catherine more, so he said nothing. He would give her whatever she wanted to keep her with him.

They talked of things Vinnie new little about, but he listened and learned, and he asked questions that she answered in words that were like dreams to Vinnie. She was familiar with European society and the wealthy of America.

She had been everywhere, to places the rich went and ordinary people couldn't afford. She told him of villas in the south of France and exclusive parties in Monte Carlo. She told him of parties in Paris. She dropped the names of kings and queens, and dukes and duchesses as if they were neighbors from down the street. She made him laugh at the antics of a group of the super-rich who drank too much on an African safari and were almost attacked by elephants as a result. And she spoke in pictures of Switzerland in the spring and Austria in the winter.

They made love on the cool silk sheets, under the ceiling fan, as they listened to the Pacific's wave's crash against the rocks below their suite. The sound of the water was so hypnotic that once they retreated to the lanai and made love on its cold tile floor just to better hear the ocean.

They lay in each other's arms that day, in Vinnie's suite, dozing in near sexual exhaustion, when the telephone rang.

"Let it ring," Vinnie whispered.

But Lady Hamilton reached over him, across his chest, and picked up the receiver.

"Hello," she said in a deep whisper like a cat purring after a good and satisfying meal. She listened for a moment or two and then said, "Certainly, darling. Please come right up."

She hung up the phone and told Vinnie, in an almost casual voice, "My husband is on his way up."

Vinnie jumped out of bed and started for his clothes that were in a pile on the floor and on a nearby chair. She laughed, pulled the sheets away and said, "Come back to bed, Vincent. It's alright. Clive understands and he doesn't care."

"Are you kidding?" he said.

"Oh, Vincent," she laughed. "I've told you that Clive prefers his boys. We have an arrangement. Please come back to bed. I want to make love to you again . . . and again."

So Vinnie dropped his clothes to the floor and returned to bed. He slid under the sheets and moved close to her. He started to pull the sheet up around them but she pushed it away so both lay completely naked and uncovered. Catherine ran her hand across his chest and reached up to him to kiss him. She whispered, "I think we should go down to the beach after Clive leaves."

The knock on the door made Vinnie jump a little; Catherine laughed and called out, "Please come in, Clive darling. The door is not locked."

The door opened, and Sir Clive Hamilton walked into the room. He was dressed for tennis in white shorts, a white shirt and a sleeveless white sweater with red and blue stripes at its V-neck. He carried a tennis racket in a bright blue case. He took no special notice of his wife and Vinnie Vasco lying naked next to each other in bed. He put the tennis case on a chair and walked to the bed.

Vinnie felt uncomfortable and wanted to cover himself but he wasn't about to give this gay bastard anything to laugh at. If Clive didn't care, then why should he. All that changed when Vinnie saw Clive staring at his penis. 'Screw him,' Vinnie thought. 'Let him wish he could have some of that.'

Catherine got out of bed and went to him, throwing her arms around his neck and kissing him softly on both of his very red, puffy cheeks. She was naked but seemingly not embarrassed.

"Please do sit, darling," she said. "Have some coffee with us."

"Thank you so much my dear, but I have a match with a sweet young man in a few minutes. I'm hoping it works out to be something, don't you know."

Vinnie sat up in bed, leaning against the bed's cushioned headboard. He pulled the silk sheets up to his chest. 'What the hell's going on?' he thought to himself.

"Hey look, Catherine," he said. "How about you put some clothes on?"

"Oh, Vincent," she said laughing again. "Don't be such a prude. I do love Clive, but he takes no interest in my body."

Sir Clive patted Catherine on her behind and said, "Actually, I need to speak with Mr. Vasco, my dear. Why don't you pour another cup of coffee for yourself and sit."

Catherine smiled seductively, patted Sir Clive on his cheek, and swayed towards the tray that had carried the breakfast. She poured a cup of coffee, took a cigarette from the pack lying nearby, and walked to the bed where she sat, very near Vinnie. Sir Clive took a gold lighter from his pocket and lit her cigarette.

"Thank you, my dear," she said. "Come sit here on the bed," she said, patting a corner of the big bed.

Thinking better of it, Sir Clive pulled an armchair away from the room's desk and sat. He crossed his legs and began, "Mr. Vasco. I do hope you are enjoying my wife."

"You're a sick son of a bitch, you know that, Clive?" Vinnie said. His gravelly voice was harsher than it normally was. He wanted to scare Sir Clive, but his scarred throat and bearlike growl seemed to have no effect on the man.

"I'm well aware of that and of who I am. But that is not the point. You see, Catherine and I enjoy a certain . . . shall we say . . . a certain rich lifestyle. Oh, yes, I have estates that provide income, but certainly not enough to satisfy both of us. And the taxes are utterly atrocious. Oh, you wouldn't believe all the money my darling little Catherine spends every year. The clothes alone are a king's ransom, so to speak. But I don't complain. I do love her, and she has never refused to appear with me at occasions when I need a wife at my side. But I need to supplement my income. This is where you come in, Mr. Vasco."

Whenever Vinnie felt the heat of vicious violence rising inside of him, a look that would terrify an ordinary man crossed his face. He felt that heat rising inside of him as Sir Clive spoke. He felt his face redden and his fists tighten. He asked, "You want I should give you money?"

"Mr. Vasco, please," Sir Clive said. He didn't shift in his chair nor make any sign that he was frightened. He said, "I know who you are. I am not a stupid man, in spite of what you may think of me. I make it a habit to be sure the men my darling wife is involved with are . . . safe I think would be the appropriate word . . . and with some semblance of wealth. I know it would be very easy for you to kill me. But upon my death, and under very strict British laws that go back hundreds of years, my title and estates, and everything else I have goes to a cousin of mine, my only living blood relative. Coleman is a very tiresome man who lives in Manchester . . . That is in the north of Britain in case you didn't know. Coleman has been a failure at every business venture he has ever tried. I have been forced to rescue him from financial disaster and bankruptcy several times. His wife, Marjorie, is a dumpy, overweight housewife; a very stupid woman with a terrible complexion and bad teeth. When Coleman inherits my title, Catherine's title goes to Marjorie. She will be left with nothing save for a little I have managed to set aside for her. Certainly not enough to support her as she wishes."

Vinnie laughed and said, "I can support her."

Catherine turned to him, reached across the bed, and

kissed him fondly on his cheek. She said, "Oh, Vincent. You are such a darling. But what would I do without a title? People treat Lady Catherine Hamilton with an element of royal respect. Doors belonging to very important people all over the world are open to me. I receive invitations from the Queen herself. Without the title I would have nothing. I could not dream of giving that up."

"OK," Vinnie said. "I can buy that." He turned to look at Clive with a fearsome look on his face. Anyone else would have skulked away, frightened for their life. But Clive sat unmoved. Vinnie wondered if Clive didn't understand or just didn't care. He said, lowering his gravelly voice yet another octave, "So Clive, how much do you want?"

"I would think fifty thousand dollars would do," he answered.

"That's a lot of cash, but I can get that in a few days. Then we won't see you again right?"

"On the contrary," Sir Clive said, sitting up a little straighter in the chair. His eyes locked on Vinnie's and he didn't blink. "Perhaps you didn't understand. We will see each other once a month when I come to collect the fifty thousand dollars."

"What! You've got to be kidding! Fifty grand a month! You're fucking crazy!"

"Then I'm afraid I must insist that my wife leave with me now. Please dress darling and pack your things."

Catherine got out of bed and said demurely, as any good wife would, "Yes, dear. Right away."

"Wait a minute!" Vinnie shouted. He couldn't lose this woman now. He knew he was in love. He had to keep her. But where the hell was he going to get fifty grand a month? That was impossible. And he realized that if he killed Clive, she would leave him, angry at her loss of her title. He had to think of something. He said in desperation, "Give me some time . . . Please. Catherine, please stay with me. I just need a couple of days to figure this thing out."

Catherine turned to Sir Clive and said, "I do so wish I could stay dear. Perhaps you could give Vincent two days?"

Clive thought for a moment, stood, and said, "Today is Friday. Monday morning I shall come back and we'll see what the future may hold."

He turned, picked up his tennis case, and left Vinnie and Catherine alone in the room. She ran to the bed and jumped on it, rolling over on top of Vinnie. She was happy, but Vinnie wasn't sure why. She kissed him hard and ran her hand down his chest and stomach and under the silk sheets. She smiled as he closed his eyes to enjoy what she was doing to him.

Two hours later they were lounging on the lanai, Vinnie having reached that point of utter exhaustion. Catherine was sipping on the champagne she had ordered and put on Vinnie's bill. She was talking endlessly of things they would do, places they would go, as Vinnie dozed, fighting off the afternoon–after sex sleep that was enfolding itself around him.

"Vincent, dear," she said, shaking his shoulder. "Vincent, did you hear me?"

"I'm sorry, no I didn't."

"I said there is a party I want you to take me to next week."

"Sure, no problem," he said, his eyes heavy as sleep was about to overtake him.

"Fine, please book the tickets then," she said. "For Saturday next."

"Tickets?" he murmured. "Tickets to where?"

"Why to Monte Carlo, of course," she said. "You bad little boy. I knew you weren't listening to me."

That woke Vinnie suddenly. He sat up straight and said, "Monte Carlo! You gotta be kidding! That's over in Europe, ain't it?"

"Of course it is, Vincent. Now, I shall need a new gown, and I certainly can't be seen in the same diamonds. We shall need to go shopping, shan't we?"

"What!" he said. "Wait a minute! I gotta buy you that stuff?"

"Well," she began. "Ordinarily my husband would receive the bill. I dare say if you were to pay him what he wants he will pay the bill and others as I need. He always does, you know. But I would be very disappointed in you if you let my husband buy me these things. I would think you would have more pride than that. And I think rather that if you don't buy me these things and you don't pay Clive what he wants, I shall have to go to the party alone in any case. Clive would demand that."

****

Vinnie and Catherine spent the weekend shopping in the best stores the Island had to offer. He spent tens of thousands of dollars buying whatever she wanted. They ate in the best and most expensive restaurants and made love throughout the nights. They didn't talk of Sir Clive until three AM Monday morning.

They lay in bed, holding each other, exhausted from their love making. Catherine rested her head on Vinnie's chest. Her hand ran through the hair on his chest and stomach, and caressed the muscles on his shoulders and arms.

She whispered, "Clive will be here in the morning . . . In a few hours. What will you do, Vincent?"

He said nothing. For days Sir Clive's demands were spinning around inside his head. He couldn't lose Lady Catherine Hamilton. But where would he get that kind of money without New York finding out? It was an impossible situation.

"I don't know," he managed to say.

Catherine sat up in bed, allowing the pale cream colored sheet to fall away exposing her breasts. "Vincent, darling. You own a business. It must be a massive business. Aren't you able to draw the money from that business?"

"I don't own the company," he said. "I just manage it."

"You don't own it?" she asked, surprise in her voice. "Who does?"

"People you don't want to meet," he answered.

"I don't understand. People I don't want to meet? That sounds like they must be criminals of some kind."

"Catherine," he tried to explain. "If I take even a small amount of money from these men . . . both you and I will die."

"Oh my God!" she said, her hand covering her mouth in shock. "Tell me about the business. There must be a way. Maybe you could borrow the money. Or better yet," she started and paused. She shifted and sat cross legged on the bed, now totally uncovered and naked. "There may be a way. Clive does have money. A great deal actually. Perhaps if your people let him buy into the business as a partner? Your people could receive a great deal of money and Clive could have a partnership share in the business. The income he would receive would certainly satisfy him."

Vinnie laughed and shook his head. He said, "You don't understand. People who invest in the company lose their money, they don't make money."

"You're right, darling," Catherine said, pouting like a child. "I don't understand."

"Look, I take money from rich people. I promise them returns on their investment. Then a couple of guys show up at their office or their home and tell them to go to hell. They're scary guys with guns. Once in a while someone goes to the cops, but before anything can happen they turn up dead."

"You mean the whole thing is criminal?" she asked. "That must mean that you, too, are a criminal."

"Does that make a difference to you?" he asked.

She thought for a moment, wrinkling her forehead, and then said, "No . . . Actually it's quite exciting. May I be your . . . . What's the word? . . . Your gun moll I seem to remember. Isn't that what they call all the ladies in those James Cagney movies?"

"Yeah," he laughed for the first time since Clive had come to see them. "If we can figure out a way to get that old fag his money, and we don't get killed doing it, you can be my gun moll."

She laughed and rolled on top of Vinnie. She kissed him deeply and whispered in his ear, "In the movies they call it a scam I believe. You are running a scam, aren't you?"

"Yeah, it's a scam," he sighed. "We steal money and kill people. That damn resort ain't never gonna be built. Pretty soon the guys in New York will shut down the operation and walk away with millions. You and me, we can do whatever we want then. You can come back to New York with me. We can live there and have plenty of money."

They spoke very few words for the rest of the night. They made love again and again and finally fell asleep holding each other. When Vinnie woke up, the sun was up and Catherine was gone. He went to the closet and all her clothes, including all he had bought for her, were gone. He ran to the dresser; all her jewelry, including the diamond necklace he had bought for her was gone. He went out to the lanai and sat. He ran his fingers across the scar on his neck.

He couldn't figure it out. Could she have gone back to her husband? Maybe she didn't want to live in New York with him. What had he done? What had he said?

He quickly walked back into the suite. He phoned the front desk and asked for Lady Catherine Hamilton's room number. He was told there was no Lady Catherine Hamilton registered at the resort and never had been.

He never saw Lady Catherine or Sir Clive Hamilton again.

CHAPTER TWENTY-FOUR

San Marcos

Betsy had sat inside the old MGB outside the Ortiz home for a long time. It had started snowing again while she was inside speaking with Mrs. Ortiz. The sky was black with storm clouds, and a heavy wind off the Pacific was blowing the snow almost horizontally.

She was determined to find the three missing girls and find them soon. Something bad had happened to the three. Were they alive? Had they fallen into the hands of some kind of serial killer? She had a nagging fear that soon there would be a fourth. That could not happen; she was determined to not let that happen. And she had nothing to go on . . . except M. The little, dirty and ragged drug dealer was her only link to the three. She had to find him. But where?

And then the thought finally broke free from the deep recesses of her brain. "Tommy DeVito," she said out loud. M wasn't the only thing connecting the girls. He had been with Sissy. He was dead because of Sissy. Sissy was one of the three missing. It was a thin connection, but it had to be connected somehow.

She had found Tommy DeVito in the warehouse. Someone had killed him. But someone must know Tommy DeVito. Someone out there must know him and that he was connected to Sissy McMillan. And that same someone may know if there was a connection between Tommy DeVito and

Diane Kohn and Mary Ortiz.

So there were two leads she could work on. Tommy DeVito would take time and questions. Finding someone who knew him and would talk to her would be difficult. She decided M was the easiest and quickest. M was a source of marijuana, and Tommy DeVito used marijuana with Sissy. He was also the source for Diane and probably for Mary, too. M seemed a logical place to go to. She would ask more questions of M and maybe even beat him until he told her the truth she needed to know. He would know Tommy DeVito and he could give her leads in that direction.

For the first time, she had what Morgan would call a 'lead', something to work on without driving around aimlessly. She smiled; satisfied that maybe . . . just maybe . . . she could find the three missing women. She started the car's engine. She sped off to the harbor once again, fish-tailing the little car down the snow covered road. M had to know Tommy DeVito, and maybe he would know why Tommy was murdered.

She slammed on the brakes causing the car to skid and fishtail just a block away from the Ortiz home. "Oh shit!" she said out loud. And again, out loud she said, "Did M kill Tommy?"

She parked the MGB at pier 3 where the Mary D would be tied up. She was in a hurry, and she slipped and skidded down the icy wood pier. The Mary D was tied where she had last seen it. It was rocking back and forth in the wind and storm.

There was a dim light behind the grimy, yellowed curtains inside the ship. Betsy approached cautiously, finally wishing she had taken Morgan's pistol with her. If M had killed Tommy DeVito . . . and perhaps even the three missing girls . . . he might kill Betsy, too. She stepped onto the deck; the ship rocked slightly under her feet. "M!" she called out. "M! Are you down there? It's me, Betsy Concanon!"

There was no answer. She put her hand on the cabin door's handle. 'Push past the fear,' she remembered Morgan saying. 'Everyone who isn't insane is scared of something,' he told her so many times. 'The trick is to push past the fear and do what has to be done.'

She threw open the door, crashing it against the stairway wall. She rushed down the three steps into the cabin. It was as cold inside the small boat as it was outside. But there was a smell inside, an odor of death and blood. In terror and disbelief, she gasped softly, putting her hand to her mouth. There, in the dim light of a single small bare bulb hanging from the ceiling, she could see M, lying on his back on the floor in a pool of his own blood. There was a bullet hole in his forehead and two more in his chest. His eyes were frozen open in the terror of facing whatever came to him after death.

****

Bob Sommers arrived with three of his officers and an ambulance. Emmanuel Bottoms had been dead for more than four hours. One of the bullets had cut into his heart, piercing the aorta. His thin, frail body had little muscle to absorb the two bullets to his chest. He had bled almost completely out before his lack of blood pressure stopped the flow. He was dead almost immediately after the bullet entered his brain.

Bob took Betsy aside on the ship's deck as his police officers were taking pictures and gathering what might be evidence. "Was I mistaken or did I tell you to go back to school and stay out of this?" he asked her. He was no longer just concerned for Betsy, he was angry.

"Yes . . . I know . . ." she started.

"Then why are you here?" Bob demanded.

"I just thought . . ."

"No, you weren't thinking. That could be you in there. That could be you with a damn bullet in your head. What the hell do I tell Morgan and Sandy if you go off and get yourself killed?" He stopped for a moment and took a deep breath. Trying to calm down a little, he said, "Now, you're going to do two things. One, you're coming down to the station and write out a very long and detailed report of everything . . . And I mean everything . . . you've done the past few days. Two, after you're done with that, you are going home and crack some books. The next time I find you out playing detective I'm going to arrest you and throw your ass in jail until Morgan and Sandy get home. Let them take care of you. I'm tired of trying. Understand?"

Betsy didn't know what to say. Inside of her there was a burning need to find the missing girls. She realized that she needed to find them because without the plain luck of finding Morgan and Sandy, she could be one of the missing. She realized that if she was still living on the streets she could be a victim of . . . anything. She realized she could have graduated from smoking marijuana and drinking beer to using some harder and more dangerous drug, and because of that she would also expose herself to more dangerous people.

The three girls were in trouble, some kind of serious trouble. She knew that. Now with a second murder of people they were involved with, Betsy was sure they weren't just shacked up somewhere having some fun with a boyfriend. No, they were in trouble.

"Bob . . ." she started but he interrupted her.

"Do you think I'm kidding? Damn it Betsy, there are now three murders here. Three, do you understand?"

"Three?" she said. "But . . ."

"You don't know do you?" he said, staring deeply into

her eyes to see if she would lie to him.

"Know what? I thought . . ."

"Another student at your college has been murdered. Do you know Ron Porter?"

"Ron? Yes. I mean I don't really know him. I was just talking to him the other day. I only talked to him once. He's the one told me about Mary Ortiz and Diane Kohn. He's dead?"

"Yes," Bob said. She wasn't lying, her face told him that. At first a red flush raced across her cheeks and then she turned very pale. Bob thought she might faint. "He was found floating in the harbor, not too far from here. He had a bullet in the back of his head."

So M was murdered, probably for what he knew about the missing girls. Tommy DeVito was dead, probably because he had been with Sissy. And now Ron Porter, who knew Sissy and Diane and Mary, who said he and Sissy had dated in the past, was dead. It seems everyone who knew Sissy was dying.

She asked, "The bullets. Do they all match up? From the same gun?"

"None of your business!" Bob said. "I'm the one does the murder investigations around here. Not you!"

Ron Porter had talked to her in the school's parking lot. That was all she knew, and she had to convince Bob Sommers of that. She pled, "Please believe me, Bob. I didn't know he was killed. I didn't know Ron; I only spoke to him that one time."

"OK," Bob said. "I guess I have to believe you. If you're lying to me, I promise you I'll put you in jail."

She asked Bob, "What was he doing? There had to be a reason he was killed."

"I'm told he was asking questions like you're doing," Bob said. "And you could wind up just like the Porter kid. Betsy," he said, his voice holding the frustration he was feeling, "You're out there doing exactly what the Porter kid did to get himself killed. Whoever killed him and Tommy DeVito and more than likely that M kid is probably out there waiting to kill you, too. Go home!"

"So you know that one gun was used?" she asked.

Bob did not answer her. He turned and went down into the Mary D's cabin to check on the work his officers were doing. Betsy slunk away, knowing there was evidence inside the cabin of the Mary D that Bob would find but she would never know about. Maybe, she thought as she drove the MGB back into the hills and to home, maybe she should take Bob's advice and just go back to school and forget all about the missing girls. She would eventually go downtown to Bob's police station and write out the report he wanted. But not yet. She had to think, to think about what she should do next.

At home, in the kitchen, as she waited for a kettle of water to boil for tea, she paced back and forth and thought of everything she had done in the last few days. Bob would insist that every detail be put on paper. She had to collect her thoughts and make sure that the statement she would write out was absolutely correct. She didn't want to give Bob any excuse to put her in one of his jail cells.

Three people were dead and three girls were missing, and she was no closer to knowing why than the very first day she set out to find Sissy McMillan. With M dead . . . and with Tommy DeVito dead and now Ron Porter, she felt she had no place left to go.

She waited for the kettle to whistle. She paced back

and forth in the kitchen, thinking, trying to find out what she was missing. The one fact she was sure of was that everything was connected . . . somehow. The gun used to kill the three was the same, Bob had implied that. But how was she to find that connection? The kettle whistled, she filled her cup and burned her lips on the hot liquid. She drank her tea slowly, but she couldn't eat anything.

Another cup of tea and more thinking, and then she drove downtown to Bob's office where she spent two hours scratching out word after word, hoping that writing it all out would cause some little bit of something to pop out, and she would have the answers . . . or at least the path to those answers. But after that time and fourteen pieces of yellow pad paper, she was right where she had been when she walked into Bob's office.

She drove home aimlessly, thinking more than driving, and finally finding herself at the curb in front of Morgan and Sandy's home. All that night, sleepless for the most part, she thought about her dilemma. As the sun began to rise in a clear blue sky, she was determined to go on with her search, in spite of Bob Sommers' threats and warnings. With the kettle on the stove once again, she ran to the front door for the newspaper. The headline was Emmanuel Bottom's murder. There was nothing in the report that told her anything new.

The paper said Emmanuel was a known small time drug dealer and failed thief with a long police record. His poor mother was mentioned towards the end of the article. That was it. A fitting epilogue for such a person, she thought.

There was nothing in the paper that morning about Ron Porter. That was strange, she thought. Maybe because he was a student. Nothing special or exciting there. He wasn't a drug dealer like M was. He was too ordinary a person for the thin local newspaper to take up advertising space to report on his murder. And Bob would not have told the reporters that there was a connection between the two.

Ron had said he dated Sissy a couple of times. He knew Diane Kohn and Mary Ortiz. And M was probably selling marijuana to Sissy. Tommy DeVito had been dating Sissy, so she was told. Everyone who was near Sissy was dead. But she would not assume Diane and Mary were dead . . . not yet anyway. Who was out there that she could talk to?

The newspaper said it would be a clear and cold day, with no snow forecast for the first time in over a week. A perfect day, she thought, to skip her classes for the day. She dressed quickly, not caring what she was wearing and drove as fast as the still icy streets would allow back to Wrightwood State College.

Leaving the MGB in the lot at the Administration Building, the lot meant for teachers and staff, she ran up the stairs of the building and into Mrs. Gordon's office. Betsy had spoken with the Dean of Students before and had seen the school files on all three missing girls. But that was the only place she had left to look, and she was sure that there was, somewhere, a connection, something all three girls shared in common besides marijuana and the three dead people.

Maybe Tommy DeVito's name would be there somewhere in some school files? Maybe Ron Porter's name would be connected somehow to the three. Maybe that was the connection with Sissy, Diane and Mary? There had to be something that brought all three girls together. Morgan had taught her that there was no such thing as a coincidence. She had to look more closely than she had the other day. Mrs. Gordon had to understand and just had to let her see the files once again.

"But Mrs. Gordon," Betsy pleaded when Mrs. Gordon refused. She sat in a chair in front of the Dean's big desk, leaning forward, hands folded as if in prayer. "This is important. I just have to see their files again." The office door was open and Betsy was speaking in a raised voice.

"Quiet, Betsy," Mrs. Gordon said. "No one is supposed to know you looked at those files. I could get in trouble for what I did."

"Is there anything I can do or say that will change your mind, Mrs. Gordon?"

"I'm afraid not, Betsy. Now you should go to your class."

Betsy sat back in the chair and locked her eyes on the Dean's. She folded her hands together and swallowed hard, and then played the only card she had. She said resolutely and slowly, "If I go down the hall and tell everyone I can find that you let me see private and confidential student files . . . would you be in trouble?"

"Betsy," the woman gasped. "That sounds like a threat."

"Good, then you understand me, Mrs. Gordon. I'm sorry but I have to see their files again. It's the only place I have to go to, and I just know there's something there that connects them."

"Betsy . . ." she started.

"*Now*, Mrs. Gordon," Betsy said in as firm and threatening a voice as she could come up with. It had to work, she told herself. The threat had to work. If she carried out her threat, if she told people she had looked at confidential student files, Mrs. Gordon would be in trouble, but Betsy would surely be kicked out of the college. Betsy didn't care. Finding the three girls was the only important thing. There were other colleges.

The Dean stood slowly, wiped a few tears off her cheeks with her hand, and said, "I have to go to the ladies room."

When she was gone, Betsy closed the office door and ran to the file cabinet that held student records. She didn't care about time; she wouldn't do what she had to do quickly. She pulled the files on the three girls and sat at Mrs. Gordon's desk, in her tall leather chair. The same pages were there, the same basic personal information, nothing was new and nothing had been changed.

She found Ron Porter's file and leafed through it. She found he was a good student, a science and math major with extraordinary grades. He would have gone far in life had he not been murdered. All the personal information that should be there was there, nothing more.

Class schedules; that was something Betsy had not looked at. Sissy was taking difficult courses, lots of math and sciences, many of the same classes Ron Porter was taking. That's how they knew each other. Betsy was taking many of the same classes, but she found it strange that she and Sissy only shared one class, Mr. Thatcher's biology. And she didn't share any classes with Ron Porter.

Diane Kohn was taking leaner courses, the kind of thing a student takes while trying to decide on a major. The kind of thing a wealthy young girl takes to waste some time until she meets a wealthy young man to marry.

Mary Ortiz was taking a full schedule of more classic studies, Foreign Languages, English Lit and even a Creative Writing Course.

But there it was, something these three girls, as diverse as they were, all had in common. Each was taking a science class that was required by the school, and each was taking 1st year biology from Mr. Thatcher to cover that college requirement.

****

Betsy hesitated at the door to the biology lab. Mr. Thatcher had a class going on inside, a class that Betsy was supposed to be in. Class had been in session for almost twenty minutes and had another twenty to go. She could, she reasoned, just walk in, apologize for being late, and take a seat. But her mind was not on biology. She needed to speak with Mr. Thatcher alone, after class.

And so she waited in the hallway, pacing sometimes in circles, looking at but not seeing the papers posted on a bulletin board, looking at her wrist watch every few seconds, biting her finger nails, and trying to think of what she could find out from Mr. Thatcher. He must know all three girls and Ron Porter. He must know something about them that Betsy could use to find them. Maybe they talked to him. Maybe they confided in him. Maybe he saw a boyfriend waiting for them to leave class.

A buzzer sounded making her jump a little. The lab door opened and students flooded out. When the last had left the room, Betsy walked into it.

"Betsy Concanon," Mr. Thatcher said, surprised to see her. "I'm afraid you're late. Class just ended." He busied himself shuffling papers and turning off his laptop computer. He didn't look at her.

"I know Mr. Thatcher," she said walking to him. His desk was on a raised platform at the head of the room, in front of three white boards. "I just need a few minutes of your time, please."

He stopped doing what he was doing and looked at her. "You're not dropping my class are you, Betsy? That would be a shame. You've got an easy 4.0 going here. That is if you don't miss any more classes. Have you been sick or something?"

"I'm not dropping the class, Mr. Thatcher," Betsy said

and smiled. "And I'm fine. I just want to talk with you for a minute or two. Do you have another class?"

"Not right now," he said. "I was just going for a cup of coffee. How about you come with me and we can talk there."

Wrightwood State has its own coffee shop modeled after every ubiquitous Starbuck's that occupies every street corner everywhere. It is usually filled with students drinking expensive espresso coffees, studying, and talking. They found a free table in a corner near the restrooms, and Mr. Thatcher offered to buy Betsy a coffee. She said a hot tea would be better.

When he returned, he sat across from her. He sipped at his hot coffee in the paper cup. She stirred her hot tea with a plastic sick and removed the tea bag. Mr. Thatcher was watching her. Her forehead was creased and she was staring down into her paper cup of tea. She slowly looked up at the teacher, and she began, "You know that Sissy McMillan, Mary Ortiz and Diane Kohn are all missing."

"I knew about Sissy," he said, a look of surprise crossing his face. "But you're telling me that Mary Ortiz and Diane Kohn are missing, too?"

"Yes, I'm afraid so." She wasn't ready to tell the teacher that Ron Porter had been murdered. She would deal with the three girls first. Ron Porter's murderer would have to be involved with the three girls. "And I'm afraid they're in some kind of trouble, Mr. Thatcher. All three are in a couple of your biology classes. What can you tell me about them?"

"Well, not much. Sissy is an exceptional student . . . like yourself," he said and smiled. "Mary is just barely passing. I know she is more creative than scientific. The only reason she's in my class is that she has to finish a science requirement. She wants to be a writer someday."

"That's interesting," Betsy said. "Did she tell you that?"

"Yes. I've counseled her on her grade in my class. Mary is very nice and quite intelligent, but she wants to be a writer, not a scientist. Diane could do better, but she isn't having any problem getting a passing grade. I think she just doesn't care, you know? She's halfway implied that she's having trouble at home, but she's never given me any details. I suggested she see a school counselor, but I doubt she's done that."

Betsy sipped at her tea as she let everything roll around in her head. She reasoned that the three girls were so unalike that they had nothing in common except the biology class. Could they all have boyfriends and could all three have run off with them? Morgan had taught her that there is nothing coincidental about coincidences. There is a reason for everything. And when something strange or suspicious happens, there is always a reason. Chance appears only when a person gambles.

"Mr. Thatcher," she said. "I think I've found out enough to know these three people. The only thing they have in common is your class. And I find it strange that you didn't know Mary and Diane are missing. Didn't you notice they weren't in your class?"

"What the hell does that mean?" he asked, suddenly angry. "Are you accusing me of something?"

"No! . . . Of course not! I'm sorry. I'm just trying to figure out what could have happened to them. All three have disappeared without leaving a message of any kind with anyone. That's pretty strange, don't you think?"

"Of course it's strange. But it has nothing to do with me or the classes I teach. Look," he said, a little calmer now, taking a deep breath. "Nothing personal, but you young girls don't take too much too seriously. I'm used to you girls skipping a class or two. Shopping and boyfriends seem to be more important than school to you young girls. You've done it yourself recently, you know."

Betsy said nothing, drank some more of her tea, and then asked, "Mary's mother told me Mary was seeing a man. Mrs. Ortiz didn't know who. Mary was very secretive about it. And she was buying a lot of clothes and makeup even though she had very little money. When you were talking with her about her grade, did she ever mention anything about that?"

"You're really intent on finding them, aren't you?" Thatcher asked.

"Yes, I am," Betsy answered. "Whatever it takes."

Thatcher drank some of his coffee, obviously thinking about what he should say. When he put his cup down he leaned forward and in almost a whisper he said, "Look, Mary did tell me something in confidence. If I tell you, I need to know you'll forget where it came from."

"Of course. All I want to do is find out if they're OK. That's all."

The teacher pulled his chair closer to the table and Betsy and said, "You're right about Mary seeing somebody. She told me she wasn't happy at home, that her parents were tough on her. She had a lot of work to do around the house, and it didn't leave enough time for studying. They wanted her to drop out of school and work in some shop or something like that. She didn't want to do that. As I said, she told me she wanted to be a writer, an author. She was very unhappy. She had started seeing a man after school, a nice guy as she described him. He buys her things and made her happy. I think she was really in love with this man."

"Did she say who this man is?" Betsy asked.

"No, only that he is very nice. I don't think he's a student because he had money to spend on her. I think maybe they've run off together, you know."

Betsy thought for a moment, filtering what Mr. Thatcher had said. She looked up at him and said, "Am I making something out of nothing here? You just spoke of Mary Ortiz and her boyfriend in the past tense . . . But you talked about the man she was dating in the present tense. And you said 'she loves him.' That's also present tense. I'm confused."

Thatcher laughed a little and said, "What are you? An English major?"

Betsy laughed a little, too, maybe nervously, but she had been taught that all too often little things mean a lot. She went on, "Did she tell you where they went on their dates?"

"No, not really . . . I think she said they came here to get coffee between classes, but I can't be sure of that," he answered.

Betsy finished her cup of tea while staring deeply at the biology teacher. If she could get a photo of Mary, she thought she might show it to the people who work at the coffee shop. But there was more she needed to know first. She might never have a chance to talk to Mr. Thatcher again. He would surely refuse her a second time.

She put her cup down and said, "Excuse me, but I don't think you're telling me everything. What are you holding back?"

Thatcher sat back and folded his arms across his chest. He looked down and to the left. Betsy, remembering all Morgan Crew had taught her, took mental notice of this. That is the body language of someone not telling the truth. She thought, 'He's either frightened . . . or lying, but he's holding something back.'

She said as pleasantly as she could, needing his cooperation, "Look, if Mary told you something that will help me find her, I need to know. All I want to do is to make sure she's OK, that's all. Please tell me what she told you."

"Are you intending to take her back to her parents?" he asked.

"No," she said. "Not at all. She's over eighteen. She can do what she wants as far as I'm concerned. I just want to know she and Sissy and Diane are OK."

"Will you tell her parents where she is?"

"No, not if she's ok and happy and she doesn't want me to."

"Who will you tell?" he asked.

"I guess I should tell the police she's OK. They have an open file on her, and if she's not in trouble, they should know so they won't waste time looking for her."

"The police are looking for her?" he asked.

"Yes. Didn't you know that?"

"No, I didn't know that. They've never come to me." he said, looking away again. He turned back to Betsy and said, "OK, I know where she is."

"Then tell me," she begged.

"I can't do that," he said. "I promised. Look, she's with someone who cares about her . . . who loves her. But I'll take you to her. I need to be there so I can explain to her why I broke my promise. And she needs to know more than her parents are looking for her. She needs to know the police are actively looking for her. If the police find her . . . she and her lover might be in trouble. I just need your promise that when you talk to Mary and see that she's not in any trouble, you won't tell anyone. Even the police."

"Alright," Betsy said. "I promise . . . If she's not in any kind of trouble. I will tell the police she's not in trouble and try to convince them not to go on looking for her. I won't tell them where she is. But I will go on looking for Sissy and Diane. Is that good enough?"

"I guess it has to be. I just don't want to have Mary taken away from her lover. She deserves some happiness."

Betsy stood and said, "Let's go."

"I have a class in fifteen minutes. Come to the class . . . A little extra learning won't hurt you. You've missed a lot and a big test is coming up soon. After the class I'll take you to Mary."

****

Mr. Thatcher's biology class droned on as Betsy sat in the back of the room, not able to listen to him. Her mind was filled with Mary Ortiz and Sissy and Diane. And there was a nagging feeling that Mr. Thatcher wasn't telling her everything. He was holding something back. He might have been trying to protect Mary Ortiz; there may have been more to it. But soon she would know what he wasn't telling her. She would be able to speak with Mary, and if she was truly alright, then Betsy would have only the other two girls to worry about.

And maybe, she thought, Mary had nothing to do with the other two. Sissy and Diane were from wealthy families, Mary was not. Sissy and Diane were interested in science, Mary was not. Maybe Mary's disappearance had nothing to do with the other two.

The class ended, and Betsy waited in the back of the room as the students filed out, all talking and laughing and not realizing that three of their classmates might be in trouble. Mr. Thatcher walked up to her without her noticing, and she jumped when he said, "Betsy? Betsy? Are you ready?"

They walked out of the building without saying a word.

In Mr. Thatcher's car Betsy only half watched where they were going until she realized they were driving slowly through the slums of North Harbor.

"She's here?" Betsy asked. "She's living in North Harbor?"

"It's not the best place, but she's happy, and the man she's with loves her. Maybe they might get a better place soon."

"But you said her boyfriend had money to buy her things," she asked. "If he has money, why are they living here?"

Mr. Thatcher did not answer.

They drove slowly, turning one corner and then another. Betsy recognized the street they were on and realized they had driven down that street just a few minutes ago.

"Where are you going?" she asked.

"Sorry," he said. "I'm not too familiar with these streets. Just give me a minute."

He took more turns and doubled back several times. Betsy saw out of the corner of her eye that he constantly looked in the rear view mirror. Finally, he pulled to the curb and stopped the car in front of a derelict old two story house that looked unlived in. Windows were broken and boarded up, and the yard was a mess of tall weeds poking through the layer of snow. Trash lay everywhere, and a feral cat ran off the front porch to disappear around the side of the house.

"Mary is living here?" Betsy asked. Maybe, she thought, Mary really was in trouble. Betsy knew the neighborhood and knew that drugs and prostitutes and thieves and drunks were thick there. Even if Mary was with a man she loved, this was no place to be shacked up in. It was possible, even likely, that Mary and her lover were also into drugs and that, Betsy knew, was trouble.

Mr. Thatcher got out of the car followed by Betsy. He led the way as they walked across the broken concrete front walk that was covered with many days of snow and ice. Betsy stepped in the teacher foot prints through the snow. They walked up the creaky wooden steps to the front door. The door was cracked and warped and had lost almost all of whatever paint was on it years ago. A cardboard box filled with trash and empty food cans lay next to the door. The teacher knocked on the door, smiled at Betsy, waited and then knocked again.

"I guess they're not home," he said. He tried the door knob. The door was locked. He reached into his pants pocket and pulled out a keychain with a dozen keys on it. He flipped through the keys, found the one he was looking for, unlocked the door and opened it. "We can wait inside for them," he said as he stepped aside to let Betsy into the house. "It's a little warmer inside."

She stood on the porch at the open door and was revolted at the smell of garbage and waste coming from inside. She looked up at the teacher and asked, "You have a key to their house? What the hell's going on here? You mean Mary is living in this place?"

Betsy was about to walk away when Thatcher grabbed her arm and pulled her into the house in front of him, slamming the door closed behind him. He threw two dead bolt locks and turned the key, locking the door.

Betsy turned to face him. His face had flushed red and a crazed gleam filled his wide open eyes, making him look like a different person. Spittle was dripping from the corners of his mouth. Betsy realized that the man was insane. He must have Mary Ortiz . . . And perhaps Sissy and Diane . . .

Somewhere in the house. She tried to step away from him. She started to scream. Thatcher's fist hit her hard across her jaw before she could. She fell backwards onto the dirty floor, hitting her head against an old wooden table, and blackness enveloped her.

CHAPTER TWENTY-FIVE

On The Big Island

Caroline sat in the kiddie pool, splashing and laughing with two other children. Sandy and I lounged back in a couple of chaise lounges under a wide umbrella and were halfway through our second Piña Colada. We laughed as only parents could laugh at the antics and loud screams of their child. Others would find Caroline's antics only normal for a child her age and too loud. But we knew she was special.

We were talking about what I had found so far. Sandy spoke softly, too many people were nearby, and said, "So it wasn't this Sgt. Aguilar who killed Lewis? Are you sure of that?"

"I'm pretty sure," I said. "His face, when I spoke to him, didn't tell me anything different. I think if Aguilar weren't such a good soldier . . . and he professed his Christian beliefs, too . . . he might have killed Lewis. But I don't think so. Someone phoned Aguilar and told him about Lewis. Aguilar was really pissed off and when he went to see Lewis, if he were a different kind of person, he might have at least beat the crap out of him. He didn't even take a swing at Lewis. No, I think he honestly reported to the CID people on Oahu and wanted them to put Lewis in jail forever."

"So do we go to the police with your suspicions?" she asked.

"The cops here hate me, remember?" I said. "No, I think I need someone else to go to."

"Who?"

"I've been thinking about that. I need to make a phone call," I said as I pushed myself off the chaise and walked back to our suite. There, I sat at the desk, and via the front desk concierge I got the phone number for Sgt. Aguilar.

When he answered the phone I said, "Sgt. Aguilar, this is Morgan Crew. Do you have a minute?"

"I'm very busy," he said. "You got one minute. Make it fast."

"I need your help," I said.

He said nothing and I waited. Finally I had to say something. "Do you care who killed Lewis Manaluo?"

"You mean Lewis George?   That son of a bitch deserter?"

"Yes," I answered. "Do you care who killed him?"

Aguilar said nothing for a moment and then said, "He's dead, right? That's a good ending for a coward. Why should I care?"

I had to convince him to help because I had no place else to go. I said, "Murder is a crime, and I believe Christians believe it is a sin, too. Without your help I can't bring the murderer to justice, and he will walk free. He tried to kill me. I was lucky. Will he kill again? Will he try to kill me again? I don't know, but if the situation ever comes up, and he got away with it once, he may well kill someone else. Now, will you help me or not?"

"Tell me what you want me to do, and maybe I'll help you. Depends on what you want me to do."

"I need some police help," I began. "The local police here on the Island hate me and won't help me. I'm asking you to phone the CID Agents you spoke with and talk them into talking with me."

"Why don't you call them?" he asked. "Why me and not you?"

"Because right now all I have are suspicions. I need some law enforcement authority to get search warrants and ask questions I can't ask. I think the Army's CID is my best bet at getting what I need to get."

"That's all you want me to do?" he asked. "Just get the CID people to talk to you? Nothing else?"

"Nothing else," I answered. "Just use your influence to get them to talk to me."

"OK," he said. "I guess I can do that. One question. Do you think I killed that damn deserter?"

"No, I've scratched you off my list of suspects. I still have a couple of people as suspects, but I think I know who did kill him. And that person is not you."

"OK," Aguilar said. "Where should the CID people contact you?"

I gave Sgt. Aguilar the phone number of the Maika'i Resort. In truth, at the time I figured it was not more than a 50 / 50 chance that anyone would phone. If the Army wouldn't help, all I could do was go home and try to forget before a second attempt on my life . . . or worse yet, on Sandy's life . . . was made. . . But I would never forget my promise to Nancy Wong and Leilani.

As I waited, I joined Sandy and Caroline for lunch on our lanai. I think Sandy could see what was tearing me apart inside by the frown on my face and the fact that my mind was a thousand miles away. She was talking to me, but I couldn't hear her, and I said very little.

Without asking me, she ordered a cheeseburger and fries for me, in hopes of cheering me up a little. From the bar in the suite she pulled two bottles of beer, some exotic German brand. I would have preferred a cold Bud from Papa Keoni's, but I drank what we had.

After lunch I sat on the lanai and ran everything around in my head once more, just to make sure what I felt was right or at least within reason. Sandy was getting our daughter ready for her nap. I would go to her and tuck her in as she liked. But I couldn't get Lewis and Leilani and Nancy Wong off my mind. I didn't know if I was right or not, but I felt sure Lewis' death had nothing to do with whatever was going on at Vasco Construction. Something was going on there, maybe Lewis had found out. But if Vasco had him killed, it wouldn't have been as messy a chain of murders as it was. And I would be dead instead of just beaten up. That made me remember that I needed to get in touch with Harry Esposito. But that could wait. There were more pressing matters that I needed to take care of.

I jumped when the phone rang. I ran to it and grabbed it up on the second ring.

"Yes! Hello!" I said too quickly.

"May I speak with Mr. Morgan Crew please," the female voice asked.

"Yes! That's me!"

"I am Special Agent Linda Hartsell," she said. "Sgt. Aguilar suggested I phone you."

"Yes! Thank you! Excuse me," I said breathing hard. "I'm a little out of breath. Are you investigating the death of Lewis Manaluo . . . Lewis George?"

"Why do you want to know?" she asked.

"Because I know who killed him . . . But I can't prove it yet. I need your help."

"You should go to the local police."

"I can't . . . It's a long story, and I don't have time to explain. Will you help me or not?"

Agent Hartsell said nothing. So I said, "Lewis was a deserter, right? That means he was never discharged from the Army, right?"

She caught on immediately and said, "Stay where you are. I'll be there as quickly as I can. I'll use an Army chopper . . . That'll be faster than a commercial jet."

CHAPTER TWENTY-SIX

San Marcos

Betsy awoke in a damp and musty room. The light in the room was very dim. There was a small window near the top of the room that had been boarded up, letting streaks of daylight filter in. It barely illuminated the small room, but it was enough for her to see the ceiling as she lay on the hard, cold, concrete floor, staring through foggy eyes. She tried to move but found her hands tied behind her and her legs tied tightly at her ankles and knees. Her jaw throbbed where Thatcher had hit her, and she could taste her own blood still oozing from her split lip.

She heard a voice, a whispered voice, filled with fear. "Who are you?" the voice asked through the wooden plank walls. Betsy looked around as her eyes became used to the dark. She found she was in a bare room, grey concrete floor and wooden plank walls. The room was not more than ten feet by ten feet square.

"Can you hear me?" the whispered voice asked. "Who are you?"

It was a female voice, a voice shaking with fear and barely loud enough to penetrate the wall.

"I'm Betsy Concanon," she said in a normal voice.

"Quiet!" the voice said. "Not so loud! He doesn't want

us talking to each other!"

"Who?" she whispered. "Who doesn't want us talking?"

"Thatcher," the voice answered.

"Who are you?" Betsy asked.

"I'm Diane Kohn. I think I know you, don't I?"

"Yes, we go to school together."

The sound of a door closing caused Diane to whisper fearfully, "Ssssh! He's coming."

Betsy struggled to push herself up and to lean against the wall of the small room. She heard footsteps coming down stairs; slowly, deliberately, one step at a time. She waited for whatever was going to happen. The door to her room opened, but no light from the outside came into the room. A dark shadow stood there, tall and threatening. He was barely visible as he blended in with the dark all around him, but Betsy knew it was her biology teacher, Mr. Thatcher. He stood for a moment in the open doorway, and then took two steps into the room.

"Hello, Betsy," he said softly. She said nothing. "I'm sorry I had to hit you. I would have been here sooner but a policeman was here. Lt. Sommers. He was looking for you. I told him you had been here but you left."

His voice was different, almost dreamlike and in a strange whisper. He was staring at something only he could see, something far away, beyond the wall of the little cell she was in. She decided that she had nothing to lose if she took an aggressive approach. She was his captive after all, in jeopardy, and there was nothing she could do to stop him from killing her if that's what he intended to do. So, she thought, why not go out as mean as she could be. At least she would feel good about herself.

She struggled to push herself up, sitting and leaning against the wooden wall. She forced a mean smile and said, trying to muster together as strong a voice as she could manage, "You have Sissy McMillan here. And Diane Kohn. And probably Mary Ortiz, too. You must be crazy, you bastard. Do you really think you can get away with this?"

"Sissy is here *with* me," he said. "Mary and Diane are *with* me, also," he said. "They're all here *with* me. They aren't prisoners. They are *with* me."

He took three more steps and stood in front of Betsy. Her eyes had become used to the dark, and she could see him now. He was smiling a weird, twisted smile while staring at the wall above Betsy's head.

"Why?" she asked.

"Because we're in love," he said, his voice almost a singsong child's voice. "I love them and they love me."

"They love you?" she asked, astonished. "You believe that? What makes you think three young girls who you're holding captive and who are scared of you, love you?"

"Oh, Betsy. You just don't understand. You see, I've saved them from terrible lives."

"Tell me about that," she said. She was struggling with the cord at her wrists. It was tight, and she could feel the warmth of her blood as she twisted the cord trying to loosen it.

"OK," he said. "I'll tell you. I'm very proud of what I've done for them. Take Diane for instance. Her parents live a thousand miles away. They have no interest in her. They think giving her money is all they have to do. With me, she can be happy."

"And what about Mary and Sissy?"

"Mary's parents want to control her, to keep her down.

Can you imagine? They want a bright, intelligent young lady like Mary to work in some sweat shop down in L.A. What a waste of a good brain. She has such a bright future."

"A bright future?" Betsy said. "Locked up in your makeshift prison? What the hell kind of future is that?"

"I've bought her the clothes she wants, and I've let her be what she wants to be," he said, his voice far away and frightening. "When I knew I loved her and she loved me, I took her away from her terrible family and brought her here, to safety, where we could be happy together.

"Sissy's parents worry more about their money than her," he went on and started walking in circles around the small prison. "She's so smart she should be in a much better college then Wrightwood State, but her parents wouldn't pay for it. I'm going to let her have the education she wants. And I love them, and they love me."

"But you're holding them captive," Betsy said.

He stopped pacing and looked down from the ceiling above, directly at Betsy. "No!" he screamed. "You're wrong," Thatcher said, his voice lowered again to almost a whisper. "I'm protecting them from their unhappy lives outside. Someday we will leave here, and we will all live together and be happy. You'll see. Someday we will all be somewhere where we can be happy. They love me, and I love them, and we can be patient. Someday we will all be together somewhere."

"You're going to live with all three of them?"

"Yes, of course. Can't you see that, Betsy? You're too smart not to understand," he said as he started to pace back and forth in front of her. The rope on her wrists was beginning to loosen. Her own blood was working as a lubricant, causing the knot to slip a little.

"You've been raping them, haven't you?" she said.

"Not rape, Betsy. We love each other, and when you love a person, a sexual relationship is a beautiful, wonderful thing. We share a beautiful thing . . . The three of us."

"Not when you hold a young girl captive and they have no choice. They can't say 'no' can they? And if they did say 'no' would you hit them like you hit me? Are they tied up like I am? Do you beat them?"

"Why would they say 'no'? Oh, in the beginning they didn't understand. They were frightened. But once they understood that I love them so very deeply and care for them, it became a beautiful thing. Now they are happy, and we are in love . . . True love."

"I suppose you took them upstairs to a nicely decorated and comfortable bedroom, with clean sheets and maybe some champagne and roses?"

"Oh, Betsy," he said and smiled. "I see what you're trying to do. You're trying to make me angry. But you can't. You see, I'm in love, and I'm loved by three beautiful women. Nothing can hurt me now."

"And what about me?" she asked. "Do I go with you and make a five-some out it?"

"I'm very sorry about that Betsy . . . I really am. You're such a smart young girl. Probably the smartest student I have this year. But you've disgraced your body with tattoos. You have a history of sin and degradation. You've lived a life of shame. You've committed sins that have blackened your soul. You are not worthy of true love like I can give you. I couldn't love you the way I love the others. Their bodies are pure and clean and soft and they've been saving themselves for me and me alone. When I make love with them it is wonderful. I couldn't feel that way about someone like you."

"So what happens to me, then?" she asked, frightened at the answer that was sure to come. But she was intent on not letting him see she was scared. She twisted her face as best she could into an angry scowl and spit out the words.

"I'm afraid that when the time comes for the four of us to leave . . . you won't."

"You mean you're going to kill me?" she asked.

"I'm afraid so," he said and smiled wickedly down at her. "But not yet. Soon, but not yet."

All this time Betsy was twisting the cord that bound her wrists. Her blood was soaking the tight cord, and the more the cord was wet, the more she could move her wrists and hands. Then, with a painful pull, her left hand was free. She didn't move, knowing her legs were bound tightly. She waited.

Thatcher paced back and forth inside the small room without saying anything, thinking of what he should do next. He was about to leave the little cell Betsy was trapped in when she said, "I have to use the bathroom."

Thatcher stopped and without turning he said, "There's a bucket in the corner. Use that."

"How am I supposed to do that? You've got me tied up so I can't move."

He turned to Betsy and took a knife from his pants pocket. He opened it exposing a small four inch blade, pitted with rust. He said, "I'm going to untie your legs long enough for you to piss. Try anything with me and I'll use this knife on you now, understand?" His voice had changed. He sounded rough and mean, insane. His eyes were red and flared. It scared Betsy but she knew what she had to do.

"I got it," she said. "I just need to go really bad."

Thatcher bent and slowly undid the knots of the cord at Betsy's ankles and knees. She kept her hands behind her as she curled herself onto her knees. Thatcher stood over her, holding the knife pointed down at her.

"I need a hand up," Betsy said.

He bent to take her by her right arm and stood her on her feet. She lashed out with her left fist across his jaw, and then a quick right as she gained her balance. Another left and then another right. Thatcher fell backwards and crashed against the wooden wall, blood streaming from his nose and mouth. His knife fell from his hand and skidded across the concrete floor.

Betsy looked at the small knife and said to Thatcher, "I'll bet that blade is bigger than your pitiful little dick." She kicked him hard at the side of his head, and as he slumped to the floor, she kicked him again in the stomach and then again in the groin.

Thatcher lay on the floor unconscious and moaning. Betsy reached down for the knife when she heard from behind her, "Don't touch that, Betsy. I'll need the prints off of it."

It was Lt. Bob Sommers. He was standing in the open doorway of the little cell Betsy had been a prisoner in. Two of his uniformed officers were behind him.

"What the hell!" Betsy exclaimed. "How . . . What . . .!"

"I knew you were here," he said. "Thatcher tried to convince me you had left. But I've been following you since you left home this morning."

"You've been following me?" she asked, astonished that he had been behind her without her knowing.

"You've been with Morgan and Sandy too long," he said smiling. "I knew you wouldn't listen to me. I knew you'd be off doing what you felt had to be done. And when you went to the school's administration building, I knew you'd get something I couldn't get without a court order. So I let you do what you were going to do anyway. Sort of like I let Morgan and Sandy do what they do. I figured you'd find the girls . . . one way or another. I never figured this guy had kidnapped them."

"How long have you been here?" she asked.

"Long enough to watch you kick the shit out of this guy," Bob said and laughed. "That's another thing I couldn't do, so I stood by and watched. There's nothing I would have enjoyed more than beat on that guy like you did. But I'm a cop. I can't do that. Police brutality and all that shit. So I let you do what needed to be done to the son of a bitch."

"He has Sissy and Mary and Diane . . ." she started.

"I know. My men got them out, and they're safe. They're on their way to the hospital now. We got them out while Thatcher was busy with you. They'll be checked over and taken care of. I think you should be looked over, too."

"No," Betsy said, rubbing her wrists. They were bruised and bleeding, but a little soap and water would take care of that, she insisted. "I'm OK. I hope you would have stepped in before he cut me though."

"Of course," Bob said. "I stood by because I needed to hear what he said to you. So my men got the girls, and I listened. It was a great confession. But I have a hunch this bastard will spend the rest of his life in a mental hospital instead of a prison. No court is going to find him guilty."

"You know you're a son of a bitch, don't you, Bob. I was scared for my life here. And you just stood there. If my knuckles weren't bleeding from hitting him, I'd punch your lights out, too."

"How about I buy you dinner tonight to make up for it?"

he asked.

"It better be a damn expensive dinner," she said. "The Country Club and one of their huge steaks would be good. And don't even think of putting it on Morgan's account."

CHAPTER TWENTY-SEVEN

On The Big Island

I once again found myself parking my rental car near Papa Keoni's. It was rapidly approaching evening. The air was being cooled by the high tide of the Pacific washing onto the black sand beach. The sun was halfway into the ocean, boiling red and beautiful. The sky was on fire. The tall coconut palms were silhouetted against it. The high tide waves crashing onto the beach were fast and loud; the rush of sound filled the evening air.

Papa Keoni's would have its usual crew of beer drinkers relaxing after a day's work in the hot Hawaiian sun. I could smell meat and fish cooking in the back room. The smell was enticing, and I wished I had time to stop and eat, and drink a couple of Mama Keoni's cold bottles of beer. From inside I could hear the music of the Islands, slow and romantic, and soft as silk being played on the CD player that sat, as always, at the back of the bamboo bar.

I stepped slowly and carefully up the wooden stairs and stood in the open doorway. If I was right . . . And I was sure I was . . . I would be able to go home knowing that I had done what Nancy and Leilani asked me to do. Mama Keoni wouldn't be happy, and her boys might mean trouble. But what I had to do had to be done.

Behind the sound of the music and the smell of the grilling food coming from inside the little thatch roofed hut, the usual guys were all talking and joking and laughing as they did every night. It all stopped when they saw me standing there in the open doorway, silhouetted against the early evening, the setting sun behind me. They could tell I wasn't happy by the look on my face. I wasn't there to buy them beer.

Mama Keoni, her entire bulk squeezed behind the small bamboo counter top of the bar, spoke loudly, "Hey! Mr. Crew! You come back again! You like my beer . . . Or maybe you like me, hey haole!"

I said nothing and I didn't smile as I looked around the room. Then I saw him. Palani was sitting at a round table with the three other men he usually sat with. He sat with his back to me. He turned when the others all turned to look at me. He alone was smiling but it was a nervous smile.

"Hey Mr. Crew!" he said. "You ever find that guy on the motorcycle?"

"Yes, I did find him," I said.

"You maybe find out who killed Lewis?"

"Yes, I think I did," I said. "I need to talk with you Palani . . . Outside, OK?"

"Hey brudder," he said, trying to laugh. "You don't look so good. What that happen to your face? Some brudder kick the shit outta' you or sump'tin'? You mad at me or sump'tin?"

"Outside, OK?" I said.

I needed to put some room between Palani and his friends and me. I stepped backwards and down the three wooden steps, not daring to turn my back on the four of them.

The black sand was soft as my feet sunk into it. There wasn't much of the beach left to walk on during the high tide. The Pacific lapped across the sand just a few feet away from the stairs. But I waited.

Palani took the steps down to the sand leaving his friends on the porch, watching. Knowing it was just Palani and me, I turned my back to him to look out over the Pacific as the last of the sun fell into the ocean. The dark sky was on fire. It was beautiful to see. I can't remember seeing anything quite as beautiful, except for my wife as she holds our child and smiles at me.

I heard Palani's footsteps crunching in the sand behind me. But I didn't turn; I waited to see what he would do. If he knew what I wanted, he would hit me from behind. And if he did, I wondered what the others would do. The footfalls stopped, and Palani said, "So what you wanna' talk about, brudder?"

Without turning I asked, "Lewis was your friend, right?"

"Hey, Lewis, he a good man. He my hoaloha ko'u . . . My friend."

"You were in the Army, right?" I asked.

"Yeah," he answered, his voice now questioning what I was getting at. "I was in the National Guard. Good times, hey brudder! Got paid for doing nothin' almost."

"Lewis got drunk one night and told you he had deserted back in Afghanistan, didn't he?"

Palani said nothing. I waited, not turning around. It seemed like a lifetime as I waited, but he finally spoke in a near whisper so the others couldn't hear him. "Yeah, he tol' me. We was alone, like. We was pretty drunk. He tol' me everything."

"Did that anger you, Palani?" I asked. "I mean, you did your service. Did it anger you that Lewis deserted?"

"Nah . . . He my hoaloha . . . Like I said."

"But you told Julio Aguilar about Lewis didn't you?"

Palani said nothing. I went on, "You found out that he had deserted under fire. You found out that the day he was supposed to return from leave, he didn't show up. You found out that a young boy, new to the Army and Afghanistan was killed in the truck Lewis was supposed to be driving. You knew that young boy, didn't you?"

I turned around and looked at Palani. He was not happy; he was sweating and he looked scared. I was taller than Palani, and I carried more weight than he did. But he was young and strong, and if it came to a fight between us . . . well, I was not sure I would win.

He said in a strained whisper, "That boy, he a haole. A blond hair surfer dude here. He a rich boy, ya' know? His makuakane . . . His daddy . . . he got lots of money. He want that boy maybe go to school, be a doctor or sumptin'. All that boy he want to do was surf and have some good fun. But he a good boy. He not a bad fella'. I like that boy. Me and him we go surfin' together and do fishin', too. I plenty mad when he get killed. An' I plenty mad when Lewis he say he hidin' out from that Army. So I look around, like. I ask some people, an' I find that Julio fella here on the Island. He there with Lewis in that place with the fightin'. I tell him. What I do wrong doin' that?"

"You expected Julio to hurt Lewis? Maybe kill him?"

"Lewis, he no good," he said suddenly, his voice now a cruel growl. "He no good . . . He got a good haole boy killed because he no good."

"I thought you said Lewis was your friend? Didn't I hear you say that?"

"You think Lewis my hoaloha? Lewis, he got that boy killed . . . For nothin'."

"For nothing?" I asked. "Lewis returned home and he lived a good life with Leilani and little Kanye. He never hurt anyone. All he wanted to do was live . . . and not hurt anyone."

"He hurt that boy because he a coward . . . he ho'ohe," Palani argued.

"So you told Sgt. Aguilar where he could find Lewis. You wanted Sgt. Aguilar to hurt Lewis, right? You wanted Lewis killed, right?"

"Yeah, that what Lewis he deserve, right?"

"But Julio is too good a person, isn't he. A good soldier and a good Christian. Julio would only report Lewis to the Army police. He wouldn't hurt Lewis like you wanted him hurt, right?"

"So what?" Palani asked. I looked over his shoulder and saw three of Palani's friends from Papa Keoni's standing on the porch at the open door. Mama Keoni stood with them. They weren't happy, but they were listening. I had been afraid of them joining Palani, but they weren't going to do that. I felt certain of that.

I spoke loud enough for them to hear me. I wanted them to know what Palani had done. My hope was he had acted alone and not with the others watching us. If he hadn't acted alone, one or more of them would come after me, or at least run.

"So you took it upon yourself to make sure the dead boy was revenged. Lewis was a coward after all. That's what you called your good friend, right? The dead boy wasn't. Lewis had fooled a lot of people around here, right? You used to think he was such a good guy, but he wasn't was he? You killed Lewis, didn't you?"

Palani was shaking visibly. Sweat was flowing freely

off his forehead, and his T-shirt was soaked. He started to backup, taking a few hesitant steps. From behind him one of the men on the porch called out, "That the truth he speakin', Palani?"

Palani turned and looked at Mama Keoni and his friends. Others from inside Papa Keoni's were behind them now, and Mama Keoni pushed herself to the front. She looked down on Palani with black anger in her eyes. She spoke in a low growl, "You kill the Lewis boy, Palani? You kill him?"

Palani said nothing. I said loudly to everyone, "Palani showed up at Vasco Construction to work as a day laborer. He did that now and then, to earn a little extra money. I spoke with the construction manager, Mario. He confirmed that. He saw Palani and Lewis leave together that day Lewis died. Palani had an old pickup truck out on the road, hidden from sight of anyone at the construction site. He had painted a fender green like Vasco's trucks. I went out to where Palani lives with some investigators from the Army's Criminal Investigation Division. We found the old truck behind his apartment building. The Army people have that now.

"When they were far enough away so no one could see them, Palani hit Lewis from behind," I continued, "as they walked away from Vasco Construction. He knocked Lewis out. With the help of the Army CID people, I checked the autopsy file at Police Headquarters this morning, too. It documents a concussive blow to the back of Lewis' head . . . That means he was hit really hard. Palani tossed Lewis and his old scooter in the back of the old truck he had stashed down the road. He drove up to the highway where Lewis died. He put Lewis and the scooter on the railing and then drove the truck into them. The green paint would point to Vasco. But the CID Investigators took samples of the green paint from the railing and from the old pickup we found. They are going to match up the paint in their lab. It won't be from Vasco's green painted trucks, but it will match the green fender on Palani's pickup truck."

"That right, Palani?" Mama Keoni asked. "That right?"

I went on, "Mikey Chung was going to talk to me. He knew something. He knew what you had done. So you killed him, too."

Palani said nothing, his knees were weakening, and he tried to back away. Mama Keoni said to the men behind her, "You boys . . . You good boys . . . Palani, he not so good a boy. You boys go get him."

"Wait a minute!" I yelled, holding up my hand to stop them. Everyone froze in their tracks. I turned and waived towards the thickets of bushes at the edge of the beach. Special Agent Linda Hartsell and her partner stepped onto the black sand. They walked past me and took Palani by his arms, handcuffing him behind his back.

"These are Army Police . . . CID . . . They'll take care of Palani," I said to Mama Keoni and the men standing with her.

"Army?" Mama Keoni asked. "Why you not call the police?"

Palani looked at me, hoping I had made a mistake. I imagine he was thinking how he could run and where he could run to if I had to take the time to phone for the police. Of course, he had no idea that the Big Island Police hated me because of my last visit to their Island and wouldn't do anything I asked them to do. That's one of the reasons I needed Special Agent Linda Hartsell. She could get what I needed from the Island Police when I couldn't. And she could get a search warrant for Palani's home.

"Lewis was a deserter," I explained. "He was never officially discharged from the Army. The day he died he was still in the Army. Palani murdered an active duty enlisted soldier. The CID examined the truck and took finger prints and DNA from it. They have the evidence. The Army wants Palani. If the civil authorities don't prosecute him for murder, he's going to spend the rest of his life in Leavenworth."

Palani, handcuffed but not struggling, walked between the two CID Agents, away from Papa Keoni's. As they walked from us, he started crying, sobbing loudly, pleading for the understanding that no one at Papa Keoni's would ever have.

I stood in the sand, the ocean now washing up onto my shoes unnoticed by me, and watched Mama Keoni and her 'good boys'. They stood looking at me without saying anything.

I waited, and then I said, "Thank you, Mama Keoni, for the good beer."

She paused and then said, "I think you go home, haole. I think you don't come back here. I think you maybe bad luck for us. Go home."

She and the others went back into the little shack and shut the door behind them. I stayed on the black sand for a long time, staring at the flaming red sky over the Pacific as the gentle waves lapped at my feet. I wondered how such a beautiful place, perhaps the most beautiful place on earth, could hold such tragedy as I had seen.

CHAPTER TWENTY-EIGHT

On The Big Island

We were enjoying the last of a good bottle of 2010 Chateau Cabredon Bordeaux. The resort's extensive wine list had the wine overpriced, but everything at the resort was overpriced anyway. That's how my family makes its money.

The evening air was cool and fresh, and carried the smell of clean salty sea with it. A bowl of macadamia nuts lay on the small table between the two chaise lounges we relaxed in. Sandy had relented and opened the jar that was in the suite's bar as a way of celebrating my finishing what I had to do.

My eyes were getting heavy as I thought that maybe an early night would be good now that I had finished my promise to Nancy and Leilani. Maybe a few days of uninterrupted fun with Sandy and Caroline before heading back to the snows of San Marcos. So far my vacation hadn't been much of a vacation.

Police Chief Daniels showed up at the Maika'i Resort that evening. He hadn't called first but I guess he felt he was above being polite. At least I guess he didn't need to be polite with me. There was a door bell at the front door of our suite. He chose to ignore it, pounding with a heavy fist on the door instead.

Sandy started to get up but my hand on her arm

stopped her. "I'll get it," I said and smiled. Without saying it, I was worried that someone . . . some friend of Palani, might have come calling. I didn't want Sandy going to the door if that were the case.

I opened the door a crack, enough to see who was pounding on it, and put my foot against it. Daniels was standing there, with two officers and a menacing look on his face.

"Open the damn door!" he growled.

"Tell you what," I said. "You show me a search warrant or tell me what the hell you want. Then I'll decide if I have to open my damn door to you."

"You screwed up my investigation!" he said.

"Chief Daniels," I said. "If you can calm down . . . take a deep breath . . . and talk rationally, I will let you in, and we can talk about it. But I have a family in here, and I have to protect them. Now how will it be? Do I close the door in your face, or can you act like a professional?"

Daniels stood there fuming and if it were possible, there would have been steam coming out his ears. His face was crimson, and he was breathing hard. One of his officers, standing behind him, gingerly touched his shoulder and said in a slow, low voice, "Chief, let's just go in and talk to the guy. He's willing to be reasonable."

Daniels shrugged the hand from his shoulder and said, trying to sound calm, "OK, Crew. Let's talk . . . Inside, OK?"

I grinned maliciously and asked as I would talk to a child, "Now, you promise to be good?" I just love pissing off people who think too much of themselves.

The officer behind Daniels said, "Cut it out, Mr. Crew. For God's sake. Just talk to the guy. We're not here to arrest you or anything."

That sounded reasonable enough, and I figured if Daniels were to fly off the handle, his two officers would restrain him. So I opened the door and said, "Come on in and have a seat. Would you like something to drink? Something to eat?"

The three didn't answer. Daniels stood in the center of the room and looked around. He probably hadn't seen such luxury before, and I hoped it would be just a little intimidating to him.

"Please sit," I said, pointing to a big couch that was upholstered in red and gold Asian silk. Daniels chose a chair to sit on, one that I had found uncomfortable and didn't use. His two officers stood, one behind Daniels and one to his left. I sat on the couch, and Sandy joined us, carrying the bottle of wine and our two glasses. She sat next to me, handed me my glass, and filled both it and hers with the last of the wine.

She looked at the three cops, one at a time, and said, "I have a young daughter asleep in the other room. Please keep your voices down. I don't want you to wake her."

I smiled and put my arm around her shoulder. "I am sorry," I said to the three. "If you gentlemen would like some wine, I can have another bottle sent to the room. It's a good wine but not terrific."

"Forget that," Daniels said. "Look, I want to know why you screwed up my murder investigation."

"I screwed it up?" I asked. "I don't get what you mean. Are you talking about Lewis Manaluo's death? If you are, the person who murdered Lewis is in custody. Isn't that what was supposed to happen?"

"He's not in my custody," Daniels said.

"Well, gosh, I guess I just never thought of that," I said just as sarcastically as I could manage.

"Morgan," Sandy said. "Please. He's here, and we need to make things right. That tone will accomplish nothing. Now please, just explain everything to him."

As usual, Sandy calmed me down and kept me out of trouble. I have a temper, I admit that. And that temper often gets me in trouble. Sandy has a way of calming that temper.

I asked Daniels, "I asked you once if I could see the lab reports on Lewis' Vespa and his autopsy. What did you tell me?"

"No, that's police business," he answered gruffly.

"You see, Daniels . . ." I started but he interrupted me.

"That's Police Chief Daniels," he said.

"Yeah," I began. "You see Daniels, you wouldn't share anything with me, so why should I share anything with you?"

Sandy put her hand on my knee and closed her eyes. But at that point I really didn't care if I insulted Daniels or not.

"The police don't share their investigations with civilians," Daniels said, choosing to ignore my attempt at insulting him.

I took a deep breath and drained the last of the red wine from my glass. I put the glass on a side table and said slowly and as reasonably as I could, "This is the second time I've been to Hawai'i. You wouldn't help me the first time, and I almost was killed. But I was able to do what I came for. I'm here this time with my family . . . On what was supposed to be a vacation. A very good friend of mine asked me to do a favor for her. That favor was finding out why Lewis Manaluo died and who killed him. It appeared that you weren't doing much because Lewis' death pointed to a big money development on the Island. So I had to go off and do it myself. When I asked for your help you said 'no'. Now, if I had come to you and asked you to get a search warrant for Palani's home, would you have done it?"

"I don't know," he said. "I don't go asking for search warrants on thin suspicions."

"But I needed to find out if my suspicions about Palani were grounded or not. I had no idea what you were doing and based on my experience with you, I just figured you wouldn't help me this time, either. I knew that Lewis was still carried on active duty with the Army, so I went to the only cops who would help. The CID listened to me and did what needed to be done. Lewis is now in their jail, and if you want to prosecute him for murder, I'm sure they will cooperate. If you don't, he will face a Military Court. My job for my friend is done."

"You should have come to me anyway," he said. "That arrest was mine. Now I have to go plead with the Army to turn Palani over to me."

"Good luck with that," I said. "I was told the Army wants him more than you do. But if you're nice to them, they might work with you."

Daniels sat staring at me. He had lost, he knew that. He sat back and crossed his legs, trying to appear normal, which was difficult for him. He asked, "OK, what about Vasco Construction? You said there might be something funny going on there."

"I still think that but I have no evidence. I really don't care anymore now that I know Vinnie Vasco didn't have Lewis killed. You should follow up on that, I suppose."

Daniels had lost once again. He knew that. He started to get up to leave when I stopped him. I said, "Please, Chief Daniels, sit down for a minute. Look, I'm sorry I made things difficult for you, but that's just who I am. I have no idea if I'll ever be back here again. If I do come back here . . . and if trouble follows me like it usually does . . . maybe we can work together . . . Like adults . . . Like gentlemen."

He said nothing. He pushed himself out of the chair and started for the door. His two officers followed, both looking rather embarrassed. Sandy took them to the door, said good night to them and closed and locked the door behind them.

She sat next to me and said, "Well, that went well. I hope the next time we come back here we won't need his help."

****

The next day I cancelled plans to play on the beach with Caroline and I took a jet to Oahu. I was in Harry Esposito's trash filled little room in the offices of Harper, Harper, Jascro, and Nettles. He had phoned me at eight that morning to say he had finished his investigation of Vinnie Vasco and Vasco Construction, and he needed to talk to me about what he had found out.

"So tell me," I said into the phone.

"I guess I'd rather talk face to face. I got results but you're not going to like it." He hung up abruptly telling me I had to go to him instead of splashing in the ocean with my daughter.

So I caught the next commuter jet off The Big Island and flew to Oahu. When I walked into his crowded and dirty little office, he struggled once again to find a place for me to sit. Dumping a pile of newspapers on the floor uncovered a portion of the ratty old couch with caved in springs. I sunk into it and waited for Harry to tell me what he had found.

He pulled a brand new cigarette from a brand new pack of Marlboros rather than dig through the ashtray for a smokeable butt as he had done the last time I was there. He lit it with his old, scratched Zippo lighter. Taking a long drag on the cigarette and then blowing it out towards the ceiling, he leaned back in his squeaky chair, smiled, and said, "So he is Mafia connected and he's running a scam. He rips off people . . . Investors . . . And then they get threatened if they want their money back. Some of them get killed."

"OK," I said. "That's what I guessed was happening. Now we need to turn your evidence over to the police."

"That's going to be a little difficult, Mr. Crew."

"Why? I don't understand," I said questioning just why the hell I had made the trip to Oahu. If all he had was words, I could have stayed on the beach and built sand castles with Caroline.

"It's kind of a long story," he said. "You see, I hired a couple of people to get inside his operation. The problem is, they did get inside and found out what was going on, but they won't talk to the police."

"What! They won't go to the police? Why did you hire them, then?"

"Look, Mr. Crew," he said. "Vinnie Vasco is East Coast mob. It would be impossible to get into his office and get paper evidence and not get killed trying to do that. So I hired a couple of really good con artists . . . Probably the best in the world. They did their job, but they won't get within a half mile of the cops. It's as simple as that. If the mob doesn't kill them, and they openly talk to the cops and testify in court, then their whole livelihood is blown wide open. Either way, they lose."

"Then what the hell do I have for my money?" I asked, feeling really angry right about then.

"You asked me to find out what was going on with Vasco Construction so you could let Lewis' woman know. Well, I did that."

"I need to speak with these people you hired," I demanded.

"That's great because they're going to want your check anyway."

"We'll see about them getting paid. I want some proof, not just a bunch of bull crap words from them. Get on the phone and arrange a meeting for today."

Harry didn't hesitate to quickly pick up his phone and dial a number. It was a local call; I knew by the number of digits he hit on the phone's keypad. So his con artist buddies were there on Oahu.

Harry pushed a button, put the phone on speaker and waited. Someone answered and said in an ever so proper, English accent, "Trent Elsworth's residence."

"It's OK, Rog'," Harry said. "It's me, Harry."

The English Public School accent dropped away quickly in favor of a Boston Irish brogue as Roger said, "Oh, it's you again. I ain't so sure he's gonna' wanna' talk t'you. You never told us the damn guy was Mafia. You know we don't deal with those kinds'a guys."

"Hey, you guys wanna' get paid, don't you? You guys are gonna make out alright. I got the client right here and he's ready to write a check." Harry smiled and nodded at me as he spoke.

"Tell him to mail it," Roger said snidely.

"No, he wants to speak with . . . You know, I don't even know his real name. Let me speak with Trent."

There was silence on the line for a full minute. As we waited, Harry said to me, "These guys don't use their real names. I doubt they even know their real names anymore. Then the man who called himself Trent Elsworth picked up the phone. He had been Trent Elsworth for so many years, running big cons all over the world that his false British accent was hard to drop. "Good morning Harry," he said lightly. Harry could hear when a person was smiling and happy. Trent wasn't smiling.

"Hi Trent," Harry said. "I need to come to your place."

"You may need what you need my old chap, but you will not pull me into yet another job that might get me killed. That, my old friend, is the thing."

"I'm sorry about that, Trent . . ."

"You may address me as Sir Trent."

"Cut the crap, Trent. You're a Kansas City street kid, all grown up and a very successful con artist. Now, I need to bring the client to your place. He wants to talk to you and get you paid. He's got a check with twenty-five grand written on it." Harry looked at me, winked and nodded conspiratorially, and said into the phone, "Maybe more if you think you earned it since the client is a rich guy with money to toss around."

"That being the case, Harry, my fee will be double what we talked about. And Mary's fee will be from you, not out of my end. Do we have a deal?"

Harry didn't really care about the money since none of it was his. He knew the Crew family's fortune was almost too big to count. He said, "Hell, Trent baby. Whatever you want. And I hope Mary is still there, too. The client wants to talk to both of you."

Mary Winchester is another confidence artist who uses sex and easily flowing tears to wrench money from old men with big bank accounts.

"Mary is still here. She is leaving for Luxemburg in the morning," Trent said. "She is about to marry a Duke. Her usual attorneys will handle the divorce settlement afterwards."

"Well, tell her to stay put. I need her there today. Tell her she can marry her sucker and do the divorce as she wants, but I want to talk to her today. The client and me are on our way over to your place."

Trent was quiet for a moment or two and then said, "Oh, alright you bastard. But bring the check or I'll have Roger shoot you in your bloody arse."

Harry hung up the phone and smiled at me. "OK," he said. "Everything's arranged. Let's get going. You got a car or should we take mine? . . . If you don't mind the trash that's inside it, that is."

"I think we'll take my car," I said. "You can drive. How far do we have to go?"

"To the north side of the Island."

"That's a long drive, isn't it?" I asked.

"That's where my people are, Mr. Crew. Now do you wanna' talk to them or not?"

"Then if you're going to drive, let's take your car. Mine's a rental and I don't want it wrecked."

Harry laughed and we left his office.

His car was worse than he had described. It was a twelve year old Chrysler with very little paint left on it. The rust was filthy with mud, and the inside was filled with fast food wrappers, old newspapers, used paper coffee cups, and assorted unidentifiable trash. It smelled bad, so I rolled down the window. "That's a good idea," Harry said. The damn AC ain't worked in a couple of years."

****

Trent Elsworth was born Hyrum Lipkowski, Jr. in June of 1960 of blue collar parents in Kansas City, Missouri. His father, Hyrum, Sr., was a sometimes carpenter, doing good work when he wasn't on a three or four day drunk. His mother, Miriam, spent those drunk days in her bedroom praying or at the Temple praying. Prayer was her world, and she never gave up hope that her prayers – one day – would be answered.

She died at the age of 81 never having seen any of her prayers answered the way she had hoped they would be answered. Hyrum, Jr. told her many times that God was not ignoring her; He was in fact answering her prayers. And His answer was "No."

Hyrum, Jr. was a reader, having learned to read everything he could get his hands on before he started Hebrew School. On the drunk days he would take two or three books into his closet and read by the light of an old flashlight, stealing downstairs in the dark of night to find food. By the time he was ten years old he had learned how to run scams on teachers, telling lies so convincingly that everyone believed him. He would show off to adults with card tricks and magic tricks, steal food from grocery stores without ever being caught and con fellow school students out of their lunch money.

Hyrum, Jr. grew up into a handsome young man, attractive to his female classmates. Athletics came easy to him, and he was able to scam enough money to buy good clothes. At eighteen years of age, he worked his way across the Atlantic on a hulk of a cargo ship, washing dishes and cleaning toilets. He was in Europe when at twenty-two, Sir Trent Elsworth was born, and Hyrum, Jr. was in his past forever. He had his first million in the bank shortly afterwards.

Trent has aged grandly. At the time I met him, he was in his mid-fifties and looked every inch the titled gentleman. He and his assistant-in-crime and sometimes body guard Roger Aymes now live in Hawai'i. The Oahu estate Trent bought once belonged to a Japanese millionaire businessman. The house is an expansive and elaborately designed home of native woods and glass, one hundred yards off Hanalolo Drive, hidden by a botanical maze of exotic plants and trees. The estate has a private beach of white sand with a hundred year old breakwater of stone inside of which coral and fantastic fish of every species and color thrive. Trent knew that all beaches in Hawai'i are public but he keeps the required public access pathway hidden just well enough that he is seldom bothered by tourists or natives.

Mary Winchester was born in a suburb of Chicago, Illinois. Her father was an accountant, and her mother was a Post Office employee. Mary was a beautiful child who grew into a stunningly beautiful woman. At an early age, she learned how to seduce boys and men with promised sex and sometimes the real thing in order to get what she wanted. At eighteen she married her first husband, and three months later she learned that with a good lawyer she could divorce men and walk away with money.

Mary now makes a living doing that. Her beauty draws rich men in, as was Vinnie, like a moth to a flame.

****

Roger brought two snifters of Courvoisier VSOP onto the lanai where Trent was relaxing in a chaise lounge, watching waves crash against the breakwater. The Cognac was for Trent and him. Mary lay back on a chaise, a crystal flute of her favorite champagne in her hand. She was absorbing some of the Hawaiian sun, topless to make her tan very even. The sky was clear, but the air portended rain that afternoon. Roger sat in a bamboo chair at the glass topped table that Trent sat next to, waiting for Harry and me to arrive.

The large flagstone lanai was surrounded left and right by three foot tall lava rock walls that were thickly covered with flame-red bougainvillea. A few coconut palm trees cast some shade here and there. Orchids of many colors in colorful Asian pots stood against the wall, and three mango trees finished the landscaping.

Harry and I arrived at the estate in Harry's dirty and dusty twelve year old Chrysler. He had pulled to a loud, brake squealing stop at the ten foot tall wrought iron gate at the entrance to the estate. He had trouble rolling down the window at his side. The car was made before the days of power windows. Once the window was halfway down, he reached out and pushed the call button on the stone pillar. He then could not roll the window back up, giving up and letting it stay as it was. I had my side window down, and the breath of fresh air flowing through the car was a relief.

We waited for Roger to open the gates. It took four very intentional and very long minutes for Roger to walk to the gate and open it for Harry and me.

Roger is a big man, broad shoulders and thick arms that put a strain on the white short-sleeve shirt he wore. He has the face of a fighter; bent nose and thick brows from too many cuts in the ring. Harry explained that Roger kept Trent safe. It was enough explanation for me to understand his job.

We drove past Roger who walked slowly back to the house where we waited on the porch for him. The house was big and very Asian in design. Red tile covered the roof.

Several marble statues – stylized lions and dogs – lined a long covered front patio. Potted green plants were everywhere, and the yard in front of the house was a manicured Japanese garden. Water flowed from a small rock waterfall into a pool, the only sound in what was meant to be a peaceful retreat. Koi swam happily in the pool.

The tall, carved mahogany wood, double doors of the house were opened grandly by Roger for us. We entered the house, and I was astonished at the luxury of the furnishings. The interior had been decorated by the previous owner with the rarest and most expensive Asian works of art and furniture. It was cool and dark inside, reminding me of an Asian palace I had once seen in Bangkok.

We joined Trent and Mary on the lanai and sat, without being invited to do so, at the table where the two snifters of cognac sat. Mary lay back, still topless, her eyes closed under sunglasses, even as she raised the flute of champagne to her lips.

Trent and Roger twirled their snifters of cognac, saying nothing and looking back and forth at Harry and me. Having played the roles of very proper English gentlemen, they were waiting for an introduction. Harry wanted to ask for some of the cognac, but he knew he wouldn't be given any, and if he was given some he would drink it too fast, rather than take pleasure in sipping as the two men did.

"So, Harry, and who is your friend?" Trent asked.

"Oh yeah," Harry said. "This is Morgan Crew. He's the client."

Trent didn't fall from his British accent; too many years of using it had made it too normal, almost as if he had been born to it. But Roger easily slipped back to his normal tough south Boston voice. "And who the hell is this Morgan Crew guy? I ain't never heard of him." Roger asked.

"He is the client, like I said . . ." Harry started.

"So, client . . . You got our money?" Roger growled.

I sat forward and said as strongly as I could manage, hoping Roger wouldn't reach over and break me in two, "I want to know what you found out. Then we'll talk about pay."

"Oh, is that right, big guy?" Roger said. He carefully laid the cut crystal snifter on the table and threatened, "You ain't leavin' here in one piece without payin' us. Got that?"

Trying to be as tough as Roger sounded, I sat back in the chair, laughed a little and said, "Oh cut the shit. You'll get paid for what you did. You try to touch me, and I will take that gun Harry carries in his belt and shoot your balls off. You got that?"

Mary sat up and swung her legs to the side of the chaise, taking her sunglasses off and still not caring that she was topless. She said, "Oh boys! Stop trying to prove who has the bigger dick. This is business, so let's get to it."

Trent spoke up, looking at the woman, and said, "You're right once again, Mary. This is business."

He turned to Harry and me and said without rancor and without dropping his British Public School accent, "Harry my old friend. You didn't mention that Mr. Vasco was Mafia."

Roger sat forward and leaned his thick arms on the table. "Vinnie 'Cuts' as his Mafia family back in New York call him. Is that the guy you sent us after?"

"Yeah . . . I guess so . . . Why?"

Trent reached for a cedar-lined rosewood cigar humidor that sat on the table. He opened it carefully and deliberately, and slowly, dramatically, withdrew a six inch long, 50 ring cigar from it. Trent had his cigars custom made, hand-rolled, by an eighty-three year old man in Santiago, Cuba. He paid a premium to have them surreptitiously shipped through Mexico to Hawai'i. They were labeled as if from the Dominican Republic so as to avoid the prying eyes of Federal inspectors. But they were the best, and Trent had come to expect the best.

He snipped the tip from the cigar with a silver cutter and lit the cigar with a polished gold triple-flame gas lighter. He drew deeply and blew the thick smoke up to the blue sky. He turned to Harry and said, "You must have been out of your mind, Harry. You know I do not run a game on the Mafia. Yet, you knew and didn't tell us."

I asked, "So the problem here is you're afraid Vinnie's people will come after you. Is that right?"

Trent answered slowly, "Yes, of course. But they will have a difficult time. We fortunately used assumed names."

"What names?" I asked.

Trent looked at Mary and she nodded. He turned back to me and said, "We were Sir Clive and Lady Catherine Hamilton."

"Is there a real Sir Clive and Lady Hamilton?" I asked.

"Yes, of course," Trent said. "Backgrounds might be run at any time."

"Did you leave anything that might be traced back to you? Clothing, anything? Did you drive cars registered to you? Did you sign your real names to anything?"

"Of course not," Trent answered, perhaps a little insulted at the suggestion. "We've been in the business for a long time, Mr. Crew."

"Mr. Crew," Mary said softy, still smiling sweetly. "In our business we have to be perfect, or people will not believe us. We do not make mistakes."

"Then you have little to worry about," I said, feeling confident saying it.

Trent huffed by way of brushing aside my conclusion. He blew more smoke towards the sky. I wondered what he would say if I asked for a cigar? I didn't take the chance.

"OK," I said. "That's out of the way. Now tell me what you found out about Vasco Construction."

"It's quite simple, actually," Trent said. "Mr. Vasco takes money from people who want to invest in his resort. The presentation made to the prospective investor is apparently very good. The money comes from very, very wealthy people. The money is sent to New York. The investor, when asking for a return on his investment . . . or if he is foolish enough to ask for his money back . . . is threatened and sometimes murdered. The resort is, of course, not a resort; merely a hole in the ground that will never be completed."

"And how do you know this?" I asked.

Mary answered, "Vincent told me, of course."

"He just came out and admitted he is Mafia and he steals money and kills people? I find that hard to believe."

She spoke as if she couldn't understand why I would ask such a stupid question. She tilted her head and frowned, finding it difficult to believe I would not simply take her word for it.

She said, "Vincent and I spent several days in bed enjoying some very good and very hot sex. He fell in love with me. Trent approached as my husband and demanded a great deal of money if Vincent were to remain having me to fuck. It was impossible for him to pay Trent, and he told me why. He told me everything because he was confiding in someone he loved. Do you understand now?"

"So there's no paper evidence?" I asked. "No bank accounts . . . No ripped off investors . . . No nothing?"

Trent said, again in his assumed aristocratic British accent, "Mr. Crew. Just how would you suggest we garner such paper evidence? Should we have burglarized his office? . . . Or perhaps his home? You are asking too much, sir."

"And Harry tells me you aren't going to give the police a statement of any kind. And you aren't going to testify in court, either," I said.

Mary said, "I am leaving in the morning. I shall spend the next year, perhaps more, living safely as the wife of a very wealthy Duke. I will be assuming the Duke's name and title. I assume Trent will be leaving for somewhere soon, and I assume he will be finding a new identity. We will be safe, and you have what you asked for. Information on Vasco Construction."

So, I leaned back in the chair, disappointed that there was no evidence, but at least I knew what was going on, and I could tell Nancy Wong and Leilani. In the end, Harry and I left Trent and Roger and the topless Mary, never to see any of them again.

I gave them a check for $25,000 which they thought was too little, but that was all they were going to get. I said goodbye to Harry and caught a jet back to The Big Island and my family.

CHAPTER TWENTY-NINE

On The Big Island

The next morning I took Caroline into my arms, and with Sandy we went to the front desk of the resort where I had arranged for a brand new Jeep four-wheel drive rental to be waiting. We drove to Nancy Wong's house on the beach. It hadn't changed much in the years since I was there last. It was, to me at least, a small bit of paradise on earth. Flowers were everywhere and bragged in every imaginable color. Birds sang and flew from tree to tree bringing music to the air. Mango trees and coconut palms and a banyan tree threw shade across the hale. The only real change was that Nancy's children had grown taller.

Nancy greeted us warmly, and Caroline ran off with Nancy's children to play. Sandy and I joined Nancy on her covered porch and enjoyed some icy papaya juice Nancy made from fruit she picked at the side of her hale. It was sweet and refreshing.

I told Nancy everything I had learned about Lewis' death. She was surprised, because she had been certain Vinnie Vasco had murdered Lewis.

"I was surprised, too," I said. "I know he's Mafia, but I don't know what Lewis knew about his operation. If Lewis had somehow gotten into Vinnie's office, he may have learned something, but I doubt he could do that. Security is too tight there. I think he just had a hunch about what is going on.

Palani confessed to the murder, so I know Vinnie had nothing to do with it."

An hour later Nancy joined us in the Jeep, and she, Sandy and Caroline and I drove off to Leilani's home. With Nancy's help I found the rutted dirt roads that took us there.

The thrown together shack of drift wood and bamboo, with the browned, thatched roof, looked as good to me as it had the other times I was there. Birds of many colors were flitting around in the trees, singing the morning away. Red chickens scratched around in the dust and in the lush green. The fresh and cool mountain air was filled with the smell of flowers. Leilani was sitting on the steps of the porch to her home, sewing white flowers into a lei. She looked at us as we got out of the Jeep, and as we walked towards her, she held up the lei and said, "For Lewis."

Nancy explained, "Leilani will take the lei up to Mauna Loa and make an offering to Pele. Pele will watch over Lewis. Until that time when Leilani can be with him again."

Sandy carried Caroline from the car and put her down on the ground. Kanye ran from inside the hale and directly to the little girl. They began playing in the dirt together almost immediately.

Nancy, Sandy and I sat on the porch on bamboo chairs near Leilani who stayed sitting on the steps. I told Leilani how Lewis had died and why, and I told her what I knew of Vasco Construction. I explained that Lewis may have been right about what was going on, but his knowing had nothing to do with his death. That fact didn't do much to console Leilani at her loss. Knowing would not bring her man back to her and Kanye and the child that would be born soon. But at least she knew. And in her religion, in what she believed, Lewis rested with the gods.

All I could do was offer her some money. She smiled

gratefully but refused my offer. She said, "Thank you, but there is fruit on the trees and fish in the water. Kanye and I will be OK."

Nancy added, "I'll keep an eye on her, Morgan. Leilani will be alright."

Inside of me, I felt jealousy. I wanted to be as free as these people, as free from want and as free as they are to live off the land and the sea.

****

That evening, back at the resort, after Caroline was sleeping happily, Sandy and I sat out on the lanai of our suite at the resort. Sandy relented once again and didn't complain when I had a second large bourbon with just a splash of club soda sent to the room, along with a vodka and tonic for Sandy. I had pulled a jar of macadamia nuts from the suite's kitchen cupboard. We sat quietly for a long time, listening to the ocean and the soft Hawaiian music floating in from the lounge on the other side of the beach.

All I could think of was what I had done and how close I had come, once again to being killed. I knew I had to do what Nancy and Leilani asked; I was feeling very tired of being called on to solve other people's problems.

Sandy, as always, read my mind and my feelings. She said, as she took my hand into hers, "You did what you had to do, Morgan."

"Yeah," I said. "It's always like that. And this was supposed to be a vacation. What did I do? I spent hardly any time with you and Caroline."

"Then why don't we stay another week or two?"

"Sounds good," I said. "I like it here. I could live like

Leilani lives. Up in the hills, away from everyone. Her simple life is something I've dreamed about for years. Remember when you and I first met? I said I wanted to ship out on a ratty fishing boat, just the two of us."

"Well," Sandy started. "I'm afraid it's not practical to run away. You are who you are, Morgan Crew. Nothing will change that. If you hide up in the hills, someone will still find you."

"Yeah, you're right, of course. But I can dream, can't I?"

Sandy finished her drink and stood. She walked to the phone and ordered a third drink for both of us, and a bowl of cold shrimp. Very unusual, I thought. She had something up her sleeve. But what? I hoped it was something good and not another dangerous quest to save somebody.

We sat in silence, waiting for the drinks. When they arrived, I started on the cold shrimp as she watched me. Finally she said, "While you were off playing detective, Caroline and I took a little day trip of our own. We went with a realtor into the hills and looked at this piece of property up there. Seven acres not too far from where Leilani and Kanye live as a matter of fact. There's an old shack, too beat up to live in. And there are rows of berries that haven't been tended in years. There are palm trees and banana trees and mango trees and papaya trees and a lot of other things like that. There's a little stream that runs down across the property. It hasn't been tended for years but it can be cleaned up. Right next door is a coffee plantation. There's an operating well and it's even been wired for electricity. You can see the Pacific from where the old shack is, through the trees."

Now that was a surprise. And it got my interest up. I asked if she had thoughts of moving to Hawai'i.

"No, not permanently anyway," she said. "Caroline has

to start school soon, and I want her to go to school in San Marcos. But it can be a place to get away to when we need to get away."

"And you want me to go look at it?" I asked, hoping that's just what she wanted.

"That would be a good idea," she said, grinning cunningly once again. "Particularly since I gave the realtor ten grand as a deposit to hold it until you see it."

****

In the morning, the three of us drove into the mountains above Kailua-Kona. The weather couldn't have been better: blue sky and a cool breeze floating gently down the slopes of the hills. Sandy seemed to know the way. She confessed she and Caroline had been there three times before giving the realtor money. She told me that Caroline loved the place. I asked if the two and a half year old told her that and what words she used. Sandy laughed and said, "No, but she runs around and plays with everything. She chased the birds and splashed in the little brook. She loves it."

We bounced along a semi-paved road. I tried to avoid as many potholes and big rocks as I could. When Sandy shouted that we were at the dirt road to the property, I braked and turned suddenly. Caroline squealed and laughed loudly as I spun the car onto the rutted road that would take us to the seven acres Sandy wanted to buy.

We turned a corner that was hidden behind thickets of bushes and trees. As we turned, dozens of birds flew from the trees, screeching their displeasure at being disturbed. But there it was in front of us. Thick green grass, tall, unkempt, and overgrown true, but thick and green anyway. A dozen rows of berries on sagging wire, uncared for like the grass. Tall palms that needed brown, dead fronds trimmed and trees full of fruit with more lying on the ground, rotting away. The little stream Sandy had told me about ran across the property and down the hillside. It didn't carry much water but it was right where it should be.

And there it was, the most dilapidated and unusable old shack I had ever seen. What was left of the palm frond roof was brown and dry, and ready to blow away at the first slight breeze. The whole shack tilted to the right on broken stone that once was a foundation. Weeds were growing through the rotted floor boards of a small porch that I imagined had once been covered but now lay open to the sun.

I got out of the car and immediately wanted the place. The property sloped down towards Kailua-Kona letting me see the Pacific off in the distance, over the trees. I could feel the clean, fresh air blowing down off of Mauna Loa, and above me birds were filling the sky and singing loudly.

I looked at the tired old shack and imagined a home built there. I looked at the overgrown weeds and vines and imagined a manicured property with Caroline playing in the sun.

"OK," I said. "Let's buy it."

CHAPTER THIRTY

San Marcos

Betsy had returned to classes after spending a day with Bob Sommers writing out another fifteen page statement of all she had done. There was a substitute instructor for Biology; none of the other students knew what Mr. Thatcher had done and that they would never see him again. Betsy said nothing in class; they would hear about it soon enough. She headed home after classes were over.

It was half past six in the evening. She was stirring some honey into a cup of tea and wondering if she had the appetite to eat anything. Her European History book was open on the kitchen table. She had a big exam coming up in two days, and she knew she wasn't prepared for it. But she couldn't concentrate on anything but all that had happened since Morgan and Sandy had gone on vacation.

The doorbell rang, breaking into her thoughts. She at first thought she might just ignore it, but it might be Bob Sommers, and she had to let him in. So she dragged her feet that were shoved in the old pink fuzzy slippers that were two sizes too big for her across the hardwood floor and opened the door. Sissy McMillan stood there, smiling and shivering in the cold.

"Sissy!" Betsy said, startled at seeing her. She had not been in class that day, but that didn't surprise Betsy. Sissy had been through a lot and needed time to overcome everything Mr. Thatcher had done to her.

"Hi, Betsy," she said still smiling. "Can I come in for a few minutes?"

"Sure," Betsy said and stepped back, motioning her into the house.   She closed the door and took Sissy's coat, hanging it on one of the coat hooks near the door.

"It's cold out there," Sissy said shivering a little. "Can I talk to you . . . Just for a minute or two?"

"Certainly. How about a cup of tea? I just boiled some water."

"That would be great," Sissy said. She was still smiling but her face exposed some sadness and pain. There were dark rings under her eyes, and her face was pale, from stress Betsy thought.

Betsy understood how Sissy must feel, and she would offer as much comfort as possible. Sissy maybe needed a friend to talk to. Betsy knew she wasn't close with her parents and she didn't have any steady boyfriends. So maybe, Betsy thought, she wanted Betsy to be that friend. The thought made her feel good. She would be the best friend she could be.

In the kitchen Betsy pulled a big mug from the cupboard and took the still steaming kettle from the stove. She put a tea bag in the cup and filled it, then pushed it across the table towards Sissy. The girl grasped the hot mug in both hands and sipped at the tea. A few tears formed in her eyes. Betsy touched the girl's arm to try to comfort her.

"It's OK, Sissy," she said. "I can only imagine what you've been through. I'm so sorry. But if you've come to say thanks, you don't need to."

Sissy put the cup down on the table and reached into

her purse. She pulled out a small semi-auto pistol and said, "Oh, Betsy. I didn't come to thank you. I came to kill you."

Betsy sat up in shock, and overwhelming fear struck her. She almost fainted but remembered the stories Morgan and Sandy told her of all the times they faced death. She pushed the fear behind her, as they often told her they had to do, and said, "You're kidding, right? This is some kind of joke, isn't it?"

"It's no joke, Betsy," she said. The smile had left her face, replaced with an expression of red hot hatred. "You screwed everything up, Betsy, and you have to die for it."

"Screwed up? What the hell did I screw up? I saved your ass, and I saved Mary and Diane, too. Are you crazy?"

"I'm not crazy, Betsy. I just love Bobby so much, and you screwed everything up for us."

"Who's Bobby?" Betsy asked. "I don't know any Bobby." Then she remembered that afternoon in the park when M told her that Sissy was with someone called Bobby. He had been right about something anyway.

"Mr. Thatcher," Sissy said as she wiped tears from her cheeks with the back of her hand. "Bobby and I are in love. And now he's in jail because of you, and we can't be together."

"Bobby is Mr. Thatcher?" Betsy asked. She was thinking, 'Keep her talking, keep her talking.'

"Yes, of course," the girl said, anger and frustration in her voice. "But you couldn't know that, could you? Someone like Bobby could never be with you. He's only a teacher to people like you."

"But Bobby and you . . .?"

"Yes, of course," Sissy said. "He's kind and gentle; he's smart and he's funny. And he listens to me. And he loves me so much."

"Sissy," Betsy started, "Mr. Thatcher kidnapped Mary and Diane. He killed Tommy DeVito and M and probably Ron Porter, too."

"That's just not true, Betsy," she said, stamping her foot on the floor. "Mary and Diane found out about Bobby and me. I knew we had to take them to the cellar to keep them quiet. Bobby didn't want to, but I knew we had to, so I asked him. I told him how terribly Mary was being treated at home and that we should buy her clothes and things to keep her quiet. But she wanted more. Bobby is so kind to me; he took her like I wanted because I asked. He'll do just about anything to make me happy, you know.

"Diane's parents didn't care about her," Sissy went on. "She would have been better off with us. I knew that, and I knew that Diane couldn't tell anybody about Bobby and me. Bobby listened to me and he took her, too."

"But he held them captive," Betsy said. "He was raping them . . . Beating them."

"They deserved everything they got," Sissy said simply.

"What about you, Sissy?" Betsy asked. "You have a good home life. You were happy."

"No I wasn't, Betsy. Oh, my folks didn't mistreat me. They bought me clothes and cars and even riding lessons. But they don't have the time for me. They use their money to keep me busy so they don't have to worry about me. And I didn't have a good boyfriend like all the other girls have. Nobody really loved me before Bobby. The boys all ignored me . . . And I have a lot to offer, don't I. I'm pretty . . . And I'm smart . . . But the boys just aren't interested."

"But what about Ron Porter?" Betsy asked. "He said you and he were dating. He seemed like a nice guy."

"All he wanted to do was go to bed with me. He didn't love me; all he wanted was sex. Oh, I gave him what he wanted, but he wouldn't take me anywhere. All he wanted was sex, and then he would up and leave me until the next time. I wanted someone who needed me and loved me, who respected me. Bobby saw that, and he understood. He loves me. And Bobby didn't kill anybody, either. He'd never do something like that."

"Then who did kill them?"

"I did, of course," Sissy said as if Betsy should have known that. "Tommy DeVito thought I was terrible for breaking up with him when Bobby and I fell in love. He stopped giving me pot to smoke. He was going to talk about it all over town. I had to kill him. And that stupid M wanted money to keep his mouth shut. Well, I shut his mouth for him alright. And Ron Porter was out asking too many questions. He had too many people wondering. I had to stop him. Like I should have stopped you, only I didn't, and you screwed everything up."

"Did you tell the police all this?" Betsy asked.

"Of course not. What good would it do for me to be in jail and for Bobby to be free? What I want is for both of us to be free . . . To love each other and be happy."

Betsy was overwhelmed and didn't know what to say. All she could do was whisper, "So now what? How do you get your Bobby free?"

"Now I kill you . . . Then I kill Mary and Diane. Then Bobby has to be released from jail because there are no witnesses and we can be together. It's really my mistake for not killing you sooner. I'm sorry, but you shouldn't have done what you did. You should have just kept your damn nose out of my business. But I'll try to make it quick. I've seen on TV that a bullet to the head is the quickest way to die. Oh, I could cut your throat but that takes a long time to die, and I guess it's quite painful. Shooting, like I did for Tommy and Ron and M, is the better, more humane way."

As Sissy slowly raised the pistol Betsy threw her cup of hot tea in Sissy's face. Sissy screamed as Betsy jumped on her and they fell to the floor. The gun slipped from Sissy's hand and skidded across the tiled kitchen floor.

Betsy was on top of the girl, holding her down. Sissy was screaming insanely, spitting and kicking. Betsy closed her fist and hit the girl across the jaw, then hit her again and a third time. Blood streamed from Sissy's jaw and nose as she lay unconscious.

Betsy got up and phoned Bob Sommers.

****

It took another two weeks for Sandy and Caroline and I to return to our home in the snowy hills of San Marcos. We had bought the property and hired an architect and a landscape designer. All the permits were approved, and we had begun to build a place to retreat to when retreat was needed.

While doing all that, I contacted Peter Jascro and the firm of Harper, Harper, Jascro and Nettles. Peter convinced the Federal Government to go after Vinnie and his construction firm. A team from the IRS, the FBI, and a half dozen other Federal Agencies descended on Vinnie in his trailer one afternoon. The whole operation was shut down and Vinnie got fifteen years in a federal prison. He decided that fifteen years was better than life for the murders of some investors. To get the fifteen years he broke the code of Omerta – telling the FBI everything he knew about his Mafia family.

On the day we got home we were sitting around the kitchen table eating a dinner that Sandy and Betsy had cooperated on. I noticed some bruising around Betsy's wrists but thought better of asking her about it right then. I would ask her when we were alone.

We told Betsy all about our 'vacation' and how I had solved yet another murder, almost getting myself killed doing it. We told her about the property we had bought and promised to take her to see it when the building was done. She was excited and told us she had never been to Hawai'i. She seemed very interested in what the surfer guys looked like. Sandy and she exchanged some sly grins as they talked about all the beach guys that were there.

We were enjoying big slices of apple pie that Betsy had made from scratch – she was becoming a very good cook – and cup after cup of very strong hot coffee when I asked Betsy, "So, how was your vacation from us? Did you do anything except go to school and study hard?"

"Nah," she said. "Nothing exciting. Pretty boring stuff. I am glad to have you guys back, though."

THE END

www.ingramcontent.com/pod-product-compliance
Lightning Source LLC
Chambersburg PA
CBHW031450260626
47154CB00016B/327